Storming Heaven

Storming Heaven

The Age of Bronze Book 2

Miles Cameron

First published in Great Britain in 2023 by Gollancz
an imprint of The Orion Publishing Group Ltd
Carmelite House, 50 Victoria Embankment
London EC4Y 0DZ

An Hachette UK Company

This edition first published in Great Britain in 2024 by Gollancz

1 3 5 7 9 10 8 6 4 2

A CIP catalogue record for this book is
available from the British Library.

ISBN (MMP) 978 1 473 23255 6
ISBN (eBook) 978 1 473 23256 3
ISBN (audio) 978 1 473 23265 5

Typeset at The Spartan Press Ltd,
Lymington, Hants

Printed and bound in Great Britain by Clays Ltd,
Elcograf S.p.A.

www.gollancz.co.uk

For Aurora, martial arts instructor, gamer,
fantasy nerd, and re-enactor

Some Notes on the World

Characters in *Against All Gods* and *Storming Heaven* express distance in paransangs and stadia (singular stadion).

The parasang is approximately five kilometres, or the distance a fit man can walk in an hour of hard walking. It's not an exact measurement. This is, after all, the Bronze Age.

The stadion is approximately six hundred feet (roughly two hundred metres, give or take). The foot is the measure of a man's foot – not standardised. There are thirty stadia in a parasang in Noa and Dardania; fewer in the Hundred Cities, more in Narmer. But don't be fooled; there are no standardised systems of measure. Every city measures everything from weights to distance, from grain to volume, in a different way. I have chosen to use the archaic Greek/Persian stadion and parasang (and the 'foot') to keep it relatively simple.

There is no money. This is a barter economy, and the relative value of gold, silver, grain or any other commodity varies from place to place and from transaction to transaction. Precious stones, like emeralds, rubies and lapis, are all useful for trade, but again, have no standard value.

There are no maps or charts, although Narmer and Ma'rib have 'world pictures' that begin to approach maps. People tend to express travel as a set of waypoints: 'I went to A, then B, then C.' Written down, these itineraries are the way pilgrims and merchants learn their routes.

Most people cannot read; the ability to read is almost a magic power. Scribes hold that power, and a good scribe can read most of the languages, 'modern' and 'ancient', of the world. There is no paper. Everything must be written on either papyrus (mostly in Narmer) or inscribed on clay tablets. Book-keeping and accounting, like reading, are near-magical powers.

Finally, the most durable metal is bronze. Iron is almost unknown, and its ownership is illegal and taboo. It is worth noting that a good work-hardened bronze blade is the equal or superior of much ironwork; only steel would exceed bronze, and bronze can be worked much more easily. This is an age of bronze, extended and enforced by the gods.

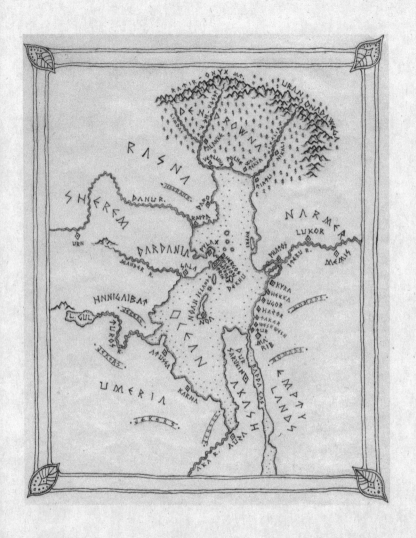

Glossary of Names and Titles

Protagonists

Atosa – Chief jeweller of the Palace of Hekka.

Daos – An orphaned child with mysterious powers. Now growing to manhood at an extraordinary rate.

Era – An epic singer and dancer, swordswoman, abandoned daughter of a godborn father and a Narmerian dancer.

Gamash of Weshwesh – Godborn aristocrat, master magos, and past tool of the gods.

Hefa-Asus – A Dendrownan smith from the far north, in Poche. A great maker.

Leontas-Zembah – A lion-killer and mercenary; a Godborn noble of Lazba.

Nicté – A tough woman of northern Dendrowna, apprentice of Hefa-Asus.

Pollon – Scribe, musician, archer and man of reason. A little patronising at times.

Zos – Godborn sell-sword, cynical and past his best.

Hakrans aboard the *Untroubled Swan*

Aanat – Master sailor, 'captain' of the *Untroubled Swan*, senior husband.

Bravah – Youngest husband of the family, a little jealous, a little too fond of anger.

Jawala – Strongest and wisest of the Hakran crew/family, senior of Aanat's three wives (and with two fellow-husbands).

Miti – Youngest in the family, independent, and stubborn, wife of the *Untroubled Swan* family.

Mokshi – Middle husband of the family, older, superb cook, steady and reliable.

Pavi – Middle wife of the Hakran family, veteran sailor and merchant.

Narmerians facing the Gods

Ahaz – Prince of Yahud, vassal of Narmer and all-round cool guy.

Ak-Arrina – A prince of the royal house and Maritaten's distant cousin.

Hehet – A junior palace functionary.

Horat – Maritaten's charioteer and informal military advisor.

Maritaten – Goddess-Queen of Narmer, although a rebel against the gods, often referred to as 'Lady of Narmer' or 'Lady of the High House'.

Mari-Ye – Chief priest of Arrina, the banished goddess, and her civil advisor.

Seti-Anu – A prince of another royal house – Maritaten's deadly enemy and occasional ally.

Timut-Imri – A mysterious and very powerful sorcerer.

Tudhal – Godborn sell-sword from Atussa, commander of the Sword Guard.

Zos's Fleet

Trayos – Lord of Dardania, Captain of the *Wave Serpent*, a merchant and a pirate and a former lord of Trin.

Daos – Probably a supernatural being. Captain of the *Trident*.

Tuwinon – Captain of *Shark*, a pirate and former Mykoan noble.

Alektron – Helmsperson of Zos' *Sea Eagle*, a veteran sailor.

Erithra – Helmsperson of *Sea Eagle*, a young fisherwoman.

Jianis – Eritha's father, an old fisherman.

Orestas – Captain of *Winter Gamble*.

Rathor of Narmer – Captain of *Revenge*, formerly a slave of the Jekers.

Stilko of Lazba – Captain of *In a God's Eye*.

Anturis – Captain of *Porpoise*. Southerner, former Jeker slave.

Leontas – Captain of *Sea Lion*, and leader of his own squadron.

Other Characters

Agon of Mykoax – God-King of Dardania.

Anenome – Godborn sell-sword; short, blond, and long-limbed, reputed the best warrior in the world.

Atrios the Great – War king of Mykoax, killed by his wife after the failure of the Holy War against the Hakrans.

Axe – Tall, dark, and old, a killer mercenary who has survived many wars. Partner of Anenome.

Bror – A stuffed bear.

Cyra – Goddess-Queen of Noa, old and powerful, and very competent.

Drakon – A big, ugly man with a mysterious past. A veteran mercenary.

Dite – A mysterious, exotic and very powerful woman.

Eritha – A fisherwoman of Trin.

Hyatta-Azi – Former Atussan prince, and a great captain among the Jekers.

Kussu – A market rat boy.

Lan Thena – A tall woman from western Dardania, a veteran mercenary.

Lawesa – A former slave and clandestine leader.

Makeda, Tisa, Theklassa – Three nomad warriors.

Mekos – God-king of Kyra, a powerful city-state too close to Narmer.

Mura of Samar – Pollon's lover and landlady, a merchant of nomad birth.

Nannu – A persistent donkey.

Persay of Mykoax – A mad former slave and failed bull-leaper.

Spathios – Scribe for the god-king of Hekka.

Taha – A former slave from Py and veteran scout.

Thanatos – God-king of Hekka, neighbour to Kyra and very rich.

The Old Gods

Antaboga – The World Serpent. The last dragon.

Arrina – Narmerian sun goddess, former lover of Enkul-Anu, now banished to the Outer Darkness.

Aurora – Goddess of Dawn and Dusk.

Nanuk – 'The old man of the sea', Nanuck by his northern name. In the south, Nammu. Sometimes a big old man, sometimes a sea monster. Also God of Horses.

Ranos – The Father and lord of the old pantheon

Shemeg – Old pantheon sun god in the Hundred Cities

Taris – Former Queen of Heaven and top god of the old pantheon, killed by Ara in the last 'War in Heaven'.

Temis – Also the Dark Huntress, Black Goddess – one of the Sisters. Lady of Animals, sometimes a goddess of death and chaos. The only one of the old gods to still hold a place in the new pantheon.

The 'New' Gods

Anzu – The winged lion-headed god of rage and insanity, a dangerous killer.

Ara – God of War and Strife. Only marginally sane. Still, a Greater God.

Druku – God of Drunkenness and Orgies, who is tired of being treated as a drunk. A Greater God.

Enkul-Anu – Bull-headed God of the Storm. Master of the pantheon. Just trying to hold it all together.

Grulu – Goddess of Spite and Envy; completely mad, or perhaps just senile.

Gul – God of the Underworld, Lord of the Hosts of the Dead. A Greater God.

Illikumi – A snake god, God of Liars, also of many merchants. Not very powerful but very clever.

Laila – A sort of demi-goddess. Apparently, just a servant. Apparently.

Kur – The Underworld, where Gul and Urkigul rule as Enkul-Anu rules heaven. Seven layers of hells, most of them rumoured to be very cold.

Nerkalush – The son of Gul, a junior god looking to increase his power.

Nisroch – Herald of the Gods, a son of Enkul-Anu with plans of his own.

Resheph – A junior god with a high opinion of himself, son of the God of War.

Sypa – Goddess of Lust; a Greater Goddess and consort of Enkul-Anu.

Tyka – Also the Blue Goddess, the Antlered One – the other 'Sister'. The goddess of death in childbirth, of fertility, of things reborn and things dying and rotting, and being healed and reborn.

Telipinu – The chamberlain of the Gods, son of Sypa and Enkul-Anu, a very junior godling.

Timurti – Goddess of the Sea, totally lost to age and madness. A Greater God.

Urkigul – Gul's wife, Lady of the Underworld. A Greater Goddess.

Uthu – The 'new' sun god. Almost powerless.

Some titles

Ra-wa-ke-ta – The champion of the god-king.

Ra-pte-re – The chancellor of the god-king.

Basilios – A great lord.

Wanax – A king who is not also an appointed god-king, a Dardanian term also used for generals and powerful lords.

God-kings – Mortals appointed by the gods to rule important centres, usually given immortal resin (ambrosia) to prolong their lives and powers.

Godborn – The literal descendants of the gods and god-kings, either the current pantheon or their predecessors. Few of them have any real powers, but their claim to superiority remains mostly unchallenged.

The Outer Darkness

Temis, the Dark Huntress, spun through the endless, featureless darkness of the void. She couldn't breathe but then, as a goddess, she didn't really need to breathe. The cold was a limitless, terrifying thing, but where a mortal body might have frozen, or exploded, she merely endured. The cold – even the absolute cold of the void – was not going to kill her.

She withdrew into herself, thinking her dark thoughts, most of which were about how her sister, the Blue Goddess, had set her up for a fall and walked away unscathed. And she spent an unfathomable aeon trying to imagine how Enkul-Anu could think she was in league with the Jekers when Temis herself had warned him of the whole plot.

That had provided her with some entertainment.

And then she began to imagine the revenge she'd wreak when she returned, but that led, with a kind of awesome finality, to the thought she was trying to avoid...

There was no return from the Outer Darkness, not unless you were released or rescued. Enkul-Anu had loved Arrina, and he'd banished her into the Outer Darkness, and the poor goddess of the Sun had never returned.

And Enkul-Anu had been obsessed with Arrina, whereas he flat-out hated the Dark Huntress.

She cursed, trying to see where it had all gone wrong.

It had seemed like any other petty crisis among the gods: Enkul-Anu had ordered the death of an over-mighty mortal, Gamash of Weshwesh. The Huntress had made use of Gamash herself; he was just the sort of ambitious fool that the gods loved.

I

But one of the insane godlings had got his orders mixed up, and killed Gamash's daughter Irene instead. Why had *that* mattered so much? Temis spun in the dark, remembering.

Tyka, the Blue Goddess, had promised the man revenge, and the two sisters had found star-stone out on the edge of reality near the Outer Darkness, and thrown it to earth. It was an old ploy – something they did to annoy the other gods. Mortals would make weapons which could harm the gods, and the gods would react with war, terror and repression. Enkul-Anu didn't know any other way. And the repression fostered further revolt, the ripples spreading…

Temis might have shrugged – the story was so familiar – if she hadn't been so utterly cold.

And there'd been one other mistake: the same godling, sent to support one mortal kingdom against another, had managed to destroy the kingdom he'd been sent to support – and had been wounded by a mortal.

Oh, how I savoured that.

In response, her blue 'sister', Tyka, had rescued the mortal along with some others. She'd had her share in the choices; all expendable mortal tools. A craftsman, a bureaucrat, a dancer, a washed-up warrior. Not the heroes they usually used.

And then Tyka had put them aboard a ship full of pacifist Hakrans. Another very strange choice. As she examined the steps that had led to her expulsion into the Outer Darkness, the Huntress realised how much of the action had been driven by Tyka. How many of the choices her silent 'sister' had made.

She winced.

I thought I was in charge.

Then Nisroch had plotted against his father, Enkul-Anu.

And the foolish godlings, Nerkalush and Resheph, had plotted against Nisroch.

And the puny human ship had washed up on the beaches of

the dead island, Dekhu, seat of the old gods. Her former friends and allies who she thought of as *dead*. And everything went straight to hell. Someone had killed the godlings; someone had released the ancient World Serpent, which pre-dated the realms of the gods.

All of the gods.

The island had exploded; the resulting cataclysm had probably hurried the environmental collapse, and it had certainly thinned the human population. The tidal wave alone would have killed so many…

Even floating alone and abandoned in the void, the Dark Huntress found tears frozen to her eyes.

Who released the fucking World Serpent?

She spun in endless, perfect darkness, alone, considering it all, as time passed.

She revisited all her own decisions, and those of others.

She repented her errors, but not her rebellion.

She imagined revenge.

She longed to return.

And more time passed.

Revisit.

Repent.

Revenge.

Return.

'How long until I go mad?' she wondered after six or nineteen cycles of repeating her own thoughts.

Not that long.

And then, with malign satisfaction: *Without me, the wheels will fall off. Even now, the whole environment is collapsing, and the Jekers are an accelerant, and the Dry Ones are creeping in from the desert edge. A couple of centuries more, and …*

That's all I can hope for? A complete revolution, with the winner

3

inviting me back. Nisroch? Not really up to it, and maybe dead, anyway. My sister Tyka? A plotter without power. Clever, though.

Sypa?

For the first time in forty cycles of self-recrimination and desire for revenge, the Dark Huntress had a new thought. About Enkul-Anu's affair with Arrina and the former sun goddess's spectacular fall from grace. She had secretly been leading an insurrection among mortals and trying to give them the secret of the resin that fed the gods.

What, five hundred years ago?

I always believed that story, the Dark Huntress thought, spinning silently in the dark. *But with nothing to do but think …*

Look at the aftermath: Arrina was banished to the Outer Darkness … Arrina, who was a threat to … Sypa.

And Sypa's son Telipinu takes over the resin works.

Fuck, how did I fail to see this?

Regret.

Revisit.

Repent.

Revenge.

Return.

How long until I go mad?

Book One

Journeys

Chapter One

Zos

The damage from the explosion of the island of Dekhu and the resulting titanic wave was visible everywhere on the headlands of Hergos in southern Dardania. The islands off the coast had been washed clean of trees and shrubs, and the floating olive trees were a hazard to even the simplest navigation; the heavy wood lay deep in the water, invisible to any but the sharpest-eyed lookout. Above them, the heavy clouds of ash and the storm of heaven hid the stars and the sun, until the world seemed to lie under an iron-grey light.

'Tree!' roared Makeda. She was one of three nomad women from south of the Hundred Cities, a proven warrior with long scars on her forehead and torso and a fluttering black veil hiding her nose and mouth; her eyes were sharp enough to penetrate the gloom and the reflections of light on the waves.

At the stern, Lord Trayos made a precise gesture, and his two helmsmen turned the damaged ship slightly to starboard. They all felt it as the keel scraped through the sunken tree's branches. Leaves boiled to the surface, as if the tree was a living monster spitting yellow-green bile.

Everyone on board had seen so much worse in the past days that no one reacted, beyond an exhausted sailor spitting over the side.

Trayos turned to the man beside him on the command deck: a tall, whip-thin man in a stained linen kilt and a gold and ivory swordbelt, bearing a sword so magnificent as to contrast sharply with the man's rumpled, filthy kilt and his salt-stained brown cloak. Trayos was more richly dressed, with two gold rings, a fabulous amulet that glowed like a peacock's tail, and a salt-stained kilt of his family's red and gold tartan, but the man wearing the magnificent sword had the perfect carriage of a dancer and the muscles of a veteran warrior, and his face was set.

Zos looked ahead, over the bow, at the sharp brown hills of his native land. As a young man he'd vowed never to return, his disgraced and humiliated mother a weeping bundle at his feet as he piloted a small boat into the Great Green, the endless sea, towards distant Lazba and freedom.

Zos could almost see that bitter young man now. Indeed, he had the strangest vision: the past overlaid on the present; the fishing smack sailing on the opposite tack...

When they passed the long point where the mountain met the sea in the shape of the great stone lion, then he'd see the enormous bay of his father's kingdom. His *dead* father's *fallen* kingdom.

And Trin, once a mighty fortress topped with a palace, would be a ruin, as it had been throughout his adolescence. Kept that way as a sort of hostage by the 'Great God-King' of all-conquering Mykoax. And yet, deep in his heart, he always expected to see it as it had been in his youth: the temples shining and white atop tall walls built of stones so huge that men said that the gods must have wrought them.

'Tree!' Makeda roared again.

The helmsmen turned the ship a little to port, and she glided over the next wave, the reaching branches of a dead oak whispering against her sides like all of Zos' ghosts asking to be remembered.

'You are determined to do this?' Trayos said.

He'd asked the same question four or five times since dawn had revealed the Dardanian coast, and it was clear that they would survive the storm.

Zos didn't turn his head, or answer.

'It's a waste, my prince,' the Dardanian pirate captain said.

He received no answer.

Pleion was the port of ruined Trin and now, of Mykoax. The huge wave born of the death of the island of Dekhu had broken on the long headland of the Lion, but the harbour had not escaped. The rising water had destroyed tavernas and warehouses all along the waterfront. Fifty war galleys were thrown high above the beach, and most were broken. The water was full of corpses and sea-wrack: wrecked ships; floating straw roofs; waterlogged bales of the famous Mykoan wool, and everything else – pomegranates and harvested grapes, half-submerged bales of grain, whole forests of cut lumber rising and falling on small waves.

Above the beach, perhaps half a hundred men moved like *gidimu*, animated corpses that necromancers used as eternal slaves. Just visible above them, a man in a chariot shouted orders.

He was motioning at the line of destruction at the tidal wave's high-water mark, but even three hundred paces away, Zos could see that his head was turned to watch the ship come in.

Zos allowed himself a small smile. He understood the man's amazement, because no ship should have survived that storm.

The rowers rowed, and the black ship crept in, her pitch-covered hull leaking in half a dozen places, her oar-banks thin on both sides from losses – dead men thrown over the side at the height of the waves and storm.

He must wonder if we are a ship of the dead.

'I'm coming with you,' said the boy, Daos.

Zos lifted an eyebrow. He'd been training the child, a little, but not enough for the boy to stand in a fight.

He shook his head, but his eyes widened.

'You've ...' He felt like a fool. 'You've grown.'

It was true. The boy, a whip-thin pre-adolescent of perhaps ten years, now looked like a muscled mid-adolescent. Narrowing waist, enhanced upper body ...

When did that happen?

Zos had spent months contending with the supernatural – gods, demigods, the World Serpent – and yet, somehow, a boy achieving five years' growth in forty days at sea seemed the most remarkable feat of all.

Daos looked down. 'It's confusing,' he admitted.

Zos remembered his own adolescence, which had also seemed to happen at a ridiculous speed, and his slight smile became rueful and broad.

'It's always confusing,' he said.

Daos shrugged. 'Anyway, I'm coming,' he said. 'I'm your *papista*.'

'Boy,' Zos said without anger, 'every *papista* I've ever had has died. In combat.'

Daos shrugged again. 'I won't die,' he promised. 'And if you take me, you won't die either.'

It was moments like this that made life with the boy so very difficult.

'The Dark Huntress told you this?' Zos asked.

The boy shook his curly head. 'Oh, no. Her voice is silent now. I just know it.'

Zos looked at the boy – really, at the young man. Behind him was Persay, the heavily muscled former slave with the bull's head tattooed on his chest. His mad eyes were too open, too glittery, to be normal. But the man put a hand on the boy's shoulder as if they were old mates.

'I'll be coming, too,' he said.

'As will I,' Makeda said. 'And my sisters.'

Zos closed his eyes and took a breath. Opened them and exhaled slowly, trying to blow the unreasoning rage out through his nostrils.

Behind Persay, the man in the chariot was motioning to the men around him, and to the ship.

Zos looked at Persay, and then at Makeda.

'It's over,' he said. 'Whatever adventure we thought we might have, it's over. The revolt against the gods? It fucking died in the volcano. The plan? Fuck it, you don't even know the plan. It doesn't matter. You're free people. Take your freedom and go!'

'Great,' Persay said. 'I'm free to choose? I'm choosing to come with you.'

Zos felt a great sadness replace the rage.

'Friends ...' he began.

Makeda shrugged. She didn't speak in Dardanian, and she didn't show any sign of understanding it. Instead, she spoke in Betwana, the trade tongue of the far east.

Pollon stepped up behind her and translated.

'You are our war leader now. We choose you. We make war when you make war.' She crossed her hands on her scarred chest. Both of her sisters did the same.

Pollon looked at her, and then at Zos.

'Nomads aren't good at taking no for an answer,' he said, spreading his hands.

'I'm going to die,' Zos said. 'Tell her that.'

Daos shook his head. 'Not if I come, you aren't!' he said. 'You don't die. And anyway, Era is still alive, and so are Aanat and Jawala ...'

Zos froze.

And then he looked down at the boy.

'What?' he spat.

'Nanuk sent a sea monster to save Aanat and the ship,' Daos said.

Trayos made a sign – a forbidden sign. 'Nanuk, Lord of the Sea, is dead, killed by Timurti,' he said. 'It is forbidden even to mention his name.'

Daos shrugged. 'Nanuk was never exactly a god,' he said in his crackly adolescent voice. Daos was cursed with sounding like every assertive young male who'd ever lived, carrying no conviction or authority at all, and most older people were immune to it. 'Nor did Timurti kill him.'

But his words . . .

'They're alive?' Zos grabbed his *papista*'s shoulders.

Daos grinned. 'And quarrelling among themselves.'

Pollon muttered, 'That sounds believable.'

Zos puffed up his cheeks and exhaled explosively.

'So,' Daos said, 'we all come with you, you will do this thing, and then you make a plan and we . . .' he looked across the sea, 'go to Narmer.'

Trayos brightened. 'I have friends in Narmer,' he said. 'But what does this boy – this *ephebe* – know?'

Zos, caught between rage, revenge, hope, and some other emotions, felt he had to defend the boy.

'He is a seer,' he said simply. 'An oracle.'

Trayos looked at the boy, touched his peacock amulet, and pulled a face.

'Of course you have an oracle,' he said. 'Boy, do I die?'

The boy looked at him. Finally, he said, 'Do you really want to know?'

Trayos flinched. 'No!' he admitted.

Daos smiled. It was a wintry smile, and it never touched his eyes.

'No,' he said. 'Really, you don't.'

Trayos looked out to sea. 'Do I go . . . with glory?' he asked.

Daos smiled again, this time with his usual youthful pleasure. 'At the moment of victory, on the deck of a ship,' he said.

Trayos snorted. 'Can't ask for better than that, lad.'

In the end, they all came: Lord Trayos; all his surviving oarsmen; the six former slave-bullies; Persay, Daos, Pollon, the three nomad women and Zos. They beached the damaged triakonter in the ruins of ten other ships and hauled her ashore over the driftwood.

As they tied her stem to a piling set well above the normal waterline, a scared-looking man approached cautiously.

'The priest-lord tells me to greet you,' the man said in careful Dardanian. 'What land are you from? Are you living men or a ship of the dead? Are you friend or foe of our god-king Agon of Mykoax?'

Zos was up to his knees in filthy water, looking at the chipped black pitch and the deep wound below it in the boards of the ship. Trayos was no slouch about work; he was also knee-deep in the water, despite it being full of dead things, but his hand was on the stern where it met the keel.

'She'll have to be rebuilt, he said bitterly. 'Or burned.'

One of the blows the ship had taken had torn the stern away from the planking on the port side. It didn't look as bad as the other damage, but it was a deadly wound for a ship.

Zos ignored the herald, or speaker, or whatever he was – perhaps just a scared slave – and sloshed over to where Trayos stood.

He waved over the harbour.

'We could build ten good ships out of these.' He pointed at a pentekonter, a fifty-oared galley floating upside down and looking like a giant turtle, or a monstrous basking shark.

'I'll wager we could right her and row her away today.'

Trayos' jaw worked. He clearly loved his own ship.

Zos glanced back at the herald.

'We're busy,' he said. 'When we're finished, I'll be happy to answer your questions. But we're living men, just like you.'

Daos, very cheerful, put a hand on the herald's arm. 'You should hide until sunset.' The man looked at Daos, who shrugged. 'It would be the best thing for you.'

Zos looked at Daos. 'Are you just going to oracle all the time?'

Daos shrugged. 'No idea. It comes and goes, you know?'

Zos smiled. 'No, thanks to all the gods, I don't know.'

The herald was still looking at Daos. But then he turned and went back up the wreck-infested beach, and a moment later they could hear his respectful tone.

Zos looked at Trayos. 'This will keep,' he said. 'If we live, we do our repairs. If we're dead, who cares?'

Trayos sighed. 'I love my ship.'

But he and his oarsmen picked up their spears and shields and followed Zos, as did everyone else.

Zos had a pair of javelins, an old bull's-hide shield that Trayos had loaned him, and no armour at all. But he led the way, and Daos carried his shield. They negotiated the rubble, the storm rack, the shipwrecks and the corpses, bloated and venting gas into the fetid air.

Zos glanced at Pollon. 'You really don't have to come, old man.'

Pollon had his bow, and a handful of arrows. He shrugged.

Zos shrugged back, then looked back at all of them. He wanted to say something grand about time, and revenge, but mostly he felt sick and light-headed and he hated the sheer waste of all the death and destruction. He wondered, with a sort of hollow guilt, if it was all his fault.

Persay clapped him on the shoulder.

'You are in a black place, my lord.'

'I am,' Zos said.

'Lay waste your enemies.' Persay smiled. 'You'll feel better.'

Zos shook his head. But the madman raised his spirits for reasons he could not fathom. And he stepped over the obscenely swollen body of an old woman, and managed not to step on a dead dog. Then he was in a clearer area with the man in the chariot and a few dozen of his workers, or slaves. They looked as if they hadn't slept or eaten; more than half were naked.

He walked towards the chariot. He still wasn't quite sure why he had to do this. But he did. Agon had to die.

The man in the chariot raised a hand. 'Stop there,' he said.

Zos kept walking.

The man's charioteer was young, but he had the haughty bearing of the godborn. The other man in the box was clearly an aristocrat – a palace bureaucrat or retired warrior, or both.

'When my lord orders you to stop, you stop.' The man spoke with casual authority.

Zos kept walking. He was perhaps ten paces away.

The man in the chariot raised his bow.

'Last warning, stranger—'

Zos threw his javelin into the unarmoured man's chest. It wasn't a perfect throw; instead of a killing shot it went in low, just over the groin, and the man rolled over it and screamed. The charioteer tried to gather his reins, but it was too late for that. He reached for his short sword instead, and Persay killed him from his blind side, a single cut up into the thigh. The boy bled out in seconds, a look of puzzlement on his face.

Zos, stepped up into the car. He hadn't been in a chariot in years, but one didn't forget; his toes engaged with the laced sinew in the bottom of the car, and the car rocked under his weight, but his knees flexed like a sailor in a storm.

'Daos?' he asked. 'Can you drive?'

Daos smiled. 'Of course, Lord Zos.'

He put the bull's-hide shield on his back and stepped past

Zos in the small car. His hands picked up the reins with the familiarity of long usage.

'Hello, my lovelies,' he said to the horses.

The two chariot horses were unremarkable but very steady, unmoved by blood and death – warhorses. They responded instantly to Daos; their heads came up, one snorted, and they both turned their heads.

Zos hardened his heart and used his right foot to dump the young charioteer's body onto the bloody gravel. The priest-lord was still alive, and his pain-filled eyes followed Zos. Zos leant down, pulled the javelin from his abdomen, and finished him. He didn't do it in anger or rage. Mostly what he felt was revulsion.

I'm not going to be much use as a warrior if I start feeling bad for everyone I kill, he thought.

The workers and slaves were open-mouthed.

Zos cleared his head, and looked at the assembled slaves.

'I'm Zos of Trin.' He hadn't identified himself as Zos of Trin since he was nine years old. 'I'm a mortal man like you who survived the storm. In answer to the priest-lord's questions, I'm from here – my father was king of Trin. And I'm no friend or ally of the king of Mykoax – I'm his enemy, and I intend to kill him.'

Some of the locals were flinching away now; none of them were smiling.

Zos leant on the chariot rail, and smiled.

'Best thing you can do is run home and hide until I leave,' he said. 'I'll be done in two or three days.' He crossed his arms. 'Unless you want to be done with him, too, in which case ...' He glanced at Trayos. 'In which case, we're recruiting, and we'd be happy to pick up seventy or eighty good men of Trin.'

Terrified silence greeted him. But one man came forward immediately, and then another, and Trayos had his helmsmen start organising them to land the best of the wrecks and see if their hulls could be dried out.

Zos nodded. Then he stepped down from the chariot and pulled his javelin from the priest-lord's corpse. It took more effort than he'd expected.

'Bring a firepot or two,' Daos said.

'What?' Zos asked.

'We may need to burn something,' the boy said, and smiled his prophetic smile.

A sailor fetched two clay pots full of coals.

'Let's go up to Mykoax, then,' Zos said.

He cleaned the head on the man's good robes. Before he turned away, people were pillaging the body.

The road from Pleion Harbour to the old citadel of Trin was straight and well-paved with huge blocks of stone. A thousand years of noble chariots and peasant wagons had worn ruts in the stone, but the ruts only made the travel easier, and the horse's hooves were hard from a dry summer and rang like iron on the old stone.

Trin remained a ruin. The walls were intact, of course, because their titanic stones would be virtually impossible to move anyway. Off to the west, Gosa towered over the olive-tree plain, the mightiest fortress of them all. The old king of Mykoax had taken Gosa by stealth and treason, massacred its inhabitants and burnt its palaces, but none of that was visible from here.

Zos considered. He knew where the survivors lived; the refugees had moved to an island in the Ocean.

He shook his head.

I won't need to plan after this. I can stop plotting.

But Narmer...

The old king Atrios had burnt the palace of Gosa, as his son had burnt Trin. No palace was allowed to stand except mighty

Mykoax, rich in gold, and for his success Atrios' son Agon had been rewarded with the ambrosia of heaven, the title god-king and the promise of immortality.

Zos looked back, amused at his own insanity. He was planning to storm Mykoax with thirty-three people.

Not so much planning to, as coming on the wings of the storm and making it all up as I go, he thought. And then darker thoughts leapt in. *Here, I saw them take my mother. Here, I was made to ...*

He had sixty stadia of chariot riding to remind him of his home, his country, and his anger. Four hours, rolling along at a walking pace with his friends walking behind him, or walking himself. The ground above Trin was too steep for the chariot to roll easily when loaded, so Zos stepped down and walked with Pollon while the boy Daos drove.

'Where did he learn to drive a chariot?' Zos asked quietly, trying to fight his own demons.

'When did the skin on the back of our hands become so smooth?' Pollon asked.

Zos looked down and felt a stomach-turning moment of shock.

Pollon, in his pedantic way, went on, 'The Dry One didn't just heal us, my friend. It gave us the ambrosia of the gods. Or rather ...' His voice held a variety of strong emotions: discovery, curiosity, anger. 'Or rather, it seems to me that the gods' entire rule rests on a single product – the blood of the Dry Ones. Indeed, I might theorise about the so-called godborn ...'

Zos, whose head had been lost in the scenes of his mother's degradation and his own endless humiliations as a boy, snapped back to the present.

'Huntress!' he spat, and then managed a smile. 'What will we do for swear words if we have no gods?' he asked Pollon.

Pollon raised an eyebrow. 'An excellent question. Perhaps

words that refer to copulation and defecation – they were quite popular with my contemporaries.'

Zos blinked slowly. 'I wasn't *really* asking,' he said, with almost a grin.

Pollon smiled. 'I know. But it's an interesting talking point nonetheless. And I made you smile.'

Zos put a hand on his shoulder, and the ghosts of his past edged away. 'Bless you, brother.'

Pollon nodded. 'But all kidding aside, I have a point.'

'Which is …?'

'We should strike their supply of resin. Somewhere, somehow, the gods must take and store it.' He looked at Zos. 'This is only a theory. But if my theory is correct, the gods are simply mortals like us, with endless access to the resin of the Dry Ones.'

'Fuck, no wonder the Bright People hate us.' Zos shook his head. 'Pollon, you are brilliant. But they aren't mortals like us. You saw them when they were hit. Monsters.'

'It's only a theory,' Pollon said. 'And look, I've made you smile again.'

'Storming heaven sounds even more foolish than storming Mykoax,' Zos said. 'Untenable. But striking against the source of their immortality …'

'Unless I'm wrong,' Pollon said.

Zos fingered his beard, thinking of the demons and the shapes they'd taken in combat.

'You know what, brother? A year ago, I thought I knew a great deal about how the world worked. It was cynical and dark, but I understood it.' He looked up at the enormous fortification of Mykoax high on the mountain above them. 'Now I wonder if I understand anything at all.'

Pollon frowned. 'I feel exactly the same. Are all godborn warriors as thoughtful as you?'

Zos shrugged. 'Are all palace bureaucrats as brave as you?'

Pollon met his eye. 'I'm not brave. I just cannot bear to desert my friends.'

Zos took in a breath of air, looking over the little army of men and women, and the road that fell away down the hills to the iron-grey sea under the iron-grey sky. Suddenly, his mood was lightened. Suddenly, he didn't want to die. Revenge seemed petty, but he could see a world beyond revenge.

'That's all courage is,' Zos said. 'Making up excuses not to run away.' He looked back up. 'But you know what? I think Daos is right. I don't think we die today.'

'Of course I'm right,' Daos said.

The road ran past the magnificent gate to the underworld that was the Tomb of Atrios, the enormous doorway capped by a monolith as large as a house.

'Incredible,' Pollon said.

'You've never been to Narmer,' Zos said.

They walked up the dusty road to the citadel of Mykoax, standing on the windswept mountain. There were people on the road – beggars, and pilgrims going to the tomb. All made way for the chariot, because only godborn men had chariots, and the godborn were lethal to ordinary folk.

Zos had remounted the chariot as they passed the Tomb of Atrios. He didn't make an offering, or salute it, which made him feel odd, as he had always done so before. When he was a hostage.

An elite slave. Face the facts.

How it all came rushing back.

Persay gave a mad laugh as he passed the enormous gate and its bronze doors.

'Dead is dead!' he called out. 'No matter what you put the corpse in.'

Pilgrims in the road made the sign of aversion, and a woman made the evil eye sign.

They walked on. The chariot rumbled over the smaller paving stones – the god-kings of Mykoax had never invested in roads as heavily as the god-kings of Trin, and Zos could feel it in his bones.

And then they took the last turn in the road, and there was the Great Gate. Above it a great god's eye in lapis and gold, and above that two lions stood to either side of a massive stone pillar, their onyx eyes gazing out at the traveller.

It was clear that even here, the storm had done damage – perhaps not the lethal damage of the great wave, but rooves had slumped off houses, and just inside the gate, a tiled, whitewashed stone house had been reduced to rubble by a titanic stone flung off the wall. The high winds and scouring pumice had driven most people inside, and a continuous wailing from the temple atop the highest citadel suggested that the rest were invoking the gods.

Zos was a veteran of this particular palace-fortress and he knew that most of these people were palace professionals: scribes like Pollon, craftspeople like Atosa, entertainers like Era, warriors like himself. He glanced up at the megaron that faced the temple. His target, the god-king Agon, the terror of his youth, would be within its red pillars.

Made it this far.

There were guards at the gate, of course – four men in bronze, none of them a day over twenty, all with the marks of a night spent on watch and a day spent in fear. They were too young to know him.

Men in armour. It was odd; in his day they'd have been bull-leaper *ephebes* – warrior-athletes in training, naked but for a kilt and a sword.

Zos raised his hand in greeting. He didn't have a plan past this point. He was still a little puzzled by the ease with which they'd come up the mountain. The mighty storm must have had more effect even than he'd reckoned.

'My lord,' said the *loxos*. 'I must ask you to dismount and hand over your weapons. This is a very … difficult … time.' He didn't smile; he clearly took himself and his role very seriously.

Zos looked at him and realised that this young man was about to die; it was almost like being Daos. There was no peaceful way he was passing this gate; there was no possibility of mercy. And he didn't like that.

But it didn't matter, because when the chariot rolled to a stop, it all unfolded as if the future really was a predestined thing. Perhaps, if he hadn't taken the chariot …

No. He wanted his revenge. He *wanted* this. Even though that serious young man had never done him any harm.

Zos shrugged. 'Kill them,' he said.

And it was done.

Because it hadn't really occurred to any of the four men at the gate that they'd be attacked, they didn't land a single blow. Persay killed one and tripped another, and the three nomad women finished them, and it was done. There was a surprising amount of blood on the cobbles, and the horses remained unperturbed.

Zos found that if he went with the inevitability, it was less unpleasant.

'Drive on,' he said to Daos.

The boy was smiling.

'Jawala makes some good points,' Zos said.

He was thinking about Jawala's insistence that all violence was murder, and never justified. She was Hakran, a pacifist. And in his current mood, his dark revulsion was still over-balancing his desire for revenge.

Daos glanced at him, a very adult smile on his young face.

'She certainly does,' the boy said. 'And yet, sometimes, someone has to put down a rabid dog.'

There had been enough bystanders to the killings at the gate that they could hear the screams in the town as the chariot rolled past the sacred enclosure, where the old god-kings were buried. In the ancient days they'd buried their kings inside the walls, and a circular tunnel led to the underworld.

Again, Zos had to fight the urge to propitiate their shades and make his reverence. He was done with all that, and the chariot rolled by with none of them making any sign of respect to the dead.

'I can feel their anger,' Pollon said. 'The dead.'

'They're about to be much angrier,' Zos said.

Somewhere above them in the town, a woman screamed, and a man called, and someone beat a bronze bell.

Zos' chariot rolled on. The horses were flagging, but it was an offence against the god-king to ride a chariot in the upper town, and Zos had always imagined entering the citadel in a chariot.

Halfway up the sacred way that led from the circle of ancient graves to the upper town's temples, a line of armoured men barred the road. The road was narrow; it ran from the magnificent stone wall on the right to the cliff's edge on the left, with a seven-hundred-foot drop to the dry stream bed far below.

'Ready?' Zos asked his charioteer.

Daos grinned. 'Born ready,' he said.

The chariot was going up a steep slope behind a pair of tired horses who'd walked all the way from the sea, and probably had walked half as far again that morning, and yet, as Daos tightened the reins, their heads came up. He said something to them in a language that Zos didn't know, and their tails swished once, making an eerie sound.

Zos didn't need to look back to know that his little war band was gathered behind him.

'Go,' he said.

The chariot horses leapt to full stride without further word or whip – fatigue falling away. The cart lurched forward so hard that Zos, trained from youth to fight this way, was almost flung from the car.

Daos, leaning forward, toes curled over the axle, looked like the living embodiment of a charioteer, reins in his left hand, and his long trident held aloft in his right.

The bronze-clad warriors waiting in two ranks across the cliffside road had perhaps forty paces to decide how to deal with the oncoming horses and chariot. It was rare a chariot attacked formed men; the cars themselves were too lightly built to survive the collision, and horses don't particularly like planting their delicate legs among squirming men and their sharp edges.

No one had told these horses, or this driver, that.

Perhaps ten paces from impact about half of the warriors, including all those closest to the cliff edge, elected to either shuffle back or away from the cliff's edge.

Zos said, 'I haven't done this in a long time,' and dropped his cloak.

Perhaps three paces from impact, he leapt up to plant one foot on the chariot rail, flung a javelin *down* into one of the bronze-clad warriors from above, over the man's tower shield, like one of Enkul-Anu's thunderbolts … and went forward *over the rail* to land on the chariot pole between the horses. His landing wasn't perfect, and he used his free hand on the offside horse's back to stay on the pole as they burst through the disintegrating formation. His second javelin took a brave man in the mouth as he tried to rally his men, and over his shoulder he saw another warrior, braver than the rest, lean out and stab at Daos.

Daos turned the thrust with the haft of his trident, just the way he'd been taught. And then he stabbed the man, his blow perfectly timed.

The man *turned to ash*.

And they were past, racing up the long curve of the Sacred Way as the rest of the men who had tried to hold the road dissolved into a cloud of dust.

Daos hauled on the reins, slowing the horses and twirling the trident over his right hand like an acrobat as he drove with his left. They trotted all the way to the top. Only the three nomad women and Persay could keep up; the rest of his people and Trayos' sailors were left behind.

'Did you see him?' Daos said. 'If you hadn't trained me, he would have killed me. Right there. I have seen it.'

Zos shook his head. He had nothing to say.

The road forked at the top of the Sacred Way; to the left and right it ran to the palace quarters, but straight on, through the High Gate, lay the palace megaron and the temple.

To the east, out over the sea, lightning flashed in black clouds, and thunder rolled high in the air.

The chariot came to a stop just short of the gate, and Zos put his back against the chariot rail and rolled back into the car.

'Are you hurt?' Daos asked.

Zos shook his head. 'Only my pride,' he admitted. 'I am not as practised as I used to be.'

In fact, his lower back was on fire and his groin...

'Let's do this,' he said.

He leant forward, the chariot rolled through the open gate of the sacred enclosure, and people began to scream.

To his right rose the Temple of All Gods, the Pantheon. Like every other pantheon in the world, its great frieze depicted all the Great Gods in their aspects: Enkul-Anu sat in judgement; Sypa, his consort, lay on a couch, divine and beautiful; Druku lay opposite her, raising a bunch of grapes; Ara, God of War, stood by in armour; Timurti somehow stood despite having a fish tail instead of legs, her arm around a dolphin. And at the other end of the portico, the Dark Huntress and the Blue Goddess were alone, angry, left out of the feast.

Because he was in the chariot car, he was almost at eye level with the priest raising his arms to the enormous golden statue of Enkul-Anu at the east end of the temple, where it could be seen from far out on the Ocean on a clear day. Behind the statue, the cliff fell sheer for six hundred feet to the rocks below. A dead boy lay across the altar in front of the statue, his throat cut, his viscera spread across the altar for augury. The carcasses of two more child-victims lay where they'd been thrown from the altar like rubbish.

Zos smiled, not because he approved of the scene, but because any lingering scruples fell away when he saw the rubbish heap of children.

A tall man in the prime of life, handsome, bearded, and wearing a long robe of magnificent mollusc red, embroidered with poppies and ravens, came to the steps, his face red with rage.

'You defile the sacred places, stranger, and for that your life is forfeit.'

Zos was not a splendid figure, as he'd often imagined himself to be in this moment; he didn't have a billowing scarlet cloak, nor a helmet of boar's tusks on his head, nor golden armour. He was splattered with blood, naked but for his filthy linen kilt.

And his back hurt.

But the smile stayed on his lips.

'I'm no stranger, Agon,' he said. 'I'm your humble slave Zos, son of Urystes, whom you killed.'

Zos stepped down from the chariot car as Daos stopped the team, and walked up the steps of the temple alone. The nomads were still in the gate while Persay stood, relaxed, by Daos and the chariot.

Agon narrowed his eyes. 'You fucking idiot,' he said.

'Kill him,' he said to his guards.

There were a dozen or so around him, and more across the great marble square, on the steps of the megaron, the palace hall. And more were coming up the side steps from the barracks.

Zos waited, savouring the moment. For the first time he *believed*. He believed they might overthrow the gods. Because he was in arm's reach of Agon, and no one had stopped him.

Two huge men pulled Agon to safety behind them, and the guards drew their swords.

And then Zos drew his.

There were some mortals who were relatively unaffected by the sword *Terror*, the sword usually carried by Ara, God of War. Men and women who'd faced their direst fears, or succumbed to them and then finally emerged, battered but unbroken: they could face the sword *eventually*.

But when Zos drew it, it was like a punch in the gut, and the more noble and thus unsullied a person was, the less resistance most of them had. The godborn guards fell away like chaff before a wind. The nobles and palace functionaries thronging the temple screamed almost as one, as if the scream were some continuation of their hymn to their distant and terrible gods.

Zos began to kill. He was sparing and cautious, like the trained warrior he was. He didn't waste energy on leaps; he used simple thrusts instead of heavy cuts.

Terror killed, and every death fed the dread sword, so that the waves of terror crashed down ever stronger, ravaging even the strongest heart. Some of the older people died in their terror; many leapt from the temple wall to end themselves on the rocks far below.

Zos didn't worry about the worshippers. He killed the guards, and out in the courtyard Persay slaughtered the other guards. The former slave was apparently unmoved by the lethal waves of fear. Even the nomad women paused in the gate, gathering themselves, but Persay *danced* and blood flowed on the white marble.

Until finally, as he'd always imagined, Zos had Agon before him, thrashing on the stained marble. The man was screaming in fear; he'd fouled his clothing, and writhed, unseeing.

Zos found it all curiously anticlimactic. He'd dreamt of killing Agon since he was fifteen, and now that he had him ... 'I only hope that your worst fear was me, returning,' Zos said. But Agon was a tool, however willing, and behind Agon stood the gods.

With the remarkable strength that the Dry One's healing had given him, Zos lifted the god-king of Mykoax, carried him to Enkul-Anu's altar, and threw him onto it, and ran Agon through the throat bole so that the great king's blood mixed with that of the children his priests had just sacrificed.

Zos looked up at the statue and raised his arms like a worshipper.

'Hear me, Enkul-Anu,' he said, and the statue flickered.

Zos still held the sword, *Terror*, naked in his hand, while Agon's blood ran down the carved channels in the altar, feeding the link to the Gods.

'Hear me, Enkul-Anu!' Zos called.

The statue's features began to grow in animation.

'Hear me, Enkul-Anu!' Zos roared like the power of the sea, the magical third time.

And the great god was made manifest.

'You dare?' the god bellowed. Only his head was animated; the rest of the statue was stone.

Zos spat into the great god's face.

'You're next!' Zos shouted.

Enkul-Anu cut the link to Mykoax and fell back onto his couch, shaken.

He was almost alone, except for the three sisters who waited on him night and day – unimportant human slaves. But none of the other gods had witnessed this humiliation. One of the slaves bent to wipe the spittle from his immortal face, and he killed her with an angry swipe of his hand, hurling her broken body across his private hall.

A *mortal worm* had dared ...

And he had Terror.

While I lie here, wounded by the World Serpent.

This isn't funny any more.

Chapter Two

Era

'We need to get out of here,' Era told her council, and Hefa-Asus nodded.

'It's like one of the hells of Kur,' the big man said. 'The hell of rotting corpses.'

He was looking out from under the big awning rigged out of one of the *Untroubled Swan*'s spare sails, spread over her long spar above the high stern. Ashore, as far as the eye could see, there were dead people and animals – cattle, sheep, dogs and cats – all washed up by the power of the titanic wave and the subsequent storm, now bloated and rotting in the now-bright sun. And the devastation continued inland for stadia on the low, flat, sandy soils of southern Rasna, home of the Hakrans. Along the beach there were six other ships. All the survivors, she suspected, of the forty ships that had sailed from Dekhu before the island exploded.

Perhaps half a thousand survivors, amid the devastation of Rasna.

Jawala looked up. Her hair was a tangle, her eyes bloodshot, and her hands were cut and bruised because she had spent the last two days burying bodies. These were her people.

'It's our fault,' she said heavily. 'We killed them. *You killed them*. This is what violence does.'

Aanat's and Pavi's hands bore the same marks. They looked at

30

each other, and then each put an arm around Jawala. She tried to shake them off for a moment, and then, as if their bodily warmth had broken her reserve, she, the strongest among them, began to weep.

Era had enormous respect for Jawala and her people – but she didn't agree at all.

'No, Jawala,' she said. 'The gods did this. The same gods who have been trying to destroy your people for hundreds of years.'

Jawala didn't raise her head.

Era went on, 'We cannot stay here. There's not enough food, and we have to mend our ships, which means docks and workers. And we, at least, have a cargo to trade.'

Hefa-Asus shook his head at her. 'We cannot try Poche. We're too weak.'

Aanat looked up from his wife. 'Don't you think Poche will be in much the same state as my poor Rasna?'

Era sat back, her chin in her hand. 'An excellent point.'

Nicté nodded sharply. 'All the coastal cities in Dendrowna will be in chaos,' she said with bloodthirsty satisfaction. 'Nanuk's balls! We should just go, take what we need, and run for the mountains.'

Hefa-Asus looked deeply unhappy. 'But the Poche kingdoms have the power to resist the gods. And the will.'

'And also the will to capture us and rip our hearts out,' Era said. 'Or so you have told me.'

Hefa-Asus shrugged. 'We will have to negotiate, regardless. But it will be better for everyone if we negotiate now, rather than a year from now, when we need to ship our star-stone weapons. Iron does not really kill mortals any better than bronze or stone – not at odds of twenty to one – and you don't want to face the Kuhl Ajaw of Nikal and his Jaguar Knights with some former slaves.'

Era shrugged. 'I've never even heard of Nikal,' she said.

Aanat spread his hands as if her ignorance was not his business. 'I'm not fond of soldiers,' he said. 'But the Jaguar Knights are ... terrifying.'

Pavi nodded. 'As are the Eagle Knights of the Tiatoni.'

Nicté tossed her head angrily. 'My people face them every season ...'

'Enough,' Era said flatly. 'I understand that they are fearsome. Very well. But the fact remains that we need to get out of here, as soon as possible. And I like the notion that the Poche states may be weak. Can we ...?' She looked at Aanat. 'Can we make a deal without bloodshed?'

Aanat narrowed his eyes. He looked at Jawala, as if Era's needs were not paramount in his hierarchy of needs, but then he looked back at her.

'It's what we do,' he allowed. 'We negotiate. And perhaps doing this, and avoiding violence ...' He shrugged. He was tired, and emotionally empty; seeing his civilisation dead on a beach had marked him.

Jawala looked up. 'I helped kill my people,' she said. 'I don't think I can live with that.'

She turned and left, climbing down the short ladder to the middle deck and the cargo holds.

Aanat watched her go but didn't follow, his face lit as much with anger as with regret.

'Pride is selfish,' he said bitterly. He looked after her with more anger than Era had expected.

Era's entire waking life was consumed with other people's problems, and there was a level at which she didn't really like people, which wasn't, apparently, a bar to good leadership. People stole, and hated and were afraid; they refused to do work that was clearly in the common interest, denied the obvious, started foolish rumours, were jealous, petty and vain. She saw it all every hour, as she tried to get the four hundred and sixty-five surviving former slaves and the crews of the ships that had survived the wave and the storm to unite, build a camp, find wood, repair the ships, gather food and prepare to depart.

It was all like wading through mud. Every problem solved led to new problems, most of them created by the people she was trying to save. She directed that they build a storage centre for the pithoi of grain that Dite was recovering, so people argued about the grain's distribution. She asked for latrines to be built, and they stared at her with dumb animosity.

'I'm not a slave any more,' one man said. And he was applauded for it.

However, Dite began to recover grain in fairly sizeable amounts – the stored grain of a generation of thrifty Hakran villagers. Some pithoi held olive oil, or salt fish, all sealed against the sea water, all recoverable, when you had a former god to do the digging. And use her godlike powers of seduction and persuasion on unwilling workers.

Era knew that loosing Dite on the former slaves was morally questionable, and she did it anyway.

And Taha, her Py scout, ranged farther and farther. He brought back a dozen donkeys, alive; then he and five more former slave-soldiers used the donkeys to range more widely. That was the day that the first warehouse to store food was finished; the day that Aanat persuaded the former slaves to dig latrines, the day that another surviving ship came ashore with seventy starving people and a pair of former slave-warriors holding them at bay with spears. And the day that Jawala put on an orange robe, walked down the beach, spread out a straw mat, and knelt, facing the sun.

Era saw her, a spot of orange against the drab beach. Everything still stank of death, even when they'd buried or burnt every body within a stade, as best they could.

33

'I hate this place,' Era said. 'I know it was your home…'

Aanat was watching his wife. Tears were streaming down his face.

Era looked at him. He was a tower of strength – always working, always steady – and here he was, weeping openly.

'Aanat, get it together. We're going to make it. The warehouse is up – we've got all the timber we'll ever need. Tomorrow we begin repairs…'

He was sobbing, and as she watched, he fell to his knees, his face a moving mask of despair.

Then, without warning, he leapt over the stern, landed on the packed sand below like a much younger man, and went running down the beach. He ran like a drunken man, or an old man – almost waddling.

Era didn't know what was going on, but her immediate assumption was that it would be bad. She jumped from the stern and followed him.

He ran down the beach towards Jawala, and she sat in orange dignity on her mat. He ran like a man racing death, and she sat, restfully watching…

She was only a dozen strides behind him when he came up to his wife.

'You *cannot!*' he screamed.

She had a nearly blank expression on her usually animated face. She said nothing.

'Jawala! You cannot do this!' he yelled. 'Jawala! All is not lost! You have spouses and responsibilities!'

Nothing.

'Jawala! For the love of all the gods, you cannot leave me alone like this!'

Nothing.

Era caught Aanat's arm. 'What's happening?' she asked, though she could guess.

Aanat pushed her away with more violence than she'd expected – anger, shock, emotional turmoil. The man was beyond distraught. But Era was a dancer, and she avoided the fall, swayed, and caught his arm.

'Aanat,' she hissed. 'I'm surrounded by people who seem to be bent on self-destruction. Don't you join them. What in all Kur is going on?'

Jawala stared into the sun, almost serene. Almost. Except that Era, through her training, could tell that the Hakran woman was listening – was, in fact, fully involved.

'She is going to die,' Aanat spat. 'Killing herself, by starvation.'

Jawala stared into the sun, which now lit her orange robe like flame.

'Fuck,' muttered Era. Very briefly, she considered striking the woman. 'Jawala, you are a leader! Every one of our people values and respects you. This is like desertion, and you're doing it in front of everyone, like a fucking attack on my authority.'

She stepped up close to the Hakran woman.

Jawala gazed into the sun.

'Damn it, woman!' Era spat. 'We need you!'

Nothing.

Era turned on her heel to find a dozen of their rescued former slaves watching.

'Perfect,' she muttered. 'Aanat, come with me.'

Aanat wasn't listening. Instead, he was kneeling in front of his wife, staring into her eyes.

Era shook her head and went back to the *Untroubled Swan*.

By evening, Aanat was also in an orange robe, staring at the horizon where the sun would rise.

Era stood on the stern of the *Untroubled Swan* with Pavi.

'Will you all follow them?' she asked.

Pavi looked down the beach, made a sign over her heart, and shook her head.

'No,' she said. 'I love the world too much, and I lack Jawala's courage. And her pride. She thinks we are the cause of all this.' Pavi shrugged. 'I think that's foolishness.'

'Can you talk them out of it?' Era asked.

Pavi gave her a look of surprise, even shock. 'Oh, no,' she said. 'It's a noble thing they do.'

Era looked at her. 'What?'

'It's not easy, starving yourself to death,' Pavi said. 'It's atonement, and it's not my place to take it from them. If they can do it...' She shrugged. 'They'll be saints.'

Era was bitter. 'Some people...' she began, but she realised that she needed Pavi and her other three spouses, Miti, Bravah and Mokshi, more than ever. So this was not a good time to belittle their culture.

She went down the beach to the shed and pen that housed both Nannu, the donkey they'd brought from Ma'rib, and Bror, the bear who'd once been a toy bear. The two seemed to get along quite well, which was definitely not the strangest thing that was going on in her world.

Era put her arms around Bror's neck, and she snuffled Era for a bit.

She cried a little, but mostly she just enjoyed the smell of the bear.

And she trusted Bror, which was more than she could say of Dite, her bedmate.

'Daos and Zos and Pollon, all lost,' she wept into the bear's fur. 'And now Jawala. I'm left to pick up the pieces.'

The bear patted her, but gave no answer.

The next morning, Taha returned with three of his scouts and two women on donkeys. They were Hakran, and they made a sign over their hearts when they saw the two orange robes, and then they came down the beach and greeted Era.

Taha pointed at them. 'I'm going to need a translator, lady,' he said. 'I went above the tideline, and there's a whole city there – thousands of Hakrans. These two are from a village right on the tideline.'

The tideline was the point, several thousand paces inland, where the great wave had reached its highest point on the coast of Rasna, and deposited its toll of corpses and straw roofs and logs and everything else it had scoured off the coast.

Pavi arrived, began to speak to the two women, and then she burst into tears and embraced each in turn.

'Rappa is not destroyed!' she said. 'The *eint ki devar* held!'

Era shook her head. 'What's Rappa?' she asked. 'And what's an *eint ki devar?*'

Pavi smiled through her tears. 'Rappa is the greatest city on this part of the coast, and the *eint ki devar*…' She was thinking hard, and it showed on her face. 'A huge wall to stop the rising floodwaters in spring.'

Era brightened. 'We should tell Jawala and Aanat,' she said.

Pavi frowned. 'They are dead.'

'What?'

'When a suitor puts on the orange robe, they are dead. One doesn't speak to them. If they fail the test, they may return to the living. But it would be rude to interrupt them now.' Pavi spoke firmly.

Era took that on board and nodded – not in agreement, but in acceptance. Later in the afternoon, she made the time to go and stand in front of the orange-clad couple.

'Your people are not dead,' she said. 'The sea wall of your great city held.'

It was a little like talking to a wall. Neither made eye contact. She wasn't even sure that she was getting through.

'Pavi says you are like dead people, and I shouldn't bother

you.' Era spread her hands. 'Jawala, you are the wisest of us, and I need you.'

Nothing.

Era had never felt so alone. So deserted. It was almost like betrayal, and it made her feel savage.

Like my godborn mother, walking off and leaving me, she thought, but that wasn't exactly fair. But she was angry, and not in a mood to be fair.

Farther along the beach, Jawat was drilling his militia of former slave-soldiers. They had a terrible mishmash of weapons, many of them made for show, but every man and woman had a good spear with a sharp bronze point, and many of them had huge shields shaped like pinched cowrie shells – a whole bull's hide.

The militia looked good; they raised her spirits a little. These were her people, and she needed their loyalty and commitment, so she walked across the sand, nodded to Jawat, and smiled at them.

'Where'd you get the shields?' Era asked. 'You, what's your name?'

A big man, perhaps the ugliest man she'd ever seen, grinned. 'Ship we came in on had a cargo of bull-hide,' he said. 'I'm Drakon.'

'And there was more dead bulls on the beach,' a small woman said. 'I'm Lan Thena.'

Era gave her a look; she wasn't small at all – she only appeared small next to the ugly brute next to her. She had only one breast; that was curious. Her 'Trade' was accented with Dardanian.

Jawat smiled. 'They came yesterday, on the floater,' he said. 'Actual soldiers.'

The giant with a face of a demon grinned at her. 'We've come a long way to join you,' he said. 'To fight the gods.'

Era just looked at him. 'Fight the gods?' she asked quietly.

'Bright People told us,' he said.

Era looked at Jawat, and then back at the giant and the tall woman.

'Welcome,' she said, and headed back down the beach. *Actual volunteers?* She suddenly felt *much* better.

The next day she oversaw repairs and found the former slaves who'd been carpenters. She thanked fortune that she had not one but two shipwrights among her flock – both careful, silent men who counted out timbers and chose tools carefully from their limited supply, and looked entirely competent. Later, as she allowed herself a breather, watching the first serious repairs on the seven ships on the beach, her lookout spotted another ship coming in. This one was in a terrible condition.

It took sixty men and women in boats to pull the dismasted hulk ashore through the surf. The captain was strapped to the tiller, and wouldn't give it up until he felt the keel grate on gravel. His crew looked as if they'd be haunted by the voyage for the rest of their lives, and there were corpses on the deck.

Era could see at a glance that some of them had been picked at. And eaten.

There were about thirty former slaves still alive aboard. The crew had put the hatch covers over the holds and chocked them closed.

'They came at us while we were trying to fish the mast,' the captain said. The man was utterly exhausted, slumped on a rug at Era's feet. 'They were insane with fear…' He shrugged. 'We had to kill some, and drove the rest below. Gods, we tried. Twelve days at sea, in that storm, no food, not much water…' He looked at her as if she could grant him absolution.

'Who are you?' she asked.

His fat merchant ship was out of some southern yard, but she didn't know him.

39

'Huy,' he said. 'Call me Huy.' He looked past her. 'I'm from Narmer.'

'How'd you find your way here?' she asked.

Pavi came and squatted bonelessly nearby. The Hakran woman gave Era a look that meant she had something to say, or report.

Huy shrugged. 'If you get dismasted mid-ocean and you don't turn turtle or sink, this is where you come,' he said. 'The wind and current bring you here.'

Pavi nodded..

Era frowned. 'I thought all these ships followed us.'

Pavi rolled her eyes. 'In a few days the other stuff will start coming ashore,' she said. 'It always does. The corpses. The ship's timbers.'

'The Jekers,' Huy said.

Era looked back at the Narmerian captain. Her heart wasn't sinking; it was going cold.

'What Jekers?' she asked.

'The sea's full of them,' Huy said. 'Dismasted, half awash, or intact. Only the gods know how many of them sunk. But there's plenty left. We saw them.' He looked at her, the fatigue making black thumbprints under his brown skin. 'The slaves who attacked us were going to turn Jeker,' he said. 'We heard them talking about it.'

'Demons of Kur,' Era swore. 'Get some sleep, Huy. When you're up to it, I'll assign you some people and you can repair your ship.'

He managed a very slight smile. 'Any chance of a cup of wine?'

She shook her head. 'Fresh water is the best I can do.'

Huy nodded, and drank more from the clay cup he'd been given.

'I am thankful for it,' he said.

He rose very slowly, like an old man, finished the water, and tottered along the sand to where his ship, the *Arrina's Daughter*, was beached. Her round hull might have been almost comical, it was so tubby, except that it had survived where so many other ships had foundered.

Era looked at Pavi.

Pavi clutched her knees. 'The two women that Taha brought in,' she said. 'Taha and I let them go with a donkey.'

Era was too tired to argue. 'Not my nice Nannu?' she asked, and then worried she sounded tyrannical. 'We're a little short of donkeys.'

Pavi shrugged. 'I'm not good at saying no to my own.'

Era nodded. 'That's not so bad.'

Pavi gave her a 'woman of the world' look. 'That's just the beginning,' she said. 'Many of the people are planning to … well, at best, to down tools and walk away.'

Era sat back and wished *she* had wine.

'What the fuck?' she spat.

'At worst, they might mutiny and kill you,' Pavi continued.

Era crossed her arms, something that she knew she did far too often. Her right hand went to the star-stone knife she wore on a cord around her neck. She made herself be calm. She thought of Jawala. The old Jawala.

Pavi shrugged again. 'Era, no one knows the plan here but you, and maybe Dite. You're utterly close-mouthed. But we all know that we're repairing the ships to run up the coast to Dendrowna, and half the people here don't want to go to Dendrowna. They want to go home.'

Era's face set hard. 'Who are the ringleaders?'

Pavi shrugged, her Hakran calm unruffled. 'I'm not an informer, Era, and that's not the way to settle this. They were slaves, and we freed them. *Or did we?*'

'What are you saying?' Era stood up.

Pavi looked up at her, squatting on her haunches, apparently relaxed. 'Are you going to hit me, Era?'

The two women looked at each other for a long moment, and then Dite came around the stern of the ship. She had a rag of brown cloth tied around her loins for modesty, and a double circle of clay beads around her waist; she had a net bag of wooden nails over her shoulder and a stone hammer in her hand, and she was shining like wet, black marble.

She smiled at Era, whose heart began to pound.

I have it bad, Era thought, and she did. *And I can't trust her as far as I can throw her.*

Which, considering Dite was taller than the tallest man on the beach, was not far, for all Era's wiry strength.

Dite, who had been a god. Or so she said.

She sat on the rug as if she'd been invited, and drew up her legs.

'Force won't fix this, my beauty,' she said to Era.

Pavi nodded at Dite. Era was immediately, ridiculously jealous. *Pavi and Dite?*

Dite's tastes were almost universal.

Era tried to get her head and heart back on her command problems.

'What do they want?' she managed. She didn't quite spit.

Dite raised her lovely eyebrows. 'They want to go home,' she said. 'As Pavi has already noted. And we should send them home with our blessings.'

'Damn it to Kur's seven hells,' Era said. 'Hefa-Asus said we needed three hundred people! If half of them go home, we'll have fewer than two hundred!'

Dite smiled. 'But the two hundred who come with us will be willing. And the hundred who leave will spread the word, which we need. We need some songs about the fight at the

42

island. We need a couple of hundred survivors out there telling people that the gods can be defeated.'

Pavi smiled very slightly. 'We need to make good on our promises to these people. Otherwise, we've just stolen someone else's slaves to use their labour ourselves. That's not "freeing" them.'

Dite smiled. 'That too,' she said in a tone that suggested that she didn't care a whit for the morality of the situation. She looked radiant, well-rested, and her eyes promised...

Era forced her rising lust down and said, 'It was never my intention to force anyone.'

Pavi took a breath, and then another, deeper breath. 'Thanks.' She hid her thoughts well, but her relief was palpable.

Era watched her go, and thought, *What am I becoming? Does she think me a tyrant?*

Dite's unquenchable eyes caught Era's as she rose to her feet. 'Just let the laggards go,' she said. 'Some of them are just barracks lawyers. Some can't see that they'll be slaves again in two weeks.' She shrugged. 'And when did you last rest? Relax? Drink water?'

Era sighed. 'I know.'

'And I know exactly how to help you with all that.'

Era shivered, but she took Dite's hand.

After an hour of lovemaking, through an ecstatic haze, Era said, 'Am I becoming a tyrant?'

Dite leant over her, her heavy breasts just touching Era's belly.

'Yes,' she said. 'I have a lot of experience of tyranny, and that's where you are headed.'

Era sat up. 'Damn it, you know how to kill a mood.'

Dite sat back. 'You asked,' she said. 'Was I supposed to lie?'

'I'm just trying to get this done!' Era said. 'They need direction!'

43

'And so said every tyrant in history,' Dite said, and then, 'That's enough political chatter.'

She went back to their former occupation with a relish that made it impossible for Era to stay angry. Or indeed, to stay much of anything.

The next morning, Era summoned her officers, such as they were: Pavi, Dite, Jawat, Hefa-Asus, Nicté, Atosa, Taha, the carpenters and shipwrights. She served them all water with her own hands, and then went around the circle and asked each for a report.

The carpenters had the warehouse up and had inventoried all the cargoes from the eight ships on the beach, which had then been moved into the warehouse, which was just a giant shed built of driftwood logs and roofed in palm fronds, in the local way. But it held all their cargoes and all their store of grain, and they were working on a second warehouse to store water pithoi.

The shipwrights reported that the *Untroubled Swan* was complete and ready for sea, as was the Mykoan merchant ship *Sea Snake*. Three more of their ships were under reconstruction.

But the term 'their ships' drew a howl of protest, and the captains and ship owners made it plain that they wanted no further part of this.

'Your soldiers forced us to carry these slaves,' Hackaput of Karthos said. He was a small, dark man with bright green eyes, a master trader of the Hundred Cities trade guild. 'Fine. We did. We risked our lives to do it. Now I want my ship repaired and I want to go. I have a family to feed. And no idea what the wave did to the Hundred Cities.'

Era looked at him, and raised an eyebrow, and he subsided.

Old Jawat, their drill master and the effective commander of her former slave troops, smiled a hard smile. Era smiled back, but shook her head slightly.

Then Hefa-Asus spoke up. 'I have most of the star-stone made up.'

Indeed, his forge had been running round the clock since they'd landed. Nicté had led a dozen smiths in making bronze items for ship's repairs; she'd even made some saws. Atosa was becoming adept at working the star-stone into fine stuff; he'd been playing with making wire, but he spent most of his time managing the carpenters because he seemed to know all the trades and skills.

But Hefa-Asus worked in secret, and they could smell the bitter tang of the star-stone as he worked.

He held up a knife very like the one Era wore around her neck.

'I've made a few of these,' he said and she nodded, excited, but not wanting to show that in public. 'We need to find the rest of the deposits,' Hefa-Asus said.

Era nodded again. 'We're working on it,' she said firmly. 'Jawat, report.'

He was the most muscular old person she'd ever seen, and slavery had done nothing to bow or break him. His hair and scruffy beard were white, and he had a scar that should have killed him, going across his face and through his nose, leaving it barbed like a fish hook.

'Fifty-nine fit for service. Training is going well – archery is the hardest. I'm taking the fat off the lardies and putting back as muscle on the skinnies.' He smiled his mirthless smile. 'I wouldn't want to take on a boatload of Dardanians or a big canoe of Dendrownans, but we're better than we were and getting better every day. And the new pair are excellent.'

Era was delighted. 'Thanks, Commander,' she said.

'Fuck, don't "commander" me,' he said. 'I'm an old *wabish*.'

Era shook her head. 'Here, you are *Ra-we-ke-ta*.'

The champion and commander. A word used by every nation and people. And titles mattered.

The old man flushed. 'At your service,' he said, obviously pleased. 'No *fucking* way did I ever expect anyone to call me that.'

Era glanced at Nicté and Hefa-Asus. Nicté smiled.

'All the star-metal is ashore, dry and stored in fleeces we took from ...' She looked at the merchant, Hackaput, and her innocent smile decorated her lips for a moment. 'We took from our friends. We salvaged everything that went into the water.'

Some of it had been swimming in the hold, and it had developed a curious red-orange rot like mould. Not the healthy green of bronze mould, but something worse.

Era sighed. At least problems were being solved, and her people – her best people – were all remarkable.

We can do this. And Dite is right – we're better off without those who want to leave.

She looked around. 'So, here's what I have to say. First, you are all doing incredible work under terrible conditions. Our having no other choice makes it no less miraculous. I saw you get the warehouses up and repair the ships, and I'm in a state of amazement.'

She smiled around. The same skills that had worked an audience when she was a dancer worked on these people. With accurate flattery, and a light tone, she could carry them with her. That, and a willingness to work harder than any of them.

'But we have problems – legions of problems. A fucking phalanx of problems. So let me share a couple. First, the ship that came in yesterday tells me that there's Jekers on the way. And the currents and tide will probably bring them here – the Hakrans say that every floating wreck in the whole Ocean comes here.' She shrugged. 'Friends, we have to be gone before they arrive.'

46

That got them talking and muttering.

'Second, I gather that a sizeable proportion of our people want to leave – as does Hackaput here. So let's get that done. Anyone who wants to go can go. We'll send the ships that want to go back to their home ports with the people who want to go. It's the best we can do.'

She held up a hand for silence, and looked at the ships' captains.

'If I hear that any of you have sold these people we send with you as slaves…' She shrugged. 'I think you'll find out how long my arm really is.'

An empty threat, so far. But … Nicté has plans …

Now the muttering became a buzz of conversations.

'And that includes the soldiers. Jawat, Lefuz, anyone who wants to go… let them go. No bullshit. Understand?'

Era smiled, because now that she was saying it, she *knew* it was right. It felt right. And besides… they'd spread the word, whether they meant to or not.

She raised her voice and cut through the babble. 'This means we need to be ready to sail by the day after tomorrow. I need the soldiers on duty and alert in case we get a boatload of Jekers before we're off the beach. And I need Nicté to make lists of who stays and who goes. Nicté, work with Pavi and Dite and choose the ships to carry them. They go first.'

Nicté was a Dendrownan, short, stocky, muscular and a dark red-brown. She wore her hair long on one side and shaved on the other, held in place by a bone pin carved with a dragon's head with a red jewelled eye, and wore a long Mykoan-style sword from a bronze-studded belt. She was a fighter, as well as a bronze-smith by profession. But she had other skills, learnt the hard way, and she was becoming the head of something… secret. More of an idea than a reality.

It had been Gamash's idea, originally, but was now driven by

47

Dite. Dite had a lot of ideas of her own, and Era wished she could trust her.

'I've spent all this time training them, and you'll just let them go?' Jawat's tone was sarcastic; he'd only been training them for a few days. But Era chose to answer honestly.

'We only want people who *want* to do this,' she said. 'We're going up against the gods. That's no secret. And it's possible none of us will live to see victory. So … let them go.' She looked at Nicté.

Nicté and Dite had cooked up some ideas that might or might not ever bear fruit, but it made the best possible use of the people who wanted to leave, and suddenly Era saw paths to victory she'd never seen before. Paths more like a dance and less like open war.

Nicté stood up. 'Every chief – go to your people, tell them the truth, and ask for a show of hands. Tell anyone on the fence they have until dawn tomorrow to decide, and get me the lists of those leaving as soon as possible. I want to talk to every one of them. Hear me?'

People were nodding.

'I'm not going to yell at them, or even try to change their minds, but I want to see them. And I'll provide them with a little scrap silver and divide them up by ships. Let's get out there and get this done. The Jekers might be just over the horizon.'

Era stood up. 'Last thing. If the Jekers come, we fight. We have no choice – we can't let them burn our ships. So make sure your people are ready and armed. We can overwhelm one Jeker longship. Two would be quite a fight.'

She waved, and pointed at the ships.

'Get going. We have a lot to do.'

Hefa-Asus put a hand under her elbow. 'What about three Jeker ships?'

Era shrugged. 'We run inland and start all over.'

Hefa-Asus grunted.

Pavi looked at her. 'And Jawala? And Aanat?'

Era hardened her heart. 'They've made their choices.'

Pollon

The restless undead hit them almost as soon as Zos sheathed *Terror*.

Pollon had had warning, and was ready with his rituals; Zos and Persay were unprepared.

The terror of the sword had driven all of the worshippers into the far end of the temple, nearest the cliff. Some had already thrown themselves to their deaths, and when the sword was sheathed, their terror of the situation replaced the terror generated by the sword.

The dead of the royal Troides, the ancient ruling family, came through the gate like an ill wind. They had no real substance, and moved like a woman's fine veil blown by a mighty gale. Pollon barely had time to ward a circle around the chariot, and the dead screamed their frustration in the realms of sorcery – a thin keening in the world of men.

He wished he had his harp – his rituals were stronger with music – and then it occurred to him that the temple harper must have been playing when they rolled in; there was an instrument somewhere nearby. He turned to the three nomad women.

'I need the harp. It's somewhere in the temple.' His Trade was barely up to it; 'musical instrument with strings' had to stand in for 'harp' or 'lyre'.

Makeda nodded and the three women, their eyes huge and with many a backwards glance at the host of the dead raging against Pollon's wards, ran up the steps to the temple.

Zos had retreated inside Pollon's wards, as had Persay.

'What the …?' he began.

'You have profaned their shrine with death and terror,' Pollon said. 'You have killed their scion. And, like many godborn, they have power even when they are dead.' He glanced at the host of the dead. 'At least, they do when close to their places of power.'

Zos reached for the deadly sword at his side.

Pollon spared him a glance. 'Not going to save us,' he said. 'And if you break my concentration …'

Zos spat. He liked simple solutions, and Pollon could see that he didn't want to rely on sorcery.

Makeda returned, face drawn, with long scratches on her left arm. She carried a small silver lyre and under her black-brown skin, she looked grey.

'One got me,' she said in Betwana.

Pollon took the silver lyre, ran his right hand over the strings, and went down on one knee. The little instrument was quiet, but it was perfectly tuned and a tinkle of notes rose.

Pollon was out of practice, both playing and casting. But his fingers remembered the way. He wasn't playing any particular tune; rather, he let his thoughts go into the ritual, his fingers producing …

'The music of the spheres,' he said, because Zos stood silent.

His circle of defence began to harden around them, and the keening of the dead rose. Pollon smiled. He was winning; his music was gathering the power, stripping it away from the dead, as he – like most court scribes – had been trained to do.

'We need to leave. They are at their most powerful around their places of worship and burial.'

Zos looked at him and shrugged. 'And we need to pass the tomb of Atrios,' he said. 'And I suppose we need to save these people.'

Persay glanced at the huddled mass of craftsmen and entertainers.

'Leave them. They spat on us. Let them die screaming.'

Pollon could tell that part of Zos agreed with Persay.

'No,' Zos said firmly. 'Bring them inside the ward. Pollon, are you up to this?'

Pollon was doing something very complicated: playing a tune and singing the counterpoint to it himself, so that the harmony floated on the keening, as if adding it to the music ... and thus cancelling it. To his surprise, Daos began to sing with him, his young voice richer and better tuned than most boys could manage. The boy winked at him, and Pollon winked back, and then turned, still singing, to Zos.

He could only answer with a shrug. He didn't know how long he could hold them; these were the most powerful dead he'd ever faced, and in the greatest numbers. In fact, the breakout of the royal dead from the tombs of the kings of Mykoax represented the very thing every god-king feared. It was the reason that every god-king had a squad of trained necromancers.

Zos led Persay and the nomads out onto the temple floor.

'Get inside the circle!' Pollon heard him roar. 'Now!'

Already, a dozen of the terror-struck courtiers were being consumed by the raging dead, slowly shredded by *almost* insubstantial claws, or that's what their screaming bodies seemed to say. One man was down, no longer screaming, and his skin was almost flayed away. And as the dead killed the living, they gained in strength, their *almost* immaterial selves filling out like pictures being painted in blood.

Zos couldn't draw *Terror*. So he flailed at the aethereal dead with one of his javelins, and there was a palpable scream.

He did it again as the floating blur withdrew from him.

'They fear the star-stone!' he shouted.

Pollon noted that and kept playing.

Zos turned to where Persay slashed at the vicious mist with his long bronze bull-leaper's sword.

'Catch!' he roared, and threw the javelin.

Persay pulled it out of the air left-handed and swept it through the cloud in front of him. He had a hundred long cuts on his arms, as if children with pins were scratching his skin. But as the star-stone head swept through the dead a scream rose, and the white fog of horror rolled back as if Persay had unleashed a sea-wind against it.

The bravest of the courtiers and palace functionaries had begun to understand, and they ran for the safety of Pollon's ward. Then the trickle became a stampede. Zos shoved Tisa and Theklassa into the circle, and Persay was back-to-back with Makeda, covering her with long sweeps of the javelin as he backed into the wards.

Zos was the last inside, the inside of one thigh flayed raw as if from a thousand tiny claws, and the keening still rose, but so did Pollon's music.

Daos extended a hand. 'Join me, lord,' he said to Zos.

Zos stepped up into the chariot, and Daos snapped the reins. The chariot went forward, faster than Pollon's walking pace.

They rolled straight through the front of Pollon's wards, and nothing came near them or the horses. Daos simply held the trident aloft, and the dead cowered away.

'Join us,' Daos said to Pollon, and went back to singing.

Pollon rose to his feet, still playing and singing, and stepped unsteadily into the car. It swayed under him, and he crouched, and then sat, so that he could trust his hands to keep playing.

'Who are you?' he heard Zos say. He looked up to see Zos confronting Daos across the space of the chariot.

'I'm your *papista*,' the young man replied with a smile.

'Are you human?' Zos asked.

Daos glanced at him, and down at Pollon, and the trident twirled in his fist.

'Is this the time for this conversation?' he asked.

The chariot gave a bump and a hop that almost unbalanced Zos as the wheels went over a dead man. Pollon felt the floor flex under him.

Zos caught his balance and stared out into the grey-white fog of the dead as it parted before them, the way the water is parted by a ship's bow.

'Yes,' he said. 'I need to know.'

'I was born to a corpse,' Daos said. 'And I am a forgotten god's revenge. And nonetheless, I am human.'

Zos allowed himself to breathe. So did Pollon.

'Mostly,' Daos added.

They rolled through the gates to the underworld and the pressure increased as they passed the tomb circles, but not so much that Pollon ever lost his voice. By then, Pollon was almost comfortable, crouched on the woven sinew floor, playing like the court musician he had sometimes been.

The wheels bumped over the softness of the dead guards by the gate, and then they were rolling along the cobbled road, and all but the strongest of the city's dead fell away.

But ahead, by the Tomb of Atrios, something towered like the funnel of a squall at sea – a roiling grey-black mass tinged with a terrible scarlet. The ground around it was littered with skeletons, gleaming in the odd yellow-grey light from the conflict between sun and cloud.

Daos spoke. 'It has stripped all the pilgrims of their flesh to make its own power. It will be quite something.'

Without orders, he stopped the chariot well short of the line marked by the recent dead.

'It will have eaten their souls, too,' Daos said. 'The old god-kings always do. It's who they are, really.'

Zos leant on the chariot's handrail, Pollon playing on at his feet singing, wordlessly, and looked at the crowd of survivors, his own wounded, and Pollon, who seemed strong.

How long can I hold out? Pollon wondered. He played fast, and glanced at Daos.

'You seem to know everything,' he said. 'Is that thing tethered to its tomb?'

Daos looked at him with real surprise. 'I'm not sure,' he admitted.

Pollon drew his tune to a close, or at least a lacuna, and the last of the dead – half a dozen recent Mykoan kings – swirled around outside his wards, but the trident and the star-stone seemed sufficient to deter them.

Pollon looked up. 'My guess is they are tethered to the tomb for power. If they break away from that, they will be much weaker. The tomb is what holds their ... identity. Without that, they collapse and ... dissipate. Or so I was taught.'

He took a long drink from his clay canteen, and then began a slower, lower song.

Zos leapt down from the chariot and walked towards the tomb. A donkey and two men lay across the road, their flesh stripped, their bones a fresh white. Zos stopped just short of them, watching the black-grey tendrils that reached for him, batting at them with his star-stone javelin head.

They recoiled.

'So,' Zos said in contempt. 'Is it tethered to the tomb, or the richness of its burial treasures?'

Pollon was deep in his fugue, and didn't want to think about it.

'How powerful is that trident, *Papista*?' he asked.

Daos smiled, still singing.

Zos nodded to Pollon.

'Keep singing,' he said.

Pollon wanted to spit at him.

To Daos, he said, 'Drive on, right to the great gates of the tomb. And then, when we get there, blow them open.'

Daos' eyes widened.

Zos shrugged. 'That trident split an island open, boy. Do it or don't. But smashing the power of the dead is part of what we're here to do. *I can feel it.*'

Daos acknowledged his words with a flip of the reins, and Zos stepped up into the chariot car, making it bounce with his weight.

The horses wanted to stop. But Daos was their absolute master, and they would have driven the car through fire if he asked it. So they passed into the red-black cloud, and then so did the car, and Pollon felt the pressure of the undead – the angry, hungry undead – like a terrible headache, as if his head was being crushed between millstones.

He sang.

Daos sang.

Zos, a man with neither talent nor magical power, sang.

And all about them was a darkness thicker than the worst storm Pollon had ever known: a terrible angry roiling grey, with scarlet veins, and a hundred angry voices shrieking.

And the horses stepped forward, brave against terror.

And the men sang.

And the undead raged around them.

On either side, the massive entry stones to the tomb appeared: blocks as large as the chariot itself, that men said had been raised by the old gods.

The tone of the keening of the raging undead rose to a fever pitch.

And a figure appeared before their chariot – tall and pale, twice the size of a mortal man. The blood of the pilgrims had given him form, so that he was like a hasty sketch of a man in armour drawn in carnelian and rose, and a high golden crown rose from his head.

'Turn back, mortals,' said the undead king. 'This is my realm forever. I curse you—'

Zos tossed his star-stone javelin. Not a hard, killing throw, but a casual toss.

The star-stone head seemed to blossom with dark fire as it passed through the pale giant.

'My curse on you, mortal! May you wither and die alone and forgotten, without family, without love, without—'

Daos raised the trident.

'None of you will leave this place. The will of Gul will be felt here!' The ghost of the king pointed a finger at Daos. 'You!'

Daos was singing now, and the trident spat something. It wasn't fire, or lightning; it was neither light nor dark. It had no substance, and yet Pollon *felt* it go. It was an illuminating experience, which made Pollon think about the *Aura* in a completely different way, as if the conditions inside the whirl of malevolent rage revealed it in a new way.

But it was dangerous to let his concentration waver. A thin filament of unlife reached for his mind and scratched at his scalp as the gout of palpable but invisible non-matter thrown by the trident impacted the ancient tomb's great oak gates.

They blew open in an eruption of the deep blue light of the auratic combat. High above them, the massive stone lintel cracked with a devastating sound like the breaking of the world and the chariot rolled through the ruined gates and into the heart of the great tomb. It was shaped like a farmer's beehive, twenty times the height of a tall man to the roof high above, big enough to house a hundred people.

The bones of the dead were arrayed on the floor, each arranged on stone couches as if attending a feast. In the centre burned a cold fire, around it were stone tables, and on every one were golden vessels; magnificent cups, worked with scenes of beasts and men and gods – dishes, bowls, amphorae: a dazzle of gold that cut through the darkness.

Pollon thought, *Is that why the undead love gold? Is it the false sun of their unlife? Colour in the darkness?*

He played a loud chord on his borrowed lyre, and used it to cover his hurried speech.

'Take the gold!' he spat. 'The heart of the darkness is in the gold.'

Zos stepped slowly from the chariot, as if he was wading through deep water. The darkness pressed in: the horror of infinite stone above ready to fall on them; the terror of ancient darkness, ever inimical to people; and the rage of the storm of death. The lintel moved, the crack widened, and the weight of the stone above them leant in.

Zos walked through it all to the nearest table, and swept the gold into his cloak. It rang like the music; it clanked like chains.

He went to the second table.

'Blasphemer! You risk the eternal torment of the Underworld! Do you not fear the gods? Gul is coming! I summon you, Lord of the Dead! The living defile us!' The undead form of Atrios rose again from the stone floor, roseate with the stolen blood of his victims.

Zos glanced up, hesitating by the third table. Pollon saw his lips move and the sound crossed to him through barriers; it came slowly, oddly accented.

'I think you're all talk,' Zos said to the undead king.

He swept gold from the third table into his cloak, and hauled it up over his shoulder – a great weight of gold. From the fourth and last table he took a single object: a massive cup with two handles that stood the height of a man's head and shoulders, and was decorated with a figure fighting a bull.

Then he sprang into the chariot, and it rocked under his weight.

'Drive,' he said, his voice a harsh croak.

A mighty stone, released from high above, fell between the horses, so close that it could have killed any of them.

'The roof is giving way,' Daos said, conversationally, as if this sort of thing was an everyday occurrence. 'Use fire. I am immune to fire.'

'Drive,' Zos repeated.

Beyond the broken doors, the world was absolutely black.

Pollon, still maintaining his shield, began to fumble with a firepot. They had two – ceramic vessels filled with burning coals.

It was as if they were driving into a void, and as the wheels crossed the threshold, the chariot gathering speed under them, the horses beginning to panic, Pollon began to lose his battle with the wrath of the undead. It seemed to him that there was nothing – no soul, no survival after death but for an icy torment – and he wondered why humans ever existed at all, and if there was any point, and if they were doomed to an eternity of cursed non-existence in the Outer Darkness…

Beware the wrath of Gul, God of the Dead, for his power is absolute, and all come to him.

The tendrils of darkness broke in on him and lashed him with whips of doubt and abnegation, and his song faltered under the onslaught… His scalp took fifty cuts…

He threw the firepot into the tomb. And death unleashed a rage of cold, a black forgetfulness, but now in its heart there was a tinge of orange. An ancient hanging had caught fire; a pile of bones or a table…

And the maddened horses burst out of the cloud of the anger of unlife and into the light of the sun.

Daos' voice lifted high, Zos croaked along with him, and behind them, the cloud rose into a tower, and thrust arms after them. The maddened horses raced along the road, free and clear as, with a roar like an avalanche, the roof of the mighty tomb fell in, the huge blocks of stone falling on the reclining corpses. A cloud of terrible dust replaced the whirlwind of the undead...

But it was just dust.

Screaming, more with relief than terror, the crowd of Mykoan courtiers and palace folk broke and ran along the road, streaming away from the collapse.

Zos motioned for Daos to stop, and he stepped down from the chariot car.

Pollon stopped playing, his fingers bleeding. The nihilism of the undead was still with him, and he looked down, at the dust under the chariot, with little comprehension of what had happened.

Zos wrapped him in an embrace.

'You are a man of many talents,' he said.

Pollon froze, and then the warmth of Zos's humanity soaked into him. For a moment, he stood still, unmoved, and then his arms raised slowly to return the hug. He looked back at the remaining crowd of weary, scared courtiers. A woman suckling a child met his eye.

'You saved something, here,' he said.

Zos shrugged. 'It wasn't my original plan,' he admitted. 'I've always dreamt of massacring the lot of them. But I was damned if I was going to let the fucking ghosts have them.'

He held on to Pollon, and Pollon knew that he was trying to hide his tears. Zos had been terrified; he had not been in control.

In Zos' eyes, Pollon saw the despair he felt himself.

'We did it,' Zos said.

Pollon thought for a moment, because it hadn't been his revenge, or his notion of... anything. Except survival. 'Next time you plan to kick a hornets' nest,' he said, 'please tell me.'

Zos pretended to laugh – pretended to be the cold, untroubled warrior – but Pollon could see through his mask and liked him better for it.

But he also admired the way Zos leapt into the chariot and put his arms around the boy.

'You are a perfect charioteer,' Zos said.

And Daos turned, his face blank.

'*In Narmer we will drive a chariot of fire*,' the boy said.

The fresh ruins along the seashore and the terrified farmers of Trin and Mykoax provided food aplenty, and Zos rode out into the countryside every day, recruiting. In three days, they had repaired or refloated and crewed five pentekonters, and they were hard at work on *Wave Serpent*, repairing her with timber from foundered ships. Most of the new crews were his own people, from Trin, but he didn't refuse the Mykoans who swore him fealty.

A delegation of farmers – prosperous men and women whose houses were far above the tideline – approached him on the third day and asked him to be their king.

'Never,' Zos said.

'But who will intercede with the gods?' they asked. 'Who will guarantee a good harvest?'

'No one,' Zos said. 'This world offers no mercy and no guarantees. And the gods are a lie.'

The delegation fled as if he'd threatened them.

Pollon stood by the ships with a stack of wax tablets, writing every detail down. They looted the ruined warehouses for cargoes, and they stripped the foreshore of timbers and masts for spares. Pollon saw Trayos work his crew and volunteers to rebuild the entire bow of his precious *Wave Serpent*, and because water doesn't ruin bronze, they could arm and armour everyone who could bear the weight.

On the eighth day, as the tide turned in the early morning, Pollon stood in the stern of Zos' long, low pentekonter. She was as black as night, her whole hull sealed in pitch, her sail a brilliant scarlet – one of Pollon's finds in a warehouse above the tide line. She carried no god's image in her upswept stern, and her bow was carved into an eagle's beak and made no homage to any deity. Zos called her *Sea Eagle*.

The *Sea Eagle* was as big as any warship Pollon had ever seen. She'd been floating mastless up the coast until Zos found her and had fisherfolk tow her to the beach, and she'd been hastily rebuilt. Her three new consorts were salvage from Agon's fleet and Trayos' ship *Wave Serpent* was now the smallest.

When *Sea Eagle*'s fifty oarsmen pulled all together, they shot off the beach and out into the Ocean, and Pollon, who had never accounted himself a sailor, felt his heart lift. It was a beautiful day, the sun rising in glory behind them in the east, the sky in the west tinted a delicate rose-pink.

'In the old pantheon,' Zos said suddenly, 'Dawn was a goddess.'

'The old pantheon sounds ... nicer,' Pollon said.

'Don't believe it,' Zos said.

He was watching the horizon, about to say something, perhaps something personal. Pollon thought that he'd changed. He could feel the change in Zos but not quite put a finger on it. He turned to face the other man.

But the warrior shrugged and let his thought go, whatever it had been. Instead, his face changed, the mask of command settling back on him.

'If we survived the waves,' he said, in a complete change of mood, 'you have to wager some of the Jekers survived.'

Pollon hadn't given that a thought, and now he shivered.

'They covered the ocean,' he said, remembering. And then, carefully, because Zos had been very different since he'd killed the god-king of Mykoax. Not unstable, exactly. Not *really* unstable, but...

He dared.

'Where to now?' he asked.

'You never call me "lord",' Zos said.

Pollon shrugged. 'You aren't my lord.'

Zos's too-bright eyes fell on him. 'Good,' he said. 'Keep it that way. It's not my intention to make myself the pirate king of Ocean, but I love the power of the sword, and it calls to me, singing a death song in my head. And people are stupid, Pollon. They'd follow me.'

'We could exterminate the Jekers,' Pollon offered.

'We might start that way,' Zos said. 'But eventually, we'd just *be* the Jekers.'

Pollon looked at Zos as if he'd never really seen him before. 'You *are* a thinker.'

Zos shrugged. 'We're going to Ma-ta-mna. On Lazba. I know people there.'

'And then?' Pollon asked.

Zos shrugged. 'I'm going to trade the king of Lazba a dead kingdom for more ships and men,' he said. 'And then we're going to Narmer, as Daos keeps telling us. And you, my multi-talented friend, are going to find us a way into the gods' store of resin, while I help the god-queen of Narmer defeat the gods.'

'Why Narmer?' Pollon asked.

Zos was watching the water. 'Rumour is that Maritaten of Narmer is already at war with the gods. Meanwhile, the Narmerians have never willingly relinquished their sun god. They're natural rebels. And anyway, it's what we discussed. We need to distract the gods, while Hefa-Asus finds the star-stone in the north and Era builds an army.' He paused, looking out to sea. 'I wish I knew more about this Maritaten. She sprang in existence like something mythic.' He looked at Pollon.

The former Writer smiled his secret smile.

'She's *hardly* mythic.' He shrugged. 'I shouldn't judge her. But she was a court toy, an erotic dancer of some sort.'

Zos rolled his eyes. 'And she's leading the war on the gods?' he groaned. 'How did she get to be Great Lady of the High House?'

Pollon looked away. 'She's the heir. The true heir. A generation ago, the gods wiped out her whole family. Someone thought it was fitting to send her to be a sex slave.'

Zos winced. 'That was almost me,' he admitted.

'But a few months ago, Enkul-Anu sent demons to crush the "new" Lord of the High House.'

Zos watched the water, and then looked at Pollon.

'I heard about that. Just before…' He winced again. 'Before you and I shared a tree.'

'And a Dry One,' Pollon said, wryly. 'Sometimes in my dreams I see that proboscis coming at me, and I wake up …'

Zos smiled a disturbing smile. 'Yes,' he said quietly. 'As do I.'

Both were silent for a moment.

And then Zos, shrugged, as if he could rid himself of evil memories with a shrug. 'But Maritaten?'

'She stepped from the palace harem to the High Throne in the blink of an eye.' Pollon mocked. 'I doubt she'll last long.'

Zos made a face. 'If she's still in power in Narmer after four months, she's got something. But as a war leader …' He made a dismissive gesture. 'So they'll need us all the more.' He sighed again. 'While I would rather be with Era, building the real army.'

He said Era's name a little wistfully.

You want to be with Era, Pollon thought. *She'll never have you. But that's not for me to say.*

He looked out over the bow, and admitted that he'd always wanted to see Narmer. After forty years of abject dullness, his life now alternated between terror and marvel.

Pollon was beginning to enjoy it.

'I should teach you some fighting,' Zos said, changing the subject.

Pollon nodded. 'I need to sharpen my music, too' he said. 'Narmer is full of the dead. And worse.'

Zos nodded. 'I don't know why Daos pretends to need my training,' he said softly. 'Whatever he is, it was born fully prepared.'

Pollon leant over the rails, watching the waves slip past. Forward, the sailors were raising the big mainsail and the rower-warriors were resting on their oars and looking relieved.

'If he asks for your training,' Pollon said, 'you should give it. It's just a hunch I have.'

Zos looked at him. 'You are not the sword-brother I expected,' he said with a hint of his old humour. Then he slapped Pollon on the shoulder. 'But you're growing on me. Right, then. I'll train him. And you.'

The little squadron set their sails and turned a little north of due west, and they ran on with the wind on their starboard quarters, as if the gods approved of their journey.

Which they most certainly did not.

Not Heaven

It couldn't even crawl. And it had trouble summoning the power to do anything – even to kindle fire.

It was consumed by fear, and hate.

It feared its many enemies, who were bent on its destruction. Its very survival implied a victory, and its enemies were by definition evil incarnate. It had been misled and betrayed, which overwrote its own history of betrayal and hypocrisy.

In between torments of panic and terror at the ease with

which its precious life could be exterminated, it had manic bouts of hatred, swearing vengeance against all of heaven and the puny human lice who had hurt it so.

It remembered its name, but it spurned it.

I am not Nisroch, bastard of Enkul-Anu, it thought with sullen anger.

It inched its way deeper and deeper into the cave it had found, when, desperately wounded, having expended all its remaining power to preserve the Jekers, it fell. That it fell to earth on an island, and not into the sea to perish, proved that it had a destiny, a promise of revenge and destruction to fulfil.

From time to time, it used its remaining hand to touch the hilt of the great sword that hung by the ruin of its body — *Godkiller*.

It grinned, a rictus grin that caused a wave of pain, because the fires of the World Serpent had lashed it when it was caught in the sky. The World Serpent, too, would be destroyed.

And Enkul-Anu.

I hate you, Father.

It needed a new name. It was not Nisroch. It would be greater and more terrible than Nisroch had ever been. It would not whisper plots — it would shout destruction.

I will kill them all. Every one of them. I will leave none alive to rival me.

I will be Kursag. I will be the destroyer, the ender, and after me there will be only the waste of chaos that began. I will it so.

Chapter Three

Nicté

Lawesa was a nice-looking man: solid, of middle height, with a good jaw, and slavery hadn't robbed him of his ability to look Nicté in the eye. He gave her an abbreviated bow and sat on a pile of palm fronds that served as a rug in her 'office', which was a corner of the water-storage warehouse. He wore a loincloth, and had all the muscle she could ever have wanted in a mate.

'You called me, lady?' he said.

She smiled. 'I want to make sure you're a volunteer,' she said. 'And I'm not a lady. I'm a bronze-smith.' She looked at him appraisingly. 'We're sending you to do something difficult and dangerous. I need to know you understand that.'

He nodded. 'I'm all in,' he said. 'Whatever it takes to get the bastards who made me a slave.'

Nicté nodded. 'Except that the people who made you a slave ... they're just the agents of the system.'

Lawesa cocked his head to one side. He had wide brown eyes that made him look guileless. Innocent. 'I know who popped me on the head and sold my arse in the market,' he said.

She smiled. She was fully aware that he liked the look of her. In fact, she rather liked the look of him, but this was business, and she'd learnt how to manipulate people in the process of becoming the only female bronze-smith that her tribe had ever produced – good enough that the famous Hefa-Asus had recruited her. Because when you're a woman, and young, being an expert in casting bronze isn't enough.

Hence the smile. 'They're just tools,' she said. 'They're functionaries serving the system. The godborn drive it, and above them, the gods. The gods treat us like cattle. Why shouldn't we treat one another that way?'

He leant back as if she'd struck him.

She leant forward, close enough to kiss him. 'What if I told you that every person is of equal value? That no one is better than any other?'

'My brother is a better farmer than I'll ever be,' Lawesa grunted. 'I don't have the patience.'

She blinked. 'Good point,' she purred. 'But the equality isn't a value. It's an ideal.'

'What does that mean?' he asked.

She shrugged, which she knew fixated his gaze on her breasts. She had some serious muscle, too. 'When the sky is dark in the afternoon, do you grab a straw rain cloak?' she asked.

'Back when I had one, you mean?' She liked his touch of humour. He wasn't all about himself, and he was smart. He nodded, to answer her question.

She said, 'But it doesn't always rain, does it?'

'No.'

'That doesn't make it senseless to have the rain cloak. Listen. Maybe people aren't equal, but it makes more sense to treat them that way than to pretend some are better and some are worse.'

Lawesa shook his head. 'Godborn are better,' he said. 'Better muscles. Some have power.' He looked at her. 'Looks. Smarts. Better.'

'Bullshit,' she said. 'And anyway, when we're done, there won't be any more godborn.'

'No godborn?' Suddenly he brightened.

She smiled. They were very close now. And yet, he had some discipline; he wasn't a fool, and he wasn't grabby.

'I'm from Dendrowna – from the mountains. You know that everywhere around Ocean, there's desert…'

'Everyone knows that.'

'Not Dendrowna. Our land goes on and on, with rivers and water and lakes and hills and forests.' She smiled. 'And no godborn.'

He blinked. 'And rivers? Sounds like paradise.'

'I admit I miss it. We're going there.' She looked at Lawesa hard. 'And if you accept this mission, you *aren't* going there.'

He swallowed. But then his eyes grew harder. 'They killed my son,' he said. 'And I'm a good hater.' He looked at her. 'I'd like to see your Dendrowna, though. I never expected to see this much of the world. It's…' He shook his head. 'I don't have the words. It's amazing.'

'So you want in?'

'Absolutely,' Lawesa replied.

'Right. Once I tell you your code and your mission, you are in. We don't swear oaths – the gods are our enemies. But if you betray us, by Nanuk's white fur and terrible claws, I'll see that you are tracked down and killed, and your body mutilated. So that if there is an afterlife, you'll be maimed forever.' She raised her eyebrows. 'Frankly, I think it's bullshit. There's no afterlife worth having. But we'll mutilate your corpse so everyone knows who did it.'

'Fuck!' He spat in revulsion, and leant back. 'I'm not…'

She smiled again. 'It's strictly business,' she said. 'I want you to know. And as you will be a cell leader, I want you to know what you may have to do to enforce discipline.'

He looked uncomfortable.

She thought, *Not a blowhard. And not an arsehat.*

'Not sure I could do that,' he said slowly.

She nodded encouragingly. 'If you choose your people with care and lead them well, you'll never have to,' she said. *Carrot and stick*. 'Remember – take your time. Recruit two people. No more. Let them recruit more, and don't let their recruits know you. Don't have many meetings. Choose your two with care, brother. And have them choose with care.' She smiled.

He missed the smile, he was thinking. Lawesa shook his head. 'If they betray me, I'm dead.'

She nodded agreement.

He whistled. 'This isn't going to be easy,' he said. 'Slaves betray each other at the drop of a chlamys pin.' She gave him a moment but then, when he didn't demur, she began to teach him the codes – a dozen secret signs like Hundred Cities glyphs; some Dendrownan stick characters that she thought were safe in the south – and then outlined his mission.

'Have your level fives identify a really unpopular godborn,' she said.

'Level five?' he asked.

'Your cell is level one. You recruit two, and each of them recruits two. Those two cells are level two.' She drew him a picture in the sand, next to the glyphs.

He nodded. 'I get it.'

'I knew you were smart.' He ate up the praise.

'This could take months,' he said.

'Years,' she said. 'We are the Secret Fire. We're not in a hurry to burn. We just want to win.'

He was still shaking his head. 'Sure. So we identify a really unpopular godborn.'

'Right. Then you kill him. Cut off his dick and stuff it in his mouth.'

Under his dark brown skin, Lawesa blanched. 'What?'

'Just a murder, not single combat. Catch him asleep or fucking – it's all the godborn ever do.'

Lawesa grunted. 'That's ugly.'

'That's the way it's going to be. Make them bleed, and make them scared and angry.'

Lawesa's eyes narrowed. 'And then what?'

Nicté shrugged again. 'Then they spare no effort to hunt all of you down and kill you, which is why your level fives need to be walled off from the rest of your organisation,' she said. 'So here's how you do that.'

Two hours later she handed him a slim star-stone dagger and a handful of star-stone nails and let him go. 'That's star-stone,' she said. 'Deadly poison to the gods. Some godborn can take it and some can't, but the god's eyes that watch us? One scratch from one of those nails and out it goes.'

That made him smile.

'There's a master code,' she said. She took her own star-stone dagger from between her breasts and held out a sharp piece of flint. 'Watch.'

She tapped the back of the knife on the flint's sharp edge and there were sparks.

He looked on with amazement.

'That's the secret fire,' she said. 'Star-stone and flint make the secret fire. We are the flint. Star-stone is our weapon. Understand?'

He nodded, fully intoxicated with her, with secrecy, with the idea and the ideal.

She smiled.

He was the most likeable, and the most beddable, of her candidates so far, but she still let him go without a backward glance.

Era came through the curtain behind her.

'How much of that did you catch?' Nicté asked.

Era glanced at Lawesa as he walked towards the distant ships. 'Just the last half an hour,' she said. 'Did you make all that up?'

Nicté's laugh was nasty. 'No, never. I'm more a doer than a thinker, Era. Hefa-Asus and old Gamash cooked it up, and your Dite added to it.' She shrugged. 'Some we cadged from Jawala and Pavi. The Hakrans have thought a lot of the philosophical stuff through.'

'They're against violence!' Era protested.

'But they're pretty good at rationalising.' Nicté's smile was cynical.

Era watched the man stumble crossing the sand, most of which was finally dry. The two merchants bound for the Hundred Cities were loaded with water and food, most of their cargoes restored. They were eager to depart.

'How do we retrieve them?' Era asked. 'Something is bound to go wrong.'

Nicté sighed. 'Gamash said we can't retrieve them. They'll all be caught and killed. That's part of the plan. As the godborn catch them, their distrust and hatred of their own slave populations will explode into a killing rage, sparking resistance and revolt.'

Era looked at her. 'That's terrible,' she said. 'Godless day, that's fucking *terrible*.'

'When I want to cast a sword,' Nicté said, 'it takes me a day to carve the beeswax for a good bronze blade, to shape it and the tang and the hilt just the way I want them.'

'I'm not sure where this is going,' Era said.

'It takes me most of another day to mould the clay – the most perfect clay – to make a mould around the wax.'

Era shook her head. 'So?'

Nicté leant forward. 'When I heat the mould, my wax melts and pours out. Is my work lost?'

Era leant back.

'When I use the mould, I pour the bronze in, let it sit for a half a day, and then I smash my beautiful mould to pieces.'

71

Nicté gave a wintery smile. 'The wax is lost, and the mould is destroyed, and *that* is the cost of making a sword.'

Era turned her head away, as if to refuse the image. She was spared the need to reply when Pavi poked her head through the curtains.

'I know this is all secret,' she said. 'But I have a problem.'

Pavi was the officer in charge of the loading of the ships; she was literate, and she'd loaded cargo all her adult life, and she had marks and seals for every ship and every load, from Hefa-Asus' special tools for working star-stone to the bales of cowhide loaded in distant Tir and now reloaded into their original ship, the *Floating Duck* of Hema, yet another of the Hundred Cities.

Era had never sat down. Now she sighed, still troubled by Nicté's apparent willingness to let others go to their deaths. But Pavi never troubled her without good reason.

'What's the matter?' she asked.

'Best if I show you,' Pavi said.

Era touched her sword. 'Do I need armour? Is this the mutiny?'

Pavi shook her head. 'No, no. That's all over – the mutineers are leaving. And I don't think that refusing to be forced labour for strangers is mutiny—'

'Spare me,' Era said. 'I've heard it.'

Pavi pulled her by the hand. They trotted across the sand from the water warehouse, which was usually almost empty of people, past the cargo warehouse, now empty and ready to be demolished, to the secret warehouse guarded by a dozen of their soldiers.

'We're ready to load weapons,' Pavi said. 'The ships going back to the Middle Sea are ready to cast off. I'm loading *our* ships. Only when I open this warehouse...'

Suiting action to word, she pulled at one of the light wooden doors.

She motioned to Era. 'After you,' she said. 'You'll understand immediately.'

Era bent to enter. She'd helped stock the warehouse, and she knew where the star-stone was, and the weapons. And the high shelves of…

'Gacgkk!' she said.

The entire western end of the warehouse was covered…

… in …

… web.

The Dry One hung in it, its outline just visible as the sun came in through the palm-frond roof.

'When did this happen?' she asked.

Pavi shrugged. 'No idea.'

Era closed her eyes.

Pavi said, 'Any idea what we should do?'

Era shook her head. 'None,' she said.

Zos

'Jekers!' Alektron called.

Zos had come to know the man well in three days: a veteran sailor, bow-legged, tougher than a bronze nail, and covered in tattoos so dense and so ugly that the three nomad women had taken to him immediately. He was a man of Trin, and his loyalty to Zos was immediate.

Zos was both touched and repelled by that loyalty, but veteran sailors were not so thick on the beach that he could spurn one.

Alektron was high above in a leather basket attached to the mainmast, a Hakran innovation that Zos had unashamedly borrowed as they refitted the magnificent *Sea Eagle*. Zos was in a despondent mood, but he loved his ship.

'Where away?' he called.

He glanced over his shoulder at his little squadron's four pentekonters and Trayos' triakonter *Wave Serpent* bringing up the rear. They were labouring straight into the eye of the wind.

'Hull down on the horizon, north by east!' Alektron shouted back. 'Sails up. Making chase, I reckon.'

There was an uneasy silence punctuated by the grunts of fifty oars being pulled by men and women who had, for the most part, never pulled an oar before. The new recruits were not godborn or warriors, or even former slave oarsmen; a dozen were fisherfolk with excellent sea-skills, but the rest were mostly recently dispossessed farmers desperate to leave the Dardanian coast for any reason. Zos' ship carried eight women, all of whom had already proven themselves capable of rowing all day, and all of whom were as desperate and forbidding as the men.

All of them knew that their proposed destination was north-east – the isle of Lazba, the Emerald Isle, the Wooded Land.

Zos glanced astern. Under anything but the most extra-ordinary circumstances, none of his five ships – save that of the old Dardanian pirate, Trayos – had enough experience to survive combat with Jekers.

He looked at Pollon. *Unless* ...

'Chase, right eno'! Three Jekers, all wind-abeam and oars in, chasing ...'

A long pause while Zos took this in and wished he had Trayos by his side, instead of five hundred paces of deep water away. Zos was a capable sailor, but he'd never actually com-manded in a fight at sea – though he'd been in enough of them to know they were hell come to earth, with the loser butchered, and the unlucky drowning. And, of course, any who surrendered would become the Jekers' living sacrifices. And food.

He had the wind in his teeth, which is why his people were rowing. It was early morning, and his people were as fresh as they were likely to be, but he knew from experience that they were days from the hardening of muscles that would make them a good and responsive crew. He had no real idea what they'd be like in a fight. He'd taken the people who'd volunteered: a few remembered him, or claimed to, but most simply wanted to escape a doomed land.

On the other hand, they were desperate, and that made them very like the Jekers, and he had the sword. And Pollon, whose archery was beyond anything he'd seen in his fifteen years of war, and was better every day, as if the resin of the gods had made him a perfect bowman.

He needed to make Lazba.

He didn't need a fight with Jekers.

After killing his mortal foe Agon, he wasn't really sure he ever needed to fight again.

'Jekers hull up. They'll be seein' us right soon, cap'n. Ah! Chase in sight. I make her … aye. Narmer. She's a reed-ship out o' Narmer.'

Narmer.

Zos stared across the sea as if he could see the chase, though the vessel was only just visible to his lookout high above the deck.

'Narmer is turning to port.' The lookout glanced down, spat over the edge of his nest, and then went back to staring north and east. 'Aye, she's around, quarter reaching on the new tack, south by west.' He sounded calm, professional – the spectator at a horse race, not a participant.

He was also the best helmsman aboard. In fact, he was an all-round expert sailor, and Zos needed twenty of him.

'Any more Jekers?' he roared up at Alektron.

There was a long wait. The sailor was patient. And cautious.

'Not where I can see 'em, cap'n. Three Jekers, an' the chase, now coming down our throat.'

Zos took that in. The Narmerian would be a difficult boat

to handle in these seas: made entirely of reeds, they tended to get waterlogged late in a voyage, and they were a little too buoyant, standing well out of the water, offering a lot of hull to a cross-wind, difficult to handle in some conditions.

But very, very hard to sink.

The Narmerian was desperate, like anyone pursued by Jekers. He must have seen their little flotilla and turned towards it in hope ... Zos' squadron would be easy to spot as Dardanian because they all bore a mainmast standing and a smaller boatsail mast forward, with a little forward deck, unlike any other ship on the great Ocean.

So the Narmerian was running for them, hoping that at worst the Jekers would go for the new target and let him slip away.

Zos felt his thoughts crystallise; he made his decision, and picked up his big bronze and bull-hide shield. He raised it on his left arm, caught the sun, and flashed it three times.

Rally on me.

They only had three signals; that was all he'd had time to teach them.

'Prepare to turn to starboard,' he said to the helm. 'Due east, if you please.'

'Aye aye,' his helmsperson replied.

She was short and stocky. Strong as an ox, short as a child. Knew her way around the steering oar. Her father was a fisherman, and he was rowing number six oar, port side.

Eritha, he remembered. *Daughter of Jiani.*

'Eritha, it's my intent to range all our ships in a tight line abreast, rowing soft and due east.'

He met her eyes. She wasn't pretty, but excitement and action made her smile magnificent.

'Right you are, cap'n,' she said.

Zos went forward to the senior rowers. 'We're going to turn three points to due east. Then you can row soft.' He looked at

Pollon, who, as a musician, was the right man to set the stroke. 'Easy and slow, Pollon.'

'Of course,' Pollon said.

'At sea, we say "Aye aye".' Zos smiled at his friend. 'It means, "I hear and understand".'

Pollon shrugged, still tapping the stroke. 'Must I?'

An oarsman laughed.

Zos spoke up, loud and clear, but not his battle-command voice. 'Here it is, shipmates. We're going to look ready to fight, but it's my intention to slip away and leave the bastards holding their dicks in their hands. If it comes to a fight, these are Jekers. Don't surrender. Don't give up. Fight like you have no other choice, because by the fucking useless gods above, we have no other choice.'

They didn't cheer. They looked at each other, and wondered if they should have stayed in Trin.

Zos understood them well enough. Too well. Exacting his revenge had emptied him. He wasn't sure, any more, what he wanted; or rather, he was sure he wanted to pull down the gods, and he had a plan to accomplish it, but he wasn't sure he had the energy to do it.

But the Narmerian reed-ship was like a sign. He was awake, now.

Zos nodded to Eritha, and she leant on the steering oar.

The long, low ship began to turn. Eritha was a careful helm; she only leant enough that the deck edge dropped away by a handspan. Some of the less experienced people cursed in surprise as their oars didn't bite the water properly; one man shot forward and smacked his head on the next bench and fell, cursing, his oar flailing in the air.

Despite the one lubber, the *Sea Eagle* made her turn neatly, and the flailing oar and the three others thrown into confusion were all on the seaward side, away from the Jekers, and thus invisible. Vital, since Zos' plan depended on looking much tougher than they were.

Astern, the second pentekonter, the *Winter Gamble*, began her turn. Trayos' former helmsman Orestas had her with fifty more fisherfolk and farmers at her oars, but his own expertise helped balance their ignorance. The ship came around as smoothly as the *Sea Eagle*.

Behind the *Winter Gamble* came the *Shark*, a Mykoan pirate salvaged in almost perfect condition, under a Mykoan captain whom Zos didn't trust but had to keep because he was so short of experienced people. Lord Tuwinon had sailed for Zos' mortal enemies. And he was a dangerous man himself.

But a competent seaman.

The *Shark* started her turn. She was crewed almost entirely by former courtiers and palace craftspeople; Zos had put all the people he couldn't trust in one hull. She had the fewest veterans and the fewest experienced sailors.

It showed. Only three quarters of her oar-loom was full, and someone misunderstood the orders coming from the command deck and got an oar in the chest, full force. They heard the scream across the water as ribs were crushed.

Zos could hear Tuwinon roaring.

But the *Shark* made the turn.

Second from last was the daringly named *Trident*: a name that had not been heard on the seas for five hundred years or more. It was a clear challenge to the gods, and most of Zos' new recruits declined to step aboard her. But young Daos, now almost six feet tall and with hair on his chin, had his own charm and a trident in his hand, and he led fifty wild-eyed fishers, coastal people with a sideline in sea-brigandage, aboard. Zos had no worries whatsoever about their seamanship, and indeed the *Trident* made her turn perfectly, cutting the water exactly where Zos' *Sea Eagle* had turned.

By then, Pollon's beat had eased, and the rearward ships began to close up on the *Sea Eagle*. Ship by ship they slipped in close, almost bow to stern, in a short, solid line, their long, low sides facing the Jekers.

Every ship had a handful of skilled archers, and they all put their oars up and reported to their archery stations.

'It's almost as if we know what we're doing,' Zos said to Pollon.

'I had imagined that it was vital not to show your long side to the enemy in combat,' Pollon said in his pedantic way. 'To avoid the deadly ram.'

Zos was looking at the Narmerian, now hurtling towards them at a good clip as they themselves moved due east at a snail's pace.

'Definitely something to avoid.' Zos was watching Trayos' *Wave Serpent* make the turn.

'But ...' Pollon began.

'When I signal,' Zos ignored his friend and turned to Eritha, 'we go from line ahead, in a single turn to port, to side by side, bow-on to the enemy. Understand?'

She looked puzzled. 'Rowin' upwind again, like?'

'Exactly,' Zos said.

She shrugged. 'Aye aye.'

'Pollon, give the drum to ...' Zos struggled for a name. 'That man there. Get your bow and prepare to dissuade our Jeker guests from coming for dinner.'

Someone laughed. Zos knew the right tone to use. He'd encouraged generations of peasants to die for him as a godborn warrior.

Poor bastards.

I'm turning over a new leaf. I'm going to keep this crew alive if I can.

'Persay, you have the ship.'

Persay laughed his crazy laugh. 'Nah, my lord. No idea what to do with it.'

Zos suppressed his instinctive *I'm not your lord*. He'd been thinking like a godborn anyway – trying to appoint the next most noble on the ship, the bull-leaper.

Instead, he looked at Alektron, who'd come down from the leather nest and was standing by the helm.

'Alektron, you have the ship,' he said.

'Pleased, Cap'n,' the old sailor replied, and his eyes kindled with something like joy.

The Jekers were turning south. They weren't as good seamen as the Narmerians, and they'd obviously hesitated, which Zos took as an excellent sign.

Kill them all, whispered a woman's voice in his head.

Zos was on his way aft, and he flinched.

Where did that voice come from?

Draw me and we will exterminate them together.

Zos blinked. Then he climbed the tall sweep of the stern and motioned for the *Winter Gamble* to come up. As soon as her bow was close, he made his leap, landing on her foredeck with a tumble to avoid going over the side. He ran aft.

The sword at his side was trying to talk to him.

Strange days, he thought to himself. He stopped at the stern, and described his plan in detail to Orestas, former helmsman of Trayos, who looked very doubtful, but Zos was already waving for the next ship to close up.

It took him the length of a long negotiation in the market to get all the way to Trayos, and by then the Narmerian was close, running down on them with the full weight of the wind behind her. The Narmerian reed-ship was enormous – long, wide and tall – and, as Zos had hoped, full of archers.

Trayos watched. 'She'll pass us downwind and run for

Mykoax,' he said with weary cynicism. 'No good deed goes unpunished.'

Zos shook his head. 'She'll join our line,' he said. 'Daos says so.'

Trayos shrugged. 'I wouldn't.'

Zos grinned, his mood restored to something like his usual excitement.

'On the contrary, my friend,' he said. 'You did.'

Trayos winced.

Zos ran forward along the benches, encouraging, patting a shoulder, calling out to people whose names he remembered, making the leap between ships again and pausing briefly on each command deck to remind his captains of the plan. He spared a few words for every archer.

This is how you lure the nice peasants to serve willingly, and give their lives. With a kind word and a pat on the shoulder.

I'm not going to lose this lot.

And all the time, the Narmerian rushed south by west with the wind behind her.

Daos could be wrong, Zos admitted to himself.

The Jekers hung back. Three ships to five was poor odds, especially as the five were all Dardanian war hulls, and the flotilla continued to creep east, forcing the Jekers to turn, and turn.

Back aboard his own *Sea Eagle* with a leap that suggested that his ageing muscles didn't need any more exercise, Zos looked at his foes long and hard. They were at the very best point of sail for their long hulls, not so different from his own, if smaller. The largest Jeker ships weren't much bigger than Trayos' *Wave Serpent*, with thirty or forty oars, a shallow draft to run on to beaches and up rivers, and a horde of ferocious, desperate boarders ready to overwhelm any defence in a close fight.

But their hesitation told, and they weren't coming on as fast as they should have. And now that they were hull up, he could see signs of storm damage.

He turned to Eritha and had her start cheating her helm to the north − just little taps, not a steady turn. Not much − he didn't want his amateur crews to get the wrong message. But over the next hundred oar beats, the line went from creeping due east to creeping north by east. It happened almost imperceptibly.

The Narmerian defied Zos' oracle and ran on, passing the stern of Trayos' ship and hurtling south with the not inconsiderable winter wind behind her. And the Jekers were still hanging back. The Narmerian was a huge prize, but the Dardanians looked dangerous.

And then, in one sudden blossoming of sail, the Jekers committed. Their ugly brown sails came up taut where formerly they'd been slack, and they were running south with all the speed the wind allowed them. It wasn't smooth, and they bobbed about like unkempt fishing smacks in a fresh wind, but they got their sails set hard.

The lead ship had a man crucified on his bow. He'd been flayed alive.

Eritha was suddenly looking pale.

Zos grinned at her. 'Never you worry,' he said, and saw her brighten.

The unfairness of the world. A godborn says it's true, and thus, it is true.

'They're terrifying, and insanely ferocious,' Zos said to the command deck at large. 'They have heavy crews because they can always eat the slaves.'

He looked back at Eritha and she smiled bravely.

Persay grinned his own mad grin. 'But …?'

'They're not that bright,' Zos said.

The line of Zos' ships had moved at a snail's pace, but move

82

they had; they'd crept east, and then cheated north-east until they were no longer 'downwind' of the Jekers. And every second of the Jekers' downwind rush actually carried the cannibals to the west of Trayos' stern, because they were headed due south.

Zos watched intently. In his bones, he felt that the critical point had already passed, but it could take an hour to play out.

He lifted his shield, glanced over his shoulder at the sun, and flashed the shield twice.

GO.

Every oar in the flotilla dipped. Every back strained.

Pollon, his great horn bow held loosely in his left hand, turned to Zos.

'You intend us to go fast, I believe,' he said.

Zos was leaning over the rail, trying to make his ship go faster with his hips. He caught himself at it and made himself stand straight and look calm.

'Yes,' he said. 'Faster.'

'But at this rate,' Pollon said, 'they'll never make the turn in time, and we'll never be in archery range.' He raised a scholarly eyebrow. 'Unless they row much faster than we can?'

Zos was secretly pleased that Pollon's eye confirmed his own.

'A pity,' he said, 'that they'll never come in range.'

'Oh, you're pleased to be *sarcastic*,' Pollon said with a snort. 'So this was all, in fact, a *trick*.' Zos allowed his secret smile to become public. Almost due west, one of the Jekers had just realised their mistake and put their helm up; the combination of slovenly seamanship and tired oarsmen was immediately apparent, and the Jeker ship was left even further behind.

South and east, the Narmerian was turning. It was a wallowing manoeuvre, rather like a fat cat searching for the perfect spot on a sunny day; but as professional as a good crew could manage, and it showed Zos what he'd already suspected: the Narmerian had a weather mage aboard, and a good one. The

83

world's wind was blowing from north to south, and over the next part of the mid-morning, the Narmerian began to sail first due east, and then east by north, following Zos' squadron without ever coming within range of the Jekers, whose three ships were now spread over twenty stadia of sea.

Eritha looked at him with something near hero worship. And he could feel the little success in the handling of the ship, in the rowing, in the glance that Alektron threw him as he stood in the command spot by the mast.

Persay finally said, 'So, no fight at all?'

Alektron barked his deep-sea laugh. 'Not unless ye want to go back.' The tattooed man spat over the side. 'They were fewkin' tired at the start, lad. Now they're killin' slaves to get another pull, and a scrap o' wind and they'll all go to icy hell.' He smiled with relish. And nodded cordially to Zos. 'Right smart, Cap'n.'

Zos nodded. He walked forward along the benches, telling the story of the not-quite-fight, making them all feel like heroes. Most of them grinned and pulled all the harder.

So easy. In a week, we'll be a crew. In a month, I'll have a war band.

A voice in his head said, ***When we have a war band, we can scour the seas, rich and powerful, lords of the waves!***

Zos paused, looking back at his flotilla.

Shut up, Terror! he thought. *I have enough dark thoughts all by myself.*

Hyatta-Azi

Once, he had been a prince of Atussa.

Once, he had worn silk and schemed to win the crown.

Now, he ate men's flesh and drank blood.

He picked up the cringing slave at his feet and opened his

throat, and the blood ran to join the huge stain on the command deck.

'Wind, Lord of Destruction!'

He didn't so much pray for it as demand it, and his rage rose to choke him.

He and his ships had fought the sea and the great wave. They'd been promised an easy conquest, and instead they'd had days of falling volcanic rock shredding their rowers and nights of high seas and ash that hid the skies.

The deeply laden Narmerian merchant had looked like a gift from Kur, but now they were denied by a squadron of Dardanians who had offered combat and then *turned away* in humiliating contempt.

'Make them row faster,' he ordered.

His lashmaster beat the nearest slave, and then walked down the midship catwalk, his whip slicing left and right without discrimination.

The favoured slave who beat the flesh-hide drum increased the beat. But the oars didn't move much faster – there was confusion on the right side. The more the lashmaster plied his whip, the more confusion spread.

By his side, a small woman in a cloak of human hair spat over the side. The human hair was not her own.

'They've had no water in a day,' she said. 'You can't make them row faster if you kill them.'

Hyatta-Azi turned to her, and she just looked at him. 'What do you plan to do?' she asked. 'Kill me, too? The fucking Dardanian coward has outsailed you, *lord*. I told you that the sea took time to master.'

He stood there, his rage burning in his throat.

'If you continue,' she said, 'we will be left adrift at sea with a crew of the dead.'

Hyatta-Azi knew she was right. But he was watching the

Dardanian squadron sail north, their oars beating together. He could see a man on the command deck of the lead warship, and he was laughing.

'I will kill him,' Hyatta-Azi swore.

'I will teach you how, if you let me,' the Noan woman said. 'But killing oar slaves won't get it done.'

Hefa-Asus

The first Jekers to come ashore were not much of a threat, as they were almost all dead. Their ship had turned turtle, whether in the storm or when the Great Wave came, and there were fifty dead men and women trapped under her, most of them wrapped in loose cordage or floating plunder. They'd seized a cargo of Akashian rice at some point, and the rice had swelled in the bilge and trapped the doomed ship upside down.

It was an ugly wreck.

There was one survivor. A big man with the scars of a Jeker veteran, and he had the strength to drag himself up the beach before a dozen of Era's 'soldiers' clubbed him unconscious.

'Just kill him,' Jawat recommended.

Hefa-Asus shook his head. He hated being interrupted, and he and Nicté had been busy making presentable but pedestrian spears and swords from their dwindling stocks of copper and tin. But now that he'd left his forge, he might as well do some good.

'No,' the Northerner said. 'No, I've always wanted to talk to one. Bind him for questioning. Offer him food and rest.'

'They're all killers.' Era, who was afraid of nothing, shied away from going too close to the Jeker. 'He has the scars of a veteran. He has *eaten human flesh*.'

'Ah, well, as to that...' Hefa-Asus cleared his throat, and Nicté laughed aloud.

'You Southerners are so odd,' she said.

Era froze.

Hefa-Asus favoured his apprentice with a glare. *Keep it between your teeth*, he almost said. In Dendrowna, war captives were usually sacrificed. If they were very brave, sometimes they were eaten. It was ... complicated. A sign of deep respect. A taking into oneself of another's greatness. Southerners were too weak to understand.

Nicté had been a warrior, in addition to being a brilliant bronze-smith. From her grin, he knew she had tasted the flesh of her enemies. So he frowned at her, and she subsided, and Era turned away, wise enough not to ask a question when she didn't want to know the answer.

'There will be more,' Era said. 'We have to get off this beach.'

'Tell the Dry One,' Pavi said, and went down the beach to bring water to her starving husband and wife, in their orange robes, apparently unconcerned by the growing desperation of their friends and companions.

The next day dawned, a beautiful winter day. Hefa-Asus had arrows and javelins for the scouts, and Taha, the scout commander, received his gratefully, making the full desert bow.

'You are a master,' he said in Py, the language of the deep desert.

'I am,' Hefa-Asus said with real pleasure.

Seeing the delight of those for whom he made some things was one of his greatest joys in life. After weeks of thinking about star-stone and even working the unforgiving stuff, the return to bronze had been a happy change, and he'd livened his work with a little art and some decoration. Taha's sickle-bladed Narmerian-style sword was inlaid and embellished in a way that Era would probably not approve of, but Hefa-Asus needed to be interested to work a project. Even the javelin heads had a line of silver wire beaten in, and each scout had a single javelin tipped in star-stone, their hafts painted a deep vermilion. Red earth was common in Rasna.

'Ah!' said Taha in delight. 'I knew you would speak my tongue! You are from Poche!'

Poche was a great city in a fold of the hills where the jungle met the mountains and the sea – the principal trading link between two very different worlds: the high desert of Narmer and the Hundred Cities, and the endless trees of Dendrowna, a vast forest that extended farther north than any man of the south could measure. The people of Poche tended to reddish-brown skin, tattoos, and magnificent woven cotton clothes that traded well everywhere on the Ocean.

The Py lived out in the deep desert east of Narmer. They were almost the only humans who lived side by side with the Bright People, the Dry Ones. Taha had dark skin, shiny in sunlight; his hair was pulled back in a tight queue, and he wore a chiton of goatskin over one shoulder and belted at the waist with a beautifully woven *zone*, or belt, Dite had given him.

Hefa-Asus smiled. 'I have a little Py,' he admitted. 'And Betwana, which is commoner in Poche. For trade.'

'Betwana is a child's language,' Taha said. 'Py has fifty words for sunset.'

'Betwana has fifty phrases for "and this way we both make a profit",' Hefa-Asus shot back, and both men laughed.

'These are beautiful things,' Taha said. 'I never expected to own such noble weapons. But they are wasted here. These are peaceful people and they bless me every time I pass. I won't fight anyone today.'

'Worry not, my brother,' Hefa-Asus said. 'When we go north, you will need all your guile and your curved sword.'

Taha bowed, hands on chest. 'I never crave a fight,' he said. 'But these weapons almost make me want to. They are magical.'

Hefa-Asus smiled to himself. *More than you know, scout captain.*

Once the scouts were gone into the dawn, Hefa-Asus and Nicté built up their fires with the help of some former slaves. Today, by design, Nicté was making arrowheads while he trained his new novices in the arcane arts of smithing. He told them no lies and exaggerated nothing, but he did work a small magic at his main fire, demonstrating how he could super-heat the coal with a small working.

'Most of our tools and our big forge are packed away,' he said. 'We're working the portable forge today, casting arrowheads for the archers.'

They were of varying degrees of ready intelligence, his new people. Atosa, of course, was a master metalworker himself, and needed no training. Tarhu, a young woman who'd worked in a forge, was eager to show both her native intelligence and her knowledge; he could see the future smith in her, if only she had humility. Mawat of Takar, far to the south, was an older man and a shepherd who could do some crude metalwork. He was slower to understand, but he retained what he was told, and he asked for things to be repeated until he understood them, and he wasn't afraid of work. The others were, for the most part, dull-witted labourers; Hefa-Asus wondered if slavery had broken their minds. But they obeyed, and pumped air, and held moulds, and carried loads, and they hadn't chosen to leave with the others.

Teaching new novices was both a pleasure, and a duty; Hefa-Asus had no idea if the great guild of smiths of Poche would ever accept any of them, but then he wasn't sure they'd take him back, either, which made him smile.

I can work star-stone as easily as bronze, copper, lead or gold, he thought without particular arrogance. *There are not many who can rival me, and none in star-stone work.*

He touched the knife at his throat – a star-stone dirk with a thin plating of tin to disguise it, something the Poche often did for bronze weapons used at sea. It was a knife he could wear anywhere, and not be caught possessing star-stone.

Nicté, head down over a row of moulds, was pouring her arrowheads from a ladle full of liquid bronze, and Tarhu was helping her, switching the moulds out under the spout with real skill. Nicté was singing an Onadawegan metal song, tapping the moulds to the rhythm, and Tarhu was humming the tune already. Atosa was making small animals in wax – because they had agreed they needed items for trade.

Hefa-Asus was pleased. Atosa's animals were beautiful; the man really was a master. And soon enough, Nicté would need to be a master herself. He had much left to teach her, but she was already skilled beyond most of the masters he knew, and she was no man's fool. She needed to be her own woman.

Her head twitched, and he snapped out of his reverie to look through the open-sided forge and see a disturbance down the beach. There was a ship coming in.

He heard the shouts, and then the drum, and then Era's voice, clear, and bronze-hard with authority.

'To arms!' she roared.

He could see her, framed in the doorway, and beyond her …

A Jeker ship, and this one not already dead.

He glanced back at Nicté, who was thorough as well as clever; she finished the molten metal in her ladle and then very carefully laid it down on stone.

'Jekers,' he said softly, and she nodded.

He pulled on a heavy, padded cotton tunic that made him seem even larger than he was, and strapped on a bronze loin-belt. He felt no fear; rather, he looked inside himself and found a sense of anticipation, like that he had before a very difficult craft operation – one with consequences. He smiled at his own rationalisation and then he picked up the weapon he'd made for himself. One of the wrecks had been full of jade, which he loved working with, and there was plenty of wood here at the edge of the Rasnan plains.

He'd made a *makuital* with it. Neither sword nor club, it was a wooden paddle that fitted his hand perfectly, and had sharpened jade teeth running all the way around the head of the paddle – the war weapon of his people.

He left his head bare, to see and hear better, then plucked up a shield so tall and so thick that most men couldn't lift it. Nicté was in her own bronze corselet in the Dardanian style, and had a pair of javelins behind her scalloped shield and a third in her hand. *She* wore a helmet.

She turned to Tarhu. 'Can you complete the pour?' she asked. 'The bronze is hot.'

Tarhu looked flustered.

'Together, we can do it,' Mawat said slowly.

'I'll watch them,' Atosa said from his straw mat. 'I'm not much for fighting.'

'Good,' Hefa-Asus said, well pleased. 'We'll see off these Jekers, and you will complete the work.'

He nodded, and stepped out of the forge shed.

There were, in fact, three Jeker ships. Together, they might have instantly overwhelmed the community's defences.

But if they came in one at a time ...

One ship was already aground, the crew ashore and trying to overwhelm Jawat's half-trained soldiers. Hefa-Asus could see the giant man, Drakon, towering over the melee, and his friend Lan Thena, carefully using her spear from behind him. Together, they were holding the charge of the Jekers, and because they stood, and Jawat stood, the rest stood. There were bodies on the sand – people he knew.

And the next Jeker ship was in close already; someone had

been asleep at their post. The third was barely hull up on the horizon, and had no sail set. But this was very bad ...

Hefa-Asus ran to where the fighting was thickest, which was on the middle of the beach. It made no sense, but war seldom did, and Hefa-Asus had been making war – unwillingly – since he was a boy apprentice. It both fascinated and repelled him; he abhorred it, but it had a horrible beauty ...

And, of course, he was very good at it.

His long legs carried him fast over the sand, and when he came to the flanks of the melee, twenty of Jawat's soldiers were trying to stem a flood of Jekers.

In a flash, Hefa-Asus understood. Jawat and Drakon were defending Jawala and Aanat, who were sitting defenceless on the beach. They continued to look in the direction of the rising sun.

Hefa-Asus loved the Hakrans, and they were worthy of being defended.

And so ...

He ran into the flank of the Jekers' attack, his huge shield breaking a man's arm. Before the next opponent could make his first swing, a Jeker took one of Nicté's javelins in the side of the head, and it went all the way through his skull, despite the man's leather helmet.

Hefa-Asus ploughed forward, and his heavy *makuital* came down, the jade ripping at a man's hide shield. The swing brought his shield down, and Hefa-Asus rolled his wrist, the sharper-than-a-bronze-razor jade flaying the man's face and eyes.

Hefa-Asus was a head taller than the largest Jeker, and he killed another with a backhand to the back of the man's un-guarded head, the jade punching into bone, the wood exploding the break, and the Jekers flinched away from him.

The *makuital* wasn't just a fine weapon. It was a weapon of terror, feeding irrational fear deep inside every warrior: the fear of being torn to shreds.

He stopped to give his war cry.

Jawat, the old man, killed an unwary Jeker with a canny spear thrust over his shield, and still the Jekers might have held. They had fierce veterans, hard men and women with little fear left in them; one leapt on to the locked shields of the amateur spear people and forced an opening while another killed. The fight hung in the balance…

Era led a charge. She'd rallied two dozen of the former slaves; they had tools, or no weapons at all, but she herself wore a quilted linen corselet and she had a spear she used… beautifully, each motion like dance. The line steadied. The Jekers called out to one another in three languages, and they pushed forward, killing another of Jawat's militia and forcing even Drakon to step back, and then…

And then Bror, the bear, waded in. Her thick fur was indomitable, her scythe-claws turned each massive paw into a mighty war club, and she stood head and shoulders above the tallest warrior. She exploded into the melee on the opposite flank and…

…in three heartbeats, the Jekers had gone from predators to prey. Now Hefa-Asus could see their despair. The woman facing Nicté simply let her shield droop and took Nicté's spear in her throat like a woman accepting a drink of water; she all but embraced her death.

Hefa-Asus gave the matter a moment's thought and then returned to killing them, his sword-club winnowing them like grain on a threshing floor. Jawat and his soldiers clearly shared his view, and in a moment the massacre was complete, and the whole of the Jeker landing party had been butchered, their blood soaking into the sand. Bror fell down on all fours, panting, and then began to lick at her paws and claws.

Jawat slapped a stunned novice-warrior on the back.

'And that's what it is, boys and girls.'

He nodded to Drakon, whose bronze sword was bent double. His partner, Lan Thena, was already in among the corpses, looking for better weapons.

The rest of the spear-people stood stunned. Some were covered in blood as if they'd bathed in it; some wore only a spatter, a trail like the tentacle of an octopus where the blood of their victim went over their shields, but none were unbloodied. None who'd lived, that was. Nine of their own lay dead in the sand.

Jawat stepped out of the huddle of shields and in front of them.

'That's what it is. You won. Congratulations – you lived to do it again. Only now you know you can win.'

Era and Nicté mustered reinforcements from the warehouses before the second ship, driven by wind and current, came ashore. It landed well down the beach, and Era began to arrange her forces.

Hefa-Asus touched her arm. 'If I may,' he said cautiously.

She looked at him.

'Let them come down the beach. They are exhausted and desperate – let them wear themselves out in the sand.'

She made a face, but agreed.

Nicté pointed out to sea. 'Another.'

'Shit,' Era replied, and had the archers string their bows.

The spear-people stood together in a clump, as if, having survived the first rush of the Jekers, they needed to stay together for comfort. Jawat exhorted them; Drakon looked bored. Lan Thena had a better spear and a good helmet.

Hefa-Asus smiled to himself. He flicked his *makuital* out to the side and cleared it of most of the blood and matted hair that had gathered in its teeth.

A man at the far end of the small spear block turned and vomited into the sand.

Jawat turned to Hefa-Asus. 'Second time is the worst. First time, you don't know what to expect. Second time, you do. It you live to the third time ...'

Hefa-Asus nodded. 'This is my fortieth time.'

Jawat looked up at him, his twisted smile emphasising his age. 'Still counting?'

Era raised an eyebrow. 'Are you two done?' she asked, with more than a hint of sarcasm. 'I'm keeping twenty of these folk back. As a reserve. And I want the big ugly man.'

'Drakon,' Jawat said.

'Drakon,' Era agreed, in a voice that suggested she wouldn't need reminding again.

Jawat nodded. 'It's a good idea. Take Lan Thena, too – they don't split up.'

Era nodded, her eyes already back on the enemy.

Jawat nodded back and turned to his archers, who were shuffling with anxiety.

'Stand still. Eyes front. Not a shaft flies until they pass the big white rock. This is target practice. Don't watch the fall of your shaft. Just loose as fast as you can.'

A woman, white under her deeply tanned skin, failed to draw an arrow from the big quiver at her side. She dropped the shaft, bent to get it, and stepped on it with a loud crack.

Quick as thought, Jawat was at her side.

'Use this one, Thera,' he said, and drew one from her quiver. 'That one was obviously cursed.' He smiled.

Nervous laughter swept through the archers.

Thera took the arrow, flushed, and nocked it.

'Steady.' Jawat wasn't a big man, and he was old, and yet somehow he projected immense confidence. 'Don't hurry.'

'Nock,' he said.

It was a wasted order; every archer already had an arrow set to their bow.

And then he waited what seemed, even to Hefa-Asus, an impossibly long time. The lead Jekers, sprinting, were well past the white rock.

'Draw,' he said calmly.

The bows came up.

'Loose,' he snapped. 'Now, fast as you can.'

As the stumbling Jekers came down the beach, the archers decimated them. Training told; Jawat had been drilling the archers for a week. They weren't very accurate or very strong, but they were fast, and the Jekers died or slowed.

Hefa-Asus was interested to see how *human* the Jekers were; he admitted to himself that he'd believed the legends. But the Jekers flinched at every arrow, shuffled like city-state militia, and some few just lay down to die...

The survivors ran in under the arrow-fall to die on the spears of Jawat's soldiers. They weren't very good either, but they were good enough to stay together and lock their huge hide shields; good enough to know they'd done this once and held. So they huddled together and the braver ones stabbed, while the old man and Hefa-Asus and Nicté did some killing.

And then, with excellent timing, as the Jekers' charge lost its ferocity and the fight became a shoving contest, Era and the big man and a crowd of workers fell on the flank of the melee and began the killing. None of the Jekers surrendered, though Hefa-Asus noted a few broke away, running back down the beach.

Jawat's archers used them for practice, decorating the sand with arrows for three hundred paces.

Pavi wept. She was kneeling in the sand by Jawala and Aanat, weeping at the blood and waste.

Jawat looked past Era to Hefa-Asus.

'Kill the wounded?' he asked.

Hefa-Asus stepped past Era.

'Kill them all.' His voice was flat, emotionless. 'Make sure every wounded Jeker is dead.'

Era looked back at the huddle of bodies that the rising ride was starting to cover. She was cleaning her bronze sword.

'Do you have to kill them all?' she spat. 'You're the one who wanted the prisoner saved yesterday.'

Hefa-Asus shrugged. His right shoulder hurt, but he was otherwise untouched.

'Yes,' he said simply.

'Why?' she asked. 'I think some might surrender.'

Hefa-Asus raised an eyebrow. 'Jekers?' he asked. 'Anyway, we have about four days' food for the people here, yes?'

Era looked away.

'Would you split the food with Jeker prisoners?'

'We could get more food.'

Hefa-Asus nodded. 'Yes. In an endless game of diminishing returns, we could spend more time here, gathering food to feed an increasing number of captives while each day more Jekers arrive.' He smiled, hoping she wouldn't take offence at his bluntness, while further down the beach, two large women were pulping a 'corpse' that had tried to rise.

Jawat was trying to get blood out of his white beard with his fingers.

'I just fuckin' hate 'em,' he said. 'Godless heavens, fightin' is harder when you're fuckin' old.'

The third ship took a long time to come ashore. She was listing badly, and had no sail set, and the current and tide only moved her sluggishly.

Tarhu and Mawat had time to finish the pour, cool the moulds, open them, and have a dozen apprentices coached by Atosa bind the still-warm heads to the already prepared straight shafts. Meanwhile the archers and a dozen children they'd brought from Dekhu plucked up arrows from the sand. The more aggressive children competed to pull arrows from Jeker corpses, as Jawat had offered a prize to the child who brought in the most arrows.

Pavi dried her eyes, but she didn't speak.

'You don't have to watch.' Hefa-Asus meant his voice to be kind, but there was a harshness to it that told him he was not as unaffected by the fighting as he pretended to be.

She nodded to him, a serious look, as if he'd just explained a particularly complex metal alloy to an apprentice who was listening *very hard*.

'Yes,' she said simply. 'I do have to watch. I am here, I am present, and I witness.'

By early afternoon, the last Jeker ship was in arrow range, and the horizon behind it was clear. By then, Era had realised that Jeker ships might be landing elsewhere up and down the coast, and she'd have to ask Taha to scout the beaches to check.

'We need to get out of here.' She glanced at Hefa-Asus. He immediately saw that they had come to the same conclusion. That pleased him.

The archery was more effective against the Jeker ship. It came in slowly, warriors at the gunwales literally biting the edges of their rawhide shields in their eagerness to get ashore and fight the soldiers waiting on the beach, but it was never a contest. Having live targets encouraged the archers enormously. They spread out to shoot, stuck their shafts head down into the sand, and took their time, loosing carefully. Era offered small prizes of food and scrap silver for good shooting, and the whole thing had a festive air that Pavi clearly found appalling.

Hefa-Asus smiled at her. 'Would you rather they came ashore and raped and killed and enslaved and ate us?' he asked.

'I would rather never watch these acts of violence. It poisons me. I will never sleep again. You people ...' She was trying so

98

hard to hold to the discipline of the Hakrans, looking at where the woman, Lan Thena, squatted at the edge of the sea, washing the blood out of the straw lining of her new helmet.

Hefa-Asus nodded. 'It is not a complex equation,' he said. 'Kill or be killed.'

Pavi looked at Jawala, sitting with her face turned away from the violence.

'It is not simple,' she said. 'You seek to make it simple with violence, but the consequences are not simple.'

Hefa-Asus was watching the fall of a flight of arrows into the floating hulk. It was almost ashore now. One brave woman leapt into the water and began to swim ashore.

Nicté ordered the archers to cease shooting.

Hefa-Asus smiled. Nicté was young and brave. He admired her. He had often wished to bed her, but she was an apprentice, and that sort of thing led to strain among the other apprentices: bickering, recrimination, and poor workmanship, the closest thing to absolute evil that Hefa-Asus accepted. So he restrained himself. But he did enjoy watching her.

She walked to the edge of the water and began to recite her clan lineage in Onadawega as the Jeker woman waded out of the water. She'd swum ashore with a shield on her back, and she was covered – *covered* – in scars. She was a veteran. And she screamed a challenge.

Nicté motioned an invitation with her spear hand and retreated up the beach, giving the Jeker woman space to get clear of the wet sand and sea-wrack. The Jeker woman rolled her shield off her back on to her arm and immediately charged, running full tilt at Nicté with a screamed war cry that pierced the ears of every listener.

Nicté's first javelin went through the woman's shield but did no apparent damage.

So did her second.

The woman ran in close, feet pounding on the dry sand, stumbling a little.

Nicté threw her third from perhaps four paces away, and her right hand swept down to close on her knife-hilt. She drew cross-body from under her shield as she flung herself forward. Her small bronze shield hooked the top corner of her enemy's square wooden shield, and she buried her knife in the other woman's chest, below and between her breasts, and used it as a lever to turn the woman, kicking her legs out from under her.

Heart-stabbed, the Jeker was dead before she hit the ground.

Nicté withdrew her knife, and licked it fastidiously. Then she pulled her javelins from the shield, and walked back to the water's edge as Jawat's soldiers cheered her.

She stood at the edge of the water, chanting her lineage again, and the Jeker ship drifted slowly in. No more Jekers clambered over the sides. They were silent, sullen.

'We cannot simply murder them,' Era said.

'I thought you agreed with me?' Hefa-Asus said, surprised at her irrationality.

Pavi was weeping again. 'I beg you to stop this. It is evil. These are people! They are tired and hungry... That woman was starving!'

'That woman would have enslaved you and every other person on this beach,' Hefa-Asus said.

'Or eaten you,' the giant, Drakon, said.

'We cannot just murder them.' Era said with firm authority.

'Walk away and leave it to us, then,' Jawat said.

Hefa-Asus saw the anger building in Era, and he shook his head.

'What will we do with them?' he asked. 'Enslave them? Set watches? What happens when more come?'

Era's face showed her struggle. But finally, she said, 'That's a problem for tomorrow. If we have to kill them, I'll do it myself. Take all of them prisoner. That's an *order*.'

Pavi clasped Era's hand.

'Bless you,' she said.

Era shrugged. 'Perhaps I'm a fool. I've just had enough death for a day.'

Hefa-Asus blew out his cheeks in disgust and he could see that old Jawat shared his feeling.

Jawat shook his head. 'You mean, some of my boys and girls have to go aboard that hell-ship, and maybe get cut or even killed to force those fuckin' animals to surrender?' he asked. 'When we could sit here and let the archers practise on 'em?' He shook his head. 'Fuck that.'

Era's voice hardened. 'That's an order.' Their eyes locked and softly, carefully, Hefa-Asus heard Era say, 'There's more to our plan then one fight with Jekers on the beach.' Her tone was light – friendly. With it, she all but begged him not to resist her.

Hefa-Asus agreed with Jawat about the utility of the thing, but he wasn't interested in mutiny. Hefa-Asus had a healthy respect for Era's skills, and her point was valid. Southerners were soft, and killing tended to make them behave badly; they lacked the discipline of the Dendrownan peoples, or so he suspected.

He put a hand on Jawat's arm. 'I'll help you clear the ship,' he said. 'Come. By obeying, we build your corps' discipline.'

Jawat took a deep breath. 'I think ye're makin' a mistake,' he said. 'But I ain't no mutineer.'

Era took a deep breath. 'Thank you,' she said.

Hefa-Asus admired her control. *She is good at command*, he thought.

In the end, Nicté joined him. They let the hulk touch the sand, and then, covered by forty archers, they went up the stern. One man attacked them and died. The other thirty Jekers surrendered. They were big men and women, out of Atussa and Haniglabat, brown and scarred and naked and starving.

'What do you propose to do with them?' Hefa-Asus asked Era.

Pavi managed a smile. 'I'm going to start by feeding them.'

Nicté shrugged. 'You are mad,' she said. 'Insane.'

Pavi frowned. 'I think the same of you. You killed that woman as if you enjoyed it.'

'The woman who challenged me to single combat?' Nicté asked.

'She didn't challenge you!' Pavi spat. 'She ran forward in a desperate hope of dying well.'

Nicté shrugged. 'I honour her courage. Against long odds, she was willing to place her body against mine.' She smiled, showing her teeth. 'I did enjoy it. I was allowed to demonstrate my skill. A public kill like that is a precious thing, especially when you are a woman.'

'She didn't need to die!'

'These are very odd things you believe,' Nicté said. 'If that had been our ship, and there were Jekers waiting on the beach, that woman would have been me, and I would have been happy to let her drink my blood if I could have had a good death. I would have attacked all the Jekers on the beach. I would not wait to be a slave.' She shrugged. 'So in a way, she is me. And now that I lick her blood, she is more me.'

'They are people!' Pavi shouted.

Nicté rolled her head, trying to loosen her neck muscles. 'Perhaps,' she said. 'Many people are better off dead.'

'I can never believe that. People have worth. People can be redeemed.'

Nicté nodded. 'Yes,' she said slowly. 'You are insane. But I like you anyway.'

Chapter Four

Zos

The island of Lazba rose out of the deeps like the offer of paradise to mortals, a green island. Its heralds were the seabirds, as the fisherfolk told the lubbers, and then the lookout, a sharp-eyed young woman named Disa, called out that she could see land. Then the visible mountains of central Lazba drew a cheer from the whole squadron, and as they closed in they could see tall trees on hills and smell the earth. And smoke. Lots of smoke, and a deep sulphur smell.

Alarm bells rang out on the coast, and watch fires sent up columns of smoke as far as the eye could see, east and west.

Zos pointed this out to Persay and Pollon.

'Jekers must have made landings.'

'Gods, they're everywhere,' Pollon said.

Zos shook his head. 'When we saw them, before the storm, there were … what – five hundred ships?'

'Didn't stop to count 'em,' Persay said with a grin. 'Too busy rowing.'

Pollon shook his head. 'They cannot have five hundred ships,' he said. 'No tribe or country could stand against them.'

Zos was looking at Lazba. 'Do you know where the Jekers came from?'

Pollon replied. 'From the mountains west of Attusa,' he

said. 'The god-king of Atussa built a great wall to defend his people—'

'To cover his own arse, I'm guessing,' Persay said.

Pollon nodded. 'Perhaps. Regardless, they came out of the mountains.'

'Maybe,' Zos said.

Pollon was not used to having his knowledge questioned.

'Maybe?' he asked sharply.

Zos was still watching the coast. 'Mountains don't support enough people to conquer a god-king,' he said.

Pollon smiled. 'You just killed one, with about thirty people at your back.'

Zos acknowledged this with a wave. 'A fair hit, friend. But the Jekers overran Atussa. And that's a lot of Jekers.'

Pollon acknowledged that.

'And then the people of Attusa began to starve,' Zos said. 'This is how I heard it. All the irrigation systems failed – the desert rolled in, agriculture collapsed. The gods did fuck all.'

Persay laughed. 'And then someone realised they could just eat each other!' he said.

Zos nodded, his eyes on Pollon. 'And then they needed more people, more cattle. Most of Hannigalbat fell ten years ago – the most powerful city-state south of Mykoax. Now Sala and the Mander river are the border, and as you may have noticed, Dardania is a tough nut to crack, so the Jekers took to the sea and fell on the Hundred Cities. Eh?'

Pollon made a notion in the air, as if he was using an abacus in his head.

'I have never heard it stated so clearly,' he said. 'Why don't I know this?'

Zos shrugged. 'Good question. I fought for Hannigalbat fifteen years ago – it was one of my first jobs. Then, I'd have said that the Jekers wouldn't last a generation. Now they have ships and leaders.'

Pollon frowned. 'So there's a god directing them.'

Zos nodded. 'We heard what Era said,' he added. 'And Nisroch himself, for that matter.'

Pollon shook his head. 'Every time I think it can't be worse …' He sighed.

'Say we saw five hundred ships,' Zos said. 'Say nine in ten were destroyed in the storm. That leaves fifty ships – more than the largest fleet on Ocean.'

Persay whistled.

Pollon frowned.

Zos watched the coast.

'Even for fifty ships, there's too much damned smoke.'

By mid-afternoon it was clear that the Jekers had landed under the towering cliffs of a small bay. And they didn't have anywhere near fifty ships.

Zos watched it, shading his eyes with his hand.

'I know this place,' he said. 'The village is way up there, on the mountain.'

'Long way to go for your fishing boat,' Persay said.

'Well, between the Dardanians a day's sail away, and the Jekers …'

'Point taken,' Pollon said. 'You don't want to live within easy walk of the sea.'

'Really don't,' Persay added.

The Jekers saw them, too. As they rowed north, past the deep bay's headland, they could see Jekers coming back aboard their ships.

'We may have caught a bear,' Persay said. 'Lot o' warriors.'

'Not the bastards we outsailed yesterday, though,' Zos commented.

Persay frowned. 'How do you figure?'

'Different ships,' Zos looked at Persay for a moment, and smiled. 'We outran them, so they can't be here first.'

Persay shrugged as if the identity of individual Jekers didn't matter much to him.

'Why fight them at all?' Pollon asked.

'We need the friendship of the king of Lazba,' Zos said. 'And we're still working up our crews.'

Persay nodded. 'Makes sense to me. Let's kill 'em.'

Pollon shook his head. 'We're killing them *for practice*? And these are the mighty Jekers?'

'They're not that mighty,' Zos said. 'They're just scary.'

Pollon went to get his bow.

Zos repeated his leaps from ship to ship, visiting his squadron, explaining his very simple plan: to flay the Jeker ships with archery and keep rowing away until the enemy were exhausted and desperate and incapable of any real defence.

'You're a vicious bastard,' Trayos said. 'I like it.'

Zos was looking south, to seaward. Far off on the horizon, he could just see the brown fleck of the great sail on the Narmerian merchant.

'I do wish he'd catch us up,' Zos said wistfully.

Trayos spat over the side. 'Why would he? We're doing all his fighting for him.'

Their five ships formed a line abreast, filling the deep bay almost from side to side, spaced out so there was no chance of their oars tangling. Only the handful of archers with heavy bows or horn recurves opened the contest.

It was a clear, almost cold day with a light wind blowing from the east, carrying a hint of Narmerian desert. Pollon loosed a ranging shot, watched its fall, and so, they hoped, did every other archer in their force.

The Jekers came on, their slaves rowing hard under the lash and the threat of becoming food.

The smoke was clouding the landward view, rolling down the bay. It stank of sulphur, and Zos and Alektron, both veterans of volcanoes, began to be uneasy.

'That stink...' Alektron had lost what reserve he'd had in addressing Zos. If Zos had godlike powers and a magic sword, it was all one to Alektron. 'That's an earth-stink, Cap'n.'

Zos was watching the land, feebly waving his hand as if the little breeze he made would clear the smoke.

'Aye,' he agreed. 'But none of the mountains are smoking.'

'True,' Alektron agreed, but unease showed plainly on his face.

Pollon's third arrow hit someone. The Jekers were two hundred paces away, and Zos had his squadron backing water. His big pentekonters couldn't back as fast as the Jekers could pull forward, but the backing Dardanian hulls frustrated the Jekers' rush, and even desperate slaves in a state of terror can only row full-out for a limited time.

At the entrance to the bay, the Dardanian ships spread out deliberately, opening wider gaps between themselves as they formed a loose crescent. The *Sea Eagle* had to struggle with the gradually increasing tide-rip, and there was a bad moment when she looked as if she would be wrecked on the Long Point's rocks, which seemed determined to drag the ship in to its death.

The Jekers gained on them as they fought the tide-rip and freshening breeze from the east. Now all the archers on every pentekonter were loosing as fast as they could; the Jekers were less than fifty paces away. They had six ships to Zos' five, but none were larger than the *Wave Serpent*, his smallest ship.

Zos had to hold himself in a tight emotional grip; he wanted to scream with frustration as his inexperienced rowers put his beautiful ship in deeper danger from the rocks with their near panic and simply by rowing badly. The rocks on the Long Point were within a spear-throw when they finally began to pull away, and so were the Jekers, and spears began to come aboard.

'Fuck,' he said very quietly to himself. Then he roared 'Sing!' and Pollon joined him, thumping the deck with his foot.

The oar-stroke picked up.

The Jekers flung their spears. A fisherman died on number nine bench amidships, and his oar trailed, crossing number seven, and the stroke began to fail. Pollon drew, his back muscles fully engaged, and loosed. At this range, Zos felt that every arrow from the deadly archer was a hit, but the Jeker ship was *packed* with red mouths that seemed to all be screaming, red-rimmed eyes watching him hungrily.

Draw me. The sword's voice was insistent, persuasive. Zos felt his hand move to the hilt.

Nope, Zos thought. He didn't want to imagine the chaos *Terror* would inflict on his oarspeople, and he certainly didn't want to unleash it – or rather, not yet. He and Persay had a plan, even if it was more like a desperate gamble...

Why did I commit to this again? For practice?
Idiot.

They had the better ships and more people. And everyone was afraid of the Jekers – he was himself – and it gave them energy.

Persay flung himself onto the bloody bench, shoved the dying man into the bilge, and plucked up the oar. More spears fell, but the Jekers didn't have that many to throw, and the arrows were hurting them.

The *Sea Eagle* backed water, slipping out to sea, as her immediate opponent hit the tidal rip.

In no longer than it took a hierophant to pray to his gods, two of the Jeker ships ran afoul of each other, oars tangled, and the distance suddenly opened up. A third ship struck the other two.

For a glorious minute, the arrows fell like bronze sleet and the Jekers could do nothing, and then Pollon said, 'Well, that's my last shaft.'

'What?' Zos asked.

It was true. They were out of arrows.

'Fuck,' Zos said with real feeling. 'How many have you shot?'

'Thirty.'

Zos shook his head. 'Fuck,' he said again.

He watched the Jekers with a critical eye, and decided on a new approach.

'Keep backing. Try to get back into line with the *Winter Gamble*,' he said to Alektron. If anyone could do it, he could.

'Aye aye, cap'n,' the man said, and the ship began to turn as they backed.

The three Jeker ships were untangling themselves faster than Zos would have liked while the other three came on. They were close enough that Zos had to watch as a Jeker warlord put a knife into a flagging oarsman and then had him pinned to the masthead, screaming.

'That's got to press her masthead down,' Alektron said with inhuman glee. 'And that weight will make her roll. And harm her mast. Look at her. Idiots. They're piss-poor sailors.'

Zos looked away. Twenty years of making war hadn't really prepared him for this, and he still intended to keep his people alive. He owed it to all the poor bastards he'd led to their deaths over the last fifteen years.

When did I get so soft?

I thought we could just row backwards and shoot, damn it to Kur!

Orestas, aboard the *Winter Gamble*, understood his manoeuvre and began to steer towards the *Shark*, so that they were gradually forming a line abreast, but on a south-westerly heading – or rather, a south-westerly *backing*, as they were moving stern first.

The three Jekers were going to catch the wind, but even Jekers weren't stupid enough to raise sails before combat...

'No …' Zos said in wonder.

One of the Jekers raised his big blood-brown mainsail, the notch clear in the winter sunlight. Suddenly he was skimming over the waves towards the *Shark* at the centre of the line, and no one had any arrows.

'So much for my plan,' Zos said. He raised his shield, and signalled *Close Action*. He nodded to Alektron. 'Get in close, let's break the bastard's oars and then pass him.'

Alektron smiled. 'Aye Aye,' he said. And then, 'We'll never touch 'im, Cap'n. 'E's too fuckin' fast.'

Pollon was getting the rowers to switch from backing to rowing forward, and for as long as a man took to don a bronze breastplate, the *Sea Eagle* was in a state nearing chaos. In the centre, the flying Jeker ship hurtled into the *Shark* with a *slam* that carried clearly over the water, and then a rattle of timbers, but Tuwinon was a canny pirate. His helmsman had managed to turn just enough that the two ships were scraping past each other, rather than the *Shark* taking the full impact. Zos hoped the *Shark* had her oars in, as a big ship running down another ship's side when her oars were out would smash the oars and grind the long shafts into the oarspeople.

The second and third Jekers were coming up fast, but not fast enough to catch the one under sail. Zos had mistimed his rush; he'd expected his rowers to reverse their direction faster, and the first Jeker was no longer available as a target, exactly as Alektron had predicted. In fact, she was already well to windward. Meanwhile, the *Winter Gamble* had turned in place and was giving chase. Zos shook his head in disgust, because if Orestas had simply held his place in line they'd have been two to one against the next ship.

'Fuck,' he said.

He watched the *Winter Gamble* hoist its big lateen, and heel as the wind took and filled it. She was out of the battle.

His entire plan was now in shreds. He considered running. But that might well be worse.

'Never mind,' he said to Alektron. 'Let's take that one.'

He pointed at the second Jeker, closing bow to bow. Amidships, the last seats were reversed; a fisherwoman showed a townie how to position her leather cushion and then pushed the oar into her hand.

He went and grabbed Persay. 'We're going to board,' he said. 'I'm going to draw *Terror*, and you're going to keep me alive.'

Persay nodded as if enduring supernatural terror was something to which he looked forward.

'Sure, boss,' he said. 'That's our *desperate gamble*.'

'That's right.'

Zos leapt back to Alektron at the helm.

'You have the ship when I board,' he said. 'I'm going to use … well, call it magic. It's going to be fucking terrifying. Look after my ship.'

'Aye aye,' Alektron had a mouth full of black teeth, and his breath was appalling. But his confidence was godlike. 'Fucking terrifying,' he added. 'Aye aye.'

As the two ships closed, Zos ran down the central catwalk to the bow, repeating the message.

'There will be a few moments of sheer terror,' he said. 'It *will* end. When it does, follow me on to their deck. The fight will be quick, and we'll be victorious.'

No one looked enthusiastic except Persay.

Alektron did something, and their hull twitched and groaned as he made two tiny course corrections at speed and they headed straight for the Jeker. 'Oars in!' Zos roared.

They did it early – too early. In some fights that would have been a disaster – or rather, another disaster – and though they *had* practised this, half a dozen lubbers did it wrong. One man got his ribs crushed as the bow of the enemy ship caught his oar and bent it back into his hands and gut.

Zos shook his head, but he was committed to the close fight now, and the loss of some starboard oarspeople wasn't going to change anything in the short run.

Draw me!

The hulls ground together. No one had told the poor Jeker slaves to get their oars in, and Zos guessed they didn't face enough warships who fought back to know what to do. Oars splintered; there were screams as people died or were maimed.

People he might, under other circumstances, have rescued.

The Jekers threw grappling hooks and heavy rocks with lines attached.

'Ready?' he asked Persay.

'Born ready,' the madman said. He was armed with a long bronze sword, and otherwise wore neither armour nor helmet.

'Don't die,' Zos said.

'Words to live by.' Persay smiled.

A grappling hook went past Zos' head, and he leapt up onto the bow-rail and, without hesitation, leapt onto the other ship.

The very last thing the Jekers expected was for their prey to board *them*.

Zos might have tumbled or rolled, but he was wearing a bronze breast- and backplate and it limited his flexibility, so he performed a three-step rush as he drew *Terror*. The three Jekers around the helm were immediately affected but, as Zos had feared, they had seen a great many terrible things and they weren't as paralysed as the godborn warriors of the king of Mykoax. In fact their warlord, a huge man, managed to get his bronze double axe into his hand and his shield on his arm, so Zos killed the helmsman – an economical thrust and a high kick to clear his weapon while the warlord tried to rid his head of the terror. As he fought it, the sword drank the helmsman's life and the fear grew.

Persay went *past* the warlord with a long leap. He stabbed down as he did, scoring a long and bloody line on the warlord's shoulder before landing on the rail and cutting down into the Jekers who were throwing the grapples.

The warlord was not finished, which Zos thought was a pity.

He cut with his axe, with more grace than Zos expected, the blade turning in the air. A good feint, and one that had doubtless killed a lot of inexperienced warriors.

Zos' counter-cut sliced off one of the Jeker's hands as Zos swayed back, using the man's momentum and shorter reach against him. *Terror* was bronze, carefully tempered and hardened; it cut through bone, and didn't notch or bend.

Together we will rule!

The man cut again, even as he understood the extent of the wound, but with just one hand his control was poor and his swing was wild. Zos danced back so that the axe whistled harmlessly past; he then stepped offline to his right and buried *Terror* in the man's head, back-handed, thumb along the blade to ensure alignment.

Nice, Zos thought in self-congratulation, and almost died as a fourth man he'd missed stabbed with desperation, over the falling body of his lord and master. He had a spear, and the spear cut a furrow across the front of Zos' bronze breastplate. Death was close.

Terror wailed its song of despair, the crescendo rising as it drank the dying man's essence.

Zos ripped it clear, killed the fourth man, who was still fumbling for his footing after his desperate lunge, and rammed the bloody magical sword back into its sheath.

Nooooo!

Zos looked down into a Jeker's rowing deck. He'd known

they were charnel-house horrors, but this was insane – there were dead men bound to oars, and another spiked to the mast with bronze nails, his rotting flesh pervading the whole ship.

No wonder the crew was relatively immune to terror.

Relatively. Most of them were still standing, petrified, or in some cases, vomiting on the deck or pissing themselves. Two had thrown themselves into the water.

In fact, the sword had bought them both a few precious seconds, in which Persay had cleared twenty feet of the rail while Zos had cleared the command deck. Now the three nomad women were coming over the side from the *Sea Eagle*; they were the first to recover. They all had armour now – good Dardanian *thorakes* of leather and bronze – and they all wore black veils that covered their faces.

No one else came, though. If the Jekers were staggered, his own people were stunned or worse, as he'd expected.

He leapt up beside Persay and started killing. Makeda had a long spear and she covered his open flank from behind. The other two closed up, and the five of them held the slightly raised platform…

…for far too long.

Zos had his second sword, a shorter, plainer bronze weapon. He used it fastidiously; this was not a situation for wild leaps, but for cautious preservation. While he had a bronze *thorakos*, Persay was virtually naked, and the nomads wore only light armour and lacked shields.

He used his own shield aggressively, pounding it into any man who tried to close, until he finally heard a weak cheer behind him. He waved his sword to draw the attention of his own boarders, who had rallied and began to cross to the Jeker's command deck. They were mostly even more dazed by terror than the Jekers, and so it wasn't a decisive charge. It took them time to clear the Jekers, and no quarter was asked or given, but with every minute more of Zos' crew came over the gunwales and onto the Jeker's bloody deck. When it became clear to the slaves that the Jekers were doomed, they joined in with reaching hands and hidden shivs, reaching up through the wooden grates that kept them in the holds and stabbing bare feet and ankles, or ripping fallen or unlucky Jekers to pieces if they fell against the slave-gratings. Persay was a whirlwind of destruction; the nomad women were like dark Fates reaping souls, and Zos made his kills carefully and cautiously, because he planned to stay alive a little longer.

It seemed to take hours until the last Jeker went down, screaming, his feet flayed from below, his side and groin pierced by spears.

When Zos looked over the side, his mind dull from combat and his senses reeling from the horror of the Jeker holds, he saw that very little time had passed. The three ships that had fallen afoul of one another had finally cut themselves free. The first Jeker, the one that had raised sail and plunged at the *Shark*, was five stadia or more to windward, and the *Shark*, the *Trident* and the *Wave Serpent* were all grappled to the other Jeker.

'Back to our ship,' he croaked. Roaring was now beyond him. *Where has my voice gone?*

His good bronze sword was ruined, the blade bent and twisted; he'd killed his last opponent by beating him to death, and when he tried to bend the blade back, it snapped by the hilt. He tried to toss it into the *Sea Eagle*'s bilges, and the hilt stuck to his hand, the blood dried like glue.

He leant over the side amidships and washed his hand in seawater until the hilt came free and sank away into the ocean, carrying with it ivory grips and silver nails.

'Fuck,' he croaked. He slapped a man on the back. 'Back to the *Sea Eagle*,' he ordered. It was Eritha's father, Jiani; the older man nodded.

'Aye,' he managed. His eyes were wild, and he had a small axe in each hand, and he was so coated in blood that Zos at first thought he was mortally wounded.

Zos had to get an arm around Persay's neck to stop him from hacking at a horribly dead corpse.

'Back to the *Sea Eagle*,' he muttered.

He held on, ready to choke his man into compliance, but the rage left Persay's eyes and he shuddered.

Eritha stood by her father, and she, too, was blood-spattered but unhurt.

'Help me get him aboard,' he said.

She picked up the big warrior's feet as if this was her everyday life and they leapt side by side, landing with the roll on the *Sea Eagle*. She looked at him and he met her eye, and they both smiled. It was no more than shared appreciation of being alive, but Zos felt stronger for it.

'Get back here, you lubbers,' he tried. Then he caught Eritha's arm. 'Shout for me.'

Her voice was piercing and much more successful, and slowly, fitfully and then faster, the weary but victorious crew came back aboard.

The three fresh Jeker ships were coming, but the wind had shifted – a small mercy – and they were having to row.

Zos made himself jump back aboard the Jeker ship. It took every bit of his not inconsiderable self-discipline; he didn't want to go. He didn't want to do anything but lie down.

But his sense of himself made him go.

I am a hero. I am not a selfish godborn. We are going to change the world.

He went to the forward slave-grating, and tried to loosen the chock that held it, and then he fetched the Jeker warlord's axe and used the poll to hammer the chock free.

The men and women beneath him stank, and they looked up at him like wounded animals.

'I don't have time to save you,' he said in Trade Dardanian. 'But you can save yourselves.'

They looked at him, ready to flinch away.

'If you follow us,' he said, 'we'll see you fed before nightfall.' No response. 'Here,' he said. 'He's dead,' and he dropped the great bronze war axe into the hold.

They all flinched away. They were like mice when a cat appears – flitting away into the shadows.

He sighed, and then, despite everything, a man went forward under him, bent and took the dead warlord's axe.

In Narmerian, he said, 'We can save ourselves.'

'Food in four hours,' Zos said, in Narmerian. 'My word on it.'

The man nodded. He was small and brown, like most Narmerians, and he didn't look like a hero or a captain, and neither did the very pale woman who came up beside him, but looks were deceiving.

The Narmerian nodded. 'Four hours,' he said. 'I am Rathor.'

'You're in command then, Rathor.'

Zos gave a sketchy salute, and, more at peace with his own inner demons, leapt for his own ship. It was barely adequate, and he was grateful for the hands that pulled him inboard.

'Brothers and sisters…' He noticed, as he began to speak, that he had a nasty wound in his shin. No idea how it had happened, and it didn't hurt, but there was a lot of blood…

He didn't have time to worry about it.

'Brothers and sisters!' he called again. 'We're not done yet. There's three more of the bastards.' He pointed west. 'Win, and we feast with King Makar tonight. Lose, and we're Jeker meat. We're five to three and we have the wind and tide with us. Victory is ours.' He pointed over the bow. 'One quick kill and we win.'

He smiled when they managed a thin cheer.

He looked down his oar deck. He had only lost five, plus the man who'd been broken by his oar. Another half a dozen were wounded. One poor woman had vanished when he drew the sword – probably jumped into the sea.

Terror had done its job. The Jeker ship should never have been so easy to take.

Easy.

'You've fought before?' he asked Eritha, who was settling to an oar.

'Once or twice,' she admitted.

He ran down to the centre of the ship, trying to wish his fatigue away, using the spirit of combat to keep himself moving. He ordered the rowers in the three mid-ships benches out, and he put them into empty spots at bow and stern, evening up the oar banks so that the ship coasted along under easy pulls, now moving downwind against the slowly pulling Jekers.

If they'd had arrows ... If gods-damned Orestas had stayed in place ...

If wishes were butter cakes ...

He went aft, to where Alektron still had the helm.

'We need a ship kill,' he said. 'The crew is too tired to fight hand to hand.'

Alektron nodded, expressionless. Then he made a face, like a man who smells something bad.

'That was fuckin' awful,' he said. 'I was afraid like I never been afraid.'

Zos nodded. 'I know.'

'Pissed meself.' Alektron was angry about it. 'That ain't right.'

Zos nodded. 'It's a terrible weapon.'

'Takes something away fra' ye,' Alektron said. 'Fuckin' evil.'

Zos had to agree.

'I'll get you a ship kill,' Alektron said. 'But I ain't sure I can serve a cap'n with a magic like that. Takes something away fra' folk.'

Zos winced, since Alektron represented almost half of his fully reliable veteran sailors. Then he banished the thought for later, and lived in the moment, as he usually did. He watched the action develop. As was usually the case, at first everything appeared to move slowly, and everyone had manoeuvre room and choices, but as the ships closed...

It was as if the hands of fate shaped reality closer and closer, narrowing the options...

His three ships were just cutting free of their Jeker. They'd clearly been victorious, but they were also slower coming off the decks of their adversaries, while the onrushing Jekers were anxious to avenge their dead, or simply to rend and tear. Zos didn't really understand Jeker motivations. But all three were going for the other three ships and Orestas and the *Winter Gamble* were still giving chase to the fleeing Jeker, far downwind and with their mainsails up.

Zos swore a few times.

'Let's see if we can ram the trailing bastard. The one behind the one with the ... man ... at the masthead.' Zos pointed.

Alektron glanced at him. 'Think the bow will take it?'

Zos took a deep breath and released it. 'Yes,' he said. 'And I don't see a better way to settle the odds.'

'Four to three,' Alektron said.

'These aren't combat crews,' Zos said.

Alektron managed a thin smile over his black teeth. 'Aye, not yet.'

He tapped his steering oars and the *Sea Eagle* went a point closer to the wind, and then he began a long curve to port.

'Have 'em row soft,' Alektron said. 'Let the Jeker hit the *Shark*. He's a right bastard anyway. We'll take her at a stand, bust the fucker in two.' He looked at Zos. 'Don't draw that fuckin' sword

119

on me, Cap'n, and I'll see ye through this.' He paused, as if smelling the wind. 'Hope our bow holds.'

'Please don't say that,' Zos said.

Alektron gave Zos a look that was full of reproach.

'Just sayin',' he muttered.

Persay clambered to his feet.

'Sorry, boss,' he muttered.

'We may have to do our trick again,' Zos said.

Persay looked less enthusiastic. 'You're bleeding pretty bad, boss, and I'm feeling like Alektron here has a point. That thing is pure evil.' He pointed at the sword. 'And I'm not made of bronze, boss.'

Zos nodded. And looked down, to see the blood positively flowing down his shin.

The second Jeker ship went bow to bow with Daos and the *Trident*, and both ships *bounced* with a crash that carried over the water. The man crucified high on the Jeker's mainmast was the death of his own ship; his extra weight at the moment of impact meant the mast snapped at about a man's height above the deck. It went over the Jeker's port side, spinning the hull to port and out of the fight.

The first Jeker bore down on the *Shark*, who barely got her bow around in time, and both ships lost oars and oarspeople as they scraped down each other's sides.

The *Wave Serpent* shot under the Jeker's stern and her well-trained crew boarded immediately, swarming the Jeker's command deck and clearing it.

The last Jeker ship determined to ram the *Wave Serpent*, and destroy Trayos' ship.

None of this was as Zos had planned; it was his fifth or sixth discarded plan of the fight.

War. Fucking war.

He liked Trayos and couldn't bring himself to sacrifice the man, so he glanced at Pollon and said, 'Ramming speed.'

Alektron gave a minute shrug, as if to say, *Here we go, then*. 'Going to be close,' Zos said, mostly to himself.

Pollon struck the deck with a spear shaft, and every back tensed. The oars went up to the check, a little ragged, then around – the dip of oar blades in the water. The skilled rowers just bit into the waves; the green rowers bit too deep and wasted energy and time.

Bam! Pollon struck the deck again. Most of the rowers had the stroke; a couple in the bow were very ragged, but that's why they were in the bow.

Bam! They hurtled forward. They were really moving now, and Zos was pleasantly surprised at how fast his beautiful ship and his new rowers had come to full speed.

So close.

The Jeker was racing for the *Wave Serpent*'s naked flank, where she lay helpless under the stern of the biggest Jeker. But they had to make a steering correction to avoid the ship with the snapped-off mast, already rammed by the *Trident*. The helmsman was good; he did the double turn just as Alektron had done it. And at some point in that complex manoeuvre, he became aware of the *Sea Eagle* emerging from the smoke and chaos to his flank.

Zos saw the Jeker sea lord point straight at him, and scream something.

He wanted to curse, but he had no fucks left to give. He managed a sigh.

The Jeker began to turn, the helmsman leaning so far it looked as if he might tumble over the side. But the oar-master roared an order at the slaves at the oars, and . . .

. . . someone misunderstood. Or someone decided they'd had enough of slavery. But where the port side oars should have dragged, aiding the turn, instead there was chaos. Oars crossed and the enemy ship actually wobbled before they hit.

'Brace!' Alektron roared.

The shock threw Zos flat despite his best efforts. He got a leg under himself and powered up to one knee, and then grabbed the rail to haul himself back to his feet.

'Bow's takin' water,' Alektron said, in a deeply offended 'I told you so' voice.

Sure enough, the black pitch coating on the hull had shattered, and water was *pouring* into the bow through a dozen sprung seams.

Zos ran forward, still trying to figure out…

The Jeker was *gone*.

No, not gone. The *Sea Eagle* had pressed the gunwale of the Jeker ship down, tipping it down into the water on its side, and it filled and sank in heartbeats. When Zos looked over the side of his own ship it was to see the enemy ship going down, and the upturned faces of the doomed rowers just a few feet below him, looking up like damned souls trying to escape a watery hell. Only there was no escape: they were locked to their oars with wooden gratings and bloodstained ropes and bronze chains.

All they could do was look up at Zos. And drown.

They fothered the bow, a trick Alektron and Jiani knew, and taught at speed to avert crisis and doom, pulling their boat sail, the smaller forward sail, tight over the broken bow. Zos had seen the Hakrans do it, but seeing it and knowing how were different, and there was a great deal more swearing, some involuntary swimming, and a lot of very rapid teaching of basic knotwork and ropework. If Zos had needed a lesson in how much he needed Alektron, this was it.

In fact, it was not a lesson he needed. But as a sailor, he learnt and helped now; the sad truth was that he was the second-best sailor aboard his ship, or perhaps fourth after Eritha and her father. He was in the water with Eritha, his wounded leg burning like fire in the salt water, trying to get the ropes of the flapping boat sail *under* the bow to pull it taut against the sea. The sail was more like a living thing than was quite right, and at one point he imagined that the vast stretch of boiled wool was actively fighting him. He'd jumped into the sea in his bronze breastplate, and fatigue threatened to drag him to the bottom.

So Zos missed the moment when Daos killed the Jeker sea lord on his own deck; missed Trayos clearing the *Shark* almost single-handedly, roaring his war cry. He even missed the moment when all the ships in his little flotilla cheered because the freed Jeker slaves from their first conquest got their sail up and sheeted home.

The fothering sail was just about done, and the lubbers were using simple pumps, or just baling, and it looked as if the *Sea Eagle* was going to make it in to port. Zos was slumped with exhaustion by the helm. Eritha had the helm; Alektron was directing the ship.

The four ships were all in a small area of sea, and the sun was setting in the west, and the weather was mild, but Zos knew they needed to get ashore. And a distant part of his mind, the remote commander, wanted to rescue all the Jeker ships. They were all triakonters, thirty-oared warships almost the size of Trayos' *Wave Serpent*. Good ships, if they could be cleaned.

Eritha smiled at him, and he managed a smile back as he lay on the deck and willed himself to move. Eventually he got to his feet, feeling every minute of his age and more.

'Help me get my armour off?' he asked.

She nodded. She had a deep cut on her forearm and a graze along her jaw that must have come awfully close to severing her head, and he found he liked her calm.

She pulled the pins in the side of his *thorakos* and helped him out of it. He felt lighter and a little better immediately, and he took it from her and was shocked to see the enormous dent in the backplate where something had not *quite* punched through.

'Fuck!' he said, finding that he did, indeed, have one more to give.

He leant out over the stern, far too tired to jump aboard any of the other ships, and with Eritha's help got Daos to understand that he needed to take his capture in tow.

Out in the sunset, the *Winter Gamble* won her fight and began to row upwind with the Jeker ship for company.

The distant Narmerian was now quite close, her sides lined with archers.

Zos didn't have the energy to savour his victory, which, at the moment, seemed utterly pointless.

Now we can rule the seas!

Oh, shut up.

He went forward, noticing that his whole right leg was now crusted in blood and there was still a trickle from the wound. Amidships Theklassa, the youngest of the nomad women, handed him a leather bottle of water with a little wine, and he drank it greedily. Her eyes were a shocking yellow gold against her dark skin, and she looked...

...very dangerous. But the watered wine was wonderful – the greatest thing he'd ever tasted. He handed it back with an apology for his greed, and she laughed.

'You need a cup of water for every cup of blood you lose,' she said, pointing at his leg. 'You can't have much blood left, godborn.'

He growled something and kept going forward until he found Alektron, who was coaching four lubbers on coiling down spare rope.

'I need you,' Zos said.

Alektron looked regretful. Zos wondered if the man dreamt

of a perfect ship, where everything was squared away and ship-shape and perhaps unused.

'Can we make it into Evropi tonight?' he asked.

Alektron looked at the land. The haze of sulphur and smoke was unchanged.

Alektron shrugged. 'Aye, Cap'n,' he agreed. 'We might ha' a go, eh?' He smiled his black-toothed smile. 'This here barky is goin' to the bottom in the first capful o' wind.'

'You are full of good cheer,' Zos said.

'Told ye that her bow was soft.'

Zos considered a host of replies, and then settled for saying, 'So you did.'

Evropi was one of the best harbours in the world, or at least on the Ocean that Zos knew: two beautiful fine-sand beaches with their own deep bays, and a tall acropolis between them, heavily fortified within the huge stonework of the distant past. A deep canal had been dug in ancient times between the harbours behind the headland, so that fully laden cargo ships could transit between the leeward and windward beaches. It was a fabulously rich city, and one of the centres for trade in the whole central Ocean.

Unfortunately, the combination of darkness and the sheer volume of smoke rolling off the land made it impossible for Zos' wounded ships to land. So they stood off the harbour mouths as several wounded people died on their decks and then everyone slumped from exhaustion.

Zos might have writhed in anxiety for his ships and his people, but he was too tired. He slept in his sweat-soaked chiton, lying by the helm bench with his head pillowed on his shield. And he woke to Alektron shaking him.

'Dawn,' the foul breath said. 'Nice day, but wind is risin', like.'

Zos went forward and woke himself up by pumping water

from the bilges. The ship had water up to the rowing benches; it didn't look as if she could be saved, and Zos couldn't bring himself to blame the men and women who'd fallen asleep when they should have been pumping.

Though the ship was in a worse condition, sleep had made many things better. Eritha and half a dozen other people joined him at work in the pink dawn, and the pumps shot water high in the air. Even ten minutes' pumping had a decided effect.

'We're gaining!' Zos shouted.

They cheered.

They pumped her all the way into the western side of the port, and she crept down the bay under half her oars while the other half baled and pumped, and Alektron ran her straight up the beach, bow-on. There was more snapping and crackling from the bow as he did so.

There was quite a crowd in the red dawn. The smoke, which was everywhere, was underlit by the rising sun, turning the morning scarlet instead of pink.

'Cap'n?' Eritha shouted from the bow. 'There's a herald from King Makar asking for ye.'

Zos was wearing the remains of his once-magnificent fighting chiton and nothing else. And, he was sorry to see, his shin was still leaking blood.

None of this was the way he'd imagined. He was supposed to arrive in golden armour, cloaked in power and wreathed in victory, as the old hymn to the War God went. Instead, he looked like a beggar – a beggar who had been roundly beaten by footpads the night before.

He leapt down into the sand below the bow, which proved to be ill-advised as his right leg buckled under him and he fell into the wet sand at the feet of the herald.

The man was tall, with dark skin like a starless night at sea, and was clearly employed for both tact and courtesy. He managed to give Zos a hand getting to his feet without appearing to do so, and then he bowed low.

'My lord is wounded,' he said.

'Aye,' Zos managed.

The hole in his shin looked like a pit; a spear had gone through his greaves and the point had bit deep. It still didn't hurt, though.

He now had wet sand on his ruined chiton, and his self-image went down another notch. He made himself stand tall.

'I am Zos ...' he took the plunge '...of Trin,' he said. 'I seek audience with King Makar.'

'Zos of Trin,' the herald said, 'a thousand eyes watched you fight the Jekers off the Long Point and the Lion's Leap, and every wound you bear is to us a jewel beyond price. The king awaits you. Food is being brought for your people – food and bandages and oil.' The man smiled pleasantly. He really was tall. 'And shipwrights,' he said.

Zos bowed to the man. Heralds came in all shapes and sizes; some were slaves, just messengers for their masters, but this one had the bearing of a lord, and the manners of the godborn, and his cloak, deep red embroidered with black eagles, was worth the value of a ship.

'Shall I follow you?' Zos asked.

The herald nodded. 'If you can come now, no time will be wasted.'

Zos looked up, and Eritha's father stood in the bow, holding *Terror* as if it was something made of ordure.

'Toss it!' Zos called. 'Also, the leather bag under the port side helm bench.'

Eritha came to the bow holding the bag.

Familiarity breeds contempt. The old fisherman threw the golden sword down, and Zos snatched it from the air and slung the undimmed gold baldric around his shoulders. Then he caught the bag from Eritha.

'I'm sure you'll have her shipshape by the time I return,' he said.

Eritha grinned.

He and the herald walked along the beach until they came to where Trayos had beached stern first, a more usual practice. The old pirate leaned out over his stern. 'I wish you the glory of your victory, Lord Zos,' he called.

Zos couldn't hide his grin. 'And yours! I hear you cleared a deck single-handed.'

Trayos grinned back. 'I thought this was where the boy's prophecy came true,' he said. 'But instead...'

'Care to accompany me to the palace?' Zos called.

Trayos shook his head. 'No thanks. I plan to be drunk between two very close *companions* as soon as I can arrange it.' He waved. 'Because I'm not dead, see?'

Zos smiled, waved, and turned back to the elegant herald.

'Lead on,' he said.

'My lord might be cold.' The herald swept the magnificent red and black cloak up over his head and, in a swirling flourish, placed it over Zos' shoulders. 'I beg you to accept this as a token of our esteem for you.'

Zos was stunned for a moment, struck by the gesture. And then he returned the herald's bow with one of equal depth.

'I am moved by your lordly generosity,' he said in the full courtesy of the godborn to the godborn. 'You have my thanks.'

The herald all but glowed. He'd just given away a piece of cloth worth a fishing village and it seemed to have made him *happy*.

Stripped of his cloak, he looked if anything, even bigger – heavily muscled. He moved with the grace of a dancer, the authority of a warrior. Around his neck was a necklace that alternated gold beads, lapis seals, and lion's teeth.

As they began to walk up through the town, he said, 'My Lord Zos...The name sounds familiar, if I may.'

Zos nodded. 'My mother and I were well received here when I was young. I feel a debt to this place.'

The cloak sat on his shoulders, the wool so well woven that it was as light as down, and as warm; the black birds were not eagles but ravens, and they almost had a life of their own they were so accurately embroidered. Some flew, some landed, a few picked at corpses.

The herald glanced at him. 'You are the king's foster-son!' he said.

Zos didn't say what came to his mind: *I hoped he still thought of me that way.* Somehow, in fifteen years, he'd never managed to come back and say...

...anything. He'd come here on the wings of the wind in a tiny fishing boat, with the shattered wreck of his mother and a warship full of rage and hate, and Makar, King of the Isles had sheltered him for a year.

I'm a selfish bastard, Zos thought. *Why did I never come back to thank him?*

Instead, he glanced at the other man's necklace.

'That must have been a big lion,' he said.

The tall man smiled. 'He was.'

Zos had seldom liked someone so well on first meeting. It was instant; the man's courtesy and competence went through his guard like a perfect sword thrust.

'You have my name, but I lack yours,' he said.

'I am Leontas, in your tongue. Zembah, in my own.'

'Lazba escaped the great wave?' Zos asked, after a bow to acknowledge the other man's name.

Leontas raised an eyebrow. 'The south coast may never

129

recover. But we have other problems, as you will no doubt be told.'

'You have problems greater than the devastation wrought by the great wave?' Zos asked.

The air reeked of sulphur and something else – something primal, earthy. And pungent. He coughed.

'I'm sure the king would prefer to tell you himself,' the herald said with careful courtesy.

'Would you humour a tired man?' Zos said. 'I'd like to know.'

They were coming to the great fortress. It stood on a rocky acropolis well above the town; sheer walls of magnificent stone rose ten times the height of a tall man from massive foundations that sat on the bare rock. Massive square bastions guarded the main gate. A dozen well-equipped spearmen stood beneath the gate, and Zos could see archers moving on the towers.

The guards under the gate recognised Leontas, but refused to let Zos past without inspection.

'No armed foreigners,' the leader said wearily.

Leontas showed a carnelian seal ring which he wore on his own sword belt.

'In the name of the king,' he said.

The guard's commander was summoned. He looked at the ring.

'I know you, Leontas,' he said with a certain reserve.

Not friends, Zos thought.

'This man cleared the Lion's Leap of Jekers,' Leontas said.

'I have a royal order to admit no armed foreigner,' the man said with relish, and Zos knew his type immediately: a man who revelled in his power over others.

He smiled and bowed, as if to a superior.

'Ah, lord, but I'm no foreigner,' he said with easy familiarity, and using the idiom of Lazba. He'd only lived there a year, but adolescence is a formative time.

'You came from over the seas,' the man said suspiciously.

'I was fostered here as a boy.'

'That don't make you a citizen,' the man insisted.

'Fostered by the king,' Zos said softly.

'Just hand over the sword,' the captain said.

Zos smiled. He glanced at Leontas, whose face was set, his pleasant expression banished by anger. It interested Zos to see the change. Leontas was ready to fight; something about this encounter had cut him badly.

Court politics.

Right. That's why I left. I'm not even in the throne room yet and I can taste it.

Zos shrugged. 'I'll just cool my heels outside the gate and keep the sword. Leontas, if you would be so kind as to ask the king for the authority…'

Leontas looked at him, his dark eyes narrowed as if he, and not the guard captain, was the problem.

My new friend has a temper.

'What more authority can there be than the king's own seal?' Leontas snapped. He raised the carnelian ring. It was carved of a single piece, ring and signet together, and the seal was big enough to decorate a sword hilt. 'This is pure folly.'

'You imply I'm a fool,' the guard captain said. 'But it occurs to me that you, too, are a foreigner.'

Leontas drew a ragged breath. The rage was controlled, but it was real.

'I am a citizen of Lazba, sir, as you well know. And it is foolish to hold this guest of the king, whom I clearly serve, as you know perfectly well – doubly foolish when the Jekers raid our coasts and the dragon hovers over our heartland.'

'Now is a good time to keep foreigners out,' the guard captain said.

Zos laughed. 'Leontas, if the king isn't too busy, maybe you can tell him I'm outside the gate? I saw a wine seller down there and I'm too tired for this.' He glanced at the guard captain. 'For what it's worth, I think you're a fool, too, and in an hour I suspect you won't have a job.'

The captain motioned and one of the guards moved towards Zos. He raised his left hand, his right on his sword hilt.

'Don't,' he said. 'Really,' he added.

Zos had commanded men for almost twenty years, and the authority in his voice was pitched to near perfection.

Draw me and slaughter them all.

Zos' hand on the sword hilt quivered, and his grip tightened as if he was starting his draw. He overcame it with an inner flinch.

Can this thing gain control of me?

That's not good.

But he maintained his composure, gave a nod of his head, and backed down the winding stone steps to the gate yard below, to wait.

Era

'We have to get out of here,' Era said. Again. How many times had she said it?

It was mid-morning, the day after the three Jeker ships had come ashore. All of her projects had come to a complete stop because everyone had fought the day before, and most people were now so tired they could barely move. She had two long cuts across her left breast and shoulder that were more annoying than painful, but she feared the red rot that could follow a wound, and she'd bathed in the sea despite the pain. Now she was tired, salt-encrusted and irritable. And she was in a dark mood; the blood spilt the day before had poisoned her in some way that she could ill define. She'd killed before, but the scale was different, and the blood soaked into the dry sand of the high beach stank, and she couldn't escape it.

Pavi nodded. The middle-aged woman had somehow grown in stature instead of shrinking; she set her mouth in a thin line and raised a wax tablet.

'If we start loading now …' she began.

If anyone can be inspired to do it, Era thought.

Miti pushed in through the loose canvas curtain that provided the stern of the ship with some shelter from the omnipresent sun.

'Someone's coming,' she said. Era imagined Jekers, and reached for her sword.

This will be the end. 'It's Taha and the scouts,' Miti added, reading Era's reaction. 'And someone in a litter.'

'A litter?' Era's mind was having trouble wrestling with ideas. *Litter?*

She went out through the canvas and looked out over the stern rail. There were Taha and a dozen scouts with mules, and among them were a dozen big men carrying a palanquin draped in white cotton that shone in the sun. The men were singing. From farther down the beach, Jawala and Aanat were watching them. That sparked something in Era's sluggish mind.

She made herself go down the planks to the sand, and then out into the glare of the sun. Jawat had come up with the guard, stumbling in exhaustion. Era thought Jawat might be a little drunk.

The men carrying the litter were singing in an alien, almost tuneless way, but their voices were in a harmony of sorts. It was not unpleasant; in fact, it was stirring. There were eight of them – strong men and women, red-brown like all Hakrans, wearing sparkling white, fringed, short linen kilts.

Someone important, then.

Era settled her sword baldric between her breasts, wincing as the sweat-stained leather went over the open cut there. Then she went forward to Taha, who raised a hand, and the column halted. The man kept good discipline; the scouts were watching for his sign, and all the mules shuffled to a halt.

The palanquin stopped.

Pavi appeared at her side.

'Bless us all,' she breathed. 'A Given.'

The Hakran word made no sense in context.

'Given?' Era asked.

Pavi nodded. 'They give themselves to the people.'

The curtains of the palanquin shifted, and a long, slim brown hand emerged, seized a cord, and the curtains parted to show an old woman with amber skin and snow-white hair. She was surprisingly tall, and her figure was athletic despite her age. She stepped onto the sand firmly, and then she turned and put a hand on each of two of her bearers and said something.

They all answered together. '*Nawah!*'

Pavi clapped her hands together. 'She thanks them for their service. And they ...' She looked at Era, eyes wide. 'It's difficult to explain. They accept.'

Era had seen a dozen god-kings and one god-queen, and this woman had more dignity than any of them. She walked across the dry sand with more elegance than Era would have thought possible. Everyone stumbled on dry sand, except this dignified woman in a spotless white sari.

Pavi knelt. Miti fell to her knees; Era had heard the expression used, but in Miti's case, it was accurate – she went down as if her sinews had been cut. Mokshi knelt with more deliberation but the same respect.

The woman walked straight to Pavi. She spared a single glance for the orange robes of Jawala and Aanat further up the beach, and then she reached out, cupped Pavi's face with her hand, and said, '*Nawah.*'

Pavi flushed.

The old woman cocked her head slightly to one side.

'I am a Given,' the woman said. 'I am here to thank you.'

Era was surprised, and her face showed it.

The old woman managed a smile. 'Did you think we don't know you are protecting us from Jekers?' She laughed without bitterness.

Era was at a loss to know what to say.

'Was it so terrible?' the Given asked. The kindness in her voice was terrible. And suddenly, Era, who thought herself as hard as adamant, had tears in her eyes.

'Yes,' she said, and in that admission was everything she'd suffered in the past year.

The Given raised her head. 'Yes,' she said. 'The acts of blood are terrible.' She nodded. 'It is better to admit that and face the consequence, then to pretend otherwise.' She looked at Pavi. 'Did you fight?'

'No, Given.'

The woman nodded slightly. 'And you?' she said to Jawat.

They were of an age – she all dignity, he strong in a different way.

'Aye,' he said. 'I fought.'

She reached out and took Pavi's hand, and then Jawat's. Neither resisted.

'There are different strengths,' she said. 'Today, I give thanks for all our people – that some were preserved from blood, and others gave and took blood for us.' She looked at Pavi. 'Are you glad to be alive?'

Pavi bowed her head. 'I am,' she admitted slowly, as if embarrassed.

She looked at Jawat. 'Are you sad to have killed?'

Jawat looked at her. It was clear that for a moment, he considered a flippant reply, but something changed in his face; the hooded eyes blinked, as if he'd been told something wonderful, or terrible.

He spat in the sand, but then his eyes went back to the Given's face.

'Lady, I am,' he admitted, and his voice broke.

The Given held their hands, connecting them.

'Let each take the other,' she said. 'Pavi, take this sadness, that people killed and died that you might live. And you ...' She looked at him carefully. 'Jawat,' she said, suddenly, as if remembering his name. 'Take this gladness, to be alive.'

Jawat stumbled as if someone had fallen against him.

'Is this magic?' he asked, anger and wonder in his voice.

'No,' the Given said. 'Merely sharing, as we practise it.'

'But killing is wrong ...' Pavi said.

The Given shrugged. 'Is being alive wrong?' she asked. 'I choose not to kill. So be it. But it is not my place to blame others for their choices. It is my place to heal.' She reached out to Era. 'Did you kill?'

Era closed her eyes and it was all *right there*.

'Oh, yes,' she said.

'I am glad to be alive,' the Given said. 'Accept my gladness.'

Era felt it – a wave of joy – and like Jawat, she was rocked on her feet. The depth of the other woman's joy was immense, and it held ...

Love. Parenting. Anger. Release, and tension; fear and its end; the lingering pain of childbirth and the purity of holding the result in her arms.

'Ah,' she said. Her mouth said it; her mind was a blank of pain-easing joy.

The Given moved among Jawat's soldiers, who had come up behind her. She joined Mokshi to two archers, hand to heart, but otherwise she distributed her own joy, and then she came and took Miti by the hand and led her among the spear-people.

Many wept openly. Drakon, the ugly giant, burst into sobs. Lan Thena stood as if rooted, gazing at nothing, with Miti's hand crushed in hers.

Era felt a wave of energy, as if she'd eaten a feast and slept for hours.

'What is she?' she asked Pavi.

'She is Given. She gives herself to her people.' Pavi shrugged. 'There are never many. They say it kills you in the end.' She looked at her hands.

Era moved her sword belt, more from habit than because she needed to; the belt made her skin sweat, and...

Her two long slashes were gone. There was not even a scar.

'Fuck me,' Era said reverently.

Dite came from the ship.

'I'm late to the party,' she said, and stood close beside Era. They didn't touch in public; Era felt such displays were bad for discipline, which made Dite laugh.

Dite giggled. And then put a hand, almost unconsciously, on Era's shoulder.

'It's healed?'

Era nodded. Dite gave a whistle, and the woman who had been a god walked across the sand towards the Given. Era had the strangest impulse to step between them.

And what? Protect who?

The Given turned when Dite was a few steps away.

'I knew you were here,' she said.

'What are you?' Dite asked.

'I am Given,' the woman said. 'And because I am Given, I am free.'

'You speak in riddles,' Dite said.

'You are a riddle, god-who-walks-in-a-woman's-form.'

'A riddle who would have your blessing,' Dite said.

'I have no blessing but what we might share.' The Given reached out a hand. 'I will share my joy. What will you share?'

Dite paused. And then, more cautiously than Era would have expected, she reached out a hand.

'Lust?' she asked.

The older woman laughed. 'Rude god, I've had my share of lust. Do I look like a maiden?'

Dite laughed with her. 'Drunkeness?'

The woman in white grinned from ear to ear.

'You think I've never been drunk, old god?'

'A song, then?' Dite whispered.

'A song is always welcome,' the old woman said.

Dite's hand clasped the woman's, and both of them smiled, their lips parting. And the woman in white began to sing quietly.

Dite withdrew her hand slowly, as if she wished to prolong the contact. Then she backed to Era.

'That one is the real thing,' she said. Dite – Dite who had been a god – had awe in her voice.

Era could only nod. Her head was full of thoughts – about her partner, about the beach, about the Given. But a simple, honest happiness washed over her, and she let the dark thoughts go. They'd still be there later.

The white-haired woman moved along the beach, touching every man and woman there. It was odd and wonderful; odd, in that sometimes as she touched them, Era could feel their... pain? Longing? Emptiness? Despair?

And then she could feel it move, like bending a steamed plank, and the moment when it suddenly was ready to be bent.

One of the people who had carried the palanquin looked at her and smiled. Several others were in among the workers and the spear-people, but this one stood alone, looking at her.

Era smiled back. She didn't even know why.

'Come,' the man said. 'She wants you.'

Era looked at Dite, and she smiled.

'Go,' Dite said. 'I cannot imagine that woman harming any of us.'

Era bowed on instinct to the man, a strange act on her part, and he returned her bow, turned, and led her down the beach. His back was utterly different from his front – an elaborate mass of curling lines of tattoos.

The Given was making her way slowly to Jawala, who was sitting up. She looked different, as days without food had hollowed her out. Her face was thin and pinched and looked like an axe blade, but her eyes were bright, and fixed on the Given.

The old woman walked straight up to Jawala and put a hand on her head. For a moment, despite everything, Era thought the Given was going to slap her.

Instead, her voice held authority, but no anger.

'Wake up, sleeper,' the Given said. 'There is yet work to do.'

Jawala's face worked, a dozen expressions crossing it.

'Wake up and follow me,' the Given repeated. 'I ask, in the name of all people.'

Jawala got to her feet. There were no miracles; a week without food had been unkind, and she had trouble standing. She stood a moment, taller than the Given, a flame of orange against the other woman's white.

'I seek only death,' she said.

The Given shook her head. 'Life needs you first.'

Jawala closed her eyes.

And then, opening them, she gave the slightest nod – the only betrayal of the struggle going on behind her tired eyes.

'Let it be so,' she said. Her voice was weak, reedy and distant.

The Given unpinned Jawala's orange robe and lifted it over her head, so that Jawala stood naked on the beach. Then the Given flung it into the sea.

139

'Let your strength flow through us all, and your pride be washed away with the robe,' the Given said. The words seemed odd; Jawala, a middle-aged woman starved for a week after months of deprivation and struggle, was more like a wraith than a tower of strength. But she smiled. It was a smile of bitterness, but also … self-knowledge?

The Given embraced her, a mother embracing a much-loved daughter.

The man who had led Era down the beach embraced Jawala, and she brightened … until he handed her a robe and she went stock-still in shock.

'No?' she asked.

'You are called,' the Given said. 'Can you not hear the call?'

The man sang a single note.

The other bearers began to gather, and they took up the note, tenors and bass: a slight harmony; a single chord.

Era took up the note, too. So did Dite, behind her. Era was filled with a longing to dance, so utterly out of place on this bloodstained beach …

When did I last dance?

The robe was white. Era could see that, and she understood; perhaps she understood before Jawala.

'I am not worthy …' Jawala said.

'No one is worthy,' the Given said. 'You were ready to die for what you believe. I call you to live for it instead.'

Jawala stood rooted to the beach, her eyes distant, until the Given seized her chin, a mother to an erring daughter.

'We are just people,' she said. 'If you wish to *give*, then give.'

Jawala gave a choking cry. And then, through tears, to nod. Biting her lip, she pulled the white robe over her head.

The men and women gathered around her, and each of them put his left hand on her so that she was at the centre of an eight-pointed human wheel. The Given stood back, and the white-kilted ones began to step around her as they sang: a powerful, almost tuneless paean. And the Given sang in a high voice. Era had no idea what she sang. Her voice was thin with age, and perhaps her own fatigue, and it wavered; then suddenly it was solid, melodious, rich and beautiful.

Dite was singing her words.

The Given grinned like a child with a sweet.

For a moment, Jawala seemed to burst into a pure white flame. The effect was blinding – that was the way Era explained it afterwards. And then she stood among them: Jawala, but dressed in a spotless white robe.

There was a sudden whirring, a sound not unlike a scream, but utterly inhuman – more like the screech of metal on metal – and suddenly the Dry One stood among them.

Era looked at it, and then back at the warehouse it had seized. There was a sizeable hole in the palm-frond roof.

The Dry One walked oddly, almost bouncing on its hideous back-jointed legs that looked as if they were carved of horn. Its mighty wings moved, twitching constantly...

Correcting its balance? Looking for obstructions?

It had landed on dry sand, and now it walked its mincing walk, the crowd parting before it, until it stood before the old Given.

The white-kilted people stood away from Jawala, who still gave off a pale white glow from her hands and face and her one bare shoulder. But the Given stepped fearlessly towards the Dry One, her right hand raised.

'Will you share?' she asked, as if it were any of the people.

One of the creature's black-taloned 'hands' lifted and touched hers.

Both of its antennae stiffened, and it fluttered its wings.

The Given sighed. But when she stepped back, she stumbled.

The Dry One leapt, and was gone. In a single leap it passed

141

high over the crowd and landed on the roof of its shed, and with a wriggle, it vanished back into its nest.

'Well,' the Given said, as if awakening from a nap.

Jawala's white light was fading. She was crying.

'You must teach me,' she said to the older Given. She was fingering the white robe.

'It's difficult to keep clean,' the Given said. 'Trust me. This is all the wisdom I have to offer.'

She touched Jawala – forehead, breasts, pelvis and hands – and Jawala stood like a statue, despite a week of fasting. And then the older woman turned to Aanat, who knelt in the sand, his eyes full of hope.

The Given smiled.

'Get up, you fool,' she said. 'You love her enough to die with her. Noble, but worthless. You are neither a saint, nor a Given.'

Aanat grinned, and wept. And stood.

He pulled the robe over his head and cast it into the surf where it floated like an orange jellyfish.

The Given joined their hands together.

'You will be the strength of these people,' she said to Jawala. And to Aanat, she said, 'You will be the strength to this woman.'

Aanat smiled happily.

'Get up and do what must be done. I say this for the People. *Do what must be done.*' She nodded. 'This is your task. *Do what must be done.*'

Aanat looked at her for a long time. Era thought that something had changed in him; his dark eyes held something she didn't recognise ... He had a distance now, so that even naked, middle-aged, he stood like something indomitable.

'What must be done?' Jawala asked.

The Given glanced at Era. 'Everything,' she said.

Jawala closed her eyes and opened them. 'We will poison ourselves,' she said, but not with anger. It was calm, and low.

The Given shrugged. 'I told you. When you are Given, it is difficult to stay clean. You are no longer your own. You belong to everyone. This is all the Gift I can make you. You stink of blood, but my people claim you. It is not rational, but it is the path.'

'But...' Jawala began.

The tall man who had led Era to the beach stepped forward and put a single finger against her lips, and then smiled.

'It is well done,' he said.

He stepped back, and joined the other bearers. The Given stepped into her palanquin as they lifted it, a perfect co-operation.

She leant out. 'Whatever you face,' she said, 'you carry all the seeds of immortality.'

Era shook her head. 'What does she mean?'

The bearers began to sing as they carried the Given away.

Jawala walked carefully along the strand to Era.

'I'm... ready,' she said.

Era smiled. 'I'll bet you're hungry,' she said. 'Any idea what she meant by the "seeds of immortality"?'

Jawala blinked. 'Can I eat first?' she asked.

Auza, Home of the Gods

The overwhelming temptation was to lie back and enjoy heaven. The ministrations of the servile were balm to his senses; Enkul-Anu had always enjoyed a good grovel, and all the more when he was wounded in both pride and body.

So he took full advantage: he revelled, orgied and relaxed.

But not for long. The press of time was heavy on him, and he had many unanswered questions. When he was strong again, when the wounds inflicted by the World Serpent were mostly healed, he strode into his Hall of Judgement and sat on his august throne, ready to hear the petty crap that his supposed peers thought of as important. But his mind was below, in the realms of Day.

He looked up from a reverie of revenge to find mad Grulu, Goddess of Spite and Envy, standing before the throne. She had bright red hair and the blotchy red skin of a pale person in a rage. Her green eyes burned with hate.

'Great God, Enkul-Anu, I seek justice!' she shrieked.

Enkul-Anu looked around for his chamberlain, Telipinu. The dark-skinned young god stiffened to something like attention as Enkul-Anu's golden gaze touched him.

'My lord God?' he asked in his magnificent deep voice.

'I ordered that Grulu never again appear in the Hall of Judgement,' Enkul-Anu said.

'Unjust!' Grulu shrieked.

'You, my dear, literally embody injustice,' Enkul-Anu said. 'You have no place here.'

Sypa rose from her couch. Today she was magnificent: lush without vulgarity, so beautiful that she was an assault on the senses, and clothed only in a gold belt around her waist, and a pair of anklets that tinkled musically as she moved. Otherwise, she was naked, her skin the warm pink of rose water candies and freshly bathed infants.

Enkul-Anu was not unmoved, but neither was he in the mood to compromise.

'I have spoken,' he said.

'What has been spoken can be unspoken,' Sypa said with a sway of her hips. 'Grulu has a tale to tell that should be heard.'

'I demand justice!' Grulu shrieked.

Enkul-Anu found that rage had overcome him in a single immortal breath. He had enough self-awareness to wonder if his battle with the World Serpent had left him touchy.

'You fucking idiots!' he spat. 'Sypa, grind your hips elsewhere. This harpy has wasted enough of our immortal time to choke the concept of eternity. When she told me that you were fornicating with Druku, God of Drunkenness, did I believe her? When she told me that Laila was consorting with demons, did I act? She is nothing but lies and spite. It is her province. It's what she fucking *does*!'

Sypa flinched, as she always did, and her proud face fell, and some of the glamour of her beauty slipped...

...and Grulu fled the hall, wailing like a child whose toy has been taken away.

She fled from the dark marble of the Hall of Judgement to the magnificence of the Halls of Day. She left a multi-language stream of profanity in her wake, rolling in eddies, so powerful in her blasphemy that a courtier fainted away and a visiting hierophant collapsed, clutching his heart.

Just outside the Halls of Day, a pale arm reached out of the shadows and drew her in.

'You seem outraged,' Lady Laila said with cooing humility. 'Tell me why, my poor goddess, and I'll do what I can to help you.'

'You!' Grulu spat. 'You ... fornicating adulteress!'

Laila smiled. 'We all have our recreations,' she said. 'But I love justice, and it's clear to me that you are being treated unfairly.'

'It's all so unfair! I live in a state of constant oppression!' Grulu said. 'Everyone is treated better than me! Even you, you slut!'

Laila's smile grew a little forced. 'And yet, I would like to help you ...'

'I will bring you all down! The whole rotten edifice!' Grulu suddenly looked through her sneer at Laila. Her change was more than mercurial – it was stunning. 'You would help me?' she said suddenly. Humbly. 'Even after ...?'

'Even after you tried to get me flung from heaven for...' Laila smiled. 'An indiscretion best left undescribed.'

'You were suborning the demons!' Grulu said. 'I fucking caught you at it!'

Laila sighed. 'Nevertheless...'

Grulu changed her mind again.

'But who's to blame you?' she said. 'At least you recognise that I'm being treated unfairly. Everyone hates me.'

Laila looked away, bit her lip, and then looked back.

'I am here for you,' she said. 'Now tell me, what were you eager to report to the Great Storm God himself?'

Chapter Five

Pollon

To Pollon's relief, Zos was at the base of the great gate towers, leaning against the ancient stone, cleaning his nails with a bronze knife.

Pollon hadn't wanted to come, but Daos had roused him as soon as the boy had his ship in order.

'I'm still his shield-bearer,' Daos, who was now taller and broader than Pollon himself, said. 'He needs me to make a good appearance.'

Pollon thought over the last twelve hours, on the desperate ship-to-ship fighting and the Jekers, and sighed, knowing courts had their own forms of combat.

'Yes,' he admitted.

He roused himself, leapt into the sea to get a little cleaner and perhaps to wash the sleep from his eyes, poured a pitcher of drinking water over his head to get the salt off, and dressed in a good wool *heton* that he had 'liberated' from Mykoax. He threw his best cloak over his shoulder and hoped no one would notice that he'd slept under it, then nodded to Daos, who looked as fresh as a new dawn and just as handsome.

'You're easy to hate, you know that?' Pollon asked.

Daos looked crestfallen. 'Sir?' he said plaintively

Pollon shook his head. 'Youth,' he snarled.

When he started up the beach, Daos cut in front of him with a bound and turned, like an eager puppy.

'This way, sir,' he said.

Pollon glared, but the boy seemed to know what he was doing, and so Pollon followed.

'I see you won your ship-fight.' Pollon didn't mean to sound so gruff.

'We did, too!' the boy enthused. 'All my people were brilliant!'

Of course they were. You're some sort of godling and we all know it.

Pollon really wanted a few hours of sleep and a little wine. He loved Daos; he didn't need to bait the boy.

His eye was caught by a god's eye painted on a post.

Uh-oh.

He walked faster. Against his better judgement, he turned and looked back at the thing. He touched it with *power* and it was live. He cursed.

'God's eyes,' he said to Daos.

The boy-man looked at him, and understanding came to him.

'Drat,' he said.

So when Pollon found Zos, his first words were, 'We passed a god's eye.'

Zos looked up. 'Good morning to you, too, deadly archer. Daos! Well fought. I didn't have much time to watch you, but …'

Daos glowed with the praise.

'We passed a god's eye,' Pollon repeated. 'If anyone was watching, they saw me.'

Zos raised an eyebrow. 'So do something about it,' he said.

Pollon sucked in a breath.

'I've seldom seen a man so cautious about using his *talents*.'

Zos glanced at Daos, who held out a clean *heton* as if he was a genuine servant. He also had an embroidered belt, and a pair of red leather sandals.

'You are the very prince of shield-bearers,' Zos said.

He stripped immediately, to the shock and suppressed delight of a passing merchantess, and pulled on the dull salmon *heton* covered with embroidery, with its double-woven edge bands in blue and yellow. The belt matched, and the sandals were clean.

'Where did you get the beautiful cloak?' Daos asked.

'Is this a fashion show or a rebellion?' Pollon snapped. 'Can we do our godborn compliment contest later and deal with immediate needs now?'

Zos slapped him on the back. 'Brother, you need to use your ... talent ... to step into the *Aura* and do whatever it is that you do. Blind the god's eyes. I need to see the king.'

'So why are you standing out here?' Pollon asked.

'Because Makar rides the tiger that is Lazba by playing court- iers off against one another and creating factions,' Zos said. 'I'd almost forgotten why I hated it here.'

Daos looked out over the magnificent bay.

'You hated it here?' he asked, unbelieving.

'No,' Zos admitted. 'But everyone played this endless game. And it got violent, and people got hurt. All the time.'

It was Pollon's turn to raise an eyebrow.

'Seems to me you'd thrive in such a scenario, brother,' he said with intended sarcasm.

Zos looked at him, deceptively mildly. 'Maybe I did, for a while.'

Pollon understood, suddenly. He reached out a hand.

'I'm sorry. I'm a touchy bastard this morning.'

'No one's civil after killing.' Zos took the proffered hand. 'Anyway, I *was* good at it. But I was young and I kept trusting arsehats ...' He winked at Daos, and he and Pollon both laughed together, the conspiracy of older men, as Daos looked back and forth.

'Never mind,' Zos wheezed. 'I'm glad you're here. This is a

good place to keep up appearances, and a bad place to look poor and vulnerable. How's the ship?'

'Alektron is a right tyrant with you gone, and everyone will be wishing for our return,' Pollon said. 'Myself, I declined to help repaint the oar benches and came away with Daos.'

'The oar benches weren't painted—' Zos caught himself.

Leontas came through the gate. He had another magnificent cloak on, and he bowed.

'The king will see you now,' he said.

Zos presented his friends, and the four of them walked through the gate. Leontas resolutely avoided addressing Pollon; it was obvious, and Zos wasn't amused. It was one of the many things Pollon was coming to love about Zos. He could be an arse, but he resented other people behaving badly, and the thought was strangely warming to Pollon.

Leontas smiled. 'This way. We can't keep the king waiting.'

'What kind of reception will we receive?' Zos asked.

Leontas made a face. 'The king has heard a great many things about you,' he admitted. 'He has many questions.'

Leontas glanced at Pollon, and for the first time their eyes met. Leontas smiled. Pollon found that smile uncomfortable.

'What kind of questions?' he asked.

'We must hurry,' Leontas replied.

Zos looked back at Pollon and gave a small shake of his head, so Pollon sighed and followed, against his better judgement.

They went through another pair of decorated gates, walls beautiful with deep blue and white tiles reflecting the sun, and into the inner courtyard. It had a dozen doors on the ground floor and an open guardroom, but Leontas led them through a crowd of supplicants and directly to the megaron.

It *was* a megaron, but built on a lavish scale, with a curtained entrance. Pollon was fascinated by Lazba, because the place seemed to straddle the cultures of the Hundred Cities and the Dardanians, the Noan Islands, and Narmer as well.

The great megaron of Lazba was famous, and for good reason. The column supporting the entrance was a richly veined green-blue marble shot with gold – an incredible piece of stone the likes of which Pollon had never seen. The hangings were staggeringly complex and colourful – better than anything the god-king of Hekka had possessed. And on the table before the king, in his throne room, there were cups, beakers and amphorae of pure gold.

The floor under his feet was decorated in elaborate designs of interlocking coloured marble.

Pollon was impressed, and he didn't hesitate to show it; he stood under the canopy of artificial stars created by the high swinging lamps, smelling the expensive incense of Narmer, and gaped like a plough boy on his first day in the city. He fell well behind Zos and the others.

The megaron was full of courtiers and slaves or servants; they were all so richly dressed that it was difficult to tell them apart. The servants carrying trays of wine cups must have been servants, but they wore wools so fine and sheer as to rival what the high-haired courtiers wore to enhance or just barely conceal their figures, male or female.

Pollon smiled at a very beautiful court lady, and she smiled back, but her smile held more amused contempt than aesthetic appreciation. Pollon sighed, and followed Zos.

Zos was in mid-obeisance. He didn't quite fall flat on the floor, but he bowed so deeply that the hand he had on the floor must have supported all his weight, like a fitness exercise or a test.

King Makar looked up from his game. He was playing Senet – a Narmerian game – against a small man with a badly twisted back. Pollon had heard of Makar all his life: one of the world's richest kings, and one of the wisest, with the dubious distinction of refusing godhood and yet remaining loyal to the system. The gods loved Makar. Or so it was said.

Which made this a very dangerous room to be in. And Pollon could see a dozen god's eyes in here, all of them active.

The twisted little man looked up, and his eyes went straight to Pollon. He smiled, and this was not a smile of contempt. It was more like a smile of recognition, on seeing an old friend.

Makar nodded to Leontas and then looked down at Zos.

'You may rise, foster-son. One might express some surprise that you are yet alive. It has been some time since you last graced my hall.'

'Great King, I wished to return when I had something worthy to share with you.'

Zos reached into his cloak and produced the leather bag, from which he drew the double-handled gold cup that had stood on the table of the mighty undead king of Mykoax. With a bow, he placed it on the ebony table at the king's side.

Guards shuffled, and hands went to sword hilts.

'The cup of Atrios,' he said.

Makar stood suddenly, his out-thrust arm motioning his guards back, throwing his light cloak back over his shoulder as he did so.

After a pause, he said, 'This is a mighty gift. Is it yours to give?'

Zos narrowed his eyes – possibly thinking of the spiritual cost they had paid for the cup, and the other treasure. But Pollon watched the warrior make himself smile. 'Do you think that revenge is justified, Great King?'

'It is a form of justice,' Makar admitted.

'Then this cup is the living symbol of my revenge on Mykoax. I give it to you freely, as it is mine by right. I took it from the dead king himself, and his tomb lies in the dust, and scavengers gnaw his ancient bones.'

As he said the words, Zos seemed to grow. And for the first time, Pollon saw something beyond tenacity and courage in the man: something like dignity. The king he'd never be.

Makar looked at him for a long time, and there was silence in the magnificent hall. Pollon began to glance around, curious, in his scribe's way, to see the courtiers' reaction to Zos' declaration.

Makar extended a hand to the cup, as if to take it, but then paused.

'And Mykoax?'

'Broken,' Zos said. 'And awaiting a new master.'

Makar looked at him, and Pollon had to admit that the burning intelligence in the king's eyes was remarkable.

'If I take this cup,' Makar said, 'I join your revenge. And in joining it, you ask me to join your war with the gods.'

Zos smiled. 'You've heard?' This was a different Zos – the light-hearted trickster.

Makar gestured at a man in the crowd of courtiers.

'A slave ship from Dekhu was your herald,' Makar said.

In the crowd of richly clad courtiers, Pollon watched a man shuffle. He thought he recognised that curling black beard and scarred face; he'd seen that face on the waterfront at Dekhu, or in the markets.

'And you carry a sword stolen from the gods,' Makar added. 'You are at war with the gods, and you bring that war here.'

'I'm at war with the Jekers, too,' Zos said, in that same dangerous, light voice. 'And I did you a service there.'

Makar stepped back without touching the cup, and sat on his throne. The throne was carved stone, with crouching lions carved into the armrests. He put a pensive hand to his beard, looking both imperious and relaxed.

'So...' he said. The hall remained silent, although the slaver shuffled. 'What am I to do with you, fosterling?' Makar asked.

'Allow me to recruit a dozen ships,' Zos said, 'and then take your army and conquer Mykoax with my blessing.'

Makar nodded. 'Interesting. I gather that you and your friends, in this conflict with the gods, provoked the World Serpent?'

Zos clearly wanted to shrug. Pollon watched his friend with some amusement, as the dignity of the occasion and Zos' relationship with the god-king of Lazba clearly precluded such arrogance.

'I don't know,' he admitted slowly. 'In truth, the World Serpent, if it was such, arose only after...' He paused. 'After our conflict was over.'

The slaver spoke up, pushing through a trio of godborn officers to gain space on the floor before the throne.

'They just started killing people! Pirates and thieves! My lord, I beg you to seize them and put them to death for the good of all.'

Makar smiled.

Pollon thought, *This is a very intelligent, very dangerous man. Not at all like the ineffectual fools who rule the Hundred Cities.*

'I find it interesting that you, a godborn, have chosen to take part in this ... rebellion,' Makar said.

His glance slid from Zos, however, to the magnificent gold cup.

Zos looked at Pollon, who took a deep breath, having made some inner decision. But Makar cut him off. 'I have troubles of my own, fosterling, and your arrival does not come at an opportune time.'

He glanced at the slaver – and perhaps his glance swept over others. Pollon tried to follow it, trying to see the currents and eddies of power in the room – worldly power, in this case, not auratic power. Though someone here had a great deal of that, and was remaining hidden.

'May I help you with your troubles?' Zos asked.

Makar smiled bitterly. 'Clear the hall. These guests may stay, and Lord Leontas, and Lord Manatha.' He smiled thinly at the man with the twisted back. 'And you, Lapotho.'

'And your queen?' asked a voice.

'That goes without saying.' Makar put a hand up, and a slim hand slid into it, and he kissed it.

Now Pollon could see that there was a veiled figure standing behind the throne. And he strongly suspected she was the source of the auratic power in the throne room. He was even more sure when that hand moved, and the god's eyes around the room suddenly went dull.

Guards escorted the rest of the courtiers away; there was no protest and no resistance.

'Some of those people have waited a month to present their cases to me,' Makar said. 'Let's make this quick.'

The man addressed as Lapotho glanced at Pollon, and again their eyes met. He was small, and stooped, and suffered from an obvious disablement, probably since birth, but he wore a short bronze sword like a warrior. He spoke up. His voice was thin and reedy, almost like a badly tuned musical instrument.

'Great King, there is no way to make this quick. These are the great issues of our times.'

The king muttered something with the word 'dragon' in it, and Lapotho smiled at the queen, who smiled back.

'I can tell you what would make this quick,' a big man, as big as Zos – Pollon thought he must be Lord Manatha – said. He was broad and looked as strong as an ox, with fiery red hair and a long beard. 'Kill these two and send their heads to heaven. The Great Storm God Enkul-Anu, may his righteous name be blessed, will reward us well.'

Makar nodded as if in agreement, and then said, 'Perhaps.' He looked at Zos. 'I have a problem.'

Zos nodded. 'The World Serpent landed here, didn't it?'

Makar laughed. 'Damn me, boy. You were always the sharp one.'

Lapotho nodded. 'Straight to the heart, eh, boy?'

Zos went to the small man and clasped hands. 'Who taught me that, eh, sir?' He turned back to the king. 'Leontas here and your dissident guard captain at the gate mentioned a dragon. And the smell of sulphur is strong out over the sea.'

Makar sighed. 'Right in the middle of the island,' he said. 'In the Vale of Jasmine. Do you remember it?'

'I remember a lion hunt,' Zos said. 'And some caves.'

Makar raised an eyebrow. 'Some caves? Priests say that the true entrance to the underworld lies in those caves. And the birthplace of the Great God Ranos, predecessor of Enkul-Anu. And the nest of the dragon he aided.'

Zos nodded again. 'Some caves,' he said with a smile. He was looking at Lapotho when he said it.

'Well, the World Serpent has taken up residence. And she's plundering the island – sheep, goats, people …' The king waved a hand to include his whole island.

'Inconvenient,' Zos observed.

Makar crashed a mighty fist down on his ebony table. The gold cup rang like a bell.

'It's not a matter for jest,' he said through clenched teeth. 'I have waited for ten days and nights for that monster to come and take my palace. And she is ravaging my people.' He looked at the cup. 'Not to mention the taxes I will never collect from the former villages of the Vale of Jasmine.'

Zos looked at his foster-father, and then at the enmity written broadly on Manatha's face.

'I am not responsible for the World Serpent,' he said carefully.

A quiet, careful voice came from behind the throne. The woman's figure remained in shadow, but her voice was beautiful without being flirtatious or seductive.

'The rumour in the Upper Air is that the World Serpent contested possession of all the earth with the Great God Enkul-Anu, and won,' she said.

'And the fucking tidal wave you people released has crushed my southern fishing villages,' Makar said.

Pollon, hitherto silent, spoke up.

'I don't think that we raised the World Serpent.'

Daos, almost invisible as a *papista*, chuckled. 'No, I did that,' he said.

Every head turned to look at the young man.

'What?' Zos asked.

'I released the World Serpent. And Era and Dite rescued her eggs.' The young man smiled.

Zos' mouth set in a hard line for a moment. And then he made some decision; his expression cleared, and he nodded sharply.

'Of course you did,' he said.

Daos' smile lit the room.

The woman behind the throne spoke again, her voice low and calm.

'As our foster-son has brought the dragon, so let him dispatch it. If Lord Zos will convince the dragon to leave in peace, perhaps the king will have the leisure to consider an alliance.'

The king sat back, considering.

Manatha shook his head. 'Just kill them? Enkul-Anu, may his name be spoken in praise, can rid us of the World Serpent.'

Makar looked at Lapotho. 'Can he, though?' He took his consort's hand again.

Lapotho smiled mirthlessly and nodded to Pollon behind Zos' back – a congenial nod. Pollon wondered why the man kept looking at him and then realized that he must be a Writer; a scribe-magos, and he recognized this talent in Pollon.

'We cannot afford to back the losing side,' he said. 'Some of the gods have already defected. And some of the old gods were not banished as effectively as Enkul-Anu seems to think.'

Makar's consort stepped forward into the light and tossed back a veil to reveal a face beautiful in age; her greying hair still full and long, a lapis diadem on her brow. 'The World Serpent wounded our lord Enkul-Anu,' she said. 'And his son Nisroch by the fallen goddess Arrina is raising his own war against heaven, or so my friends tell me.'

Manatha narrowed his eyes. 'This is folly, Lady. The gods are the gods – they decide our fates ...'

Zos shook his head. 'That's not true,' he said. 'The gods are a collection of powerful mortals masquerading as immortals.'

The bent man smiled. 'You are wise, warrior. Where did you learn this dangerous wisdom?'

The queen looked at Pollon, and then at Zos. 'They are still very powerful, foster-son. Do not deny their power because you've been fortunate. But ...'

She raised her hands in the way of invocation and prayer, then opened them, and between them came a picture – a detailed image. Even Pollon, who knew how it was done, felt the breath pulled from his chest in surprise.

For as long as a pious worshipper would pray, and make sacrifice, they watched the World Serpent, as big as twenty ships or more, and the Great God of Storm, fight over the sea.

She closed her hands.

'That is power which no mortal of our generation has, or is likely to have, Lord Zos. Even you, or your friends.'

Zos bowed his head to her.

'But,' she said, addressing Manatha, 'the gods are failing. Listen, Manatha. I know you think I'm a ... what did you say? "An old witch with sagging tits"' Manatha stiffened in shock. 'But I can listen to the wind and learn,' she said. 'Just as I can listen to you when you think you speak in private.' Manatha looked as if he might melt into the floor. 'The gods are failing. Every harvest is worse than the one before. The fields are dying and the desert is taking the coasts. I have seen it. And the Bright People, the Dry Ones, encroach every year, closer and closer. Yet the gods do nothing. Plague and famine in Narmer, sent by the gods! Because of some petty quarrel with Maritaten. Jekers assail our coasts, and grow in strength by eating human flesh. Imagine where that ends, Manatha, and tremble. Our world is *dying*, and the gods are unwilling or unable to save us. And now this.' She lowered her hands.

Makar looked at her as if seeing her anew.

'So what is the answer?' he asked.

She shook her head. 'There is no *answer*. But slavish obedience to the gods is no longer a guarantee of survival.'

Daos nodded. '*If Zos takes an army to Narmer, Lazba will never be invaded by Jekers again.*' His bright, boyish voice was full of prophecy. '*And I will drive his chariot of fire.*'

The lady looked at the boy. 'What god speaks through you?'

Daos grinned, an impish boy defying his parents.

'I'm not allowed to say,' he said.

Makar looked at the boy, and then at Zos.

'You have some interesting companions,' he said. 'This is my word – if you will go to the World Serpent and send her away, I will…' He paused, and looked at his wife. 'I will take my fleet to Mykoax and place it under my protection. And lend you what I can spare of my fleet.'

'I fail to see the benefit to me,' Zos said. 'After I survive chatting with the dragon.'

Pollon noticed that his smile was genuine, and so was his good humour.

Makar raised a royal eyebrow. 'You know what it will mean, boy,' he said. 'Be content. I'll find you some recruits if you rid me of this troublesome dragon.'

Daos smiled. 'I dreamt you said that. Except you said, "Will no one rid me of this troublesome dragon?" and Leontas, here, volunteered.'

Leontas looked at Daos, and then nodded.

'I will go, if Lord Zos will have me.'

Zos looked at Pollon. 'What language does the World Serpent speak, do you think?'

Pollon smiled. 'Old Akkad?' he said. 'Old Narmerian?'

Makar leant forward. 'You'll go?' he asked suddenly.

Zos nodded. 'I suspect it's my fate.' And then, with a twisted smile, 'We'll ask the ancient serpent that once fought all the gods to quietly leave the island. What could possibly go wrong?'

Aanat

Aanat woke in his hanging bed in the aft cabin of his beloved *Untroubled Swan*, with his wife Jawala snoring lightly beside him.

He lay for a moment, savouring the wonder of it.

And then he rolled his feet over the edge of the bed and went through the leather curtain and onto the deck.

It was dawn. Out east, over the ocean, was a beautiful sunrise; Aanat imagined the goddess Dawn preparing herself and rising from her bath. It was a fine image, for all that he didn't really believe that there was a goddess Dawn.

Era was looking out over the stern, and he walked up behind her, his bare feet silent on the broad boards of the deck.

'Good morning,' he said.

Era turned. 'Damn, it's good to have you back.' And then, as she'd clearly been too emotional, she added, 'Hardly anyone else is an early riser.'

'I'll make a hot cup of something,' he said.

'Pavi's cooking on the beach. I want us to leave today.'

Aanat nodded, looking at the sea. 'It won't get better than this. My weather sense says we have three, maybe even four days of fine weather.'

'And I regret every lost minute,' Era said.

Aanat smiled, and thought of the thousands of minutes he'd spent starving himself to death.

I will awaken to every sunrise. I will savour every minute, he thought.

Era's mind was clearly elsewhere. 'Did you get the Dry One stowed?' she asked.

Aanat winced. 'It won't leave the bear and the donkey,' he said. 'So I put it off until today.'

Era made a face.

Aanat shrugged. 'I was busy dying. In fact, I'm still hungry and thirsty.'

And tired. His mind was very clear, but his body was something else: full of aches and pains as if he'd aged twenty years.

He worried that he had – that he wouldn't get his vitality back.

A small price to pay.

Did I know before, that I loved life so much? I certainly do now.

It was mid-morning before they knocked down the last warehouse, having loaded the last pithoi of grain that they could fit aboard their six ships. One of the Jeker ships had been stripped and rigged as a cargo galley, just so that they could get more food aboard.

Aanat was watching his jury-rigged masthead-sling sway the huge grain pithoi aboard when the shouting began on the beach. He turned to see Jawala, clad in white, walking with deliberation down the beach, trailed by Era.

He couldn't see the action, whatever it was, around the former Jeker galley. But as soon as he saw the pithoi vanish into the bilges without either sinking the ship or snapping the over-pressed lateen yard, he trotted around the stern of the partially beached ship and saw the crowd.

He kept pressing forward until he stood behind his wife. He could see her white clothing illuminated with a clear blue light. It was piercing, overwhelming, like the light of the sun when you looked directly into it, something Aanat had done so much of that he still saw spots before his eyes.

He put a comforting hand on Jawala's shoulder. People were shouting, exclaiming, or even praying.

She put a hand in his and pulled him forward.

'What the ...?' he managed.

'Shhh,' she said.

The Dry One stood on its back-hinged legs in the centre of a hemisphere of blue fire. Bror, the bear, lay at its feet, as if dead, or asleep, and Nannu, the donkey, stood to the side, watching intently – a very human look.

'How long has this been going on?' Era asked.

'A little while,' Pavi said. 'I was going to lead them aboard like you said—'

'Kur's seven hells,' Era spat. 'We *need to get to sea.*'

If the Dry One could hear them, it made no sign.

Aanat said, 'I can tell you that there's an incredible ... emanation from the Dry One. It's not just auratic power, but ...' He looked at Era, her face illuminated a livid blue. 'It's gathering power.'

'What?' she asked. 'The Dry One?' And then, 'I can feel it. It's too long since I cast anything.'

Aanat nodded. He shook his head, raised his hands, and made

a small invocation. A burst of brilliant blue light appeared between his hands.

He banished it. 'The power is everywhere,' he said.

'The Dry One is summoning,' Jawala said. Her voice was flat, without her usual emotions.

'That's fine,' Era said. 'And what about my nice bear?'

As if in response to her words, there was … a connection. Every person on the beach felt it, like the pop of static when they touched wool in winter, magnified in spirit.

The thin, brilliant blue line, like lapis fire, connected the blue hemisphere to the heavens. It vanished out of sight over their heads, and appeared to flow to infinity …

… and then it was gone, and with it, the brilliant hemisphere.

Aanat blinked.

Bror stirred at the feet, or chitinous appendages, of the Dry One, and everyone released long-held breaths.

'Can we get aboard and get to sea?' Era asked. 'Without any more supernatural events? Please?'

Bror raised her mighty head.

'Of course,' she said.

The Outer Darkness

Regret
  Revisit.
  Repent.
  Revenge.
  Return.
Temis wasn't insane yet. She clung to memories, although they were fading in the endless cold, and she was increasingly aware of how tenuous her hold was on concepts like 'I' and 'me'. She tried to imagine Arrina, who'd been in the Outer

Darkness a lot longer than she, and for a while, she tried to contact the old Sun Goddess, but there was…

…there was nothing.

I am my own universe.

Gods, it's cold.

How did I miss the purpose behind Sypa's malevolence?

Regret

Revisit.

Repent.

Revenge.

Return.

… and then, after a couple of dozen eternities and some terrible dreams…

Temis?

It took her some time to accept she was hearing a voice, not imagining it. Temis wanted to believe, but she was very cautious about allowing herself to admit she had gone insane.

Temis!

The voice tried again. She'd made up a good Arrina, but Temis was increasingly sure it was just her own…

TEMIS!

Interesting. That was loud, and it had the same sensation she remembered when…

When…

When…?

Nammu?

TEMIS!

A blue light flashed in the void, a magic so powerful that it could live in the darkness of the eternal abyss.

And Temis was… *somewhere.*

I'm a bear!

Best we could do, Tem. Listen. We have a lot of work to do.

You're dead!

Eh, heh heh ... Well ... not as dead as all that.

But I'm a ... bear! Powerless! And mortal? And you're a DONKEY?

Tyka might have enough juice left to put you back in the Outer Darkness, if you like.

You're an ass!

A donkey, darling. Donkey.

Chapter Six

Zos

The cave was surprisingly dry and comfortable. Zos had a fire going, and Leontas had brought in a pair of freshly caught rabbits, newly dead. They were two days' hard walking from the palace, and the small cave in the flank of the valley was the most comfortable they'd been since they walked out through the king's beaded curtain.

'We used to camp here when I hunted with the king,' Zos said. 'And Lapotho. He was King's Tutor then.'

He was changing the bandage on his right shin, where something had gone through his greaves during the fight on the ships – a deeper wound than he'd thought. He didn't like the look of it, and it was hot to the touch.

'Lion hunting?' Leontas said.

He looked out over the shelf in front of the cave. There was smoke higher up the valley, to the north, and a strong smell like eggs left too long in a basket, but in the dying light of the sun the Vale of Jasmine looked like a stony hell designed to punish anyone so foolish as to cross it.

Leontas stretched his long form on the sandy cave floor. 'In my country, we hunt lions from chariots.'

Zos glanced up from his fire, and smiled. 'A chariot wouldn't last half a stadion here, friend.'

'You hunted lions on foot?'

'With spears and shields.'

Leontas nodded. 'We'd finish them that way, but only when they were full of arrows.'

Zos nodded. 'We used dogs to harry them.'

'Rough on the dogs,' Leontas added.

He was spitting his rabbits on green branches cut from an old holm oak that stood above the cave, while Daos came up the rough path with an armload of rough grass for bedding.

'Where'd you find that?' Zos asked.

'Pollon found it, the other side of the ridge. He's bringing more...' A few minutes later Pollon appeared, all but buried under a load of grass.

Leontas looked at Zos. 'I'm not sure why you brought a scribe on such an expedition.'

Pollon got that expression Zos already knew well: clamping down on his feelings; refusing to be insulted.

Zos shook his head. 'He's as much a warrior as you or I,' he said.

'He's scarcely godborn. The boy, I admit, is clearly...'

Zos carefully swept his coals into a pit he'd dug. He had a little clay pot, fire-hardened, but he was still careful with it. He knew from many campaigns how easy it was to crack a clay pot when cooking. He filled it with water and then set it gently in the coals. Then he looked up.

'Pollon is as much a warrior as you or I, Leontas. And pardon me, but most godborn aren't worth a shit, in a fight or anywhere else.'

Leontas' face closed as if he'd been slapped.

Pollon came and sat cross-legged by Zos.

'Lord Leontas is quite right,' he said. 'I'm no warrior.'

Zos wanted to roll his eyes. 'Who put an arrow in a god?' he asked. 'Who just stood his ground against five pirate ships?'

Pollon smiled. 'You don't stand on ground when you fight

at sea.' He realised that sounded pedantic. He smiled ruefully. 'I learnt my archery in a town militia. And every time you lead me into a fight, I want to lie down and hide. I hate it.'

Zos patted his shoulder. 'It gets easier.'

Pollon frowned. 'Maybe that's your experience of battle, Zos. Mine is that it gets worse every time. I have a better and better idea of how ... Of what ...' He stopped, staring into the flames. 'Of what death will be like.'

'And yet,' Zos said, determined to support his friend, 'you never flinch.'

Pollon smiled. 'You're blind if you think I never flinch. This whole thing terrifies me.'

'Then why are you here?' Zos asked. 'You could have stayed with the ship.'

Pollon looked away.

Leontas laughed. He had an excellent laugh, a big, rolling laugh that sounded like a trumpet call to mirth.

'Now, you stung me with that cut at the godborn, Lord Zos.'

'Just Zos,' he said, annoyed.

'Listen, just Zos.' Leontas grinned. 'You stung me. I have worked, sweated, lied and killed to be included among the godborn.' He looked at Pollon. 'You make the error, master scribe, of thinking that we are any different. You know why I am here? Because I can't admit fear in the face of my king. Am I afraid of the World Serpent? Gods, yes. I could piss myself, I'm so afraid.' He looked at Zos. 'You?'

Zos nodded. 'Pollon, if you think we're not afraid, you're not as observant as I thought. And maybe it's not facing the battle that gets easier – maybe it's just managing the fear.'

Pollon looked at both of them for a moment.

'Perhaps,' he said. 'But as far as I can see, you two live for this stuff. And I, begging your lordships' pardon, would prefer to sit in a well-run scribal office and manage your accounts.'

Leontas nodded. 'And I, begging your scribal pardon, would prefer to lie on a couch with five beautiful women and eat pomegranates and fuck until I die. Perhaps with some breaks for getting drunk and eating lotus flowers.'

Zos fingered his beard, because it was a moment that called for truth, and not a performance of his role as 'Zos, hardened warrior'. He turned the clay pot carefully on the coals, heating the whole surface. The water was warming, then he looked up.

'I think …' he said. 'I think I'd like to have a merchant galley, and trade like Lord Trayos.'

Leontas looked at him. 'What about the soft couch and the women?'

'I love the sea.' He shrugged. 'When I face a man in combat, I'm afraid. But when I face a storm at sea … I'm still afraid, but I'm also in love. I can't explain it.'

Pollon leant forward. 'But you could have that now,' he said. 'Or any time in the last ten years, if what I hear about you is true.'

Zos caught himself making a face. 'It's difficult to explain,' he said.

Leontas laughed his booming laugh again, and it sailed out into the falling night and rebounded off the walls of the Vale of Jasmine.

'I think I can explain, Pollon.'

Zos noticed that it was the first time Leontas had used the scribe's name.

The big man rolled up on one elbow. 'When I was young, I killed a lion. Until then, I was nobody … *but I could have become anyone.* Once I killed the lion, I was a lion-killer. I was invited on every lion hunt, on every war expedition. By the time I was nineteen, I'd killed four lions and a dozen men. I was a warrior. And there was no escape. Now I have to be that man.'

Zos nodded. 'Exactly.'

Pollon shook his head and began sorting grasses on a piece of wood; Zos realised he'd foraged wild thyme and oregano while he gathered bedding.

He looked up. 'I've never heard you talk like this, Zos,' he said quietly.

'When I killed the king of Mykoax, something ended. I know – they all tell us that revenge is a worthy thing, a great goal. All the epics have revenge.' He smiled at Daos, who'd made up four beds and now came and sat by the fire. 'And I won't say it was empty. It was...' He rotated the clay pot once more. 'It was a fulfilment. A completion.' He looked up, at Pollon. 'But now? Now, I think, I have to be someone else. Not a famous sell-sword and not a vengeful son. I'm still not sure who that is.'

Daos said, in his sing-song prophecy voice, '*Now you are Zos-Against-the-Gods*,' and leant forward. 'I understand your words,' he said in his own voice. 'But I like fighting.'

Pollon ruffled the boy's hair and made him squirm.

'That's because you are some sort of god-in-waiting,' he said. 'You think you're immortal, and you have an immortal weapon. Think of the dogs harrying the lion.'

'Think of my last twenty-two *papistas*,' Zos said in a harsher voice.

'So...?' Leontas said the following morning. His 'so' conveyed a great deal of meaning; in effect, it asked *How are we doing this?*

Zos had slept well and felt... excellent. It wasn't a common feeling for him on waking, and he savoured it: the lack of aches, the clear head, and the sense of... purpose.

'We go unarmed,' Zos said crisply. 'We offer no threat.'

'And it eats us,' Leontas snapped.

'I'm not sure that a couple of spears and a big shield would change that.'

Leontas looked at him for a long time, and then, with a sigh, took off his sword and laid it carefully on his grass mattress.

'You can't just leave *Terror* sitting in a cave,' Pollon said.

I will find a better master – someone cruel and mighty and worthy of me.

Zos looked at the mighty sword with something close to loathing. Since he'd taken it, it had fashioned itself into his very dream of a duelling longsword: the blade apparently solid gold, almost as long as a tall man's leg, with a hilt of ivory, crystal and gold, and the gold enamelled with a tiny scene of a herd of cattle in a stampede.

When he put it down, Zos knew a frisson of fear, and found that he'd picked it up again.

Daos' clear, sweet laugh dispelled his tremors. 'The one place Enkul-Anu will not come right now is the Vale of Jasmine,' he said. 'No one will come here.'

And without hesitation, the boy took the sword and placed it on the ground.

'A wandering shepherd...' Pollon tried.

Leontas shook his head. 'What shepherd would wander here right now, master scribe? Only a fool would face the dragon.'

Zos nodded to his friend. 'Pollon, would you stay and watch our kit?'

Pollon folded his arms over his chest. 'I'm a brave warrior,' he said. 'I'm coming with you.'

'Fools,' Leontas said again, and his laugh boomed over the valley. 'We are fools.'

Daos smiled his adolescent smile. 'Not really. We have something the dragon wants.'

Zos frowned. 'We do?'

Daos grinned. 'Dite has her eggs,' he said.

★

They had to walk all the way up the valley to its roots in the ancient volcano, just as Zos had expected. It was a hard walk; the Vale of Jasmine was full of small stones that seemed carefully crafted to get between the sandal and the bare foot, and there were spiky plants of every description whose only purpose appeared to be to ruin a man's day. The famous jasmine, which grew all along the little watercourse at the bottom of the gorge, was bare and almost lifeless.

Despite which, even in the early winter sunshine, it was beautiful.

They halted for a bite of sesame cake and sausage when the thin winter sun was high, and then plodded on.

'Long walk back tonight,' Pollon muttered.

'You're an optimist,' Zos countered.

'I am?' Pollon asked, and made Leontas laugh again. It rolled back and forth across the narrowing gorge ahead.

'He means, you think we might be alive to walk back.'

Pollon cracked a smile, and they all kept walking.

Nothing molested them; in fact, almost nothing moved but a couple of stray sheep high above them, and once, a fox darted across the trail and vanished into the jasmine. But with each step, the tendrils of reeking smoke became ever thicker fog, and then thicker yet, until they all bound their cloaks over their faces, which, of course, made the now-steep uphill walk much harder.

When a breeze rose and lifted the smoke a little, Zos peered up and thought he saw a cave mouth, well above and to the left side of the valley.

'The mouth of hell,' he said.

'Nice,' Pollon said.

'No, really,' Zos said. 'The priests say it is the mouth of hell.'

'It's definitely the source of the smoke,' Pollon said.

'I can feel the World Serpent,' Daos added. 'She's watching us.'

172

Leontas looked back at Daos, and then at Zos.

'Does he just prattle on, or do we take him seriously?'

Zos sighed. 'He's usually right. Which is annoying as hell. Usually, you can just ignore an adolescent, but in this case, no.'

Leontas rearranged his cloak and peered up. 'And we just walk into hell?'

Zos coughed.

'You first,' Leontas said, bowing deeply.

They set off again. The little trail cut back every twenty or thirty steps, and there were little side trails, probably cut by generations of sheep and goats, and then, just a hundred paces below the cave mouth, there was an enormous pile of red bones, the shreds of meat on them rotten and stinking.

'It eats a great deal,' Pollon said slowly.

'*She* eats a great deal,' Daos put in. 'And she can hear everything we say.'

'You are full of good cheer, boy,' Leontas said.

Pollon wrapped his cloak tighter, tried to take a deep breath, and gagged.

'Fifty sheep?'

'More. And that's a man. Oh, no. More than one man.' Zos' gorge rose.

Eight men.

Zos froze. The voice was clear in his head – a female voice, redolent with sorrow, and rage.

'Are you the World Serpent?' he asked.

That is the name you give me, O man.

Daos spoke up. He was last in line; they were still in single file on the narrow switchbacks of the track.

'Our friends rescued your eggs,' he said.

A blast of red-underlit smoke rolled out of the cave like the first warning of an active volcano.

What?

Daos' voice was strong with the insistence of youth. 'There were five eggs. I saw them. All like milky crystal.'

Zos felt a wave of heat against his bare legs – at first, quite pleasant on a cold day, and then, quickly, much too warm.

You interest me. Bring them to me.

Zos looked at Daos, but the young man didn't have anything more to say, so he shook his head.

'We don't have them.' He looked at Pollon, who shrugged. 'It's a long story.'

I have nothing but time. And that my eggs may still exist is easily the price of your lives. I invite you to my cave. I fear it is none too clean, but my invitation is a guest bond.

Zos had hoped the eggs might be a key to open the door, and his reason reminded him this was why they had come, and there was no cause to back down now. But the reality . . .

He realised that his knees were weak, and his hands trembling.

He made himself climb all the same.

The fear he fought was not like the terror the sword caused. There was no remembered horror, no failed test. Instead, he walked through fear the way a shepherd might walk through the pouring rain, hunched forward.

Behind him, he could hear the sound of sandals on gravel. But he wasn't really listening; mostly, he was just enduring.

And then, suddenly, it was gone. Not the smoke, or the vague but real sense of doom. But the wall of fear was gone, and he was at the entrance to the cave.

'That was unpleasant,' Leontas said.

Pollon grunted.

Daos pulled himself up onto the ledge.

'That was terrible,' he said.

Pollon said, quietly, 'Welcome to my world.'

Zos felt his lips twitch, took a look at his fellows, and made himself walk into the cave.

Welcome, said Antaboga, the World Serpent.

The mouth of the cave was perhaps the height of ten men, and the width of ten horses, tied nose to tail. A huge cave, which went back and back into full darkness. The entrance was littered with fresh bones, and the smell was horrific.

And deep within, two great eyes glowed. It was like looking at a giant cat in a dark alley. The eyes were a golden green, and they transfixed him, but their distance apart defied belief.

Pardon the smell, O man, Antaboga said. *It has been a thousand years since I fed well and my kind do not thrive in isolation.*

Zos gagged, trying to speak. He thought, *Gods, I'm going to fail and be eaten because of the smell.*

Pollon spoke, his voice thin with fear. 'Our friends have your eggs. They are far away.'

Anyone might say the same, to save their skins.

Daos piped up. 'But we know you had five eggs, and we know what they look like. Who could say the same?'

Who indeed? asked the voice. *Bide.*

A wind of death and carrion swept over them. The dragon had exhaled without fire, and as the graveyard stench faded, so did the smoke and the reek of the carcasses.

Zos drew a breath. 'We landed—' he began, and Daos spoke over him.

'You toy with us, Great One,' the young voice said. 'You know the trident freed you, and I wielded it.'

In the gloom, Leontas darted a glance at the boy.

If you wield the trident, boy, should I fear you?

'Zos said we should bear no weapon. I left it in a cave.'

You show either great wisdom or incredible folly. You left Worldbreaker in a cave? The World Serpent wheezed, and Zos wondered if she was laughing. But it seemed a good sign; the longer he was alive, the more likely it appeared that they were negotiating.

'World Serpent—' he began.

I hate that name, man.

'What should I call you?'

A roll of smoke, this time smelling like burning cedar – a good, piercing, smell.

Antaboga will do. My true name is as long as the ages I have lived.

'I am Zos of Trin,' he said. Suddenly the 'of Trin' part seemed natural. 'These are Leontas and Pollon and Daos.'

I know all these names, Zos of Trin. I was aware when you killed the gods. Indeed, I helped the Traitor keep them in check.

'The traitor?' Zos asked.

Never mind, Zos of Trin. Where are my eggs? Nothing else matters.

Pollon made a motion with his hand, and Zos nodded, happy to pass the position of spokesman.

'Great One ...' Pollon began.

Antaboga. Titles offend.

Pollon nodded. As an expert on court etiquette it made perfect sense to him that a creature as powerful as the World Serpent had her own rules.

'Antaboga,' he said, 'when you rose from the island, we all fled in different directions, in ships. Not every ship survived. But our friends took your eggs for safekeeping. Indeed ...'

He looked hard at Zos, who shrugged helplessly, having no idea what his friend was asking.

Pollon took a breath. 'I believe it was the one you call "traitor" who insisted on taking your eggs. The former god, Dite-who-was-Druku.'

Silence.

Zos had time to think, *Will I even see the wall of fire that comes down the cave?*

As his eyes adjusted and the smoke dissipated, he could see more than eyes now; he could see the whole of her enormous, magnificent head. He'd seen the rise of the cedar smoke from her nostrils. They were only about ten horse-lengths away.

At least it will be quick, he thought.

Hefa-Asus

'That thing stinks like carrion,' Nicté spat.

Hefa-Asus had cut a big circle of demon skin from the hide he'd taken in the fight at Dekhu. He'd kept it rolled tight and salted, on the principle that anything that worked on cowhide would work on demon skin, and it had, sort of. The hide was dry and incredibly tough, hard yet yielding, like the best boiled leather, and he had to wet it to form it, and now it stank worse than any hide he'd ever prepared.

'Did you take its brain?' Nicté asked.

She had her hands on her hips, and she was, without a doubt, the most annoying apprentice he'd ever had. Also the most attractive. He banished that thought.

'I was busy—' he began.

'Every creature carries enough brain to tan its skin,' she said impatiently.

'What a pleasant people yours must be,' he said. 'Think of the experiments you've done.'

She grinned wickedly.

'Regardless, I'm not planning to tan it,' he said. 'I want it hard and thick.'

'Rawhide,' she agreed. 'It might be even stronger if you boiled it in wax.'

'Godless heavens!' Era spat from the command deck above them. 'You will not boil that thing in anything aboard this ship.'

Hefa-Asus was tempted to be petty. 'I wasn't planning to,' he growled slowly. 'I was planning—'

'You don't want to waste it,' Nicté said. 'Demons are hard to kill.'

Era grunted. 'Something tells me we'll get more, though,' she said.

The first day out they saw an unknown sail on the far horizon, well north and east – too far away to determine if it was a Jeker. The second morning brought three more sails, and the closest bore the deadly notch that identified her as a dangerous enemy. But as the flotilla bore almost due north on the world's wind for Dendrowna, the Jekers would have had to decide to give chase instantly – a long chase against high odds. Era's squadron were all merchant ships, but six tubby merchants made a difficult target even for the rapacious Jekers.

Hefa-Asus paid little attention to the potential threat once it was clear they were unlikely to face imminent combat. Instead, he worked on a dozen projects that had languished during their weeks on the Hakran beach. The tough, chitinous demon hide was only one of them, and he continued experimenting with the star-stone they had aboard, both finished and ore.

He mostly worked on the broad amidships deck of the *Untroubled Swan*. The Dry One had settled itself into the fore-peak, once again walling itself into a cocoon of dense webbing. Hefa-Asus quietly harvested some of the web fibre and experimented with it, and succeeded in making an incredibly strong cord after several experiments with drop spindles. At one point, he had Nicté and two new apprentices each twisting a thread in their hands while spinning it in the opposite direction as the three threads were bound into a thicker cord, but the process was tedious and the result uneven.

Throughout, Jawala sat in a little shade under the mainmast, dressed in white. Sometimes she watched them, but mostly her eyes were unseeing, her legs crossed, and Hefa-Asus assumed that she was deep in meditation. The process interested him, but the potential of the Dry One's silk interested him more.

On the fourth day they touched at a river delta on the coast of Rasna. The land thrust out boldly from the sea here, with towering cliffs and deep bays very different from the flat sandy lands to the south, but the villagers were Hakran. The tidal wave had struck here, but aside from destroying all the carefully built stairs from the villages down to the sea, and some boats which had been badly stowed, it hadn't done any damage to the people living high on the cliffs.

They traded for food, and Jawat took his soldiers well upstream of the villages to get fresh water – including two of the captured Jekers, now silent and dour conscripts who weren't trusted by their mates. Hefa-Asus knew they'd be watched every minute, but including them was an experiment, like his work with the demon hide.

Hundreds of villagers came to the beach, risking their hastily rebuilt stairs, to see Jawala and hear her speak, but she spoke little, only sitting on the sand under the magnificent cliffs, staring at nothing.

Meanwhile, Hefa-Asus traded for tools, built a small oven, and cast bronze on the beach to the delight of the locals. Nicté built her own oven, and when Atosa produced a fine bull out of wax, they cast fifty of them and sold them to the villagers, along with mirrors. Bronze mirrors were very difficult to make, because the casting had to be perfect and so did the polishing, but there was a very fine stone, a volcanic pumice, that was available locally. Atosa set a dozen untrained refugees, all former slaves, to polishing while Hefa-Asus looked on approvingly.

Hefa-Asus wasn't the only one who approved. Era exclaimed in delight at the bull, which was small and fat and beautiful, comfortable in the palm of the hand, and well suited to the traditions and art of the Hakrans.

'I thought we were going to run out of trade goods,' she said.

'Eventually we'll run out of bronze,' Hefa-Asus said. 'If the Jekers hadn't made such significant contributions, we'd already be running short.'

Era's delight became irritation, which was her usual look, lately.

'Where in Kur's seven hells do we get more bronze?' she asked.

Hefa-Asus shrugged. 'The Poche of Waxtekka have copper. The Tiatoni and the Nikali have tin – not much, but enough to trade. The Caktul of Lakamha are swimming in tin. We can buy it at Vetluna.'

Era made a face. 'Sometimes I think this is all fucking impossible,' she said. 'How do we buy copper and tin?'

Nicté raised an eyebrow. 'The best tin comes from the west, upriver. As Hefa-Asus says, Vetluna is the main tin port.'

Era looked thoughful. 'Where have I heard the name Vetluna?'

Dite, who was helping cast bronze, turned her head.

'Gamash of Weshwesh smashed the Dardanian fleets there, thirty-odd mortal years ago.' She smiled. 'On the surface, it was a petty quarrel between the gods. Actually, it was a fight for tin resources. Even the gods need tin.'

Hefa-Asus had been making a small file from star-stone, scoring it with obsidian to make the grooves. Now he looked up.

'Why don't I know that?'

Dite smiled sweetly, her extravagantly beautiful face a little unsuited to her patronising tone.

'Your Nikali and your Tiatoni and the upriver Caktul helped Gamash fight the Dardanians so that they could continue their near-monopoly of tin. You think the tin comes from Nikali. A little of it does. But as Nicté says, the best tin is from far upriver beyond Vetluna.'

Hefa-Asus thought for a moment. 'Even a small cargo of

tin would buy us almost anything we wanted in Waxtekka,' he said. 'The grace of the ajaw, for a start. The Nikali strangle our metalwork. It's one of the reasons I emigrated.' He looked at Dite. 'How do you know all this?'

She smiled seductively. Or maybe that was her normal smile and she couldn't help it.

'I helped plan it all,' she said. 'I mean, I was drunk and male at the time, but it was my idea to deny the Dardanians access to the tin.'

Era leant forward, fascinated. 'Why?'

Dite shrugged. 'I needed to create a solid reason to make Enkul-Anu avert the destruction of the Hakrans.'

Jawala, startled from her trance, looked at the former god.

'Why?' she asked.

Dite batted her eyelashes. 'I have a soft spot for people who don't make war and do write manuals about exciting sex,' she said. 'Also, Sypa was pushing for the destruction of the Hakrans.'

'Why?' Jawala asked.

Dite shrugged. 'Why do the gods do anything? Maybe she had a dalliance with the god-king Atrios? Maybe Enkul-Anu was ploughing some furrow in Rasna and she was jealous? Maybe it was a whim?'

Jawala looked at the former god of drunken revels as if seeing her for the first time.

'So you have been conspiring against the gods for some time,' she said.

Dite's peal of laughter was long and loud. 'My dear and re- vered Jawala,' she said when she'd stopped laughing. 'All the gods *do* is conspire. That's it. It is every one against all the others. Don't offer me any praise for it – I was playing my own game for my own ends.'

'And now?' Era asked, hands on hips. 'Are you still playing?'

Dite lay back in the sand. She was wearing a sort of sari that left little of her to the imagination, and the sand clinging to her lower legs was somehow all the more enticing, at least to Hefa-Asus, who had to put his head down and apply himself to making his small file as if it required his complete concentration.

'Of course I'm still playing,' she said. 'But I've chosen a side.'

Era didn't want to have this conversation, so she was surprised to hear herself ask the next question.

'And will you change sides again?'

Dite crossed her legs and lay back. 'I understand why you might fear that, my love. But there is no turning back, now. We are committed to pulling down the established order. I have done things that make me unforgivable.'

'We?' Era snapped.

'I have a few allies,' Dite said. 'Don't enquire too closely, there's a dear.'

'I really don't like being patronised,' Era said slowly. 'And as the self-appointed leader of this expedition, I think I need to know.'

Dite made a face. 'I have already said too much. It's not my secret, darling. And you worry too much.'

Era, who had been sitting cross-legged on the sand, rose. Her face was red with anger.

'I'm carrying the needs and hopes of two hundred people,' she said.

'But you like that sort of thing. Let's have a cup of wine.' Dite's face looked open, cheerful ... alluring.

'Fuck you!' Era snapped, and walked off.

'Any time,' Dite said, but then made a tut-tutting sound to herself. 'I didn't do that well.'

Nicté laughed. 'No, you didn't.'

★

A day later they were back at sea. The wind was from the west, and they had to reach, tack, and reach again – a slow passage, but the unusual west wind guaranteed that no Jeker would see or chase them.

Hefa-Asus had finished his small file of hardened star-stone, and he used it carefully on the small bronze cogs he'd cast, making them crisp. The idea had come into his head a piece at a time: a way to turn a handle and make three dowels rotate together while counter-rotating individually. He'd seen cogs before – big ones in mills and once, in Narmer, in an irrigation pump.

His first model was hopeless, and he realised that the tolerances required were much finer than he'd expected. He started again, while Jawala watched, and was working on a bronze baseplate to keep all the little axles in place when Jawala spoke.

'The world is dying.'

Hefa-Asus was using a punch, working carefully to avoid deforming his piece. When his hole was the right diameter, he looked up.

'I'm not particularly surprised.' He took Jawala seriously, a respect he didn't pay to many people. 'How do you know?'

She glanced at him, very much the old Jawala – sharp as a good spear, and a little annoyed to be questioned.

'I can feel the world,' she said.

Hefa-Asus found the little bronze axle rod in a fold of his kilt and began to fit it to the backplate.

'Ah?' he asked.

'If I concentrate, I can feel the world,' she said. 'It is a different level of consciousness, I suppose. I think it was always there. I think I understand why we don't take life, or eat meat. It's particularly obvious when we're at sea.'

'And the world is dying?' He motioned to Era, on the

183

command deck, and she looked at him. He beckoned with his left hand, trying not to draw Jawala's attention.

Era came down the short ladder and handed him a cup of fresh water, which he drank off greedily.

Jawala didn't look up. 'It's dying almost everywhere,' she said. 'The gods are killing it. They take too much from the *Aura*, from the ground, from the people.' She looked at Era. 'Using magic is killing us.'

Era rolled her eyes. 'Using magic is killing us?' she repeated.

'The world... no, that's too simple. But as a model... the world makes the *Aura*. And when we use it, we take from a diminishing pool.' Jawala looked disturbed by her insight.

Era settled on the deck. 'And you just discovered this?' she said, in what she'd probably intended to be a frank tone. Instead, she sounded disgusted.

'The people who chose me to be Given gave me—'

Era's eyes narrowed. 'How much magic do we consume, compared to the gods?'

Jawala's black eyebrows furrowed. 'Very little, of course, but in principle—'

'Spare me any more principles,' Era snapped. 'We're running a revolution. Maybe we should deliberately run the world out of magic. That would even the scales.'

'Era!' Jawala said. 'That would be a sacrilege!'

Era smiled grimly. 'No. That would be a strategy.'

Later, Hefa-Asus met Era in the forepeak, he collecting more web and she delivering food to Bror and Nannu, who stayed close to the Dry One.

'I'm sorry,' he said. 'But I thought you needed to hear what Jawala is saying.'

Era nodded. 'I shouldn't have been high and mighty with Jawala,' she said. 'But we're not getting through this without oceans of blood, and worse. She has appointed herself my conscience, and I don't really need one right now.'

Hefa-Asus smiled grimly. 'I've never felt the need myself,' he admitted.

On the ninth day off the Hakran lowlands, Hefa-Asus turned the handle on his new machine, and Tarhu and Mawat fed Dry One web into each of three counter-rotating quills.

'Careful!' he snapped. 'The thread must be …'

'Fine and even,' Tarhu said cheerfully.

And it was. They had made hundreds of feet of it. Then they cut the thread into three lengths and put one into each quill, each held by a piece of wood, and Tarhu turned the handle, and the thread was bound into cord – a hundred feet of it, no thicker than a grain of rice, which glowed an attractive silver-grey.

With one end tied to the mainmast, the three of them couldn't break it.

'That's marvellous,' Era said. 'What's it for?'

Hefa-Asus shrugged. 'No idea,' he said. 'I just wanted to see if it would work.'

Nicté smiled at him. 'Me, too.'

The Bear and the Donkey

'Is he with us or against us?' Temis, the bear, asked.

'Who?' Nannu, the donkey, muttered.

'Druku?'

'More *she* than *he*, just now,' the donkey brayed. 'And I don't know.'

'But they know we're here?' Bror growled.

'Yep,' Nannu grunted.

'But we're not on the same side!'

Nannu turned his head so that two dark eyes both fixed on the powerful bulk of the bear.

'I'm not sure *you and I* are on the same side,' he said. 'You joined the new lot as soon as they were winning.'

'I wasn't powerful enough to do anything else. And I'm rotting them from inside!' After a pause, Temis growled, 'Or I was. I don't have a plan now.'

Nannu brayed a laugh. 'That's all done, sister. I don't have a plan either, just a sort of wild gamble. My guess is that a wind called Antaboga came up and blew everyone's cards right off the table.'

'So what do we do now?'

'Lie low and hope no one notices us,' the donkey suggested. 'Anyway, I like these mortals. So there.'

Zos

Zos made himself walk deeper into the cave. He wasn't sure why; perhaps as an indication of trust, or perhaps because he was always proving himself. To himself.

He made it a few steps, so that he could see the outline of the nostrils and the shape of the World Serpent's head. Two great fangs emerged from its upper lip, each the height of a man.

'We don't know where our friends are,' Zos admitted.

So my eggs are lost?

Zos shook his head. 'No. I doubt it. I *can* tell you where they are headed. Would you swear not to harm them?'

A scent of burnt meat rolled over him and he realised the behemoth had exhaled slightly.

My kind are naturally duplicitous, man. Why would you keep a bargain with a gnat?

Zos considered that.

Behind him, Daos said, 'Viewed through human eyes, you are in our debt. We freed you.'

Indeed. Although I suspect you were the unwitting agents of another power.

Zos snorted. He couldn't help himself.

'You have that right,' he admitted.

Deep in the shadows, he could see that the creature's massive head was lying on a pair of taloned forefeet, not unlike a dog waiting to be fed. The sight steadied him. He was growing used to the scale of the serpent.

'Why do you hate the title "World Serpent"?' he asked.

I am a being like other beings. I did not make the world and I am unlikely to break it.

'Like other beings?'

Indeed. Once my kind filled the skies. Here and … elsewhere. Now I am the last. But when my eggs hatch …

'We are not your foes,' Zos said.

The great eyes blinked. It was as if a lantern went out and was relit, and Zos realised that the eyes actually shone with some inner fire.

I admit that it is possible we are not foes. After all, I have not killed you all.

Zos' mind was moving like a runaway horse. He thought of Makar; he thought of his intention to take an army to Narmer. He thought of Era and Hefa-Asus.

He thought, *Nothing ventured, nothing gained.*

'I would propose an alliance,' he said.

Would you make an alliance with dung beetles, O man?

'I would, if by doing so I could take down the immortal gods.'

He forced himself to stand straight. *I am negotiating with a dragon.* He had a moment of curious distance, as if he stood watching himself.

If you make me laugh, I fear all of you will be drowned in smoke, burned to cinders, and flung out of the mouth of the cave. Antaboga's eyes were on Zos, and they blinked again. *My kind are subtle and duplicitous, but we prided ourselves on returning good for good and evil for evil. I will credit you with releasing me from an aeon of torment and imprisonment.*

Zos released a breath he hadn't known he was holding.

And it is surprisingly pleasant to converse, even in your painfully slow way. Tell me your proposal. For my part, the worst I'll do is refuse. Your lives are safe.

Zos pondered. What alliance did he want with this creature?

'I suggest...' he began, and hesitated. He could be condemning Era, Jawala and Aanat to death.

He shook his head. 'When mortals make alliances,' he said, 'each has something to gain, and most often, each has some hold on the other. There is some mutual benefit.'

When mortals make alliances, they do so from immediate expediency, and they betray each other the moment a new circumstance arises. You are mortal. I am mortal.

Zos contemplated this. Behind him, Pollon said, 'You are mortal?'

I will die. You will die. Enkul-Anu will die. I have never met a creature who is not mortal. Death can be cheated for a long time, but in the end, there's always something. If I had but world enough, and time, I would show you that all things have an end.

Zos considered that.

'We share a common foe.' He didn't say it with emphasis; he wasn't sure it was true.

Indeed, O man. Enkul-Anu imprisoned me. I would like to see his kind gone.

'His kind?' Pollon asked, but Zos ignored him and drove over the scholar's words.

'I can tell you where to meet our friends. You would have to negotiate with them for your eggs. And then, when you have your eggs, you join us against the gods.'

The so-called gods are still very powerful.

'A handful of mortals killed three of them,' Zos said with pride.

With my help and the help of two rebel gods, you killed two. Nisroch still lives, and will emerge stronger than when he fell.

'Oh,' Zos said.

Two weak and foolish gods.

'We released you, Antaboga.' Daos spoke confidently.

And when we join forces to destroy your so-called gods? What then? Are my brood and your scuttling hordes to live in peace and harmony?

Zos shrugged. 'Perhaps,' he said. 'I doubt that we're powerful enough to harm you.'

By the time you bring down Enkul-Anu and his legions, you will be powerful enough to harm me. That is the way of the game, O man. Think! Once they were as you are now. Then they stormed heaven and made themselves rulers. And the rulers before them fought my kind and won. They were all once men and women like you.

Zos chewed on this in shocked silence.

I have seen many aeons of this world, O man. So it goes.

Daos said, 'There is one who does not change. And she is our ally.'

Nothing is stranger than her role, Daos, except perhaps your own.

Daos grunted.

Zos raised an arm – a godborn habit, the way orators were trained to speak.

'So be it,' he said carefully. 'You are hiding in a cave, fearing Enkul-Anu's wrath. We slink from island to island, hoping to foment rebellion. What do we have to lose from working together? If you leave Lazba, I can raise an army here. If you go to Dendrowna, you can find your eggs. Each of us has something we didn't have before.'

Dendrowna, O man? That is a distant place I haven't seen in aeons. But I give you this — it is a place where I might live safe from our common foe.

Zos winced as he realised he had surrendered information and received very little in return.

'I could write a letter,' Pollon said. 'For our friends.'

Go, the dragon said. *Return tomorrow for my decision.*

Zos fought his own eagerness to be gone.

'Will you guarantee our lives, tomorrow?'

Why would I? I gave you no such guarantee today, and yet you came.

Leontas, who had been silent all this time, said, 'She is toying with us like a cat with a half-chewed mouse.'

Nay, lion-killer. I never play with food. Go and return.

It was full dark when they reached their own cave to find everything exactly where it had been left. Zos uncovered the coals he'd left in a pot with fire-fungus, and built them a roaring blaze while Pollon laid out the makings of a simple soup: sausage, parsley, barley. Daos heated the clay pot. Zos constantly wanted to advise him, to make him go slow, but the boy managed to heat the water without cracking the pot, and he threw the rabbit bones in.

'We can tell stories until the broth is ready for the barley,' Leontas suggested.

'We could decide what to say to the dragon,' Zos replied.

Pollon watched the broth for a few minutes, carefully adding wood chips and twigs to keep the fire just the right temperature under the pot.

'I'd prefer the storytelling,' he said. 'Nothing we decide here will make any difference. It's up to the dragon now.'

Daos spoke up. 'Once upon a time, there were many dragons.

There were so many that they filled the skies like ducks in the delta of Narmer, coming upriver at nightfall.'

'Go on, boy,' Leontas said.

'When did you go to Narmer?' Zos asked quietly.

'Where does this story come from, Daos?' Pollon asked.

'From me,' Daos replied. 'Listen. The dragons filled the air and every mountain had a nest, and then they made war against one another – for nests, for lineage, for pride and for sport. And men were few and wary, like mice in a granary full of cats. They made simple weapons of stone, and moved in full daylight only, because the dragons saw them better at night.

'Interesting,' Leontas said. 'Is that true?'

'Most things that I say are true,' Daos said with some humour. 'One evening, a lone hunter was late dragging a deer carcass back to his cave in the hills – perhaps this very cave,' he added.

Pollon smiled. 'Careful, lad. Don't strain the credulity of your listeners too much.'

Daos looked down like a bashful maiden, and then went on. 'His name might have been Krnos, or maybe it was Ranos. Whatever his name, he took too long, and was caught in the valley at nightfall. Even as he thought of ways to hide, there was a shrill cry that froze him, the rush of wings, and he was plucked from the ground and carried away.'

'Excellent,' Leontas said. 'This is definitely the story I wanted to hear before I slept.'

Pollon lit a taper of twisted bark and raised it high to look into the pot in the gloom of the cave; it was like a star rising.

'Water's boiling,' he said.

He began to put herbs into the pot and stirred it carefully.

'I wish we had a spoon,' he said.

'I am before you.' Leontas held up a stick and a bronze tool like a curved knife, but without a point. He was carving a spoon.

Zos silently handed the scribe a pair of wooden tongs, cunningly made from two sticks and wrapped in vine. He tried them experimentally, and then began fetching the denuded rabbit bones from the pot, being careful not to damage the delicate clay.

'Go on,' he said to Daos.

'The dragon fetched him to its nest, beside a cave at the head of a valley.'

'Perhaps this very cave,' Leontas put in.

Daos grinned. 'Perhaps! Anyway, hours passed as Krnos waited to be eaten, but when day came, the dragon lay down and went to sleep.

'Several hours later, while examining the rocks around the nest for any possibility of escape, the man heard the rush of wings out over the valley, and there were two dragons, apparently hunting by day. They flew very low, and their cunning hide matched the stone, but the hunter was trained to see things that moved, and he saw them. In a moment, he knew that they were coming for the nest.'

'Ahhh,' Leontas said.

'And the man asked himself, "Do I flee, or do I awaken my captor?"'

Pollon was smiling. He was adding barley now, and some wild carrots and salt.

'Good story,' he said.

'What do you think?' Daos asked.

Zos scratched his beard and worried about lice.

'Thorny problem,' he admitted. 'Wake the dragon, hope you're right and it's grateful for the warning. Slip away and leave it to its fate, hope that in the tussle you're ignored.'

Leontas grunted. 'Take a sharpened stick and poke out a dragon's eye,' he said. 'Just as the other two come in. Prove yourself worthy.'

Pollon shook his head. 'Hide under the nest or in the twigs and await events.'

Zos was shaking his head. 'Not enough information. How hard is it to climb out of the nest?'

Daos smiled. 'Almost impossible. Very risky. And the twigs it's made of are full-sized trees.'

'You're making this up,' Leontas accused him. And then, with his wide smile, 'I like it.'

Daos spread his hands. 'The man woke his captor. The dragon – *his* dragon – immediately flew off and deterred the others, before it returned.'

'And had him as a snack,' Pollon laughed.

'And sent him home alive,' Leontas said.

'And they became allies,' Daos said triumphantly. 'The man and his clan protected the dragon by day, building a fort of earth around the nest. In turn, the dragon protected the man and his family, which grew and grew.'

Zos smiled grimly. 'I'm not sure I like where this is going.'

Pollon was stirring a thickening soup with the new wooden spoon Leontas had handed him.

'Eventually, the dragons with human helpers triumphed over the dragons who had none, raiding their nests, killing them or destroying their eggs.' Daos seemed to be in a trance. But his voice was good, like a good harpist's voice, or a *rhapsode*, a singer of epics.

'So dragons fought among themselves?' Leontas asked. 'That must have been … awe-inspiring!'

'And then what happened?' Zos asked.

Daos smiled. 'And then humans were well fed and prosperous. They had time to make things, to sit and think. Then dragons taught them the properties of stone and metal, and men became smiths, and then dragons taught men about the *Aura*, and people became mages and sorcerers.'

'I see,' Zos said.

'Bet this doesn't go so well for dragons,' Leontas put in. 'Given how many we are, and how few she is.'

'And so gradually there came to be more people and fewer dragons,' Daos said dreamily.

'Gradually?' Zos asked. 'As in, there were aeons of conflict?'

'Dragons enjoyed fighting among themselves as much as people do,' Daos said. 'But there were never as many dragons as people.'

'Druku's sacred balls.' Leontas laughed. 'So they did themselves in?'

'In part. Now, mostly the dragons ate a form of wild bull – the aurochs. But men slaughtered them in great hunts, and finally there were no more herds. Too late, the dragons who were left decided to wage war against the men. But there were powerful women and men who could contend with the dragons – the ancient great ones, of whom we are forbidden to speak. Their names were Theni, Goddess of War, Shemeg, God of the Sun, and others. They broke the dragons' power.'

'Shit,' Zos said. 'The gods before these useless gods made war on the dragons? Don't you think we needed to know this yesterday?'

Daos shrugged. 'I didn't know this yesterday.'

Pollon grunted something, and stirred the soup.

'And as our great serpent said,' Daos said, 'before they were gods, they were humans.'

'Perfect,' Leontas said. 'How's the soup?'

'Done,' Pollon said.

Zos' dreams were full of fire and blood.

Never leave me, the sword moaned. **Never leave me again. Or I'll find someone better.**

Six days' travel up the increasingly rocky coast. Six days of careful food rationing and careful management of the wind, which grew weaker and more whimsical the farther north the *Untroubled Swan* led her little flotilla of mismatched vessels.

Two days out from Vetluna, by Aanat's expert estimation, the sea was a darker blue, deep and cold when she dipped a bucket for a morning wash. Off the starboard side, a pod of whales slipped alongside the ships – a dozen great creatures. One leapt the height of a man above the sea, its whole bulk, four times the length of a chariot and team, crashing back into the sea in a cloud of spray.

Era was reaching for a spear when Jawala put a hand on her arm.

'We love the whales,' she said. 'They are no threat.'

Era let the words *sea monster* die on her lips. The vast animals, so big that they fooled the eye and made something atavistic inside her head want to cringe away, slipped playfully in and out of the water.

Aanat came on deck and began to smile, and soon all the Hakrans were watching them. Miti stripped her tunic off and dived in fearlessly. Era saw her surface well out from the *Untroubled Swan*, her naked back reflecting the sun as she slipped through the sea as effortlessly as the big whales. She caught the dorsal fin of one and it pulled her along and she shrieked in joy.

Era thought it was the bravest thing she'd ever seen.

'Makes me wish I could swim,' Nicté said.

'You *can* swim,' Pavi said.

'Not like that,' Nicté said in open admiration.

Pavi stripped and leapt into the cold water, and Jawala and Aanat followed. Under orders, Mokshi took in the mainsail and brought the ship to, rising and falling on a heavy swell, as every Hakran in the flotilla swam with the whales.

'The Dardanians kill them in vast sea-hunts,' Taha said to her. He and half a dozen of his scouts were aboard the *Untroubled Swan* after a terse conversation with Jawala. He glanced at Nicté, whom he clearly admired. 'I, too, would swim, if I had the skill.'

Nicté favoured him with a grin. 'It would be a mighty thing, swimming with these happy monsters.' She was watching them intently. 'How do the Dardanians kill them?'

'It takes ten or twenty boats,' Taha said. 'Many spears, and long ropes. I was an oar slave for one such hunt. A single cut from a great tail can smash a boat and kill a dozen men.'

Drakon, the giant, came to the rail. His weight made the ship heel just a little more. He watched the whales with a smile that lit his face. Lan Thena hesitated for a long time, and then slipped out of her short *heton* behind the mast and leapt into the sea on the far side while none of them were looking. But she shrieked when she hit the water, unprepared for the cold.

Era ran to the weather side and leant out.

'You all right?' she shouted.

Lan Thena was kicking and coughing, but not drowning.

'It's … fine … when … you … get … used …' she managed, and then rolled, kicked and was gone, swimming under water.

Hefa-Asus had joined them at the rail by the time Era recrossed the deck. In fact, the *Untroubled Swan* and every other sailing vessel in the fleet was listing, as virtually everyone on board watched the whales spout and disport off the starboard side.

'My people hunt them, too,' he said. 'A dozen boats and some brave people.'

Era was shaking her head. She looked forward, and there was Bror, leaning on the rail like a human, watching the whales, and then, to her astonishment, the bear slipped over the side into the sea as well.

'Bror!' Era felt a strong possessiveness towards that bear; Bror had saved her life in the fight with the gods. Lately she had begun to act with something approaching human attention, looking at people, sniffing the air appreciatively at mealtimes, and sitting with Era once on a starry evening.

The bear also avoided Dite as if she had a dread disease, and the feeling was clearly mutual.

Era ran barefoot along the deck, looking over the side every third step, but the bear was gone. She only saw her again when she was almost to the bow.

Big and heavily furred, the brown bear was a clumsy figure aboard ship. But in the water she was surprisingly agile and very fast. And graceful, Era saw, when Bror's snout broke the surface for a breath as the powerful legs drove her along.

…and then Nannu went over the side as well.

Era froze. *Did the donkey just glare at me?*

She leant over in time to see…

That can't be right.

All the hair on her head seemed to stand up, and the back of her neck tingled as if from the tickle of lightning. Whatever was passing under the ship was vast beyond the huge size of the other sea creatures. As she watched, a dorsal fin passed under her, and that fin was the size of the ship. Era had never, ever felt her insignificance more powerfully.

Has that terrible thing eaten Nannu?

I loved that donkey.

She realised that she had screamed. The whole ship rocked as everyone at the rail leant over to watch the leviathan pass under them.

Where is Nannu?

And then, very suddenly, the massive creature dived, even as sailors were calling out to each other – not in fear. Definitely not in fear.

Era looked at Mokshi, standing at the steering oar.

He grinned. 'No better luck than to see him! The lord of the sea, we call him.'

When she looked down again, she could just see a giant fluke disappearing into the fathomless darkness. The sight made her feel very small, very insignificant.

And where is Lan Thena?

Era was still looking for the donkey when Aanat came back aboard, cold, dripping wet and unashamedly naked, and he took charge of the command deck. The Hakrans were training all the others as sailors, and he used the occasion as an opportunity to teach a dozen newly liberated people how to get the ship underway. Era watched with amazement as she saw Tarhu holding the sheet with cautious competence, letting it slip through her calloused hands until the mainsail was drawing and the ship had resumed its course. Taha was at the steering oar.

Era, who had no real status at sea because she lacked the requisite skills, approached Aanat cautiously. She didn't want to step on someone else's authority; she knew where that led. But…

'We have a lot of people… still over the side,' she said. 'And Bror, and Nannu.'

Aanat grinned. 'Hakrans are strong swimmers,' he said. 'So are bears. And the donkey is coming aboard again right now.'

He pointed amidships, where Nannu suddenly brayed with all his might as Mokshi and Bravah got him in a sling and raised him to the deck.

Era ran to him, patting its wet hide. 'Where did you go?' she asked.

The donkey brayed again. People were coming over the side now, and Era looked at the man-high swell, the occasional wind-driven whitecap, and the spouting whales, and shook her head. She couldn't imagine going into those dark depths on such a day, and Jawala, twice her age, had stripped and dropped in as if going for a bath.

'The bear...' Era began.

Aanat nodded. 'I saw her. Better swimmer than me!'

He found his kilt on the deck, went below, and came back almost immediately with towels. He rubbed himself all over, getting the salt off, and then tossed Jawala a towel as she came up the side. She was almost red with the cold, but her grin was the purest Era had seen on the Hakran woman in weeks. Era grinned in response.

'You've made all of us who cannot swim very jealous,' she said.

Nicté joined her immediately.

'That was beautiful!' she said. 'I long to swim with the glorious fish! And that monster! I will never imagine myself important again!'

Aanat laughed. 'We'll add swimming to the sailing courses,' he offered.

Jawala was glowing, and she kissed her husband on the nose.

'Only the best men think to have a towel for their wives,' she said.

Aanat's grin looked like it might crack his face open, and Era felt an urge to look away. Aanat's open face had revealed all his fears: that his wife was lost to him in this new role as a Given. But some deep question had been answered in the last half an hour. And Era breathed an inner sigh of relief. The time on the beach had revealed how dependent she was on her Hakran navigators. They weren't just good at sea. They were good at almost everything.

Looking at Aanat, standing in his kilt by the port side steering oar, watching over the flotilla and clearly waiting for everyone to recover their swimmers and get under sail, she made a face, and realised that Nicté was watching her.

'They are very complete people,' Nicté said. 'I would never have thought that I could so admire people who do not fight.'

Era nodded silently, not sure exactly what she wanted to say.

Hefa-Asus grunted. 'Fighting is overrated.'

Nicté all but spat. 'Easy for you to say, big as you are. Who could threaten you?'

Era watched the shimmer between the two of them – a tension like that between two good dancers, or sparring partners in the fighting ring – and turned her face away so that they would not see her smile at them. Hefa-Asus obviously admired the Northern woman. Nicté ... Era was never quite sure what Nicté was thinking, except when it came to devious war strategy.

'Where do you think our deserters are now?' Era asked, to change the subject.

Nicté smiled deviously. 'Somewhere far away, and if we are blessed by fortune, already making trouble.'

She leant out over the rail and got Lan Thena's hand in hers. Era hadn't even seen the Dardanian woman approach the ship. Then Nicté snatched a cotton towel from Aanat's hands and wrapped the Dardanian as she came up the side.

Era wanted to raise an eyebrow, but instead she saw a thoughtful look change Drakon's face from bestial to ... almost handsome.

'Thanks,' he said to Nicté.

Era looked a question at Nicté after the unlikely pair walked back across the deck.

'She thinks she is ugly,' Nicté said. 'She doesn't like us to look at her.' She shrugged. 'My mother was clawed by a bear. She was the same.'

Era smiled, because her people were binding together, and that was ... wonderful.

Before the sun began to drop from the sky, Bror came over the side amidships, where the *Untroubled Swan* was closest to the water. Miti came with her, cold through and needing a woollen blanket, but beaming with joy. Bravah came and put his arms around her until her lips had a little life in them. Everyone aboard laughed when the bear shook herself and blasted water over all the people who'd tried to stay dry. Then she cuddled up to the donkey.

Aanat put an arm around Miti's shoulders. She was crying – not with grief but plain joy.

Era felt a deep pain in her chest.

When have I known simple love like this? Would Dite hug me when I cried for joy?

She dismissed such thoughts with a shiver at her own temerity.

Above her, on the command deck, Aanat gave a shout.

'Dendrowna!' he called.

Just as for the whales, everyone came to the rail – this time in the bow.

Only the sharpest eyes could make out the sliver of land, a mere line of black that came and went on the swell.

But suddenly Era could smell Dendrowna, and the rich, piny scent mixed with the salt sea which filled her with something not unlike Miti's joy, and stayed with her for the rest of her life as one of the finest scents she'd ever experienced.

'I love it, too,' Dite said, putting her arms around Era that night. 'Of all the scents of mortal earth, this is the best. Better than all the foolish perfumes of heaven.'

Era was tempted to ask why, now, Dite chose to admit that she knew how heaven smelt. But the arms around her were warm, and Era wasn't interested in conflict just then. She burrowed closer, listening to the snores of a dozen people around them. And soon enough, she was asleep, too.

Chapter Seven

Zos

The trip back to the World Serpent's cave seemed shorter. Zos was familiar with this effect on trails, and he moved along, despite the annoyance of the wound in his leg. It had been weeks and the hole in his shin wouldn't heal, and it hurt when the vegetation caught at it.

He was surprised to find that he had achieved something like fatalism; he wasn't particularly concerned about the dragon, though his sense of danger fully admitted the possibility of nearly instant death at the claws and flame of the World Serpent, whatever she called herself. It wasn't that he didn't care; it was that, as Daos and Pollon had agreed, it was clear that it was all up to her. She held all the knucklebones, and he held none.

Today he wore *Terror*, and Daos carried Earthbreaker, and neither was meant as a threat. Zos felt that they'd been foolish to leave such mighty artifacts behind, and his dreams had been too clear to be forgotten easily.

Daos carried the clay pot and they all had their cloaks; whatever befell them today, they were either dead men, or headed for home.

Well up the gully to the dragon's cave, the feeling of fatalism vanished, and Zos felt a sudden spike of fear. He almost smiled to himself.

'I prefer the fear,' he said.

'What?' Pollon asked.

'Never mind.' Zos pushed himself up to the lip of the clearing before the ancient cave. Today it smelled like a priest's burnt offering of a sacrificed animal – at least to Pollon and Zos, it smelt clean.

'Antaboga,' Zos called.

Here, O man.

'You have decided?' Pollon said.

'She decided yesterday,' Daos said.

Leontas laughed. And it was unforced, and in that moment, Zos rather admired the bigger man. He could not have managed a genuine laugh, just then.

'She may not play with her food, but she did play with us,' he said.

I agree. I find you amusing. Or perhaps I'm just delighted to have someone to talk to. An aeon trapped in a volcanic vent is not as pleasant as you might imagine. What if I'd gone mad?

That was not an idea that Zos particularly wanted to contemplate.

I accept your offer, and I will formally call you friends. My kind are slippery as snakes and fast as eagles, but we don't often lie directly. So I will speak plainly. I will go to Dendrowna – this simple act will show that I am doing what we have agreed. If you understand that I place the safety of my brood above any plan of yours, or even my own, then you have the measure of our alliance. I can scarcely be more open or honest.

Daos stepped forward and said, 'Friends like the dragon Daltarova and Krnos the Clever?'

There was a flash of fire; the whole cave filled with smoke. Zos choked, and Pollon tried to hide his mewl of terror.

Someone is a lore master. And who benefited more, little godling?

Somewhere in the smoke, Daos stood his ground. 'Krnos was never disloyal.'

203

And you will defend my nest, Earthbreaker?

Zos spoke into the silence and the smoke. 'We'll do better. We will turn the eyes of the gods away from you, and away from Dendrowna.'

I find you worthy, Zos of Trin. Go well. And know my blessing carries weight. Leontas Lion-killer, I do not see far into the future – if I could, no one would have buried me in a volcano. But I see this – with Zos or without him, you die a happy man. And that is no small blessing. Daos the godling, you I cannot see. Be merciful when you can, and remember that in the end, they will turn on you.

'I know,' Daos said. 'I don't mind.'

Remarkable, the dragon said. *Best be gone, mortals. When I slither out of this hole, all hell may break loose. Bah. Why prevaricate? I'm blocking the route to hell. Do you mortals even know how dangerous is Gul, God of Death? He is not like the others. Trust me in this.*

Pollon stepped forward, with a tablet of baked clay.

'I wrote a letter to our friends,' he said. 'Will you carry it?'

Leave it on the stone and I will commit it to memory, scribe. I won't carry anything when I leave. I may be busy.

Pollon bowed.

'Are you leaving now?' Zos asked.

Daos laughed. 'Tonight. She is Lady of Night. And she's waiting for something.'

That night, they were far down the Vale of Jasmine. They didn't have a cave. All they had was an overhang.

'Here she comes,' Daos said. He'd been watching while Pollon and Leontas cooked.

All four went to the ledge. The sky was packed with stars – so many stars that it looked like a jewelled carpet, but no earthly carpet had such magnificent detail or the endless spill of light. The Gift burned like green fire; the moons were both up. The

Maiden was in the Gate almost directly overhead. It was, by Zos' reckoning, the longest night of the year.

And there, far up the valley, was a lick of flame like a distant campfire, and then a titanic shape that blotted out the stars even as it launched itself into the air.

Zos felt his heartbeat race.

For some reason, he'd imagined that Antaboga would move in silence, going in stealth.

Instead, she screamed a challenge to the heavens, and beat her healed wings as she rose, and so powerful were those dread pinions that the dust rose from the Vale of Jasmine, even below their ledge, fifteen stadia to the south.

Chapter Eight

Enkul-Anu

The Great Western Desert was a barren, awful and awesome place even for the gods, who were well aware of its many dangers. Amot-Thait Oasis was much fought-over, the only good water on the long caravan route from Kyra and the Hundred Cities north into Narmer. The coast road was too easy to close, and had to cross the dozen branches of the Iteru river, requiring both boats and logistics.

Enkul-Anu was too impatient for any of that. He ordered his vassals and their legions out of every one of the Hundred Cities that had warriors; he ordered them to rally at Kyra and then march north and east to Amot-Thait. And they were, for the most part, on their way. The process had started months ago – just as soon as it was clear that the established order in Narmer had been overthrown and somebody needed her arse kicked.

Maritaten. How the fuck did my idiot priests let this happen?

None of the God-Kings were worth a crap when it came to battlefield command, which was all well and good as a policy to prevent revolt, but when it came to something like war with Narmer, he needed some human leadership. Experience had shown that humans didn't really follow gods. They worshipped them, but they also ran off and left them on battlefields.

He landed on the sand by the chariot of his two chosen generals.

Axe bowed his head, and Anenome stepped down from his chariot car and knelt on one knee.

'Great God,' they said.

'Generals,' he replied. He liked them as much as he could ever manage to like humans. They weren't obsequious or rude; it was as if working with him was just business, for them. Which it was, as he was paying them.

With immortality.

'Are we ready for Narmer?' he asked.

Axe was one of the largest humans he'd ever met. In his current, bull-headed aspect, he was well over ten feet tall himself; bigger than the mercenary captain, but no that much bigger.

But it was Anenome who replied. 'Great God, Narmer is a deadly enemy. They have the best army in the world, and most of your vassals from the Hundred Cities aren't worth ...'

'Shit,' Great God Enkul-Anu said. He nodded. 'I know. That's why I have you two; to make something of this army.'

Axe looked at the endless masses of peasant infantry whose rude huts stretched out along the flanks of the oasis. He raised an eyebrow. 'They're fodder, and worse yet, they know they're fodder. Great God, we need to offer them something.'

Enkul-Anu looked at the big man. 'Speak, mortal. What do you have in mind?'

Axe glanced at his partner. 'Lower taxes for the survivors?'

Enkul-Anu thought a moment and glanced at Telipinu, his steward and chief of staff. 'Make it so,' he said. 'Anything else?'

Axe grinned. The man certainly didn't lack confidence. 'We need more spearpoints. Of bronze.'

'Get them, then,' the Great Gd snapped.

'There's a shortage of ... bronze,' Anenome said.

Enkul-Anu wanted to roll his golden eyes, or vent fire, or just swear. 'Get some, then!' he snapped.

Anenome bowed.

'I want the Army of Narmer destroyed. I want this done in a way they remember for generations. That is my will!'

'Yes, Great God,' they said together.

Enkul-Anu was looking forward to making an example of Narmer, and he'd come to lead his host in person. He was short of really powerful gods just at the moment, so he'd brought Illikumi and Telipinu as god-apprentices. He didn't think much of either, although Telipinu was at least good at organising mortals.

'Get them more bronze,' he snapped.

Telipinu raised an immortal tablet, on which he could write almost as fast as thought; he was, after all, the Chamberlain of Heaven.

'Most High Storm God,' he said.

Enkul-Anu raised a hand. 'Just Enkul-Anu, in the field,' he said.

Telipinu nodded. 'Very well … Most High. I wanted to express … That is—'

'Out with it, pup,' Enkul-Anu had an absurd impulse to ruffle the other god's hair.

'They don't have enough food.' Telipinu held up his immortal tablets. 'They don't have enough food to march on Narmer and return.'

Enkul-Anu barked a genuine snort of derision. 'But they have enough to get to Narmer, yes?'

Telipinu nodded. 'Just. By my calculation, Great Storm God. A few of the wiser god-kings have more …'

Enkul-Anu put an arm around the young god's mighty shoulders and looked Illikumi in his snake-like eyes.

'Boys,' he said, 'I think you need to understand something.'

Both young gods looked at him with awe, which he enjoyed.

'They don't have to come back,' he said.

Damn, it was like the old days, instructing young Apep-Duat on the ways of war on alien worlds. Aeons ago, when it had looked like they'd conquer the million suns and shatter the crystal spheres...

'But... we're promising them lower taxes...' Telipinu met Enkul-Anu's golden eyes.

The Bull-Headed God sighed. 'There's always more where they came from. And it's best to thin out the warriors every couple of decades.' He smiled. 'And we don't really need peasants who don't pay taxes, do we?'

'But they are our *people*!' Telipinu said.

Enkul-Anu nodded, but said, 'No, boys. They aren't people. Remember that. They're just meat puppets we use, the way ants use grubs. And whether they know it or not, every one of them is actually our enemy. Trust me here – give them an inch and they're in revolt, sabotaging and undermining us... even when it's directly against their own interest.' He shrugged. 'Too many warriors, and they could really test us. This is a difficult time, but if we can wreck Narmer and also thin out the Hundred Kingdoms... well, then, everything will be *fine*.'

And if I can just get a generation of you lot trained and competent... I was lazy – that shit's over. A little work now, and we can sun ourselves and gorge for aeons.

He stretched his true body, feeling the scarring in his thorax where the gods-be-damned World Serpent had hit him.

'You two need to handle some serious fighting. I don't want to just defeat Narmer. I want them crushed, and I want the survivors whispering about the wrath of the gods for generations.'

The two looked eager.

'I have great gifts for you both,' he said, and grasping them, he rose into the air and flew deeper into the western desert, out of reach of the curious.

There, sitting at the crest of a titanic dune, were a pair of chariots. One appeared to be drawn by four magnificent white horses; one by four golden stags.

Telipinu, who, as eternal chamberlain, knew the contents of the armoury, gave a sigh of wonder.

'The sky chariots,' he said aloud. 'The chariots of the gods.'

'The old gods,' Enkul-Anu said. 'They made a lot of marvellous things, but none of it saved them in the end.'

'How do they work?' asked Illikumi. 'They're so beautiful!'

He walked over, putting his hands on one of the horses. All four stood like statues.

Enkul-Anu waved a hand. 'They run on pure *Aura*. That's all we need to know. Listen, until you two are strong enough to fly on your own, you fly these. Don't go too high – there's something about the interaction of the *Aura* with other fields ... Anyway, don't fly too high, or directly towards the sun. Otherwise, have fun.'

Telipinu was already standing in the car drawn by stags.

'A war bow!' he said.

'Which looses veritable thunderbolts,' Enkul-Anu said. 'I made those myself. Shoot a couple for practice – save the rest for battle.'

The Great Storm God raised a wind storm that howled like a hundred demons and set it up as a distant whirlwind to hide them. The young godlings flew their toys up and down the sand, loosing thunder javelins and lightning arrows, skimming the crests of the dunes, and talking to their teams.

Illikumi was grinning like the great cobra he sometimes resembled.

'I want a charioteer!'

Enkul-Anu shrugged. 'So get one.'

Telipinu looked puzzled. 'But you said...?'

'Oh, as individuals, they're loyal enough. Easy to buy *one*. A taste of immortality and unlimited gold usually does it.' He winked. 'Pick a pretty one, give them a taste of resin, and you own them.'

The boys practised until full darkness ruled the skies, while his sandstorm surrounded them, hiding them from prying eyes. Enkul-Anu wanted them to be a complete surprise. Narmer was always a thorn in his side; he was sure they'd have something special ready. He didn't expect Narmer to be easy. But he expected to win.

And anyway, he was lord of the storm, and while the storm raged, Sypa couldn't find him, and he had a little entertainment planned.

Outside his mighty spinning storm, the World Serpent screamed her challenge, and Enkul-Anu never heard it. As she rose, she repeated it again and again, screaming her wrath.

Auza, Home of the Gods

High on Mount Auza, deep in the many-halled mountain where the gods resided, the World Serpent's challenge rent the air. However distant and impossible, her high, shrill voice spoke the ancient words of ritual, demanding that a god meet her in combat.

Enkul-Anu was busy plotting war in Narmer; he was not in his own halls, but far to the west. Sypa cursed her bad luck and wondered for a fleeting moment if her consort was simply *ignoring* the monster. He'd never shown a trace of cowardice before, but then, Antaboga had slashed him cruelly.

The thought made her lick her lips.

Sypa was not the kind of god to face the World Serpent. Druku was a mighty warrior when he chose, but he had gone. Gul and Urkigul pleaded mourning for their murdered son. And Enkul-Anu had always been careful about letting Gul unleash his powers. She knew that, and why. Gul was a Power. Death was real. And unleashed, death could become Death.

But she needed a champion.

It was not a pleasant scene in heaven. Sypa watched the gods scurry to make excuses to avoid facing the great dragon as she, curse her, rose higher and higher, turning lazy circles and calling her challenge with increasing degrees of contempt.

'She calls us false gods and cowards!' Grulu whined. 'How dare she?' She turned her brilliant green gaze on Timurti, Goddess of the Sea. 'Why don't you face her, Great One? Surely you aren't afraid?'

Sypa stepped past Grulu. 'I ought to smack you, you green-eyed bitch. Timurti has never been the same since we fought for this place. By my own name and my unsagging tits, I'll fight the fucking dragon myself, if I must. I remember how to kill a dragon. Anyone else?'

Laila drew herself up and stepped forward. 'Great Goddess Sypa, I am not a god but a handmaiden.' She bowed. 'But I, too, remember how to kill a dragon.'

Sypa nodded, her face registering both surprise and pleasure. 'Then the two of us will...'

Inwardly, Laila cursed her own impetuosity – but it was in her nature. She had no interest in fighting the World Serpent, or in helping Sypa... and yet...

'No,' said mad Ara, God of War. 'No. This is *my* war.'

Laila, who knew too much of too many plots, wanted to stop the old killer.

'Your sons stole your sword,' she said gently, which was the best she could manage without revealing everything she knew.

His smile wasn't mad at all. 'I can kill a dragon without *Terror*. Indeed, she'd be little use against a wyrm.' He raised a spear, long and needle-sharp, and apparently made of a single piece of crystal. 'This will suffice.'

Laila stepped back.

Sypa couldn't help but look relieved, but whatever you said about Sypa – and a great deal had been said in the last aeon – she wasn't shy. She was a war goddess in one aspect, and she was good at war. She hadn't become the Storm God's consort on looks alone.

'I can join you, with Laila,' she said to the Great God of War. 'The three of us together will bring her down, and we can have a good laugh at the Great Storm God.'

Ara shook his head. 'No, Great God Sypa,' he said.

Laila looked at him in surprise. *When has he ever called Sypa 'Great God'?*

'Don't you hear her challenge?' Ara shook his great head ruefully. 'These young godlings have never faced a dragon. They don't remember the old war.'

He bowed to Laila and she wanted to cry, because he'd been insane for so long that she scarcely remembered this gallant god, the one they'd tricked into facing the goddess they'd all feared.

She'd been in on that plot, too.

He gathered his mighty scarlet cloak around him and reversed the crystalline spear.

'This kind of combat is not a new role for me,' he said, and eagle wings sprouted from his back, and he leapt into the *aether*.

Deep in his own cave, Kursag the Destroyer heard the World Serpent scream her challenge and instantly knew that his hated father would come against her, and he rejoiced. He flexed the talons he'd grown to replace his missing hand.

Could it be this easy?

It could. He was Kursag the Destroyer. It would be as he wished.

He made his way to the mouth of his deep cave, on an islet west of Pylax, somewhere out on the Great Ocean. High, high above him, the World Serpent screamed her challenge, and far to the south, a winged thunderbolt leapt from the very peak of Auza and flashed through the air.

He had a smile on his ruined face, and he deliberately turned his wings and body a matt black: teeth, eyes, talons – all black.

It was all a matter of timing, really. And he had the advantage of being master of the Nexus, the informational net in the *Aura*, as he had formerly been the Great Herald God – master of all the spies and priests. He watched the two combatants close on each other through a thousand eyes and a hundred spells. Everywhere among the Hundred Cities courts, astrologers, deranged sorcerers and lone hermits turned their eyes and spells to the two fiery forms winging at each other at the very edge of the *aether* that nursed the million spheres. And many of them used the god's eyes to communicate. Kursag – who had been Nisroch, Herald of the Gods – looked through them. When he was done, he sent a bolt through the god's eyes that left the watchers' brains burnt-out relics in the wake of his auratic passage. A whole generation died that night, the plague of sorcerous death flowing like a wave from south to north, and before they died, not one of them got a good look at what appeared to be mighty comets burning through the starry heavens. Few guessed, before he boiled their brains, what they were seeing.

He didn't need to kill them. He just did. He was the Destroyer. It was his pleasure to do so, and he fed on their deaths.

It was fun. And anyway, Enkul-Anu was a fool to let mortals use the *Aura* and live.

Just before the two burning comets merged, Kursag beat his black wings and rose into the air.

His only concern was that one might triumph over the other before he could reach them, but timing was everything in this, his simplest and best plan of revenge. Up and up he rose, changing his aspect and his shape to maximise his lift, but always remaining a dead black that tricked the eye, reflecting nothing.

He needn't have worried. They were canny enemies, and this was not their first joust. As he went higher and higher, they flew at each other; the dragon scoring with fire and talons, the god with his crystal spear, so that gouts of dragon blood, burning hotter than the hottest forge fire, fell on the sea below and blew massive clouds of steam into the air. Nor was the god unmarked; fire had burned him to an unrecognisable hunk of winged flesh, and talons had marked him. And yet he fought, valiant and powerful; yet he struck his foe, driving her lower, pushing her to consider flight.

Kursag wondered why she'd dared rise and challenge the gods. It seemed foolish. Hopeless. Though he admitted to himself that early in his healing he'd considered just such a hopeless course, and it held a bleak fascination.

Perhaps the World Serpent was a kindred spirit, after all.

Kursag wondered if his plan to destroy the world could tolerate an ally, dismissed the thought, and suddenly saw the obvious flaw in his simple plan: after he murdered Enkul-Anu, *he* would be alone facing the murderous dragon.

Best be quick, he thought. *Perhaps later we can make a bargain.*

He was close. The marred shape of the Great God, now forced into his natural form, was huge, if not as vast as the dragon, a hundred legs battering, the crystal spear held in great scarlet foreclaws still plunging home...

Kursag came out of the total blackness of the ocean far below, and plunged *Godkiller* into his father's broad and chiton-plated back, and watched the blue fire eat his flesh. But he didn't linger; as soon as the sword had gone deep into the god's vitals, he dropped away, ripping it free, falling... forcing a shape change, so that he became like a spear, an elongated teardrop of living matter plummeting towards the sea immeasurably far below.

As he plummeted, he planned. It was time to rally the scattered Jekers. He had no rival for their affections now, and as Kursag...

...how they would worship him.

Kursag purged the last of Nisroch's weakness and rejoiced, having killed the Great God.

Antaboga

Always deceive. Always deceive. Always deceive. Always deceive.

The World Serpent rolled, feigning terrible injury, aware that her foe was not Enkul-Anu but Ara, the most dangerous of the gods, armed with the most dangerous of spears.

But none of them were a match for her one on one, high in the air.

And they all know that. The outsiders are wise in the ways of war, ancient enemies of my race.

So who is deceiving who? And where is the trap?

She fought cannily, cautiously, watching the air around her, the stars above, waiting for Enkul-Anu to manifest, or one of his endless brood.

From the beginning, her only intention had been to deceive

– to aid the gallant and doomed mortals in their little war by drawing the full attention of the gods for a few days. It was the least she could do. And she meant to leave a massive and utterly false trail before she went for her eggs. She meant to give the War God his victory, and feign her own death. None of them knew how far she could fall without harm.

Dead, they would not search for her.

Dead, they would never find her eggs.

My eggs! My future!

She owed the mortals. Her kind reckoned, and paid, their debts.

And they call us deceptive.

Always deceive. Always deceive. Always deceive.

She rolled, always better in the air than any of her opponents, and because she was wary, she saw something...

No idea what that is...

She climbed, which she could always do faster than they, and beneath her, something *utter* happened. It was like a flash of lightning, except that it was totality, and it was grim reality – auratic and real.

She was almost vertical when it happened, her mighty wings outstretched to catch the faint remnants of air this high, though she could fly in the *aether*, too, if need be.

Whatever had happened below, it was dire. She rolled over on her back, the rim of the world passing below her like the rim of a warrior's shield rising behind his head. She had forgotten how it felt to have the wind of the *aether* pass under her wings, its silky touch singing to her of travel between the spheres.

Between the spheres...

Unbidden, a cry of joy came into her throat.

We used to fly in the aether. *Why did we cease?*

A long scream of ecstatic joy came from her long throat and rippled through the complex semi-reality of the raw *aether* between the stars.

And then she looked *down*.

Her god-foe was *falling away*. As if mortally wounded.

She rolled, flexing her tail to turn with a snap that would have broken the spine of a lesser creature, and dived, her great luminous eyes trying to pierce the shroud of night. But even as she dived, crossing the boundary between *aether* and air, she heard…

… She heard…

Something called back across the Outer Darkness. Something answered me.

I am imagining this. I have been alone too long.

She banished her thoughts, because danger was suddenly imminent.

Unlike most creatures of air and wind, Antaboga was perfectly willing to accelerate her dive, and she used her wings and her innate skills with *aether* and air to plummet beyond the limits of wind and friction. She used her power to build a thin envelope of pure *aether* around herself, flowing perfectly against the pressure of air, and she used other powers to push herself faster.

Down and down.

The god was dead.

She got close enough to his blasted corpse to see the wound. He'd died in his true shape – that of the star-spawned monsters which had exploded across the worlds a dozen aeons ago.

I didn't do that.

But she did reach out and take the crystal spear that had fallen alongside him.

Now that's old. Older than I am. And wicked beyond belief.

Where the hells did the Apep-Duat get this thing? This is almost as old as the gates …

She plummeted down and contemplated having faced the best of them. An honourable foe, he'd fought her in the air, one to one. Of all the enemy, he was the one she'd liked best.

And something murdered him.

It was not the first time in her aeons of existence that she'd faced a mystery beyond her understanding, but she knew one thing: anyone who could murder Ara, God of War, was a danger to her as well.

Always deceive.

She began to slow her descent, first ridding herself of her shield of *aether*, because that was not a secret she was prepared to share, and then by carefully using her wings; and then she allowed herself to tumble. The apparently artless manoeuvre rolled her north, and north again, as the air friction warmed her skin until she glowed like a falling meteor.

Her greatest performance. And in her *death* she fell into the mountains of northern Dendrowna, as far from the realm of the gods as could be imagined, though she didn't, in fact, smite the earth in her fall, but rather vented her breath and the speed of her passage in the snows beneath the highest mountain of the north. Steam and snow flew so high that it looked as if a volcano had lit the snowfields, and even seen from the peak of Auza, her fall could be marked.

Always deceive. Always deceive.

She found a snow cave, deep and pale, and under it, a lake, cold and deep, except for one end, which held a hot spring.

An excellent place to raise young. And to hide the spear.

Auza, Home of the Gods

Sypa looked out from the very peak of Auza, above the highest halls of the gods. She felt cold, and she allowed Laila to embrace her to keep her warm. Auza was so high that the gods could smell the *aether*.

'He is gone,' Sypa said. 'And so is she.'

Laila looked out across the purest night, wondering if Ara had gone knowingly to his death. And she wondered, with a certain experience of combat, how two such mighty adversaries had actually killed each other. She couldn't remember another such encounter.

It seemed unlikely. But she decided not to comment, and she wondered if Sypa had noticed the slip in time that marked someone's use of *Godkiller*.

Laila looked out across purest night, and wished that someone would tell her whose plot had just reached fruition.

Book Two

The Narmer War

Chapter One

Maritaten

Maritaten shook out her hair, which had been confined by the crown of Narmer. She had a great deal of hair – brown and curly and apparently endless, even when sweat-soaked.

'Give me a charioteer's helmet,' she said.

'That is unsuitable for the Beloved of Aten-Arrina, Ruler of the High House, Oras Rising in Strength, Favoured of the Two Ladies…'

Maritaten glanced at Mari-Ye, the High Priest of Aten-Arrina, the forbidden cult of the sun goddess whose worship had started this whole thing, and without whom she would still be a slave girl in the palace harem. He was tall, dark-complexioned, and looked like the incarnation of death, his bony face not unlike a living skull.

On the one hand, she was nothing without his faction.

On the other, if she lost the battle today, she was dead, and none of it mattered.

Mari-Ye offered her a low crown, like a helmet of bronze and gold, atop the Khat crown, with an aventail of woven linen. It was a beautiful thing, and, technically, a crown of Narmer.

Mari-Ye had not risen to leadership in Narmer without making some compromises, and Maritaten pursed her lips and nodded. The Khat crown secured her sweat-soaked hair, and a slave discarded the scent-cone. When he went to replace it, she motioned him away.

She had to smile a little, battle and all. Less than a year ago, that might have been her with the bag of scented cones. And she was already used to this service: the perfect, silent slaves and priests.

Far better to die as God-Queen of Narmer than live as a sex toy to a fool, she said to herself.

A year of practice had made her a marginally competent chariot-fighter, but the Royal Guard chariots around her held the very best her kingdom had to offer.

It was the centre that worried her. She kept looking that way, but the battle-haze of dust and blown sand obscured the centre and the far right, where Seti-Anu and his brood, her rivals for power, led their vassals. Nothing could be seen through the dust but the occasional brilliant reflection of light from polished bronze or gold. Seti-Anu had more gold on his chariot than Maritaten did, and she'd put him on the right, where by custom she would have been, an honour that soothed his insatiable pride for a day.

Her charioteer, a scarred veteran with a permanent leer where a Py stone-knife had notched his lip, nodded to her.

'Great Queen,' he said, very quietly. His name was Horat, and she took his advice when it was offered, despite his lack of honorifics or titles.

She followed the jut of his chin.

Opposite her position was a flat plain stretching off to the south: hard, packed sand and gravel for two hundred *parasangs*, with an occasional stretch of deep sand. Just off to the right was a scrub of acacia and a fringe of date palms along the seasonal watercourse that ran down to the river Iteru. The muddy stream divided her army but covered the flank of her infantry, and the screen of trees had allowed her magi to lay their trap for the gods.

Fucking gods.

There was a rumour among the magi – a gossipy group at the best of times – that one of the gods had fought the World Serpent in the heavens the night before. Maritaten had other things to worry about.

She focused on the massed chariotry of Kyra, Ugor and a dozen more of the Hundred Cities, just opposite her. Five god-kings in person, leading the largest force of godborn warriors the Hundred Cities had ever produced. Over on her right, facing fucking Seti-Anu, would be more – godborn chariot-warriors from as far away as Ma'rib. The Storm God Enkul-Anu had spent weeks preparing this army.

She waved her whip at Mari-Ye, who bowed, and the entire palace staff fell on their faces.

'The Lady of the Sun shines bright in the heavens, and victory is assured,' he said.

The Lady of the Sun was banished to the outermost void a long time ago. Whereas Enkul-Anu, may his name be cursed, is right over there somewhere, waiting for his moment to throw thunderbolts. And unlike the blessings of Arrina, the thunderbolts of Enkul-Anu are palpable.

She made a clucking noise, and Horat snapped the reins and the royal chariot rattled forward. It was a light car, made of cunningly bent wood and leather and sinew; her horses had more armour than she did.

'Well?' she asked her charioteer.

He shrugged. 'Anything they can do, we can do better. Until the gods get involved.'

'One step at a time?' she asked.

'Exactly. If I might be bold enough to advise your divine majesty …'

'Horat, what have we said about such titles?'

The old charioteer chuckled, making his ugly face even uglier.

'Then let's go at 'em. Everyone's bolder going forward, and the one thing we absolutely have is better chariots.'

A considerable number of the godborn aristocracy did not support her, or the Narmer-wide popular rebellion in favour of their traditional gods. She was short on warriors she trusted: she expected her godborn to fight and die. That was their place, and they knew it. But she didn't trust them for advice, except perhaps Prince Ak-Arrina from the south.

Which is how a virtually unknown chariot driver with forty years of fighting behind him had become the de facto architect of her battle strategy. She was better at choosing perfumed oils for someone else's bath.

'Do it,' she said.

They rolled over the smooth ground, and she crouched slightly, her feet on the axle, her heels on the rawhide netting that was stretched tight as a floor for the car. She'd been trained as a dancer and acrobat, and riding a fast chariot wasn't a tremendous stretch of her talents.

Besides, the wind of their passage cooled her a little, and as her chariot dashed forward through the ranks of the Royal Guard, they cheered. And she enjoyed that.

They rolled to a crisp stop exactly by the great golden hawk that should have been Ak-Arrina's standard. The mighty sun disc stood on the right with fucking Seti-Anu.

Ak-Arrina leapt from his chariot and bowed, his gold and lapis scale armour flashing like a dragon's skin in the brilliant sun.

'Great Queen, Goddess come to Earth!' he called, and the Royal Guard roared.

Maritaten enjoyed it, and if this was the last time then she was going to bask in it for another minute.

Then she took a deep breath. She knew perfectly well she was a beautiful woman; she'd ordered the palace armourers to make sure her armour revealed her figure. Sex was a kind of power – not the best kind, but she needed every scrap she had, and Ak-Arrina didn't love her for her law-making.

She spread her arms, raising her bow high.

'We attack!' she shouted. 'Let the petty kinglets of the south make a carpet under the wheels of our chariots!'

'Not bad,' Horat murmured.

There was the usual minute of jostling. Horses weren't people, and even the best trained chariot horses tended to fret, drag cars out of line, chew their bits . . .

Soon enough, Ak-Arrina turned his head and gave a wave of his riding whip. *Ready.*

Maritaten looked across the field, at the dust cloud in the centre, and the apparently endless tide of chariots and horseflesh opposite her.

She looked at Horat. 'Don't let me be taken alive,' she said. 'That's an order.'

He nodded.

She had a curved sickle-sword, a dozen javelins of the finest make, and her bow – lighter than a godborn's bow, but the heaviest she could pull and still aim well. She had more than a hundred arrows, three of which were made of ancient sky-iron, the star-stone that even the gods feared. Possessing them was a crime against the gods.

Interesting that even my god-mad predecessor had a few as an insurance policy.

He literally worshipped them, and they sent demons to rip him to pieces.

Message received.

By contrast, the charioteer had a simple, hooked bronze knife thrust through his sash. His only weapon.

She savoured it all one more time. Took a deep breath, and winked at Ak-Arrina. Who knew? They might win, and then she'd need his lust for her to balance Mari-Ye and his desire for a theocracy, and…

Fuck it.

She raised her right hand, holding her golden bow aloft. The sun caught it and made it burn like a fire of the gods.

'Forward,' she said in her normal voice, and a dozen trumpets rang out from behind the standard, brazen and high.

As one, the Royal Guard of Narmer's chariots rolled forward and, further to the left, another four hundred chariots of the Northern Kingdom, and some allies from beyond the delta.

My horses are rested and watered, and theirs will not be, she thought. *My chariots are lighter and my warriors better.*

We are outnumbered two to one and the enemy has literal gods with unholy powers.

It was difficult to despair when you were the god-queen of a mighty people, and their ages-old power was made manifest in horseflesh and bronze, rolling forward at your command.

They moved at a good trot; to her left, a guard chariot bounced into the air over an anthill and the charioteer and warrior bounced with it, sticking the landing with calm skill. The line to the left was already fraying. The ground fell away there, slowly but steadily, to the marshes, and slopes made for difficult driving.

Everything has been decided.

She looked to her right, where all the infantry of the Hundred Cities was locked with her own infantry. They had a mix of godborn and useless conscripts, and she had some professional soldiers … and some useless conscripts. The gods, for all their many failings, had kept massed warfare to a minimum since the Battle of Vetluna, thirty-odd years before. No one had seen a battle on this scale in…

She spat dust and gripped the railing as they hit a patch of soft sand.

It doesn't matter. There is only now.

The mass of enemy chariots was seething like a disturbed nest of roaches; some scuttled forward, and others hung back.

The Narmerian left wing rolled forward in a single wave. Every squadron left a gap between itself and the next to the left; over among the less-reliable northern nobles, the gaps weren't as wide or well kept.

It doesn't matter.

She wished she knew what Enkul-Anu had planned, or where he was.

And suddenly, the chariots of the Hundred Cities were *much closer.*

They were still boiling about. She thought she could see individual contingents; off to her own left, a big group rolled forward in good order, a wall of horses, but to her immediate front, the enemy was boiling like water in the giant palace kitchens' cauldrons. But suddenly she could see individual chariots, and the colour of their horses, and the flash of bronze and gold. There was a standard in front of her – a massive wooden statue of Ara, the God of War, gilded and held aloft on a pole the thickness of a young tree. It stood high above a heavy wagon that looked as if it was made of solid gold, and rose high above the chariots in front of it. The huge wagon was lined with archers.

Ak–Arrina had suggested their tactics for the chariot fight, and Horat had silently nodded his approval, so they were going to—

'Halt!' Ak–Arrina roared. A trumpet sounded.

The entire line of Narmerian chariots went from the trot to a full halt in three horse steps.

No one waited for further commands.

A sheet of arrows was launched from the Narmer warriors' heavy, deeply curved horn bows. There were perhaps two thousand chariots on the left flank, in four lines; the lead chariot warriors punched out five light flight arrows in as long as it took a priestess to sing the morning prayer to Arrina-Aten. Dozens of them had heads that shrieked as they fell.

They were two hundred paces from the boiling mass of enemy chariots – long range by any standard.

Maritaten had never seen the effect of her nation's famous archery before, and it was devastating. Two thousand arrows fell along the enemy front; perhaps one in ten struck home, most of them hitting horses.

The enemy lines exploded forward.

'Caracole to the rear,' she said, and Ak-Arrina repeated her command, just as they'd discussed.

With a snap of the reins, Horat started forward, but he immediately turned the chariot to the left, following Ak-Arrina's chariot closely, and the rest of the rank of chariots followed them until they were in the open space between squadrons. Still in a line, they turned to the left together – a nearly flawless manoeuvre, carried out in the face of the enemy. Then they retreated rapidly, all in a line, and passed the next three lines of chariots and went a further hundred and fifty paces before turning hard to the left once more and rolling back in behind the fourth squadron.

Up ahead, almost five hundred paces away, the second squadron of the Royal Guard was just launching its fifth arrow.

Off to the left – she could tell from the sound – it was not going so well. One of the Hundred Cities princes or god-kings had simply charged and, tired as his horses might be, he was going to throw the Northern nobles into confusion.

It doesn't matter.

She wasn't good at fatalism, no matter how often she told herself she should be.

She looked at Horat. He was impassive. The horses breathed heavily after their short run, and they gleamed with sweat. The sun, supposedly their patroness, beat down unmercifully.

The second squadron passed them, rolling by to their left in a long, uneven line, and then pulled in behind them.

'How are we doing?' Maritaten asked nervously.

Horat glanced at her and shrugged. His perpetual leer suggested that he was ogling her, but she'd been ogled since her breasts budded, and anyway, she knew it was just the scar.

Off to the left, another squadron – the third – passed them, rolling to the rear.

'Not bad,' Horat said.

Together, they watched the fourth squadron launch its wave of arrows, then pass across their front and retire. As they parted like a curtain in front of her, Maritaten saw the enemy chariots were quite close, spread across her entire front, and had been thinned the way chariot hunters thinned a herd of gazelle.

'Our turn,' she said.

This time, the range was close enough for her to shoot. That took her mind off other things. She wasn't a good archer, and she had to spend a moment getting it all right – the thumb ring, the grip. Her first shaft was a terrible shot, short, and wasted.

Welcome to battle, sister.

She thought of her first dance performance in front of shouting men – not her best. But she'd got through it. This was the same.

She was fitting her fifth arrow to the string and suddenly the chariot was in motion, turning…

She'd been too slow to shoot five. She turned in the car the way the chariot-master had made her practise. Moving in the chariot car was her best chariot skill; she had all the balance of an acrobat. She put her hip against Horat's hip, drew and loosed over the right side of the car, her bow held flat to avoid the syahs slapping the light rail.

As she aimed, she was a little shocked to find that she could not only pick a chariot, but in fact, could pick the driver, just twenty paces away and racing for her.

She felt Horat's hip move and knew they were turning with the rest of the squadron to the left, to run. She balanced on the back of the floor, toes curled over nothing, legs flexing naturally. There was no back rail on a Narmerian chariot; one mistake and the goddess-queen of Narmer would end up face down in the sand, waiting for the enemy charge to roll over her.

She drew a heavy arrow from one of the crossed quivers on the left side, stepped back so that her left leg was tight against Horat's legs, and shot the driver of the enemy chariot just behind them. It was personal, and she saw her arrow strike home − centre of mass, as she'd been taught. The man lost the reins and fell backwards, knocking his warrior out of the chariot in a tangle, and the empty chariot raced along after them for a few paces.

She felt a wave of elation like nothing she'd ever known before, even after a full aerial somersault before a crowd of 'suitors'.

She felt Horat begin to lean. She got her centre of gravity low and used her right hand to steady herself as they turned very tight to the left, but there were no longer any chariots behind them.

This time, when they stopped, Horat leapt down and gave water to each horse − just a couple of mouthfuls. Every charioteer in the first squadron was doing the same.

The second squadron thundered past, and Ak-Arrina stepped

down from his car as if he didn't have a care in the world. He walked over.

'A beautiful shot, Lady-who wears-the-crowns-of-Narmer.' He made a full reverence.

She was never sure whether Prince Ak-Arrina just wanted to get her naked, or whether he actually admired her. Just then she thought he might be admiring her shot – but she knew men well enough to suspect it was mostly amazement.

She turned the full power of her smile on him, and he was dazzled.

'I enjoyed it,' she said. 'Let's do it again.'

He laughed, and swung back into his chariot. Around her, the warriors and charioteers of the first squadron grinned at her.

'Are we winning?' she asked Horat.

'We're not to the battle, yet,' he said. 'But the bastards we just shot up are definitely losing.'

'Third squadron is signalling,' Ak-Arrina called. 'We shot their formation to pieces. Our immediate opponents are all dead or broken. No need to continue the drill.'

'What do we do now?' she asked.

Ak-Arrina grinned. 'Now we charge.'

'No,' Horat said quietly. 'Let Squadron Three charge. We'll stay in support.'

She turned to Ak-Arrina. 'Let Squadron Three have the glory. We'll hold.'

A shadow crossed Ak-Arrina's face, but his one really winning quality was the habit of obedience. She could tell that he wanted the charge for his own glory, or his desire for excitement. He pouted for a few heartbeats, but he gave the order, and the trumpet sounded, and his golden hawk standard rose and dipped.

She looked to her right, but beyond the date palms, it still looked as if there was a dust storm raging.

She looked to her left. Chariots appeared and disappeared into the dust. As she watched, a dozen chariots – heavy-wheeled, and thus the enemy – appeared from their left, and began to form a line.

She pointed with her whip.

Ak-Arrina nodded crisply, as if she'd told a good joke, and called an order.

The First Squadron wheeled to the left by sections, an order that she was pleased she recalled, although hers wasn't the voice that gave it. Now they were in a column of sections of twenty chariots, facing to the left. Immediately, the back of the column began to roll forward, to the left again, extending the new line. The speed of the manoeuvre was uncanny, and it clearly took the enemy by surprise.

'And that's why we don't all charge together, dipshit,' Horat said quietly.

'Are you calling me as a dipshit, Horat?' she asked.

'Nope,' he said. 'Although you could learn a thing or two. That was for *Prince* Dipshit.'

The new line faced the victorious chariots of the Hundred Cities, who had apparently driven off some or all of the Northern nobles and their vassals.

'Does that mean we're losing?' she asked.

He shrugged. 'Start shooting, Great Queen.'

She did as she was told. They rolled forward at a walk, and she shot over the rumps of her team, aiming carefully. She was shooting into the dust and seldom had a real target, and suddenly a trumpet sounded and they were moving faster.

'Dipshit's going to have his charge,' Horat said. 'Hang on.'

Suddenly they swerved so fast that they went on one wheel for some paces, but she kept her feet and bounced with the car as they came down. Horat had just evaded the wreck of a Northern noble chariot, both animals dead in their traces.

234

Maritaten nocked another arrow.

And suddenly there were chariots everywhere. They were almost at a gallop, and so were their opponents, running against one another, the two forces threading through each other, although here and there, dust and ill luck caused two teams to collide, rearing or fighting or falling in their traces, spilling their warriors into the dust to die under the wheels of other cars.

Maritaten shot and shot. Only once did she have the satisfaction of seeing her shaft go home to the fletchings in a horse; now she understood why the archery master had made her shoot at so many moving targets. She missed a dozen shots. Her right hand and arm were heavy and tired, despite her extensive training.

And then there was another rush of chariots, this time from her new left; her instant reaction of panic was replaced by relief that they were clearly Northerners. It was mostly luck that she was still fumbling for a fresh arrow and didn't put a shaft into one of her own.

A noble she didn't know pulled up to their left, came out of his car and knelt in the sand. There was cheering all around her.

She stood there, breathing hard.

Horat handed her a canteen of bronze.

'Drink, Great Queen. We're in the shit now.'

'Are we winning?' she asked.

He shrugged. 'We're still alive.'

Enkul-Anu (Western Narmer)

'What the fuck is going on?'

The Great God of Storm waved a live thunderbolt over the battlefield at his feet. He hated working directly with mortals – they were all so fucking stupid.

The hierophant of Ma'rib prostrated himself.

'It's very difficult to see ...'

Enkul-Anu waved a hand, and a blast of wind blew through the centre of the battlefield. Men were blown off their feet, and fronds were ripped from the date palms.

In the centre, the two infantries were locked in a grim pushing contest that had already cost thousands of lives. But the Narmerian infantry was being pushed out of the muddy stream bed and back up the far side of the little valley.

'Now tell me what's happening,' the great god said.

'Great God, God among Gods ...!' The hierophant was screaming over the storm.

'Uh-huh,' Enkul-Anu grunted. 'Taking too long. This is supposed to be a thrashing, not a contest.'

He leapt into the storm, his wings letting him soar like an eagle over the carrion below.

He flew to his left, where the professional charioteers from Ma'rib contended with the nobles of southern Narmer. He looked down into the maelstrom of chariots until he found one he favoured.

He waited until the big man in the chariot used his spear to cast his opponent to the ground, and then he used a well-aimed thunderbolt to blow the next few Narmerian adversaries into splinters and charred bone.

Anenome pulled hard on the reins, and Axe saluted his god with his spear, dismounting to kneel in the bloody sand.

Enkul-Anu hovered, mere paces above them and, in a dazzling display of might, used three thunderbolts to clear twenty contending chariots, most of which were Narmerian.

Pieces of burning horse were still falling when he addressed his favoured warriors.

'Well?' he asked.

'Doing our best,' Axe said. 'These Hundred Cities godborn aren't worth much.'

Anenome nodded towards the far right.

'That's not their god-queen,' he said. 'That's an old enemy of ours – Seti-Anu, a prince of Narmer.'

Enkul-Anu nodded. 'Get on with it,' he said. 'Win.'

He rose in the air.

Far below, a single Narmerian chariot archer raised his bow and loosed; his arrow struck the rising god under the left wing. Being bronze-headed, it did no damage whatsoever.

Nonetheless, Enkul-Anu rained fire on the blasphemous man's chariot and every chariot around him, before flying to the great royal standard of the sun disc, beside the gold car of a great noble.

He batted an arrow from the air out of habit. 'Seti-Anu!'

The noble's charioteer fell from the car, clutching his ears and kneeling in the sand, and Seti-Anu raised his hands in supplication.

'Feel my wrath!' Enkul-Anu raised a thunderbolt.

'Hear me, Great God!' Seti-Anu said. 'I never wanted this foolish rebellion!'

Enkul-Anu knew a whining turncoat when he heard one.

Humans! Offal! he thought.

'Why have you taken up arms against my divine majesty!' he roared, and Seti-Anu fell on his face by his chariot car.

Enkul-Anu had to use his unnatural hearing to catch the words mumbled to the sand amid the roar of war. He used the time to throw a thunderbolt into the very midst of the Narmerian reserve, destroying a hundred years' worth of chariot-fighting experience in a single flash of red fire. He began to play with them, the temptation too strong for him; he flayed one chariot officer, taking his skin and leaving his skinless musculature to scream itself to death; he turned reins into snakes, and horses into lions. It was great fun.

And then, suddenly, he was being held.

Rage threatened to smother him, even as he felt the tethers binding him. He ripped one free, sought the mortal sorcerer at the end, and boiled his blood.

This was a *trap*.

Enkul-Anu wasn't amused. Resistance was like a drug for humans; let them have any success, any at all, and they would build a hundred years of further resistance on it.

Thunderbolts flew.

So did something else. Some filthy, unsanctioned mortal manipulation of the *Aura* ... and it was dangerous.

He concentrated on breaking free. He snapped his bonds like whips, and a few of the powers holding those whips were extinguished like oil lamps in a wind.

But they still held him.

'You *dare*?' he screamed, and the mighty wind leapt from him, smashing friend and foe alike as he sought the mortal powers who dared ...

... *where the fuck are they?*

He was actually beginning to feel the edge of panic. He could feel one mage in particular, who was very, very powerful. Damn him. Something hurt him – hurt him badly. Something dark and malevolent crept up his bonds and stabbed him, exactly where the World Serpent had stabbed him; a jolt of pain.

He snapped his lashes again, attempting to overload the bonds, but this time they tightened, and he slew just one of the enemy sorcerers. It was like being attacked by insects – except that one of the insects had a dangerous sting.

And then ... there was a rush of air, the sound of the deep twang of an enormous bowstring, and Telipinu's chariot swept by him, trailing fire, and the sound of his great bow was music to Enkul-Anu's ears.

Telipinu circled, the four great golden stags glowing like the sun itself, and his bow loosed again, and there was a titanic explosion deep in the enemy centre.

Go get 'em, boy! Enkul-Anu thought.

To his right, Illikumi swept through the air, dropping thunderbolts of pure fire into the shattered remnants of the central infantry. One such flashed against a magical shield...

There.

Cunningly hidden. And shielded masterfully, in the broken ground behind the reserve.

Not the way I wanted this to go. Fucking mortals.

He raised his own powers, summoning from the *Aura*. Around him, men died as their souls were sucked from them; ancient date palms blackened and turned to ash, and the scythe of death swept over the battlefield, devastating a generation of Hundred Cities peasants until Enkul-Anu was *filled* with power.

Then he released it.

The firestorm was an absolute red hell that blew through the right side of the army of Narmer and into the centre, burning the standing acacia and sycamore and the date palms; burning the bodies of the men and women fighting over the muddy banks of the stream; rolling like a desert storm of towering flame over thousands until it reached the hidden sorcerers' shields.

They held for less than three beats of a human heart, and then the fortress of their massed minds began to fall into panic. The fire storm rolled over them.

Most of them.

Enkul-Anu had not been particularly indiscriminate in his rage; thousands of his own devotees had perished, but the sorcerers were mostly eradicated, and neither Axe nor Anenome nor the prostrate Seti-Anu were used for their *Auras* or burned as fuel. The damage to the enemy centre was, unfortunately, about equal to the damage he'd done to his own.

But he was free.

A sudden and absolute silence fell over the part of the battlefield that had just been burnt flat.

Enkul-Anu lowered himself, until his golden sandal touched the cowering Seti-Anu.

'Did I hear you say that this *slave girl*, this *rebel*, isn't even the rightful heir of Narmer, mortal?' he asked.

Seti-Anu raised his head. 'The priests chose her. But I am the rightful heir.'

Enkul-Anu allowed his true weight to crush the mortal to the desert, filling his mouth with sand.

'Then you, little sand-louse, are now god-king of Narmer. Bring me her head.' He rose majestically into the air.

Maritaten had probably burned to death with her sorcerers, but this would keep the little louse of a god-king on his toes.

I want the one who hurt me, though. Who the fuck was he? The fucker with the dark magic. He tasted like ... Temis. I always have to worry about the ones who might crack the barrier and make it to the big leagues.

He scanned the *Aura* for a major player, but his own massive spell had made it a whirlpool of chaos. He shook his mighty bull's head, and lifted himself into the air. The Narmerian centre was broken, and when his own cowardly mortals recovered, they'd finish the Narmerian rebels. He himself was wounded, and his bright blue ichor was falling on the sand.

It was humiliating, to get wounded by some mortal worm, but he liked that the boys had come through. Even now, they were massacring the rest of the helpless infantry of the enemy centre; a generation of young Narmerians were dying with their Hundred Cities enemies.

Enkul-Anu rose and rose, because he'd just blown his entire

store of power, and he didn't need to get hit again. Much as he needed a victory over the *fucking useless rebels*, he was fully aware that there were troubles at home in heaven as well.

We're going to turn this thing around, and it starts here.

He watched the boys deal death. Illikumi was elegant, cautious, but also had a fine eye for the flow of the battle. He helped the two mortal mercenaries complete the envelopment of the Narmerian right flank, where the royal standard had been taken and the best of the chariots would have been concentrated.

Telipinu was wilder, bolder, faster – surprising in the cautious, organised chamberlain. And he was less discriminating. More than a few of the chariots and warriors of Ma'rib and Noa died under his bow. And then he backed off, spiralled up, and joined the great Storm God. He'd donned a hawk's head as a nod to local custom, and Enkul-Anu approved.

'I leave you in command here. Slaughter the Narmerians. Kill half. More. Make this a day of slaughter they never forget.' He pointed to the north. 'Looks to me like the king of Kyra got his arse whipped over there. You'd best go and clean that up first.'

Telipinu raised his bow and rejoiced.

Enkul-Anu leant close. 'I'm setting up a local fool to be a petty tyrant for us. But you … The hawk's head is very good. You can *be their god*. And their saviour. In a few years, stomp on the tyrant and set yourself up as god-king, and then rise majestically into the heavens. I can spare you as chamberlain, and the Narmerians will fucking love you.'

'I am honoured by your trust!' The godling dipped his head.

Enkul-Anu hovered as the younger god darted north, already readying his great bow.

'That's how the gods win battles,' he said to the cowering hierophant. 'Someone get me some wine.'

And as he drank it off, he thought, *I have one useful apprentice.*

He watched with satisfaction as Telipinu swept forward. His

arrows were nowhere near as deadly as Enkul-Anu's thunder-bolts, but the boy had real promise as a killer. Every arrow seemed to have a different effect – clouds of gas, flashes of fire, walls of smoke – all enhanced with auratic power, all devastating on a local level.

Nice. Imaginative. My kind of youngling. How did I miss all this in the kid?

Enkul-Anu was tired, and the wounds he'd taken from the World Serpent burned like fire, and he didn't like something about the new wound.

And where is this louse of a mage?

But for the first time since the fight in the high air with the Serpent, he felt satisfied that he was on top of things. Crushing Narmer would allow some rebuilding, and finding a cringing stooge to fill the dual crowns of the rebel queen would allow for a continued flow of taxes – a stroke of luck that reminded him of the old days when everything had seemed to flip his way. He smiled, and watched Telipinu destroy the chariot of one of the Narmerian princes, marked by an eagle, where they'd tried to turn his centre.

Fucking mortals.

Enkul-Anu allowed himself to rise a few paces into the heavens so that he towered directly above the scurrying priests.

'Time to go home,' he said to the hierophant. 'Telipinu is your god now.' He smiled, as wistful as he, as the Storm God, could allow himself to be. 'Arrina is never returning. Make sure the rebel Narmerians see that. But Telipinu, the Hawk that Rises with the Sun, will be your new protector.'

Enkul-Anu rose into the sky, which had been a crisp blue and was now filthy with smoke.

So he didn't see the expression on Illikumi's face.

It took time to realise the scope of their victory. Her northern princes had been defeated, but by some miracle, instead of fleeing through the camp, they'd sorted themselves out and re-entered the fray just in time to wreck the Hundred Cities chariots that had turned to roll her up. In the aftermath of the wheeling dogfight of the chariot battle, a confused horde of her subjects had turned into the flank of the enemy infantry and literally rolled them under their chariot wheels.

But Ak-Arrina and Horat were in agreement that she'd done enough.

'We become the reserve,' the prince intoned.

'Inspired leadership, arsehat.' Horat spoke so quietly that only Maritaten could hear him. 'But absolutely right,' he added.

Ak-Arrina and his staff worked on rallying the four squadrons of Royal Guard chariots, trumpets blaring brazenly as the palace staff trumpets joined the prince's. Ahaz, one of the tributary princes Maritaten had never met, was showing a certain grim enthusiasm for rounding up the northern princes and their prisoners

'All luck,' Horat said quietly, with a shrug. 'Good luck – just luck.' He bowed to his mistress. 'But I'd rather have a lucky god-queen than almost any other kind.'

'Speaking of god-rulers,' Maritaten said, 'how about that?'

A line of dejected men was marched by, including someone obviously very important.

'I am the god-king of Kyra!' declared an overweight man, stripped naked. His fingers showed the marks of rings. 'I demand the return of my sacred raiment!'

Maritaten looked at him coolly.

'Someone get him a kilt,' she said. 'And treat him with ...'

'Every courtesy?' One of the palace functionaries was at her elbow – Hehet, once her mistress and a noble lady, and now one of Maritaten's underlings.

'Ah…' Maritaten said. 'Hehet.' Hard to forget, actually – a chamberlain named after the old goddess of measuring. Someone who'd been many levels above her in the old days, when she herself was a slave. 'Just some minimal courtesy. You have a knife?'

The junior chamberlain produced a good bronze *khopesh*. Its blade had the elegant sickle sweep and was inlaid with silver. She took charge of the defeated kings and led them away.

The Royal Guard had fallen back all the way to the camp, and ahead three of the four Royal Guard squadrons were reforming. Her Guard of Swords, all foreigners from Dardania and Atussa and farther to the west, stood off to her right, watching the line of trees. They were infantry – hired killers who protected her person and her palaces and didn't get involved in politics.

Or that was the hope.

Horat was motioning to her. Off to her right, there was the sound of rolling thunder just beyond the Guard of Swords.

'Here we go,' Maritaten said with confidence.

I am winning!

A victory here would cement her reign for years. She could ignore Seti-Anu and take a lover of her own choice for a change. A year of political abstinence had worn heavily on her. But lovers had sticky fingers, as she knew all too well.

She smiled at the tall bronze back of the captain of the Guard of Swords.

I even have someone in mind…

Her brief daydream of victory was rocked by a flash of lightning and then a blast of wind.

Horat made a face. 'Gods entering the fray, over on the right. Just as you planned.'

Maritaten was not the sort of ruler to snatch credit from

underlings; she'd seen enough of that crap when she'd been an underling.

'Just as *you* planned,' she said.

Horat wiped the back of his hand over his straggling moustache as a hundred violet strands leapt into the air.

'And there we go,' he said.

Even the old veteran sounded hopeful. Maritaten's heart was soaring. She was going to restore the glory, drive out the foreign gods, and ...

For as long as it took Mari-Ye to chant the Sunrise Prayer, she was victorious. Her sorcerers and astrologers were puissant, and their desperate ploy ...

was ...

Two winged chariots hurried near, passing over the battlefield like lightning-fast carrion crows or deadly vultures, and disgorging fire.

'What the sacred name of the Sun?' she said to the sky.

There was a titanic bloom of fire off to the right, and a vast cloud of smoke rose over the woods.

Mari-Ye looked at her. 'We have failed,' he said. 'Enkul-Anu is in the field, and even now he is destroying our centre. Our powers are dead.'

'No!' Maritaten shouted. Maybe she screamed it.

'Shut up!' Horat barked.

He didn't touch her, or put a hand over her mouth, but his order, as sharp as a whip, cut through her anguish. He was watching the sky to the south, where a flying figure, majestic and immanent with auratic fire, floated above the smoke.

'We've lost. Your choice, Great Queen? Either die here, or run.'

The two flying chariots were magnificent, untouchable, godlike.

Maritaten had never felt so puny, as fire and death rained

down on her people. The smell of charred man-flesh rolled over her and she retched. It was too much; a moment before, she had had victory in her grasp.

'What went wrong?' She was going to cry. 'Fuck!' she screamed at the heavens. She was *not* going to cry.

Fuck this.

'Die here,' she said.

Horat shrugged. 'Fine, if wasteful.' He considered for a moment. 'You're going to tell Ak-Arsehat to face the Royal Guard to the right.'

'Wasteful?' she asked.

He shrugged. 'You die here, most of us die, too. This isn't some pissant southern kingdom. We're fucking Narmer. This is the Royal Guard of Narmer. I'd wager not one of them lives if you stay. We're loyal to your salt, Lady. No one is going to walk away if you don't.'

That was a long speech, for Horat.

Maritaten looked at him.

He shrugged. 'Also, you're competent. And you take advice. Fuck, even Prince Ak-Arsehat isn't that bad. Whatever comes next…' He shrugged. 'Higher taxes, random shit. The gods. Fuck 'em, says me.'

Maritaten's mind was completely empty – a dark mixture of self-pity, panic and determination.

'Tell me what to do,' she said.

'What are you – some fucking slave girl?' Horat's voice lashed her mercilessly. 'You're *the Chosen of Arrina*. Tell *me* what to do.' His voice went down to a whisper. 'Do it, Lady. Run. Fight another day.'

If she wept, all the kohl around her eyes would run, which was not how she planned to die. She drew herself up. She wasn't tall; in fact, she was small, perfect for an acrobat. But she knew that a straight spine improved almost everything.

'Horat, dearest subject, absolute defeat in battle exceeds my experience and I need your advice.' She even managed a smile, surprised to find that she was still queen in her head.

Horat smiled with half his face – the full ugly leer. 'That's my girl,' he said. 'Look you, Queeny. We won our flank. The northerners, most of them, are loyal. So they turned straight into the enemy centre, where they're making meat.'

'Making meat?' she asked.

'A northern expression,' he said. 'Killing the enemy. Here's my point, Great Queen. They're far from the gods and keeping everyone busy. We sacrifice the Guard of Swords, put the palace people in the chariots and run for the river. Maybe we save the whole administration.'

'What for?' she asked. 'So we can fight another battle?'

He looked at her. 'I have no more idea than you. But why let 'em all die today when we can put it off until tomorrow?'

Maritaten was thinking of the river.

'But Enkul-Anu or one of his carrion crows ...'

Horat was watching the sky.

She looked back. 'Dying here on the sand sends a message,' she said bravely.

Is it courage? Or do I just want it over with?

'Does it?' He shrugged. 'Let me read that message – you're dead, so the so-called gods can write anything they like. The false queen-slave-whore died crying her cowardly heart out. Or whatever they want.' He looked at her. 'Something *really* ugly, no doubt.'

Her lips were trembling. It was partly anger, but it was also just plain fear.

She took a deep breath.

Queen. I'm goddess-queen of Narmer, anointed by the gods. The old gods.

She saw Hehet standing off to her right, serving palm wine

247

to the god-king of wherever. She had captured three of the bastards.

Hehet had been good to her, in a distant, professional way, when she was an erotic acrobat for the Great House. Everyone knew that Maritaten, daughter of a fallen great king, was to be humiliated, and yet, Hehet never had.

Gracious Sun, the woman even has a sense of humour.

She didn't deserve to die on the sand so that Maritaten could make a statement. And Horat was right; that statement wouldn't survive the day.

'Very well,' she said. 'We run.'

Horat nodded.

'All officers,' she snapped to the trumpeters. Voice steady; eyes dry. It was just a performance, and she was an expert performer. She was immediately impatient to *get on with it*. Over to the right, a firestorm was killing her people, and the appalling smell of fried pork drifted from the wreck of the centre.

I have dealt with worse.

But the officers came. If they were panicked, they gave little sign; three squadron commanders of the Royal Guard chariots, and the tall, ruddy-haired man who commanded the Guard of Swords, and Prince Ak-Arrina, and the northern tributary, Prince Ahaz. He'd rallied his own contingent – all foreigners from Yahud – and a handful of other chariots.

'We're beaten,' Maritaten said with deliberate brutality. 'We set a trap for Enkul-Anu and it failed. I've been convinced not to stand and die here. So we're going to run.'

No one questioned her. This was definitely the advantage of a strong tradition of absolute power and sacerdotal rulership. Every eye was on her, and she knew from their demeanour that her performance was impressive.

'Count the rest of the Royal Guard chariots and the northern princes as lost,' she said. 'We run north to the river. We take the chariots across the Iteru, and then we move north into the Delta.'

She expected Ak-Arrina to argue, but he took off his helmet and bowed deeply.

The captain of the Guard of Swords was a tall, very strong Atussan named Tudhal. When he led them in battle, they fought on foot, usually with a contingent of Royal Archers, but right now the archers were all in the centre.

'We're not very fast,' he said in his deep voice.

She looked at him. 'I need you to stand and die.' She held out her hand.

He took it, knelt, and kissed it – an immense honour for a foreign mercenary. She wanted to tell him that he was her first choice for a bedmate, but that was never going to happen now, and her eyes remained dry.

'Save me,' she said.

Tudhal nodded. 'We'll get you clear. That's why we get paid so much.'

He gave her a hard grin and got to his feet, a tower of bronze, and walked off towards his men. The Guard of Swords were almost all big men – an old tradition, and one that died hard. They had long spears, and swords, heavy armour, and both auratic magic and lots of amulets. They were rightly feared.

She watched him walking across the gravel, and then turned to the rest of her people to speak imperiously, her voice high and strong.

'Every chariot takes a servant, a slave or an official. Leave the camp *empty*. Tell the slaves to bring grain or fodder. Move!' Maritaten turned to Ak-Arrina. 'Fetch Hehet and make sure someone gets Mari-Ye,' she added.

Horat nodded, and she relented.

'I'll fetch Hehet,' she said. 'Then … back to the ranks, wheel to the left, and ride for the river. A retreat, not a rout.'

The other officers saluted and strode for their battle-cars; Ak-Arrina, who was almost smiling, remained. He nodded to the south, where the Guard of Swords were re-deploying in four ranks. They moved with a sort of organic flow very different from the Royal Guard chariots' attempts at precision. They just flowed into their new formation, as if they were one organism.

'You think you are still queen,' Ak-Arrina said.

Maritaten almost bridled. But instead, she turned her head slowly, looked him up and down as if considering him at a slave auction, and then nodded.

'I am the goddess-queen of Narmer.'

To her complete surprise, he fell to his knees and then face down, the full *proskynesis*.

'I will pray for a new dawn, Goddess-Queen of Narmer.'

'Rise, Prince,' she said. 'And let us live to fight another day.'

He nodded. 'Damn, we were close,' he muttered.

'Not that close,' Horat said.

Perhaps for the first time, the two men looked at each other, and Ak-Arrina surprised Maritaten again by shrugging.

'Perhaps not, Charioteer. But we tried.'

'So we did, Prince,' Horat said, as Ak-Arrina followed the other officers.

'Was that so hard?' Maritaten said a moment later.

'I don't like him,' Horat said.

'You don't have to fuck him, and I may have to before this is over. So work with him.'

Horat scowled. 'I don't like it when you talk like that.'

Maritaten looked back to the south, and came to a sudden decision.

'Take me to Hehet,' she said, ignoring him.

The chariot crunched over a patch of gravel. Palace stable slaves changed their horses, and then mounted the tired horses they'd unhitched and began to ride slowly north to the river, under the orders of the Lord of the Stables.

Maritaten looked down into Hehet's face.

'Kill all the captive kings,' she said.

Hehet smiled. 'Yes, mistress.'

'Nice,' Horat said.

'You don't approve?' Maritaten asked.

To her right, Hehet beheaded the god-king of Kyra with a single competent blow. His blood was very red against the white sand, but it didn't spread very far, no matter how much gushed out of his neck. The dry sand just soaked it up.

'If they were commoners, I wouldn't,' Horat said. 'Kill all the big-hats you like.'

'Sometimes I'm not sure we're on the same side,' Maritaten replied. The god-king of Takar was cringing, his pale skin already burnt by the sun.

'No!' he screamed. 'No! I am immortal! No! I beg—'

Hehet's blow didn't quite take his head off, and his airless mouth moved for a few seconds, then a strong stench of faeces and urine rose as the god-king of distant Loxis fouled himself in his last moments. Hehet wrinkled her nose and slew him, carefully raising the hem of her linen gown.

'That should fuck with the gods' control of the Hundred Cities, at least for a little while,' Maritaten said.

Hehet cleaned her sword on the king of Kyra's loincloth.

'Ride with me,' Maritaten said.

Hehet joined them, and Horat started the chariot forward, now burdened with a third person, but Hehet wasn't much taller than her mistress. Her right hand was red, and she had blood under her nails.

'Thank you, Mistress. Many blessings.' She looked at her hand. 'That was … very satisfying.'

Horat's smile grew wolfish, and he snapped the reins, and the royal party began to move faster.

'Wait,' Maritaten said.

If she was going to be defeated, she could make her defeat into victory by saving things.

When I was an erotic acrobat, I saved my soul by being the best. Small wins for sanity. Anyway, I like him, and good soldiers aren't all that common.

'Go back to the Guard of Swords.'

'If we go back—'

'Just do it, Horat.'

He looked at her and turned the chariot. All around her, Royal Guard looked at her.

She waved. 'Keep going!' she shouted as her car gathered speed in the other direction.

They didn't. They were the Royal Guard, and they would not be ordered away, even by her.

The Guard of Swords were just a few hundred paces to the south. As she rolled up, hundreds of her own archers, interspersed with Py mercenaries, were streaming past them. A few stopped and formed up by the Guard – mostly naked Py with tall plumes in their hair and empty quivers.

Tudhal stood under his cloth dragon, a banner allowed by his rank. He smiled to see her.

'Don't die,' she said. 'If you can make it to the Iteru, we'll get you out.'

He looked back towards the open ground and the billowing smoke and his mouth twitched in something almost like a smile.

'We'll see what we can do,' he said. 'Get clear, Heaven-Sent.'

She flashed a smile and nodded at Horat.

'Let's go,' she said – and one of the flying chariots came for them.

A god with the head of a hawk, sacred to Narmerians, swept

over them, and his great bow slapped forward, and an arrow the size of something from a siege weapon plummeted towards the Guard of Swords.

A golden bubble, thin and immaterial and very beautiful, sprang into existence over the Guard of Swords.

The god's arrow struck ... and exploded in a gout of dragon-fire.

Maritaten didn't even feel a touch of heat.

'Back step!' roared the captain.

As steady as if they were changing guard at one of her palaces, the barbarian mercenaries backed away from the line of trees they'd been watching, spears at the ready.

Tudhal glanced at her. 'Best go now, Great One.'

Maritaten was fishing in her crossed quivers for the ancient arrows. The star-stone arrows.

Horat saw the iron glint and put a hand on her bow arm even as the flying chariot turned tightly out over the river and came back at her.

'Using those ...'

Maritaten shrugged, because she was the goddess-queen of Narmer. 'Hanged for a lion, Charioteer!' she said cheerily.

Really a good performance, if I do say so myself.

'Seven fucking hells, Great Queen. Is that fucking star-stone? Begging your pardon.' Tudhal was looking at the arrowhead.

The flying chariot was coming around again. It was more than five stadia away, having finished its turn, and she could hear it. It burned in the sun like pure gold ... like the sun. And the godling in the flying chariot had the impudence to wear the head of a hawk.

Blasphemy. They're mimicking our true gods!

Anger filled her.

'You an archer?' she asked the captain.

A corner of his mouth turned down. 'When I have to be,' he said.

'Take the shot.' She handed him the bow and the dreadful arrow.

Tudhal looked at Horat. Horat looked at Maritaten, and the winged chariot parted the heavens as it raced for them.

And then, even as Maritaten thought the mercenary had waited too long, his mighty left arm went down, then up. He pulled her bow so far that she thought it would snap, forcing the recurve into a teardrop, drawing the long, heavy arrow to the head, and loosed.

The god-archer had thrown a deadly shaft into the Royal Chariots, destroying a dozen vehicles and killing her veterans, but he'd had plenty of time to fit a second deadly shaft, and he released almost straight down. His shaft struck the magical shield and Maritaten could *see* the enchantment unravelling.

Tudhal's shaft went up into the belly of the chariot and had no effect at all.

The god swept over them like the hand of doom and raced south, already beginning his turn.

Tudhal handed Maritaten the bow.

'Sorry,' he said.

The Py archers were forming up. Maritaten wanted to tell them to run. Two of them were carrying an old man who looked very out of place on a battlefield, especially as he wore the long robes of a Hundred Cities courtier, and a long, thin beard.

I've seen him before ...

'Put me down, you louts!' he shouted in pure Delta Narmerian. 'Where's my staff?'

One of the tall archers handed him a staff.

On the day the demons destroyed the palace. He tried to save the god-king.

Far off to the south, over the wreck of Maritaten's infantry, the god's chariot turned, shining in the sun. She could follow it, and when the smoke began to clear in its wake, she could see a dozen demons, the gods' elite monsters, feasting on her people.

'Let's go, Great One,' Horat said.

'No, no,' the old man said impatiently. 'Stand here a minute. Do I look like I'm dead?'

Maritaten felt as if she'd fallen into a comedy.

'You have the advantage of me,' she said archly.

'You're the goddess-queen? I'm the great sorcerer.' He waved. 'The rest got fried.'

The harshness of his statement was only matched by the harshness of his tone.

'Here it comes,' Tudhal said. 'Do you have another arrow, Lady of the High House?'

Maritaten nodded. 'Two more,' she said, and drew one.

'You damaged it,' the self-announced sorcerer said. 'It's bleeding power in the *Aura*.'

'The what?' Tudhal asked, but he'd already taken back the bow and nocked. He raised it, already at full draw, and the chariot was on them.

He loosed.

This time Maritaten saw the god, his hawk's eyes a glassy black as he drew, aimed at her, and loosed.

The sorcerer made a slapping motion with his hand, and the god's great arrow was batted to the ground and burst, spraying all of them with hot sand.

The godling-archer gave a choked scream that rang across the whole battlefield.

And the chariot itself began sinking.

'How I hate them,' the sorcerer said. 'I'm Timut-Imri, by the way. I served the old god-king, although he mostly ignored my advice.'

Maritaten smiled at him.

Why not? I really need a sorcerer.

'And look where that got him,' she said.

'Exactly,' he spat, in a tone so patronising as to almost be comic.

She gave him her most practised withering glance. 'I'm the goddess-queen of Narmer, Lady of the High House, Chosen of Arrina,' she said. 'And you may say all of those titles before you use my name, Timut-Imri. I am Maritaten.'

He nodded. 'Sure.' But his smile, while quick, wasn't derisive. 'I am at your service, Lady of the High House, Chosen of Arrina. And by the way, we should get the hells out of here.'

Her charioteer grunted.

Off to the north, Illikumi watched his rival find and then attack the beaten Narmerians' rearguard. He was considering outright betrayal – or simply flying home in a snit. Enkul-Anu wanted their loyalty, but he only ever gave real power to his own seed.

I thought today would be different. We saved his worthless old arssse.

And then he heard his rival scream and saw Telipinu's chariot sinking to the desert surface, and he began to grin.

How perfect!

I'll just go ssssave him, poor thing.

Horat turned the chariot and started back for the river Iteru at a trot.

'I can walk, Lady of the High House,' Hehet said, her first words in a long time.

'Nonsense,' the queen snapped. 'We have fresh horses and less than ten stadia to ride. You, Timut-Imri. Get in.'

'Do you know who I am?' he asked. His arrogance was on a par with any arrogance Maritaten had ever witnessed.

Hehet looked at him as if he was a dung beetle.

'No,' she said. 'But my mistress is offering you a ride, and if you care to walk back to the delta, you are going about it the right way.'

Maritaten was tempted, despite everything, to giggle.

The sorcerer muttered something and climbed into the chariot with a natural agility that belied his age. But his smile was rueful, and that made him a little more human.

Behind her, the Atussan mercenary captain bellowed an order in an alien tongue and the Guard of Swords began to walk backwards, facing the smoke. Off to the south, Maritaten could see the gold gleam of the downed god and his chariot, and the other hurrying to him.

I should have taken the shot myself.

No, I shouldn't. I have people for that.

'That was well done,' Horat said quietly.

She nodded. 'Let's save what we can,' she said briskly.

I am the goddess-queen of Narmer.

Chapter Two

Nicté

Vetluna towered over the ocean, high on the cliffs, a walled city that could be seen for a parasang over the northern seas. Its port was a deep bay with three good beaches set on either side of the rushing waters of the river Limdas where it met the sea. There was a waterfall just upriver, visible from offshore, ten times the height of a man, and the cold northern waters rushed over in an endless torrent, and the roar of it carried for miles.

Nicté was low on sleep, having watched… whatever they'd seen from the aft deck last night. Shooting stars tangled in combat? Gods fighting for supremacy? Whatever it was, it had been strangely beautiful, but she wasn't sure she should have stayed awake to watch.

Old Jawat came on deck, glanced at her, and then came to the rail. She favoured him with a smile. She definitely liked this one – tough as an old hide and covered in scars. He looked out over the bay and rubbed the top of his head.

'You are troubled, old man,' she said fondly.

'In this bay,' Jawat said, 'we fought the Dardanians. Longest day I've ever seen.'

'You were here?' Nicté asked.

Jawat made a face. 'Me and every other unfortunate bastard that Gamash of Weshwesh could beg, borrow or steal,' he said.

'And a lot of Nikali and Poche from Waxtekka. Even some of yours, Nicté.'

'A sea battle?'

He nodded. 'They came to take Vetluna. We came in right behind them and trapped them in the bay.' The old man watched some fishing boats, clearly lost to memory. 'We thought we were fighting for a new world,' he said. 'Turns out we were just peons in some game of gods.'

Hefa-Asus had climbed out of the aft hold, and now leant his bulk against the rail, which creaked.

'Well...' He spoke like a teacher. 'You were also helping us save the tin trade.'

Jawat made a sour face. 'Tell that to the dead, smith. Twenty thousand or so, ours and theirs. Godless skies, there were sharks and killer whales coming into the bay all night, eating the meat we'd provided.' He shook his head.

Nicté looked up at the walls high above them.

'And the Hakrans fought?'

Jawat shook his head, glanced at Aanat by the steering oar, and said, 'No. They watched. Some of the northern Dendrownans put a garrison into the town to make sure it didn't fall, but the Hakrans just watched.'

Nicté made a contemptuous sound. 'Yes,' she admitted. 'I have heard of this battle from older warriors.'

Now the bay was full of small craft, and the beaches were crowded with fishing boats and merchants: a few Dardanian craft with long black hulls, and some of the round Hakran trading vessels like the *Untroubled Swan* herself, as well as big log boats and hundreds of the northern outrigger canoes. A couple were catamaran double hulls with wide decks. On the southern beach was a long Noan ship, her paddlers just preparing her for sea; it was clear she'd recently been repaired from the new paint on her sides, bright and blue the way the Noans liked it, and they were testing her seaworthiness.

'The storm and the wave caught them, even this far north,' she said, over the cry of gulls.

Jawat pointed at the big island that didn't quite fill the mouth of the bay.

'Telebor will have caught most of it. That's where I fought – on the island. It took us all day to clear it – there was still fighting at night.' He shuddered.

'We'll get news of home here,' Hefa-Asus said, with some caution.

'We'll get drunk and laid,' Jawat said. 'Or at least, that's my plan.'

Hefa-Asus smiled and Nicté grinned, because once again she was in agreement with the old warrior. These were, in fact, proper thoughts.

Jawat was one of the first to go ashore, which meant that when Era wanted him to guard the prisoners … he was gone, and so were most of his soldiers.

'Who's going to guard them now?' Era asked.

Nicte glanced at her. 'We should just kill them.'

The thirty-odd Jeker prisoners were a bone of contention. It was work to guard them; one had escaped and killed a former slave, a good worker, before he was put down. A few had joined their militia, although no one trusted them yet, and two had started to work as carpenters, and one had committed suicide. The rest required food and water and took up space while remaining sullen and dangerous.

And their silent fury was a challenge to everyone.

'Who is going to kill them all?' Era asked.

Hefa-Asus glanced at her. 'I will, if it must be done,' he said simply.

Nicté nodded. 'I'll join you.'

Pavi put a hand on Era's shoulder.

'Jawala will never forgive you,' she said. 'Nor would I.'

'So what exactly are we to do with them?' Era muttered.

Jawala, robed in white and looking hale and beautiful, came up from the single cabin.

'Let me have them,' she said.

Era looked at the Given for a while, and then looked away.

'Very well. But only with guards.'

Nicté was just as eager as Jawat to get ashore.

'Almost home,' she said to Hefa-Asus, who gave her a long look that, from any other man, she'd have taken as an invitation. 'To get news,' she added, since that was clearly on his mind.

That proved to be true. That morning, after landing their whole flotilla on the northern merchants' beach and paying a toll to a Hakran official, Aanat and Pavi led them up the hundreds of stone steps to the city above. There were no guards; people walked through the big gates with complete freedom.

On the beach, Jawala had all the Jekers sitting in a circle. Nicté kept looking over the railing as they climbed the apparently endless steps up the cliff, waiting to see what would happen.

'And no one has come and taken this city from you Hakrans?' Nicté asked.

Hefa-Asus barked a laugh. 'All of the northern kingdoms have tried. The ajaw of Waxtekka tried ... oh, almost a complete calendar cycle ago.'

'How long is a calendar cycle?' Mawat asked.

He was along to carry purchases, and because he and Tarhu were now fully recognised apprentices. Atosa was also with them. The jeweller was gaping openly at the beauty and cleanliness of the city.

Hefa-Asus nodded. 'An excellent question. The *Haab* is

fifty-two of your years. We have other calendars. It is very important to count the days, as the wise know that events repeat.'

Era looked exasperated. 'Can we stick to business?'

Hefa-Asus raised an eyebrow. 'What could be more important than discussing the count of days?'

Pavi went off to buy supplies, and Aanat led them to a 'visitors' house', a sort of tavern for merchants. There, a dozen languages were all being whispered, discussed, or shouted in a chaotic common room where a hundred foreigners from fifty different lands argued over everything from the power of the gods to the latest price of an ingot of upriver tin. There were niches around the walls with the images of hundreds of gods; the food on the tables made Nicte's mouth water.

'Wine!' Atosa said, with the fervent hope of a true believer.

'No god's eyes,' Nicté noted.

'The gods are not well loved in the Hakran lands,' Hefa-Asus said. 'In Waxtekka you'll find a few, although we have our own names for them.'

'In the mountains, we fear these gods, but no one worships them,' Nicté said.

Hefa-Asus took Mawat and went to see if they could trade for tin. Nicté had hoped to find some of her own people, but she didn't see anyone from the mountains, and followed Era when she went to sit with a dozen merchants from the Hundred Cities.

All the talk was of the great wave, the destruction of the slave trade and the island of Dehku.

'Lot of opportunities out there,' said a grizzled captain from Ma'rib, 'for those with the balls to take them.'

A weather-beaten, middle-aged woman, tall and slim, wearing a tight, tailored jacket that emphasised her naked breasts, laughed.

'Don't need balls to make a profit, old man!'

He grinned. '*You* – calling me old? Your boobs were already hanging to your knees when I was puking green.'

It was obvious that they knew each other.

'May we sit?' Era asked.

'Free to any sailor,' the woman said. 'Where you from, honey? Narmer?'

Era waved vaguely.

The Noan woman with the tailored jacket looked at Nicté.

'You're Uran!' She was admiring what she saw.

Nicté smiled in a way that showed her teeth without indicating pleasure.

'Onadawega.'

Her hand went to her sword hilt. The Uran were her hereditary enemies.

The Noan captain smiled back with as little mirth.

'Whoa there. No harm meant, I'm sure.'

The man from Ma'rib ignored Nicté for Era.

'You're with that motley bunch that came in yester e'en.'

'Motley is a little unkind,' Aanat said. He'd apparently beaten them to the tavern; he already had a cup of wine.

'News for news,' the Noan captain said.

It was a trading tradition all around the Ocean, wherever trade was done: the last-comer offered news of the world, and others would respond.

Nicté glanced at Era, but it was Aanat who nodded.

'We're new come from Rasna,' the Aanat said. 'The walls there still stand. The *eint ki devar* held, and the city is recovering.'

The Noan woman looked pleased. Another man, with a maimed face and a missing eye, leant over from a neighbouring table.

'What's an Inky Dipper?' he asked.

Hakrans didn't do sneers, and they were seldom intentionally patronising. Aanat's smile was steady.

'The *Eint ki devar* is a massive wall of fired brick at Rasna, built to hold the river in its banks,' he said. 'Apparently it held back the wave.'

Everyone at the tables around them had the good grace to look pleased.

'Don't I know you, Captain?' the Noan woman asked.

Aanat turned and smiled. 'We shared the customs line at the port of Noa, some weeks ago.'

She nodded. 'Right you are!'

'More news!' called a Hundred Cities captain.

Aanat looked around. 'As far as I could see, the coast is devastated. I would guess five thousand died on the coast of Rasna alone.'

A man groaned.

'See any Jekers?' the man from Ma'rib asked. 'We're looking at forming a convoy to run south. We heard there were a *lot* of Jekers.'

Era spoke proudly. 'We fought the Jekers. We defeated four of their ships.'

The Noan looked astounded. A couple of men shook their heads in disbelief, but the crowd around them grew deeper.

'With a crew of Hakrans?' the Noan asked.

Nicté smiled. 'Not *all* Hakrans.'

The skipper from Ma'rib put a hand to his gold and lapis earring as if for luck.

'Come on,' said the third. 'You bested four Jekers? The sodding Dardanians would be hard put to do that with a dozen warships.'

Nicté smiled, showing her teeth. 'They weren't at their best,' she said slowly. 'And now they are dead.' When they all looked at her, she nodded. 'I, Nicté of the World Turtles of the Wolf Mountain Onadawega, bested their *ra-wa-ke-ta* in single combat. This, perhaps, is news.'

No one smiled back. Nicté wondered if she had looked *too* fierce. Hefa-Asus never criticised her for such things, but southerners were often weak as well as pale – easily intimidated.

Era spoke into the silence. 'I think ... the Jekers have other interests besides the northern seas. For some days, their hulks drifted on to the coast at Rappa, and then, no more came.'

'That's useful news,' the captain from Ma'rib said. 'I'm Tukas, captain of the *Manta Ray* out of Ma'rib.'

'Era.' She hesitated. 'I'm the *nauarch* of our ... convoy.'

The Noan woman looked at Era and smiled.

'Good for you, honey,' she said. 'I like to see more girls in the trade. I'm Poppea, daughter of Likina. I have a hundred-paddle trading craft down there under repair – the *Sea Lady*. But isn't that a Hakran ship you're on?'

Aanat spoke up. 'That's the *Untroubled Swan*,' he said. 'Everyone here will know her.'

That proved true, and more captains came over – mostly men, but a handful of women. Aanat told the story of their voyage, leaving out almost everything, and suggesting – without an outright lie – that they had merely passed close to Dekhu before the wave caught them.

Pavi came back in with two big sacks of green vegetables. She retold a few of their tales, but she was as clever as Aanat at leaving things out.

Tukas was impressed – they all were – and Nicté was pleased to see her friends praised by these foreigners.

A short man in a colourful headscarf came and stood by her.

'Killed a Jeker champion hand to hand?' He had a hard face, a great many muscles, and a viciously curved dagger in his sash. 'I'd like a piece o' that.'

He tried to put his arm around her waist, which she didn't like, but he had a good smile so she avoided the arm but did him no harm, looking him up and down.

'Ah, it's Bad Krul,' Poppea said. 'Don't take any of his shit, Onadawega. He's just after your cunny.'

Nicté nodded. This Noan was difficult to dislike and Nicté leant against her.

'He's not unattractive,' she said to the other woman.

Krul, who'd been set to glower, managed another smile. 'Hear that, Poppea? Someone thinks I'm *not unattractive*.'

The Noan captain rolled her eyes. 'It's a low bar.'

'Why are you "bad"?' Nicté asked.

He was a little shorter than she, stocky and strong, and had tattoos all down his arms. He wore an expensive wool *heton* covered in embroidered flowers, but it had seen better days. He had a silver amulet of a trident.

'He's a killer,' the Noan snapped. 'And probably a pirate.'

'Fuck off, grandma,' Krul said. To Nicté, he said, 'I had some trouble in Narmer.'

This was greeted with general laughter, but no one explained.

The next hour was full of news, most of which was rumour and gossip, some of it barbed. People exchanged what Nicté might have viewed as mortal insults, except that these explosive words were greeted with more laughter than violence. A few times, people touched their knives, but no blood was shed.

The gist of it was that trade had come to a virtual standstill, and the ships at Vetluna considered themselves lucky to be alive and afloat. Any news from beyond the harbour was good news; the newcomers enjoyed a gentle popularity just for being alive.

Hefa-Asus returned soon enough, and his news was mostly good.

'Tin is going cheap,' he said. 'The warehouses are full and all these fine folk already have their cargoes.' He looked at Krul. 'Who is he?'

'A pirate,' Nicté said. 'He fancies me.'

A strange look passed over her master's face, and in a northern man she'd have taken it for jealousy.

'Uh-huh,' Hefa-Asus said, with failed impassivity. To Era, he said, 'I have other news not so good. A month ago, the ajaw of Waxtekka declared a ...' He paused. 'A war. To take captives.'

'Oh, gods,' Krul shook his head. 'I was there, big man. If we hadn't been warned by our factor, we'd have been on the ball court for sure.'

'You know the ball court?' Hefa-Asus asked.

Krul shrugged. 'Not personally.' His eyes flicked to Nicté, clearly interested to see if she was still in the conversation.

Poppea raised an eyebrow. 'Ball court?' she asked.

Hefa-Asus nodded. 'Various ... undesirable ... people are sent to the ball court. The losers are always executed. Sometimes the winners are also executed. And the very ... unpopular get to be the ball.'

Krul laughed. 'Now that part I didn't know,' he said.

Nicté was pleased. She liked the pirate. He was not without manners, he had a good body, and he was obviously dangerous. He had a set of scars; he'd used his left hand as a shield, and paid for it, and then he'd had tattoos run around each scar, using them as part of the decoration. He'd also smiled at her a dozen times, but not leered once.

'They sacrificed every foreigner they caught,' another sailor said. 'We ran, too. We were going to trade for copper, but—'

'This is what I heard,' Hefa-Asus agreed, looking at Era.

'Fuck,' Era muttered.

Nicté listened to more of it – including a rumour that the Feathered Serpent himself had flown over the Northern Sea just a night before. Hefa-Asus was unbelieving, demanding details.

The Noan captain shook her head.

'It wasn't just a comet,' she said. 'It was big. There was some sort of fight in the stars – half the room saw it.'

Era nodded, as did Pavi. 'We saw it, too.'

Nicté closed her eyes and slowly opened them, trying to avoid anger in front of the handsome pirate.

'You think we saw the Feathered Serpent?' she asked quietly.

Era looked as if she might give way to anger, but then saved herself.

'No,' she said. 'Pavi and I saw two comets hurtling through the heavens and into the sea.'

'Well, one went into the sea,' Pavi said. 'The other fell into the mountains of the north, or that's what it looked like.'

'I didn't see that.'

Era looked at her, and Nicté remembered that Pavi was usually the lookout and had remarkable eyesight.

'And were either of them the Feathered Serpent?' she asked.

'You know I can identify a Jeker on the horizon long before any of you,' Pavi said. 'Yes?'

Era agreed.

'Useful skill,' Krul said. 'I could use ...'

Pavi smiled gently. 'At night? Looking at stars? I would guess they were fifty parasangs away. Maybe more.'

'So ...?' Nicté asked.

'No feathers. No shapes, even. Just bright lights in the sky. The whole Feathered Serpent thing is a local rumour.'

The discussion became louder and louder as the wine flowed, suggested that the deadly Tiatoni, the oldest and most sinister of the northern kingdoms, were also at war, but that their war was aimed north.

'Your Uran enemies are probably getting their villages burnt,' a grim sailor put in.

Nicté loathed the Uran – child stealers, with filthy eating habits and terrible songs, but ... 'There's a saying in the north,' she said. 'A mountain is a mountain.'

Krul raised an eyebrow. 'Meaning, you all hate the south together?'

Nicté narrowed her eyes. 'Meaning most southerners can't even tell us apart, and when the Nikali or the Tiatoni come to take captives, they don't seem to know the difference either.'

She glowered at Hefa-Asus. It was completely unfair, but her blood was up. The Tiatoni Eagle Knights would be going up against her warriors, and she was *here*…

The whole idea came to her in a flash of hatred. She took a deep breath; the conversation had moved on to speculation about the end of the island of Dekhu. She waved a hand at the others and tapped Hefa-Asus on the shoulder.

They'd worked together for so long he needed no urging, and she walked outside. Krul followed her.

'Not now,' she said to him.

'He your husband?' Krul asked.

'Would I be burning your skin with my eyes if he were my husband?'

The pirate, if such he was, grinned. 'I hate to get these things wrong. You seem pretty blunt.'

'I am. Now go back inside,' she said. 'When I want to ride you, I'll tell you.'

He flushed. And then bowed his head and went inside, a slow smile spreading across his mouth.

'Damn,' he muttered.

Hefa-Asus waited, his arms crossed on his chest. 'Walk with me,' she said, and they went out into the streets; they were lit, because every house kept a canvas lantern burning all night. Nicté stopped and admired the sight for a moment, and then walked on.

Hefa-Asus walked beside her, a tower of muscle.

'I have an idea,' she said. 'Why don't we go inland from here? In canoes.'

She glanced at him, prepared to explain, but he pleased her by smiling.

'Yes,' he said, his right hand making a hammer motion, as if he was shaping metal. She knew that motion well. 'Yes. Why didn't I think of that?'

She shrugged.

'If we cannot land at Waxtekka and trade, why go there at all?' she asked.

'It's my home.' His smile turned wry. 'I may even miss it.' He looked at her. 'So all my time working to buy tin was wasted?'

She smiled at him. 'We'll need tin for making, won't we?'

Hefa-Asus settled his mighty shoulders into a corner between two whitewashed buildings.

'I'm still not clear *what* we're making,' he said.

She leant forward until she could see him clearly, and he, her.

'We're making an army to storm heaven. And equipping that army with star-stone.'

He nodded. 'Sure... but...' He shrugged. 'What army? We have fewer people every day.'

Nicté admitted to herself that she'd had the same worry.

Hefa-Asus raised an eyebrow. 'I suppose I imagined that we'd get warriors out of your people and mine,' he said. 'But if we don't go to Waxtekka...'

'Weren't you threatened with the ball court if you ever returned?'

He shrugged. 'I was not Hefa-Asus the smith then.' She loved that he said it with no intention to boast – a simple statement of fact. Then he turned to look at her, his eyes dark in his broad face. 'How hard would it be to go up the Limdas?'

She looked at the whitewashed building behind her; there were no signs anyone had pissed on it, so she leant against it.

'Buy river boats above the falls – there's a town called Forest

Port. Move any cargoes we need to save. Start paddling.' She shrugged. 'Maybe ten days to Palanke-Lakamha, and then into the mountains. Then over the mountains. It would be the Kautlin people here in the west.'

'I have traded with Kautlin, and made war there,' Hefa-Asus said. 'Your people call the forest city Lakamha? Not Palanke?'

She nodded. 'And from there to the Saswatatan River, and the lakes. Twenty days?' She shrugged. 'But at the end of the journey, the Great Falls and my people.'

Hefa-Asus leant close. 'Are we really going to your people, Nicté?'

That froze her.

'I think we're going farther north,' he said. 'Over the mountains. To the ever-snows.'

She looked at him, seeing her image inverted in his eyes, lit by the canvas lantern behind her. In the inn, people were singing – a remarkable harmony of seventy voices.

'My people are close to the snows,' she said.

He nodded. 'I agree with your plan. Only, once we reach your castles, we'll still have ten days' travel north.'

'Less,' she said. 'Every year the snows come closer.'

He hesitated, and put a hand on the wall to stop her moving. 'I have something to say.' He was too big for her to evade him, unless she hurt him, which she didn't contemplate. She had come to him a good tribal smith; he'd made her like a god by comparison.

'I think it's time you were promoted to master,' he said.

She straightened up, even under his arm.

'Really?' she asked. And then, 'Fuck, yes!'

He smiled. 'We should do it before you go home,' he said. 'Might as well be here.'

She was grinning from ear to ear. 'Me? Master! I still don't know how you make the enamel flow over bronze the way you do …'

'I will show you,' he said. 'Again.'

They walked back into the inn. She watched him for signs of jealousy, and saw none, which was good, and when he took Era off to a corner to suggest a massive change in their plans, she wished him luck.

Master!

She couldn't stop smiling. And she walked over to Krul, now listening to Pavi.

'Let's fuck,' she said in his ear.

'Where have you been all my life,' he said.

He was funny. And he was a killer.

Perfect.

Era

Era walked back down the hundreds of steps to the beach feeling better than she had in weeks, and worse, at the same time. The hangover was real, but so was the sense that they were getting somewhere. The day was magnificent and so was the setting: seabirds wheeled against the cliff; the sun shone brilliantly for all that it was winter; the sea was the purest blue. Above her, the walls of Vetluna shone an almost pearlescent white – something that they put in the whitewash here. And below, lines of ships pulled up on all three beaches like giant sea turtles basking.

The air was cool, almost cold, and the salt-sea and pine smell raised her spirits with the cool air.

'I could live here,' she said to the air.

She felt better and better as she descended. She bought a cup of fruit juice from a vendor and drank it off on a platform a hundred feet above the beach, crowded with merchants: women with various nuts roasting on small clay braziers; men selling fresh flatbread, hot tea or cider, cold juice or wine or mead.

They were invariably polite. She was coming to appreciate every aspect of Hakran society, and these small merchants epitomised the people. The platform had been built by the city, for them; it aided their prosperity. And there was a sort of channel down the middle of the platform that no one crowded, so that through traffic of stevedores and crew was not impeded. There was even a canvas awning stowed away; clearly the space was covered on rainy days.

She sighed.

I'm going to behave more like a Hakran, she thought.

Mature, careful, slow to anger, polite. All good command principles.

I can do it, she thought. *No room for frustration and annoyance with three hundred people depending on you.*

Her good mood evaporated when she looked over the side of the merchants' platform to see the *Untroubled Swan* pulled fully onto the beach and turned on her beam ends so that the black hull was uppermost. There was scaffolding over much of her stern, and a dozen local workmen on the hull. All of her cargo was sitting under boiled woollen sheets at the back of the beach, hard against the stone of the cliff.

'What the seven hells of Kur!' she spat at Aanat as she came up the pebble beach.

Aanat smiled down at her from the scaffolding. It was all built of wood; in the Hundred Cities it would have been a fortune in pine and maple. She'd never seen wood used so wastefully.

'What are you doing?' she called up.

Aanat clambered along the makeshift structure and dropped

to the beach next to her like a boy. Up on the hull, Jawala waved. She wore white, but it was badly stained with tar.

'Repairs,' Aanat said. 'We had water coming into the bilge. Too many times on and off the beach at Rasna. Anyway, we've been at sea for months. We need to dry the hull and—'

'Dry the hull?'

'You're not a sailor,' Aanat said fondly. 'All hulls gradually take on water, and water is weight.'

Jawala dropped to the shingle next to Aanat with a boneless grace that showed that she, too, was feeling much better.

'We usually do this at the mid-point of the voyage. Strip the pitch off the hull, dry it in the sun, put a fresh coat of pitch on her. She's a good ship – she deserves our care.' Jawala smiled at Aanat and he put an arm around her.

'Get a room,' Era growled.

Jawala smiled. 'We did. Don't take offence, but it was so nice last night with everyone out of the *Swan*.'

Era glanced up and down the beach. 'And where the *fuck* is everyone?'

So much for her morning resolution to behave more like a Hakran. She regretted her tone instantly.

Jawala smiled. 'No idea,' she said. 'Once Aanat and the other captains agreed to beach and dry our hulls, they wandered off. Oh, there are your *captives*.'

She pointed to where the miserable Jekers sat among the neatly arranged items of cargo. A single bored sentry stood guard.

'Old Jawat arranged a payout of the loot from the beach,' Miti said, sliding down a wooden support and spitting when she got a splinter in her hand. She held up a silver sun disc. 'This was my share.'

Jawala looked away.

Era thought, *At least I'm not the only one to be irritated.*

'Jawat gave them silver?' she snapped. 'Godless heavens, we'll never see them again.'

Aanat shrugged. 'If they're like hireling sailors,' he said cheerfully, 'they'll return ten minutes after you'd planned to sail, drunk as lords.' He kissed Jawala. 'I need to get back to work.'

'Where's Dite?' Era asked.

Miti smiled. 'She went to find you. Last night.'

Era took that in. Her lover had never showed up.

Era glanced at Aanat. 'I'm sorry to ask it,' she said, 'but I need you to meet me at the Traders Taverna in the upper town. We're having a meeting. You and Jawala both, if you can.'

There. She'd put it as politely as she could.

Aanat looked at her for a moment, raised an eyebrow, and then shrugged.

'Sure,' he agreed. 'Let me get a little more work done first. Miti and Bravah can keep it going.' He smiled at Jawala and climbed the hull.

Miti climbed back up the scaffold, leaving only Jawala. The Given looked happy and a little less thin. Better in every way.

'Of course, I'll come,' she said. And then, without apparent thought, 'What are you planning to do with the Jekers? We do not allow compulsion, Era. And we won't accept making them slaves.'

Era sighed. She felt the justice of Jawala's comment; a wave of guilt at simply forgetting the captives for so long, and the consequent annoyance from being called out on her failures. She took a deep breath, erased the crease between her eyebrows with deliberate effort, and nodded.

'I'm sorry,' she said. 'I'll go and see to them.'

Jawala beamed. 'Thanks!'

She went back to the hull, humming to herself. High above, Bravah started to sing and all the Hakrans, including the workmen Aanat had hired, joined in.

275

Era sighed again. She plodded up the beach, the effort of walking on loose gravel somehow apt to the day and the task. The big tattooed Jeker was sitting with his back to the deeply planted piling of a wharf that stood well above them and gave a rather frightening testimony to the height that tides could run here. The others sat in clumps, but he sat alone.

The sentry was Lefuz, who was at least a dangerous fighter and a reliable man.

'Thanks for sticking this out,' she said.

Lefuz nodded. 'I'm going to need someone to take a few shifts,' he said. 'And I don't think Jawat's sober enough to remember I exist.'

Era nodded. 'I'll send a relief in an hour.'

Lefuz nodded. His voice was cool; it was obvious he was annoyed.

'That'd be good,' he said.

Era went over to the Jeker chieftain – *former* chieftain, she reminded herself.

The Jeker was a very big man – almost as big as the Poche smith, Hefa-Asus, but not in the same league as Drakon. Many of his teeth had been filed to points, but then, so had some of Nicté's. She tried on a smile.

'Good morning,' she said in Trade Dardanian. 'Have you been fed?'

He grunted. 'Just fucking kill me?' His tone was utterly matter-of-fact.

She followed her new Hakran courtesy and answered bluntness with bluntness.

'It's unlikely that we will kill you,' she said, and got down on her haunches by him. 'Want some hot wine?'

He looked at her for a long time, as if unbelieving.

'You're the *wanax* of these people?' he said.

She nodded.

He considered her for as long as a priest would give a long prayer. His eyes weren't uncanny – just very bright.

'Sure,' he said.

Era walked up to the platform and from it, looked down on the beach. She didn't see anyone she knew – not even old man Jawat. Not a marine, not a refugee, just Lefuz and the Jeker prisoners, and the Hakrans working on the *Untroubled Swan*. A couple of the other boats, captained by Hundred Cities men, were turned turtle on the beach and had work-crews, but their owners – or thieves – were gone.

She bought a wooden canteen for some scrap silver and then had it filled. Wood was everywhere; in the Hundred Cities, canteens would have been made of fired clay.

She carried it down to the Jeker and watched him drink it off. He didn't take it in one long pull, as she'd expected; he drank in sips, obviously savouring every one.

'Well,' he said.

She'd guessed he was originally Atussan; that's what he spoke with some wine in him. His eyes met hers. The look went on too long; usually, men who did this wanted sex, and she wasn't interested at all. But his gaze was surprisingly mild, for a Jeker.

'You speak Atussan?' the man asked.

She shrugged. 'Enough to sing epics.'

He drank again, looking out over the sea. 'Just kill me,' he said. 'When the wine's gone. Best for everyone, really.'

She wished she'd bought herself wine.

'Why?' she asked.

He shrugged, drank again. 'I could kill myself, if that made it easier on you soft-hearts.'

'But …?' she asked, because his tone implied a 'but'.

'That one, the Hakran, she won't leave me enough chain to strangle myself. Fucking Hakrans. They're cruellest.'

She shook her head. 'No. They just have beliefs, like most people.'

He was getting drunk. 'Yeah,' he said. 'I had beliefs. I believed we should all be free.' He managed a terrible smile. 'Look how that turned out.'

Era left him drinking on the beach and went back to Jawala.

'He wants to die,' she said.

Jawala looked at the man and then back at Era.

'It is every sentient's right to die whenever it pleases them,' she said. 'I can teach him to do it, if he is receptive. All of them, if they like.'

Era started. 'Teach him to do what?'

Jawala looked at Era as if she was a child. 'To turn himself off. To die by his own will. It is a thing many of us work to perfect.' She smiled. 'Let me tell you a harsh truth, Era – I didn't want to die on that beach. I was hoping you, or someone, would find me a way out. I'm a coward.' She smiled happily, as if her cowardice was a delightful thing. 'I know how to die. I could have donned my saffron robe, sat, and been dead in an hour.'

Era didn't know what to make of this confession.

'But …?'

'Life is beautiful,' Jawala said. 'And terrible.' She nodded, as if it was all perfectly clear. 'Shall I teach them?'

Era wanted to shout at the woman. What was it about Jawala that constantly set her teeth on edge? Instead, in her new-found wisdom, she bowed.

'If you can reach them, make the offer,' she said. 'Their only possible ways out of this are to decide to join us, or I have to kill them. Or they can choose to kill themselves.'

'You could just let them go,' Jawala said cheerfully.

'To rape and murder Hakrans? You *are* cruel.' Era glowered.

'That would be their choice to commit evil, not yours.'

Era didn't buy it. 'I'm going to find Dite,' she said.

Jawala nodded absently, called out to Aanat, and began plodding up the beach.

Era looked up the hundreds of stone steps and cursed, spoiling her record of an hour. And then she started up.

She was tired by the time she walked back through the long sea gate of Vetluna. The night before, she hadn't taken in the glorious mosaic set into the ceiling, but now she did. It was magnificent, showing a sunrise, and it was also placed where most cities would have had their murder holes – an unsubtle comment on Hakran society. She regretted that her legs, honed by ten years of dance, had so taken to the sea that she was tired by the climb, and she determined on the spot to go back to her exercises. Every day.

There were many things about command that she enjoyed. She liked helping people shape their lives. She liked being in charge, she'd found. But there were many aspects she hated, and one was the lack of time. There was always something. Once people grew used to your authority, they expected every banal decision to be made for them.

I don't dance. I don't work the Aura. *I never sing. I haven't worked the* auros *in ages, except to light a fire.*

She walked through a flower market, grinned, and bought an arrangement of what she was told were forest flowers.

After an hour of prowling, and the purchase of a really fine silver and bronze brooch for her heaviest cloak and another for Dite, she gave up her search and went back to the sailors' inn, where, of course, Dite was leaning against the long serving table that functioned as the bar. Every male in the place seemed to be gathered around her.

Dite's obvious enjoyment of their attention – or rather, their drooling – set Era's teeth on edge the way Jawala's effortless moral superiority did. Worse, Dite didn't even look up, her

279

long-limbed beauty transfixing the mariners. It was as if she was drinking them in.

Era walked through, pushing away a wandering hand, so she could put the flowers in Dite's lap. She did so aggressively, instead of lovingly.

Dite's eyes met hers, and her glance was *almost* blank with what? Ecstasy? Drugs?

'Are you on something?' Era spat.

Dite grinned, her gaze sweeping her circle of admirers.

'Perhaps, my love.'

But then she put the flowers to her face and inhaled, and looked so delighted that Era's anger dissolved.

'Excuse me, gentlemen,' Dite said. 'But now that I've found what I wanted, I find I want her very much indeed.'

She led Era through the little crowd and a mumble of lewd comments, up one of the sets of side-steps and along a railed open corridor to a small room with a bed and washstand.

Dite pulled the pins out of her long chiton, dropped it to the floor and reached for Era.

'Where were you?' Era asked.

Dite was pulling Era's pins from her shoulder-knots.

'Do we have to do this now?'

Era looked at her and spun from under her hands.

'Yes,' she said. 'I went down to the ship, and everyone was gone.'

'I wonder what they're all doing now?' Dite asked with a lustful smile.

'I was here. Where were you?'

'Here and there, love. Are we really *not* making love?' she asked, somewhat piteously.

Era crossed her arms. In fact, she was aroused herself; but she was, at a root level, tired of being led by Dite. She leant against the rickety door frame.

'Where did you go?'

'Are you jealous?' Dite asked. 'Because first, I'm a terrible person to be jealous over, and second, I haven't touched another woman. Or man. I mean, not recently.'

Era tried to breathe. Was Dite doing this on purpose, to cloud her judgement, or did it just come naturally?

The other woman knelt on the bed, and put her arms up to repin her hair.

'You are angry. Let me help you with that.'

Era closed her eyes. 'You left the boat last night. Now you're here. I suppose I expected you to come here directly.'

Dite laughed. 'I had an … errand.' She smiled. 'I can't hold this pose forever.'

Era was crossing the room before she'd made a conscious decision, but she managed to stop short of actually touching the other woman, which she knew would be the end of her. That skin was … so lush …

'Dite,' she breathed. 'You were a *god*. You are not one of us. I need to know what you do. You need to build trust …'

Dite smiled, and opened her mouth just a little, and Era leant forward unconsciously …

… and was lost.

Zos

Leaving Lazba was harder than he'd expected. Leaving the king was harder still, and he found himself weeping as the headland fell away behind him.

He had loved the king as a father. But he hadn't expected the noble gifts, or the king's warmth – his vitality. Or the queen's obvious care, or Lasotha's wisdom.

Pollon smiled at him from the stern bench.

'It's like leaving home, isn't it?' he asked.

Zos reached into the leather bag at his feet and took out a helmet. It had been a present from Makar: a magnificent war-hat made from the fangs of forty boars, woven together with rawhide so that it was supple yet hard, light yet incredibly strong. And this one had the feel of magic, and powerful magic at that.

'A kingly gift,' Pollon said.

'More than you know,' Zos said. 'This was my father's helmet. And that ...' He pointed at the round shield covered in bronze and gold. 'That was my father's shield.'

Pollon took the shield between his hands, and Eritha, on duty at the helm, leant over him. From any distance the shield, almost flat, but with a strong rim, looked as if it was covered in gold. But the closer you went, the more detail was revealed – ivory inlay, lapis, scenes of incredible complexity: a line of Dry Ones all the way around the inner rim, each carrying jars of resin; a lengthy scene of the siege of a Narmerian city, with a strong resistance from the people on the walls; and outside, barbaric warriors, and then, amid trees and towering marsh plants, an army in ambush, each soldier beautifully realised though only the height of a fingernail, in shining armour with weapons, crouched as if waiting to spring. And then inside that band, another, done in black niello and silver and copper: a wedding feast with dancers, men and women, leaping and turning with such precision of execution that the viewer's eye was caught and the dancers seemed to move. A man ploughed a field of jade with a magnificent ox of solid gold; a beautiful woman sowed silver seeds into a spring field of emerald and peridot, and then, at the centre of it all, a shield boss made in every way like the sun, with rays of gold-plated bronze that ran out into the shield, strengthening it.

Eritha sighed at its beauty.

Pollon just shook his head.

Zos took the shield, and held it in his left fist.

'My father had this from his mother, and she from her grand-mother. It is said that this is the shield of the old queen of the gods, stolen from her by Ara before the Great War. Ara hung it in his own temple in Narmer, which my great-great-grandfather stormed and sacked.'

Pollon winced.

Zos shrugged. 'Let's face it. Before there were Jekers, there were always Dardanians.'

'Kingly presents,' Pollon said. 'I can feel their power from here.' He smiled. 'And in this.'

He plinked away at a lyre he'd been given by the king. It was a fine instrument, tortoiseshell and silver and electrum, and he was obviously pleased with it.

'Did you ever try influencing the god's eyes?' Zos asked, mostly to cover his own display of emotion. His eyes were full of tears; the shield blurred, until he could see it most clearly in his mind's eye, hanging over his father's throne.

Pollon looked at him. 'In the whole *one day* we had between talking to the ancient monster and readying a fleet for sea?' The sarcasm dripped from his tone.

Zos winced. 'I'm sorry. I'm … in a strange mood.'

'Well, I did,' Pollon said with a smugness that made Zos laugh.

The scribe looked aft. They had twenty warships now; Leontas the Lion Killer had his own squadron, and there were more – sell-swords that the king had rented them, and three shiploads of Lazbian adventurers, and some former slaves of the Jekers bent on revenge. The royal army of Lazba was going the other way, to seize as much of the former Mykoan empire as they could.

Zos could just make out Leontas sitting by his own helms-people.

Pollon's words finally reached him and he turned so suddenly that he left a notch in the wake of his ship.

'You did?' he asked.

Pollon stretched like a cat. 'I did, too. You were right – I'm too timid. It was my job for ten years, after all. I went in through the main network. It's easy. I can do it from almost anywhere, though not at sea. It's surprisingly difficult to cast or channel across open water. I wonder how Aanat does it.'

Zos shook his head. 'You mean you can just... enter the system?'

Pollon played a bit of one of the Atussan epics – just a couple of lines – and then looked up.

'Yes,' he said. 'But... the choir – that's how I always think of it – the choir is a mess. Something's happened in the south. A lot of nodes are down, or empty.'

'I have no idea what you are talking about. Choir? Nodes?'

Pollon nodded. 'Imagine that a storm comes up, and half these ships are missing in the morning.'

'Could happen.' Zos smiled grimly. 'It's fucking winter. It probably *will* happen.'

'Now imagine you are in a long line, signalling by flashing your shield, as you did before battle.'

Pollon pointed at Zos' magnificent shield, the bronze face layered in brilliant gold. It lay abandoned under a bench.

Zos nodded.

When did I stop paying attention to my magnificent equipment?
Not a pertinent observation...

'Yes,' he said.

'And imagine that six ships between you and the farthest are suddenly lost,' Pollon said. 'So that even though the southern-most ship is still there...'

'I cannot reach it with a flash,' Zos agreed. 'So there are … what? Chains of these … Sorcerers?'

Pollon shrugged. 'No one would call me a sorcerer. But there is bureaucracy even to the use of magic.'

Zos agreed. 'There's a lot of bureaucracy to making war, and most people think it's something dashing.' He looked aft thoughtfully. 'So what can you do?'

Pollon was playing a chord. He narrowed his eyes.

'I've been thinking,' he said. 'I could listen for information.' He paused. 'But …'

Zos grinned. 'Here it comes.'

Behind the former scribe, Eritha smiled, and so did Persay. Both were stripped to the waist, fighting with padded poles. Since the last Jeker fight, Zos' crew took hand-to-hand combat a great deal more seriously.

'Why are you all smiling?' Pollon asked.

Eritha laughed. Persay looked away; for a madman, he was surprisingly tender of other people's feelings.

Zos leant forward and put a hand on the scribe's shoulder.

'Because every time you propose something new, you are just like this.' He mimicked Pollon. '*I've been thinking … but …*'

Every man and woman in the stern laughed.

Pollon looked around, and chose to be amused.

Zos wanted to smile again, but no one likes to be teased all the time. So he busied himself with the hole in his shin, which continued to leak blood and pus.

'Tell us your idea,' he said.

Pollon rolled his eyes. 'I was only thinking …'

Eritha giggled, an odd sound from so tough a woman.

Pollon pressed on. 'I think that I could place false information into the system.'

Zos looked at him. 'Ahh.'

'Ahhh?' Pollon asked.

Zos shrugged. 'No idea what it will be useful for,' he said easily. 'But any time you can feed your enemy a falsehood, you are winning.'

'Are we still going for the ...' Pollon leant close. 'The resin supply?'

Zos fingered his short beard, looking aft again.

'I don't know,' he said. 'I don't know what's going on. I don't even know if Era's still on the plan, or if Maritaten's still alive. In fact, I need information more than anything else.'

'Land me in any town and I can get you the *Anaphora*.'

'*Anaphora*?'

'Scribes and scholars prepare a daily report for the gods,' Pollon said. 'About everything from taxation to war and pestilence.'

'And you can just ... get it?'

Pollon shrugged. 'I think so.'

'But you didn't get me a daily report just now?' Zos asked.

Pollon was clearly annoyed. 'I broke into the god's eye system, and found a way to access it from anywhere,' he said. 'And maybe a way to trick it. While helping you track all the supplies and all the men and armaments we loaded.'

Zos withered under Pollon's rant. 'You did.' He raised both hands in what he hoped was a placating gesture. He looked out over the bow, as if the coast of Narmer might already be in sight. 'We'll raise Jennah in another day or two. You can tap in there?'

Pollon clearly didn't like the prospect, but he nodded.

'Excellent. Then we'll head for the delta, find someone from the Narmerian High House to tell us what's happening ...' He shrugged. 'Listen, Pollon – we're making all this up as we go, you know that, right? All I can do is react. I wanted to help Maritaten against the Jekers – mostly because the Narmerians, if they're really in revolt, will be the strongest force on the board, aside from the gods.'

Pollon nodded, mollified somehow. 'May I ask you something?'

'Ask me anything,' Zos said, relieved that Pollon wasn't actually angry.

Pollon raised an eyebrow, as if questioning whether Zos would actually answer anything, which Zos agreed was probably fair.

'Why Lazba?' the former scribe asked. 'I mean, so ... we have ten more ships.'

'Fifteen pentekonters is a major force,' Zos said. 'I'm not even sure I can keep them fed.'

'With gold, all things are possible,' Pollon said, referring to the bars of solid gold that sat in the bilges below them.

'Maybe,' Zos agreed.

'So all you wanted was to increase your forces? We could have raised this many in Dardania.'

Zos took his turn to look smug. 'Maybe – the Lazbians are more experienced and more reliable, at least as long as I feed them.' He nodded aft. 'But really, I wanted to offer eastern Dardania to my foster-father.'

'Because he raised you?' Pollon asked.

Zos smiled wickedly. 'He was the first man to behave decently to me,' he admitted. 'But no. Because now he's a rebel, too. His greed for Dardania will overcome his duty to the gods. You know it, and I know it.'

Pollon blinked.

Zos waved his hands. 'It's not a war, Pollon. We can't win a war. Any time we stand and fight, I guarantee that the gods can pound us to bone and ash. Dekhu? We were lucky, and we had the help of at least two gods and a dragon. You heard what the World Serpent said.'

'I'm not sure we can trust her, even in that,' Pollon said.

Zos waved a hand. 'I don't trust the fucking dragon as far as I can throw her, but she speaks the truth in this. We were lucky, and we were also *tools*. The gods are fighting *one another*. We're a third force, or a fourth or fifth.'

Pollon looked away. 'So how do we win?'

Zos smiled thinly. 'What are humans the very worst at?'

'Love? Faith? Sexual abstinence? Altruism?' Pollon asked. 'Discipline?' Zos was laughing. 'Accepting advice?' Pollon went on. 'Saving grain for the future? Obedience? Rulership?'

Persay leant in. 'You got to admit he has some valid points here.'

Zos managed, between guffaws, to say, 'Patience!'

Pollon stopped. 'Oh, that.'

'He who says "patience" often says all the rest of these,' Zos said, serious now. 'But we can only win through patience. Every rebellion costs them twice – once in lost revenue and again in the effort to suppress it. If we can get Narmer and Dardania in revolt at the same time, that's got to hurt. That's a third of the world.'

Pollon picked at the beautiful silver strings in the high range of his lyre and didn't speak for a bit. And then he raised his face to Zos.

'That's an excellent plan,' he said. 'And I can think of ways that I can help foment revolt *and* help the gods mismanage it. But I still think the resin store is key.'

Zos nodded, then shrugged. 'I see why, but I can't see how.'

Pollon nodded. 'I'm still … looking at the data.'

Zos nodded. 'Now we're having fun.'

Chapter Three

Hefa-Asus

Going to Vetluna was almost like going home. There were shops run by Poche people, and when he left the Traders Taverna, he went to a tiny drink shop, mostly because they served a tolerable balché and he could speak his own language.

And, because he was a ruthlessly honest man, so he didn't have to see Nicté throwing herself at a worthless piece of sea-trash.

I'm not jealous, he reassured himself. *I'm concerned for her.*

Liar. You're jealous. Dishonesty ill-suits a craftsman. What if such dishonesty led to misjudging a piece of work?

'Another round, here,' he said.

He'd listened to the gossip from home: it was obvious that the port of Waxtekka was closed, and that the gods had played a role in closing it. He wondered if the other northern ports were similarly closed, or if a major war was brewing; a trader from Waxtekka had said as much. He'd hosted half a dozen such men, but now his table was empty.

He waved airily at the two dozen Poche and some assorted Hakrans and other foreigners crammed inside the little place.

'A round for everyone,' he said, a little to his own surprise.

But he'd traded a dozen good bronze knives for some hack silver, and he wasn't feeling cautious.

The owner, a small low-caste Poche, approached cautiously.

'If my lord would...' He hesitated for a long time. He was trying to read Hefa-Asus' tattoos – trying to read the man. 'A round for the house is very generous, my lord, but...'

He was actually wringing his hands.

'You're out of balché?' Hefa-Asus asked.

The man looked daunted. 'Not at all, my lord...'

'I'm no one's lord,' Hefa-Asus said.

In a Poche place, it was a foolish thing to say, because he was wearing a short sword of his own make, a Mykoan wool tunic with colourfully woven edges, and a gorget of bronze and gold worth the cost of the entire tavern. He *looked* like a lord. He *intended to* look like a lord.

'Yes, my lord,' the taverner said.

Poche society was rigidly hierarchical, and lords said and did funny things, especially when under a *geas*. They both knew it.

Hefa-Asus nodded, mostly because it was obvious even through the cloud of drunkenness that the taverner was an intelligent man.

'What, then?' he asked.

'I think he wants you to pay up front, most noble,' said a woman.

She wasn't Poche; she was a little more like Nicté than was quite right, but taller, and with heavier eyebrows. She had four war-scars on her face and a very elegant tattoo over her eyes. and long black hair in an elaborate Nikali dressing that was completely at odds with her quilted cotton war-coat and leggings. He'd looked at her twice – mostly because Nikali women seldom left home and almost never served as warriors, but she'd been busy playing knucklebones with two Poche who appeared to be mercenaries.

Her words pushed slowly through the fumes and into his thinking mind, and he grinned.

'Ah!' he said. 'Mine host, you are an honest man, I'm sure. Take what the round will cost out of this.'

He dropped a handful of hack silver on the greasy table. His magpie mind noted a fine jaguar with a pin on the back.

Belt ornament? Decorated shield? Excellent work by someone.

The host picked through the little pile, taking the jaguar – naturally – and six pieces of what had once, most likely, been a heavy Noan cup.

A rhyton? Was that a bit of ram's head?

He realised that he had snatched that bit back and the taverner had stepped well back out of his reach.

'My apologies, host.' He handed it back without explanation.

The host knew a drunk when he saw one, and smiled easily.

'Most noble, let me convey the thanks of all of my guests.' He bowed.

Hefa-Asus was not yet too drunk or too arrogant; he rose and returned the bow.

'Care to play?' the Nikali woman asked.

Hefa-Asus held out his hand. The Nikali woman dropped the six knucklebones into his hand, and he felt them. They were curiously heavy, good solid bone, well polished by both craft and use.

'Salgut?' he asked.

Salgut was one of a dozen northern versions of the game, and what he thought they'd been playing. The player laid out a pattern on the table, and tossed one reserved knucklebone into the air, catching it on the back of his hand or top of her fist while simultaneously snatching one of the five remaining bones. The players took turns; missed throws required the failed player to drink.

Hefa-Asus wasn't too drunk to know he was drunk, and the woman was less intoxicated than he, but he was a big, heavy man and she was half his weight.

'Drink off the balché and I'll play with you,' he said.

She smiled. She had sharpened incisors, like Nicté, and she took the cup of drink the host handed her and drank it off.

Then she laid out a pattern, and threw, catching the bone perfectly on the back of her hand. She was fast as a snake, and she hadn't even brushed the other pieces, which Hefa-Asus noted she had placed close together.

Given the size of his hands, it made the game much more difficult. He failed his first throw, actually knocking a piece onto the floor. She grinned. It was a war smile.

She was out for his silver.

He drank his whole cup off, more than the game required, and waved to have it refilled. Most of the guests were watching now; when he raised his eyes, two Poche traders made bows of thanks, raising their wooden cups.

He ignored them.

She grinned again, her Nikali head shape making her grin a little like a jaguar skull.

I have jaguars on the brain.

Or some god is trying to tell me something.

She tossed her bone high, scooped *two* of the bones, and caught the falling knuckle with a beautiful swooping motion.

She's showing off.

He tossed badly, losing the bone altogether. A trio of his well-wishers crawled under tables to find it, and he drank again.

She made an easy throw and scooped both of the last bones to win.

He paid down five pieces of scrap.

She leant over the table.

'You're too drunk to play,' she said.

He nodded. 'Very true, milady.'

All Nikali thought they were lords.

She looked around for another victim.

292

'But I'll play again,' he said.

She looked at him, a slight smile on her face. 'Too easy,' she said.

He shrugged. 'What would make it more interesting?'

'A larger wager? I'd like that sword. It's beautiful.' She smiled.

He shrugged. 'What do you have to place against it?'

She thought for a moment, putting one finger to her lips. Then she went back to the bench where she'd been sitting, and picked up a bundle and unrolled it. It proved to be a black fox cloak, the hide side painted magnificently in complex patterns, like the rugs of the south.

Hefa-Asus wanted it instantly. He even thought of offering a straight trade; he could make another short sword.

But he'd seldom spoken to a Nikali, and almost never to a woman.

She looks like Nicté.

She does not actually look like Nicté. Forget jaguars, you have Nicté on the brain.

He looked at the cloak carefully. It wasn't that he needed to see it better; it was that he'd noticed that when she was bored, she drank. He kept her waiting for a long time, until some of their audience drifted away.

He called the host and paid for another round.

'If you are so generous, most noble, you can just give me the sword.' She smiled again.

He nodded, waiting for the balché to arrive, and then he affected to find a flaw for long enough to make her drink again.

The rules said that the winner held the bones. So when he waved his hand and gave her back the cloak, she set them very close together. It was legal ... if rude.

He kept his face impassive. She made her throw with the same grace as in the first game, and snatched two bones from the pattern, leaving three very close together.

293

Hefa-Asus narrowed his eyes. 'You are a difficult woman to defeat, milady.'

She accepted the compliment. 'I'm sure you play better when sober, most noble.' It was a very Nikali thing to say – an insult hidden in an apparent compliment.

He leant back and managed to spill his cup, and time was wasted while he got another cup, from which he took an immediate slug. Then, having delayed as long as he could and with every eye on him, he tossed the bone. He tossed it less than the width of his palm, and his left hand took all three bones just before the bone settled onto the back of his hand.

He almost lost it – he was that drunk – and one of the bones was stuck between two fingers; it was sheer luck that he hadn't dropped it. But he'd done it, and her beautiful brown eyes narrowed to slits.

She was very angry.

Hefa-Asus leant back, so that his stool creaked, and put his back into the corner of the wall.

'My cloak,' he said gently.

Nikali, like Poche, prided themselves on not giving way to public displays of temper. Her carriage was rigid, but she forced a smile and handed over the cloak, rolled tight.

'You played me,' she hissed.

'A noble gift,' he said, playing to the crowd. 'A queenly gift, indeed. You are most gracious, milady.'

She was barely keeping the rage off her face. The jaguar was *right there*. Interesting to see, now he was no longer nearly so drunk.

He reached to his chest and unbuckled the narrow leather belt that held his short sword. The buckle itself was a fine thing – bronze, with two stones set in to emphasise the quality. Northerners almost never wasted metal on fastenings; a buckle was a rarity here.

He handed the sword over the table.

'Your sword, milady,' he said.

He watched his gesture hit her like a blow. First she was angry; then chagrined, and finally pleased. All three reactions showed only in the skin around her eyes.

She rose, and bowed.

He rose and returned her bow.

'Play again?' she said.

'Another time.' His night was much better now.

'How did you do it?' she asked.

How exactly was she so like a big cat?

He considered. Side bets were being paid off in drinks; their audience was dwindling, and her two gambling companions were arguing loudly in Nikali. He leant forward.

'With pleasure, milady. You are a warrior, I see.'

She nodded. 'The best you'll ever see.'

Hefa-Asus thought of Zos, Era, Persay and Nicté, and begged leave to doubt it, but this wasn't the place or time. He nodded.

'Does fighting excite you?' he asked.

She shrugged. 'When is one more alive?'

Hefa-Asus nodded.

Typical Nikali.

'When I want to clear my head of the balché, I think of fighting,' he said. 'I remember my last kill. I let the war-spirit fill my blood. It drives out the balché. It takes a little time, but it has never failed me.'

She smiled, and licked her teeth. 'So all that time you spilled your cup and looked at my cloak—'

'*My* cloak,' he said.

Rising, he threw it over his shoulders. In the northern cold, it was like a mother's embrace. And it was long.

'I look forward to seeing you again, milady,' he said, and walked away with his dignity intact.

It was mid-morning when he arose, and only then because Pavi stuck her head into his tiny cubicle and roused him.

'We're having a meeting,' she said. 'There's hot ka.'

She placed a cup with a metal straw by his sleeping mat and withdrew. He drank it off with relish; he hadn't had *mate* in years. It helped clear his head, but he'd been mostly sober when he went to bed.

Down in the common room, Nicté looked smug; he wasn't going to be jealous. He was happy for her happiness.

He closed his eyes and opened them again, and it was so. Mostly.

Era appeared, also drinking ka. The taverna staff served them flatbreads with olive oil, herbs and little jars of olive paste, and Hefa-Asus ate his with relish. So did Nicté. Pavi licked her fingers and they all laughed. Dite joined them, and she was almost glowing with vitality. Hefa-Asus greeted her courteously and she leant over.

'Where did you get that beautiful cloak?' she asked.

Nicté wrinkled her nose. 'It stinks of Nikali.'

Hefa-Asus remained outwardly unruffled. 'It is Nikali,' he said. 'I won it in a game.'

'And lost your sword,' Nicté said. 'Did you leave it in the bastard?'

'The Nikali was a woman,' Hefa-Asus said.

Nicté made a face. 'Where's the sword, then?'

Hefa-Asus was pleased to see Aanat and Jawala pushing through the curtains; he wasn't sure why Nicté was snapping at him.

'I gave it to her,' he said.

Era laughed, and slapped her thigh. 'I've heard it called "giving her the sword", but I've never known a man *actually* give a woman his sword.'

Nicté looked angry. 'I liked that sword,' she said. 'Where did you meet this Nikali whore?'

Jawala settled next to Nicté.

'I can't imagine anything less likely than a Nikali whore, and among Hakrans we don't—'

Nicté cut her off. 'So you met a high-born Nikali woman *here*?'

Era cleared her throat. 'I'd like to get to business,' she said. 'I tried to get old Jawat and the other captains, and I couldn't find them.'

No one met her eye.

Nicté looked at Hefa-Asus. 'They're finding whores, I guarantee it, whatever Jawala calls them.'

Era shrugged. She was obviously annoyed, and holding it in check.

'Nicté, let's hear your idea,' she said.

Nicté leant back, gathering her thoughts. She had a line of very red bite marks on her neck, and Hefa-Asus looked away.

'It's not complicated,' she said. 'Our best information says that we can't get into the north country by landing in any of the city-states. So ...' She took a fortifying sip of ka. 'So I suggest that we send all our cargoes that matter up the falls, buy riverboats, and paddle north.'

'Godless heavens – in winter?' Era asked. Like all southerners, she expected northern winters to be ferocious.

Hefa-Asus met Nicté's eyes. 'It won't be winter, precisely, for another month, and maybe more. These are good months to travel.'

'Especially if you have a fine fur cloak,' Dite said.

'And a Nikali girl to lie between you and the ground,' Nicté said. There was ice in her voice.

Hefa-Asus was stung, as he'd been trying to help.

'I'm sure a pirate will do as well,' he said evenly.

'What's that supposed to mean?' Nicté asked, half-rising.

Era took a deep breath. 'Nicté, if you and Hefa-Asus could stop arguing, we'd like to hear your idea.'

Nicté shrugged. 'We can go up the Limdas as far as the Second Rapids,' she said. 'No point going farther than that. Then we carry them around the falls and head west into the mountains. We can probably keep the boats up the Sable River, at least for a while. Across the divide and into the Saswatatan in two days. Perhaps twenty days' travel to my people's lands. And none of it should be a fight.'

'Except for fighting the current and the weather.' Dite smiled benignly.

Nicté shrugged, as if she no longer cared. 'We could just overwinter right here,' she said. 'Maybe the ajaw of Waxtekka will get over himself and let us land.'

Hefa-Asus looked at her, trying to understand. She was angry. *Why? And why is she angry at me?*

He sighed. 'It can be done. In many ways, it's better than going to Waxtekka. It's a little longer, but any way we went north from Waxtekka ... we'd look like a war party.'

He looked Nicté in the eyes, willing her to understand that he wasn't against her.

She looked away. But then she looked back.

Era looked around. 'I like it,' she said.

Hefa-Asus was surprised; Era was usually more cautious.

Aanat shrugged. 'We can load a cargo and be gone south before the bad winds come. We were only ever your ride,' he said with a smile.

Jawala thought and then said 'No.'

Aanat froze.

Jawala rose. 'I was made a Given for this task,' she said. 'I am going with you to the end. And this *is* a good plan, mostly because it is possible to go a long way without fighting, and you are all prone to fighting.' She said the last with humour, and everyone, even Nicté, managed a return smile. 'And not least, because I'm the protector of your captives, and we all know it.'

Era bridled. Hefa-Asus wondered what that was about.

Aanat looked up at Jawala. 'Silly me,' he said. 'I thought we were going back to real life.'

He was giving his wife a hard glare, and she was ignoring him.

Dite raised a beautiful hand. 'But,' she said, 'wouldn't it be *much* shorter to go to Waxtekka?'

'Yes,' Nicté admitted.

Dite smiled at all of them. 'What if I could … ease … your way in to Waxtekka?'

Hefa-Asus thought of the Poche trader who'd whispered that the gods themselves had ordered the Flowery War against foreigners. He looked at Dite carefully, the way he'd look at a mould he suspected of having a flaw.

Era glanced at her lover and shook her head. 'Flowery War?' she asked.

Hefa-Asus spread his hands. 'A war made to take captives,' he said.

'So that they can be sacrificed,' Nicté spat.

Era snorted. 'Well,' she said, 'upriver sounds like less risk.'

Dite frowned. 'You only say "no risk" because lovely Nicté hasn't mentioned the rapids, the rising and falling waters, and the insect life.'

Era looked at Nicté, who shrugged. 'Not so many insects at this time of year. And no Bright People.'

Hefa-Asus leant forward. 'All that is true,' he said. 'But it's still less risky than landing at Waxtekka.'

'I can be very persuasive,' Dite said.

Era looked at her, and it was an odd look, almost as if Dite had said something that had gone against her own argument.

299

Pavi looked around. 'I'd love to see Waxtekka,' she said. 'But upriver isn't that hard. I took a cargo upriver when I was a girl. We bought tin.' She smiled at Jawala. 'Before I married you all.'

Dite shook her head, and Hefa-Asus felt the force of her personality.

'I really think …' she began, her voice unctuous.

'Vote,' snapped Era. 'All in favour of a voyage upriver?'

Every hand went up, save only Dite's.

'Unanimous,' Era said.

'I'm most definitely against,' Dite said.

Era smiled, but her voice was anything but pleasant. 'You are not an officer.'

Dite's head snapped back as if she'd been slapped.

'If you want to employ your various *arts*,' Era went on, 'help me find our people. They must be spread across the city by now.'

Dite smiled, but now it was malicious. 'Some of them will be on board ships headed elsewhere.'

Era locked eyes with her partner and asked, 'How do you know that?'

Dite shrugged. 'It's obvious, Era. You may be set on this expedition, but they aren't.'

Era

'I'm *not an officer*?' Dite snapped. 'I saved the lot of you on Dekhu! I was a fucking *god*!'

Era was sitting on their bed. She wanted to search for her crews, but Dite had insisted, and …

'You know why I left fucking Enkul-Anu? Because he treated me like useless baggage! Even when he adopted my suggestions, he pretended I was too drunk to participate. By Kur's rotting demons, Era! That was nasty, and what have I done to deserve it?'

'Maybe Enkul-Anu didn't trust you,' Era said carefully.

Dite's eyes almost literally caught fire. 'What's that supposed to mean?'

Era got to her feet. 'I'm going to go and look for our people. I'd like to go before one of us says something we'll regret.'

'You don't trust me? Is that it? You, the erotic dancer, don't trust me, the former god?'

'I wasn't an erotic dancer,' Era said, her jaw clenched. 'I was a classical dancer.'

'Maybe if you'd been an erotic dancer, you wouldn't be so high and mighty with me.' Dite burst into tears.

Era bit her lip to keep herself from joining in. Instead, she used the pain to get her out of the room and down the steps.

Do I love her? Era asked herself. *Or do I just love that wonderful body?*

And then, almost gratefully, she dismissed the thought and went in search of her people. A problem to solve was always better than dealing with her own problems.

Maritaten

The full scale of the disaster had only become clear when they reached the Iteru, and the boats. Most of the navy and hundreds of river-trading vessels had been required to move her army, her palace people, and all the food and water…

According to Mari-Ye, it had taken only seventy-three ships to take them back downriver. Seventy-three big river craft: the best of her navy and the largest trading ships, built to go overseas to Dendrowna for wood and to Ma'rib for spices and oils.

'The remains of my empire,' Maritaten said to herself.

A palace maid, Hotashut, was undressing her. Maritaten had sweated through her war-gown, but the linen would clean. There was a spatter of blood, just a few drops, over her back where the *thorakes* of gilded scales hadn't covered it; she wondered whose blood it was, and how it had got there.

I could just kill myself.

She looked that thought in the eye. It had been a real possibility every day since she'd reached womanhood and been handed straight from the High House nursery to the Halls of Pleasure. She kept it in reserve – a little mantra she told herself: *I could just kill myself.*

She was pretty sure she could, too.

But she thought of Horat and Hehet and even Ak-Arrina, and found that wearing a bronze scale cuirass all day had strained her back muscles in ways hours of dancing had never done. Hotashut got her clothes off and cleaned her with olive oil, and then massaged her. She just let it happen. At some point, she started crying and it was all vivid: the corpses; the man she'd killed almost face to face; the dead horses; the empty ships; the rising column of smoke behind her...

'Horat says you killed many foes today,' Hotashut said.

Even in the midst of darkness, Maritaten found that the idea that Horat had praised her, even to her maid, caused her to smile. Although, knowing Horat, he was trying to please Hotashut.

But honesty won over vanity.

'One,' she said. 'Maybe as many as three.'

Hotashut made an unaccustomed noise and Maritaten rolled over to find her body-servant laughing.

She instantly fell to her knees.

'Oh, Chosen One! Queen of the High House! I didn't mean...'

Maritaten lay back down. 'I will not punish you if you keep taking the knots out of my lower back. What made you laugh?'

Hotashut took a long time. 'The image of you killing grown men,' she said. 'This one hopes she does no insult to say, they must have been very poor warriors.'

Maritaten rolled over fast enough to hurt her own back. 'They were not!' she snapped. 'And they beat us hollow, in the end, so ...'

The young woman was back on her knees. 'Ten thousand apologies, mistress.'

Maritaten lay back down. 'I used a bow,' she said. 'It's true, Hotashut. I could never fight sword to sword. I'm tiny and they're all huge.'

'I shouldn't have laughed.'

Maritaten stretched. 'I probably shouldn't have tried to lead an army. But this is not seemly, Hotashut. We don't laugh at the Queen of the High House.'

Cautiously, Hotashut said, 'I laughed only at your enemies, I swear, goddess-queen of Narmer.'

But wouldn't it be nice to have a friend here? A girl I could laugh at and who could laugh at me?

Sure would. And it is funny — little me hacking away at some great Hundred Cities warrior ...

She contemplated it.

Hotashut stopped kneading her aching flesh and helped her sit up. Then, shyly, she put a hand near, but not on, Maritaten's bare thigh.

'Is there anything else I can do for you, mistress?' she asked.

Maritaten took the hand and kissed it gently, as she had been taught. And then she gave the servant girl her hand back.

'Remember where I came from,' she said in a low voice. There was anger there — a great deal of anger. 'I will never take sex from my servants,' she said carefully, enunciating each word.

'Oh, mistress!' The woman burst into tears.

Later, on the deck of the long warship, Maritaten sat and was fanned while fifty sweating men rowed with the current so that they fairly flew upstream. Hehet came and stood by her.

'What can I do for you, Great Queen?' the woman asked.

'As the great chamberlain and the great steward are apparently lost, I'd like you to be Master of my Household. We'll see how it works.'

Hehet was not the sort of woman to show surprise. 'Of course, Great Queen. I've already seen to your dinner.'

'And Hehet,' Maritaten said, 'send Hotashut to serve someone else. Someone nice. This is not a punishment. Am I clear?'

Hehet nodded. 'Very clear. You do find her adequate, but you do not want her to serve you.'

'Better – she's a delight. Have her delight someone else.'

'Your will is always my command, mistress,' Hehet said.

Maritaten nodded, and went back to watching the banks of the river race by.

In the morning, it was obvious why the sunrise had been so red.

The temple city opposite Lukor, on the south bank, was on fire.

Maritaten cursed.

Mari-Ye raised his chin a fraction, which, for the old priest, was quite a sign of emotion.

'Curse them,' Maritaten said.

It was obvious one or more of the gods had done it. The devastation was the kind of thing that only the gods could manage, although, in her new-found wisdom, she noted that the slums along the river burned much better than the houses of the rich high above the banks, and the gods' great temples were untouched, except the Great Temple of Arrina, which had been smashed apart by thunderbolts.

Lukor itself showed some signs of damage, but hadn't been hit as hard.

'You know that Arrina and Enkul-Anu were lovers for a century,' Mari-Ye said.

Maritaten couldn't have been more shocked if the skull-faced priest had slapped her.

'What?'

He nodded. 'It's not well known, but we know. It's the only reason we ever inclined towards the new gods at all.'

Only in Narmer, Maritaten thought, *would a pantheon that had risen to power a thousand years before still be called the 'new gods'.*

'What happened?' she asked.

Mari-Ye shrugged. 'Someone told Sypa,' he said. 'The lovers were very careful, and only a handful of mortals and gods knew the secret, so someone betrayed her, and Enkul-Anu had to cast her out. The new sun god is as weak as a kitten. I won't say that Arrina's banishment is the only reason that the sun is failing, and the desert is encroaching on our valleys, but—'

'That part I knew,' she said.

'I want you to know because…' Mari-Ye looked at the destruction of what would be, in normal times, *his* temple. 'Because if you ever have the chance to negotiate, we'd like Arrina back.'

'I know,' she snapped. Mari-Ye made her feel like a real queen; this must be the annoyance of every patronised ruler. 'Life in the Halls of Pleasure doesn't actually erode the mental processes, priest.'

He looked at her mildly enough. 'What I want to say is subtle and secret,' he muttered. 'I mean no offence. We know you are very intelligent. We chose you.'

So you did, she thought.

'So say it,' she said.

'Narmer usually defeats her enemies, but when she fails to

win on the battlefield, she wears them down with grain and gold. Gods are no different. We can accept these gods, as long as they return Arrina. Everything else is priestly prattle.'

'Ahhh.' Maritaten hadn't known that. 'So in exchange for Arrina, we can trade away all the rest of the older gods and all our liberties?'

Mari-Ye shrugged. 'Arrina knows something,' he said carefully. 'Her release from the Outer Darkness would probably reveal who betrayed her.'

Maritaten was losing interest. Theology was far too much like the bitchiest gossip in the Halls of Pleasure, except it was about immortals.

'Will anyone care?' she asked.

Mari-Ye frowned at her; she'd gone too far.

'I think it might divide heaven,' the old priest said seriously. 'There are many very old divisions among these new gods.'

She looked at him sidelong.

'Very well. If we can ever negotiate anything, we'll go for Arrina, may the sun rise in splendour.'

Her automatic obedience to the sun ritual clearly pleased him.

'You are pure at heart,' he said.

You might be surprised, she thought. But instead, she said, 'Tell me some good news.'

He thought for a moment. 'I have no good news.'

'Then why do you press all this godlike garbage on me now?'

'I had a dream. I believe it was sent by the Blue Goddess, and in it, you were triumphant.'

She smiled. 'That's good news.'

He raised an eyebrow. 'The Blue Goddess is anything but dependable.'

She saw that his attention had been diverted. He was looking down the deck of the reed ship, watching the old man they'd rescued. At least, Maritaten assumed Timut-Imri was an old man. He moved quickly enough. He was doing elaborate stretching exercises amidships, using the mainmast for some of them. The busy sailors and the equally busy servants tried to avoid him, but he brought many stares.

Even as she watched, he finished his exercises and bowed to the sun, and then collected his clothes and walked up the deck towards them. He was naked; she saw that he had the body of a younger man, and only the hint of a belly and some wrinkled skin told his true age. He might almost have passed for handsome, except for the ridiculous long beard.

He bowed. While nudity was not uncommon in Narmer, one didn't usually appear before the Lady of the High House in the altogether, and eyebrows were raised.

'Great Lady of the High House,' he said in the High Tongue of Narmer. 'Favoured of Arrina, whose hand raises the sacred waters.'

Maritaten had thought him an arrogant old fool, but she was beginning to suspect he was merely an original. An eccentric. She favoured him with a smile.

'You speak the High Tongue beautifully,' she said.

Next to her, Mari-Ye nodded agreement. The old man was obviously a foreigner, and yet he spoke the sacred words of the old language.

He shrugged as if it was of little moment. He rose from his deep bow, and at her nod, climbed the last two steps to the command deck and the royal dais.

'How may I help you, Timut-Imri?' she asked.

He smiled. 'Now that's new,' he said. 'Your predecessor was only interested in my ability to perform party-tricks.' He looked at her. 'I never met you, Great Lady.'

'I was, at the time, a party trick myself,' she said, unruffled.

He nodded. 'Ah,' he said, as if that sort of thing could happen

307

to anyone. 'You know that if Enkul-Anu comes with his lightning bolts, he'll sink your fleet. I can't stop him.'

She shrugged. 'I know. I'm playing the knucklebones as I
find they lie.'

He met her eye, which was discouraged among courtiers.
'You are rebelling against the gods?' he asked. 'Before the battle,
I thought perhaps you were just defending yourself against some
capricious attack.'

She sat back. 'I will answer your question, mage, but one
really does not interrogate the Lady of the High House.'

The old man looked at Mari-Ye.

'I can help,' he said. 'But only if I know what you are attempting.'

'Who are you?' Mari-Ye asked suddenly.

The man smiled. 'I'm a student of the universe.'

Maritaten allowed herself an eye roll. The man had a long
beard, but otherwise seemed very like a teenage boy.

'Spare us,' she muttered.

The man spread his arms, as if asking what else he could
have said.

'I'm three centuries old,' he said. 'I've learnt a fair amount
about the underpinnings of the system by which we live. I have,
up until now, stayed in the shadows, but the bastards, by which
I mean the gods, wrecked… Never mind all that.'

'Oh, no,' Maritaten said softly. 'I wish to know.'

He shrugged. 'I was in love with… someone.' He looked away.
'And he's dead now.' Perhaps Timut-Imri realised his explanation
was insufficient; he blinked, and looked back. 'He died in the
collapse of the palace. I tried to save him. And his useless father.'

Maritaten leant forward. 'I saw you,' she said. 'I saw you raise
a… a bubble. Of light.'

He nodded. 'When the demons cut through my spell, my

308

beloved was already dead. In a few heartbeats, so were the god-king and god-queen. I left before they ate me, too.'

Maritaten was young, but she was expert at reading people, especially men. He was ashamed: ashamed that he had run; ashamed that he had failed; bitter, angry.

And thus, almost certainly loyal.

'Welcome to my very limited kingdom,' she said. 'I accept your service. I will appoint you a royal councillor. In exchange, it is…' She paused to fold away her smile. 'It is usual for those close to the throne to wear clothes.'

Timut-Imri bowed again. 'I am sorry.' He didn't sound sorry. 'One more thing,' he said.

She nodded.

'I believe we'll find that the World Serpent has escaped and risen to fight. My reading is that the World Serpent has killed one of the Great Gods. The new gods.' He spread his hands. 'It's not a guess. There are signs.'

Mari-Ye made a gesture of aversion. 'The World Serpent?'

Timut-Imri smiled. 'Yes. A giant dragon the size of four warships laid keel to keel, four or five thousand years old, with all the wisdom of a hundred generations of men and all the wickedness of a legion of demons.'

Maritaten took a deep breath. 'Another nail in our coffin.'

'I was thinking more of an ally in rebellion,' purred the old man.

He bowed, tossed his raiment over his shoulder like a towel, and strode off down the deck, still nude.

Maritaten watched him go, her mind reeling at the thought of allying with one of the world's most ancient evils.

She sighed. Mari-Ye cleared his throat. 'The Jekers are landing in the delta,' he went on, as if the sorcerer had never been there. 'Prince Ak-Arrina wanted me to keep it from you until tomorrow, but I think it's better—'

Instead of further depressing her, the news was like ice water in her veins. She sat up, her face as hard as stone, her mouth set.

'First, *priest*, you may have made me, but I, not you, am Queen of the High House.'

Mari-Ye looked at her steadily, and then, without being asked, made a full obeisance. She thought she heard his bones creak.

'I offer ten thousand apologies,' he said from the deck at her side.

'I accept them all,' she said. 'Now get up, and never do that again. I *always* hear first, not Ak-Arrina, who is neither my consort, my secret lover, nor King of the High House.'

'Yes, Great Queen.'

'Fuck yes, priest. Understand me. Or replace me.' She met his eye, and he was rueful. She went on, 'Ak-Arrina is probably good at commanding armies, but he's not a good politician and sometimes I may not want *him* to know what's happening. Understand me?'

The priest stood taller. 'Events forced my hands, mistress. I agree with you in every way. We received the news together, from scouts.'

She nodded, mollified. 'Very well.' She looked at him. 'We will fight the Jekers.'

He looked towards Lukor.

'There are reputedly thousands of them,' he said.

She looked, too. 'You think I should stand and fight for Lukor?'

Mari-Ye shook his head. 'Hopeless.'

Maritaten stretched. 'I agree. But the delta ...'

'We can raise fresh levies.' Mari-Ye sounded tired. Or perhaps hopeless.

'Levies won't do much against Jekers except die,' she said, and realised how true it was.

'They might buy time for your chariots to defeat them,' Mari-Ye said. 'Or we will all die facing them.'

She shrugged. 'Perhaps we will die. But the Blue Goddess sent you a dream that I triumphed. And anyway, if I cannot protect my people from fucking Jekers, I might as well be dead, eh?'

She was watching the slim brown figure of the old man as he went down the central hatchway.

'I imagine our sorcerer might be effective against Jekers,' she said.

'We have perhaps two thousand warriors, almost no food, and no supplies. Most of our archers don't even have arrows, and Lukor is exposed to our foes.' He shook his head.

'We have the guards – most of the chariots, the Guard of Swords, and half a thousand Py archers.' She looked at him. 'Jekers won't have chariots.' And then, after thinking for a moment, she asked, 'Why haven't the gods just sunk us on the river, as old Timut-Imri said? Enkul-Anu must be able to see us.'

'The gods move in mysterious ways,' the priest said. 'Usually foolish ways. Whatever drives the Great Storm God, he spent a day destroying his former lover's temple … instead of finding you.'

'Gods,' Maritaten said. 'Just like a fucking man.' She looked at the banks of the river. 'Hide us by day – use the swamps north of Lukor. We'll only travel at night.'

'Where do we stop? Phatos? The palace?' The old priest sounded almost wistful.

Maritaten looked out over the bow as if she could see her whole kingdom.

'For supplies, yes. Otherwise, no. Definitely not the palace, and not the capital. I would be lost there – pillowed in comfort until the enemy took me.'

Mari-Ye sighed. 'Perhaps you are wise,' he agreed.

'We take every soldier from the capital, and go to Thais, in the delta. It's on the main branch of the river, and we have river power, at least until the gods or the Jekers take it from us. Let's use it.'

'Thais it is, Great Lady of the High House.'

Maritaten allowed herself a smile. Despite everything, it was a pleasure to rule, and to be obeyed. She pushed her doubts down, and dismissed her fears.

Until it was time to sleep, when they would all come creeping back.

Auza, Home of the Gods

'What the fuck happened here?' Enkul-Anu bellowed. His rage was all the more pure because he'd allowed himself to believe that things were getting better.

Only Laila had the courage to face him directly.

'Ara went to face the World Serpent,' she said simply. She let her arms fall by her sides.

Enkul-Anu looked at the frozen faces of the other gods. Grulu looked angry, but she always did. Timurti wore an absent look and spittle trailed down her face. Gul and his consort looked like the dead, but that was their business. Enkul-Anu didn't trust Gul; he didn't really trust any of them. But there was something about Gul...

He realised he was looking for Druku.

Fucking traitor. You'd be a big help now.

And there was Sypa, who, if anything, looked pleased.

Enkul-Anu raised his arms to heaven and unleashed a scream of rage that carried his anger and loss out into the *aether*. More than a brother – Ara had been a war comrade across almost eternity. Gallant, honourable and easily led.

The best of us.

And we broke him.

I fucking broke him. Dammit.

Enkul-Anu's mourning was sincere, and total, and he took himself into the Hall of Emptiness and slammed the great black stone door behind him. Heaven shook.

Time passed. Heaven went on. And Sypa took to running it.

'Any news?' Sypa asked Laila, her handmaiden.

Laila shrugged. 'The battle in Narmer is a total victory,' she said. 'I'm reading the hierophant's report on the Nexus. Ah, the goddess-queen of Noa has sent her tribute.'

'What did Cyra send me?' Sypa snapped.

In Sypa's oft-repeated view, the goddess-queen of Noa was a little too successful, had ruled too long, and thought too highly of herself.

'Cyra has sent the full tribute of Noa, mistress – two hundred and seventy-two bars of refined gold, nine hundred and seventy bars of refined silver, seven hundred and six male slaves…'

'What did she send *me*?' Sypa asked in a voice of thunder.

Laila looked at her. 'It's her tribute, mistress. To all of heaven.'

'What did she send Enkul-Anu?'

Laila could see where this was going, and she hesitated in her answer.

'One hundred black bulls, mistress, with horns gilt, and crowns of roses. And fifty trained acrobats to leap them for the Storm God's pleasure.'

Sypa leant forward, her voice soft and dangerous. 'And what did she send to the other gods?'

Laila sighed inwardly. 'For… For Ara, one hundred godborn warriors with the long bronze swords, to fight for his pleasure.' She went on, her voice barely audible. 'And a suit of armour'

'And *what did she send me*?' Sypa all but shrieked.

'It must be an oversight, mistress. Although you … you … you are not on the tribute list of Noa.' Laila sounded as if she didn't want to say the last.

'That overweening arrogant witch. I'll have her entrails,' Sypa spat. 'How dare she?'

Laila blinked and could be seen to count to ten. 'Mistress, you have never been on the tribute list of Noa.'

'How well I know it,' Sypa said. 'Now that will change.'

A brief time later, as heaven measured it, Illikumi came to heaven with a wounded Telipinu in his arms.

Sypa met them, saw to Telipinu's healing by handing him to Laila, and ordered slaves to repair the sky chariot.

'We need a craft god,' Laila said, looking at the relatively minor damage. 'Sypa! This is a star-stone injury! I can feel the sickness from here!'

They were standing on the ledge of the great 'Portal of Air', the gate into heaven used by flyers.

Sypa flinched away. 'Fucking mortals. Disgusting. It's a sickness.'

Laila was very brave, whatever other tendencies she had, and she leant down and sniffed the wound. It was small: an arrow prick in the heel, where a mortal shaft had gone through the light floor of the chariot car, through the young god's sandal, and into his foot. The immortal heel was almost purple-black, and the flesh around it looked as if it had been burned, and even as she watched, corruption was spreading over the ankle.

'And a healing god,' Laila said. 'We *really* need a healing god.'

Sypa shrugged. 'We're not very good at fixing things, are we, my sweet? Mostly, we're good at breaking things.'

Laila sent for resin-laced ambrosia. And then, moving decisively, she took a sharp knife from her bosom and cut into the

314

wounded godling's heel, and began sucking and spitting out the blood with her own immortal lips.

'That's disgusting,' Sypa said. 'Stop.'

Laila ignored her mistress. She could see the advance of the corruption slowing, and she knew she was winning.

'Laila, do that somewhere else.'

Laila looked up. Telipinu's godly ichor, some of it nearly black with the poison, ran down her chin. She looked like a monster several times over, her own beauty now turned to horror.

Sypa backed away.

'I'm saving his life, Great Goddess,' Laila said. 'If I take the time to move him to a more aesthetic location, he might die. Even as I speak to you, the corruption gains again.'

Sypa didn't even raise an eyebrow. 'I order it. Do not do this in my sight. Gods must be incorruptible. You look like a mortal just now. Go.'

Laila took a deep breath, and then, the perfect handmaiden, lowered her eyes, lifted the young godling, and carried him away.

'And you?' Sypa said to the snake-headed godling. 'Are you wounded?'

'No, Great Goddessss,' Illilumi replied. 'I am unmarked.'

'And Narmer?' Sypa asked.

'Beaten. Beaten badly, with hideousss lossssessss.' Illikumi's snake-mouth formed a wicked, fang-toothed smile.

'And that little whore, Maritaten?'

'May be dead,' Illikumi said slowly. 'We certainly cooked all her ssssorcerersss. Enkul-Anu laid wassste to the whole centre of her army.'

'But you don't *know*,' Sypa snapped.

Illikumi shook his head. 'I don't. But when it'sss light, I'll go back and burn their river fleet.'

Sypa was entirely uninterested in river fleets.

'I have different orders for you. Take this case of thunderbolt javelins, and destroy the Temple of Arrina in Lukor. Turn the stones into sand. Make it impossible for anyone to miss the message.'

'Perhaps the Great Ssstorm God—'

Sypa smiled. 'The Great Storm God is mourning his brother. I want the Temple of Arrina levelled tomorrow morning.'

'And the river fleet? A consssiderable number of rebelsss essscaped.' Illikumi leant forward intently.

Sypa offered a seductive smile. 'And where is my son's chariot?' she purred.

Illikumi frowned. 'I left it on the sssand. We are triumphant—'

'Demons!' Sypa snarled, and motioned at a demon guard. 'Fetch it immediately, before some mortal gets ideas.'

The demon bowed. 'Great Goddess! Your will is our will.'

Sypa turned back to the snake-headed god.

'My young friend,' she said, and stepped up close to him, 'a few mortals here or there will not alter the game, but the destruction of the Great Temple of Lukor will tell every fucking peasant in Narmer who's in charge. Do my bidding, and I will arrange a magnificent reward.'

Illikumi's snake head grinned again.

'I will do your bidding, Great Goddesssss.'

'And what do you want as a reward?' she asked, staring deep into his snake eyes. Her voice was a soft caress; her skin was warm and lush …

'Narmer,' he said. 'I want to be the god of Narmer.'

'A snake god of Narmer?' She grinned. 'Perfect.' Her smile was terrifying.

He took her offered hand, kissed it, and then, with incredible daring, turned it over, and Sypa felt his forked tongue, rough and delightful against the palm of her hand.

'Perfect,' she sighed.

316

Bashmu pulled at the golden chariot.

'What the fuck happened here?' he muttered.

He stood as tall as three men, his scale armour glowing in the sunset. The desert was carpeted with corpses for as far as he could see.

'Big battle,' Gallu said. 'And us not invited.' He stepped into the car, and the four golden stags came to life.

'This is fucked,' Bashmu said. 'The gods need to stop fucking around. Put us in, we'll fuck the mortals up.'

Namtar showed his fangs. 'True words, boss.'

Gallu had the damaged chariot off the sand now.

'Things are fucked in heaven, boys' he said. 'The Storm God is bawlin' his eyes out and we're playing fetch an' carry.'

'Losin' 'is grip, maybe,' Namtar growled.

'Stow that shit,' Bashmu spat. 'Storm God will put things right. Lost 'is best mate, eh? Stands to reason.'

'I'm just sayin' it's all fucked up, boss. We got to show the mortals who's in charge.' Namtar cowered a little, aware he'd said too much.

'We do what Sypa said, and then maybe we tell her it's time to send in the Legion,' Gallu suggested.

'Which of us goin' ta tell Sypa any such shit?' Bashmu demanded. 'You, Nashtar? Goin' ta tell the Great Goddess who to run a war? You know what happened to the captain, eh, lads?'

Silence greeted that.

'Let's get this heap o' crap back to heaven and wait for the Storm God to come out,' Bashtu said into the silence. 'An' maybe, just maybe, I'll say som'in' to him.'

'Fuck me,' Gallu said. 'There's thunderbolts in this thing. In the quivers.'

All of the demons looked at the lethal tools of Enkul-Anu's power.

'Don't be getting' any fuckin' ideas,' Bashmu growled.

Gallu shrugged. 'I didn't say nuffin',' he murmured.

Nashtar leant over and drew a thunderbolt from one of the javelin quivers.

'Fuck me,' he said. 'You know what these things can do?'

'Put it back, fuckwit,' Bashmu ordered.

'Come on, boss,' Nashtar said. 'They'll never miss one. Save it for a rainy day, like.'

Bashmu took his whip off his belt, and then thought better of whatever he was going to do.

'One, then,' he said. 'Only one. We'll hide it.' He nodded to Nashtar. 'You never know.'

'Ya' don't, at that,' Nashtar said.

Era

Of course, a third of her rescued former slaves had wandered off. Worse, a dozen had already taken ship and left, and no amount of moral posturing from Jawala and Pavi could make her feel better about it.

'When we're taking our boats upstream over the rapids, you'll miss those twelve strong backs,' Era spat.

'They *aren't* slaves,' Jawala insisted.

Era just walked out. She wasn't sleeping with Dite; she wasn't really sleeping well at all, and she was beginning to hate everyone, with the possible exception of Aanat. Old Jawat insisted on his absolute right to have a drunken orgy in a brothel and ignored her demands that he do any work. Jawala prated about morality and the Jeker prisoners. Nicté and Hefa-Asus were having a destructive spat of some kind that made them both useless. Era had the cargoes of six ships to transfer up the falls, river boats to buy and porters to hire and *it was all on her.*

And Aanat. For a man who had declared his unwillingness to go upriver, he had thrown himself into the work with an intensity that might have amused or threatened a different Era. He had found them a dozen big log canoes, and traded wool cloaks and scrap metal for them. He had found a way to ship the Dry One's great cocoon up the falls without giving away the contents, and he had found a way to get the bickering bear and donkey to co-operate long enough to walk up the long road around the falls to the top, to the amusement of every local who saw the two animals together.

'We should have charged, like a circus show,' Aanat said.

'In what? Scrap metal?'

'Cacao beans. Almost everyone here uses them and the little cowrie shells.' Aanat held out a handful. 'Somewhere in the world, there's a beach covered in these little brutes.'

That made Era laugh, and very little made her laugh these days.

The effort of sorting the cargoes, and shipping them up the winding road through the forest and up a very steep incline – almost a full parasang – to the landing stage north of the falls where they could transfer to the river, took every soul she had available, and they worked hard. Atosa grumbled, but he helped; he knew how to organise people.

But more of them wandered off. They took jobs. One married a local man and settled down.

Era seethed. 'We're never going to reach the star-stone,' she complained to Aanat.

The two of them were in Forest Port, the fairly prosperous town that had grown up at the top of the falls. Two major products came down the river: wine and tin. Both were traded throughout the Ocean, and so the long portage around the falls was an economic as well as a geographic reality.

They'd ended up in a tea shop, of all places, tired and modestly triumphant at getting to the end of the load-out. Aanat and Era sat and drank some of the mountain tea that everyone drank in Vetluna. And Era glared at him.

'I'm so tired of this,' she spat, suddenly furious. 'We're trying to make the world a better place, and half of my people are fucking off and doing no work. Some leave us—'

Aanat's eyes were mild – almost as if he was amused.

'You find this funny?' she asked.

He shrugged and sipped his tea.

'Say something!' Era said.

Aanat spread his hands. 'You will only say that I sound like Jawala,' he said. 'But they aren't as committed as you are. And if you consider the pressures they've survived in the last two months, you might understand that they need a break.'

'*They* need a break? Does anyone know how hard I'm working?' She was instantly regretful. 'And you. I think you've outworked me.'

He shook his head. 'They wouldn't follow me. They follow you. But you can take a break. The world won't collapse.' He paused, and his smile vanished. 'Actually, it might. But not because of you. This thing you and Gamash and Zos planned – it's going to take years. Years!'

Era put her head in her hands.

'Are you planning on running flat-out for years, Era?' Aanat shook his head.

'We're racing the winter upriver,' Era said through clenched teeth. 'Time is a driver. But so is the need to keep all *these people* together. And sometimes I feel that I'm surrounded by lazy idiots.'

Aanat sat back. 'My mother used to tell me that when no one

wants to obey you, that's because they have something better to do. I've had hired sailors aboard, and I pay warehouse keepers and longshoremen all over the Ocean. Mother was correct. If you push too hard, eventually you lose everyone.'

'So, what. Overwinter here?' Era's tone was derisive. 'Lose the winter?'

Why the fuck can't they see this the way I do? We need to move!

'You catch more flies with honey than with vinegar,' Aanat said.

Era leant forward, ready to tell him what she thought of coddling malingerers, and then she caught herself, and after a brief but titanic inner struggle that caused her to flush…

She sat back and sipped her tea, and said nothing.

Aanat was very good at silence, so the two of them sat together for a quarter of an hour. The year was growing old, and darkness would fall early.

'The arrangements are made,' Era said. 'What if I declare the day after tomorrow a day of rest, and we pay for a party? And then, with aching heads, we leave the next morning?'

Aanat smiled. 'That might work.'

The bear and the donkey

'What's the traitor *doing*?' the bear shouted at the donkey.

The two of them had 'escaped' from their pen and ambled to the low stone wall that prevented children from falling into the massive waterfall. The rush of water was louder than a thousand war cries, and it was almost impossible to be heard, which was why the bear had chosen it; that, and because to her left, at the base of the falls towards the city of Vetluna, she could see a series of caves, including the one they were both watching.

The donkey shook his big head and his ears twitched as he rid himself of a late-season horsefly.

'I can't see much,' the donkey said.

'Can we steal some better bodies?' the bear asked.

The donkey made a half whinny, half *chuff* of contempt.

'The traitor is watching us just as we watch them,' the donkey said. 'They'll know. And the Dry One – it's sharp, and its auratic abilities are well honed.'

'I hate this body,' the bear muttered.

'Imagine life as a donkey. I was Lord of Horses!'

The bear grunted. 'And I was Lady of Bears,' she said.

The rush of the water covered their thoughts for a while, and then the donkey said, 'There! The traitor is moving.'

'Carrying something,' the bear said. 'What are they hiding?'

'We'll work it out when we start upriver,' the donkey said. 'Although I hate to leave the sea.'

The bear made a loud noise – almost a roar – which carried over the sound of the water.

'We're far off the plan, now,' she said. 'How do we get back to the plan from here?'

The donkey started up the wettest path away from the falls, but stopped and looked back.

'We don't. We just make it up as we go. No plan ever survives contact with these humans, anyway. I already miss the sea.'

The bear put a paw on the donkey's flank. 'I was *in the Outer Darkness*. I couldn't go back there again. I'd go mad. I almost did…'

'So?' the donkey asked. 'I'm trying to be two entities at once.'

'So, I can't afford to lose.'

'Who can? All my people are depending on me to save them. And I'm stuck *on land*. And I still don't see anything that will make any change. They're so *slow*.' The donkey gave a quiet honk. 'But I'll find a way.'

They landed at Kanun, the provincial capital of Yahud, just north of the river delta – one of the 'Northern Principalities' that was firmly under the thumb of Narmer. It was a good-sized town, clearly very rich, and their arrival caused immediate panic; Pollon watched as long columns of camels and horses fled into the desert to the west.

It took the better part of a day to establish that they were not Jekers, nor were they a danger to the people of Kanun or Yahud. Their prince was away with all of his chariots and most of his men, serving the goddess-queen of Narmer. They had nothing to resist Zos' fleet; so many warships and warriors that Zos might have had the town in an hour.

Zos paid out some of his vanishing supply of precious metals to buy food and reassure merchants. Pollon left him to it, and walked up into the town. Like most parts of Narmer, Kanun was warm, and the town looked like a pile of mismatched building blocks, all painted the startling yellow that was some local variation on whitewash. The acropolis was magnificent, high above the town, the only rocky outcrop to be seen for twenty stadia along the coast. The palace was at the top, as were the temples.

Like most of the Northern Principalities, the town boasted a rich collection of temples: one to the dominant pantheon; one for the old Sun Goddess Arrina whose cult was so popular in Narmer; and a scattering of other temples to gods no longer worshipped anywhere else, or to gods who were apparently in a different aspect, including the Nikali gods, their distant but ever-present neighbours to the north. The Nikali God of death, Miklantikuitl, looked like a feathered version of Gul, but the Feathered Serpent God of Wisdom, Kwatzalcotl, looked like no one from Auza. Pollon, fresh from the encounter on Lazba, was suddenly struck by how much the Feathered Serpent looked like…

…like Ataboga.

Pollon was still considering what, if anything, that might mean when he was searched by a pair of very professional guards, and then allowed to wander the sacred enclosure. After he'd looked into the other temples, he approached the Temple of All Gods, with the usual imagery over the great bronze doors: Sypa on a couch, Enkul-Anu standing over her, right in the centre, and the other gods spread to either side, including a couple that Pollon didn't recognise. A new statue was being hauled into place while he watched: a hawk-headed god with a golden bow. The statue was replacing the 'Two Sisters', Tyka and Temis.

Pollon smothered his thoughts and plunged into the cool gloom of the nave. The floor was polished marble – thousands of perfectly cut pieces forming a rich black and white mosaic. Squat, heavy pillars lined the nave and supported the marble roof.

And there, high on the first pillar, was a god's eye.

Pollon glanced around. A junior priest, accompanied by two acolytes, was waving a thurible over one of the sacrificial altars, purifying it and scenting the air with something spiky and musky, and much better than the reek of butchered meat that it was replacing.

Pollon moved along the centre of the nave in plain view of all three celebrants, making his obeisance to each god's pillar in turn. At the pillar dedicated to Sypa, the priest glanced at him with approval. Then, his task complete, the young priest gathered his acolytes. The three went back to the sacred space around the high altar and vanished through a door.

Pollon looked around and then made his way up the line of supporting columns, at what he hoped was an unhurried pace.

At the entry to the inner sanctum, the *naos*, he paused and listened, and found his heart was beating very quickly indeed.

No one could enter the inner sanctum of a temple to the Gods of Auza except the anointed. Pollon felt as if there was a barrier of bronze, even though he could see that the middle of the three doors into the inner sanctum was open a crack.

He peeked in.

Empty.

He slipped into the inner sanctum to see a detailed mosaic floor, and walls that at first glance appeared to be solid gold. The sunlight, reflected from the vault overhead, with openings high in the clerestory and a dozen enormous bronze mirrors, dazzled his eyes, and it took him a moment to realise that the walls had hangings of cloth of gold. The effect was magnificent, and literally awe-inspiring. It was sheer good fortune that there was no one there to see him as he sucked in a long breath, stunned by the splendour. And then, he got his head around what he was doing and made his feet move. He took a long look at the nearest shining curtain of cloth of gold, was reassured to find it threadbare towards the top, and dusty. He slipped in behind it.

He couldn't stop his knees from trembling, but, after a few breaths, he began to search for doors. There had to be one…

In fact, there were half a dozen doors hidden behind the cloth-of-gold hangings, and four were locked. One was an office of some sort, the mingled smells of fresh papyrus and wet clay taking him back to his own scriptorium. The images summoned by the scents were so powerful that he stood frozen for a moment, ready to hear Spathios ask for orders.

Spathios. Mura. Dead? Enslaved?

I scarcely think of them any more. I feel as if I've lived another life since my city fell. Ah, Mura…

Indeed, Pollon's entire life before being tortured and left for dead seemed like a tale told by someone else.

He looked around for a niche or a closet dedicated to the use of the god's eye network, but there was none, so he kept trying doors until he found a second one that opened. Behind it was a purpose-built casting chamber, with a variety of silver and gold patterns inlaid into a cedarwood floor. And on the wall, at head height, a familiar sigil.

There were voices out in the *naos*, or perhaps the outer temple.

Pollon stepped in, almost unable to breathe, and made himself go straight to the sigil. He breathed on it...

And it lit up. And recognized him.

Despite his fears, Pollon went to work, scrutinising the Nexus and searching... searching for... he wasn't sure what. And the voices came closer.

There.

He had, as usual, overthought the matter. In his own scriptorium, he'd created methods of 'filing' each of the day's *anaphora* reports. It was all about fine control of the *Aura*, and he'd adjusted the flow until he could drop and retrieve reports in order. That was the way his mind worked

It hadn't occurred to him that others wouldn't do the same. And so, the complete chaos of reports and messages that greeted him on this node was an ugly surprise. He had to fight the urge to organise them – that would be noticed.

'Eminence!' said the voice outside. 'Surely you see the potential for conflict?'

Pollon thought his heart might explode on the spot. They were just the other side of the cloth-of-gold hanging and he'd foolishly left the door open. It would leave a bulge in the fabric – anxiety dropped him out of his trance and contact with the *auratic*.

A slighter voice, heavy with dignity, replied, 'Our first duty is to the gods.'

'Even if that means betraying our prince?' the deeper voice asked.

'Don't imagine that I haven't had these thoughts, Ben-Turuk. I have. Our prince is capable and fair. I'd hate to trade him for some god-appointed placeholder. But—'

'But what? Hierophant, they want us to raise the city against the prince!'

Despite the voices, Pollon managed to regain his contact.

Pollon found the *anaphoras* for the last ten days and began to memorise them. He'd spent his youth learning to memorise; it was an essential scribal skill, which might have become a little flabby the last few months.

'If Sypa asks it of us, it is our duty.'

The deeper voice said, 'You have heard of the slave revolt in Ma'rib?'

The one he'd called 'Hierophant' said, 'Yes. Of course.'

'What if…? What if it was us against the gods, Eminence?'

'If you go on like this, Ben-Turuk, I will have to remove you from office.'

Pollon began to wonder if there really was a goddess of fortune. If so, she was riding his shoulder.

Memorisation while listening to a conversation and being terrified: definitely a challenge. And the complete confusion of the files made it…

He found a report that caught his attention, even through the fear and the other considerations.

And he found the report's attached reply.

And the reply to that.

Someone in heaven had ordered a huge supply of resin to heal an injured godling, a storehouse reported their supplies were low, and something called *Nest* had filled the order.

Nest.

A choked cry and a heavy fall out in the main chamber

snapped him out of his trance again. Pollon had missed something; the intensity of his concentration had drowned out the outer conversation and his own fear, which came rushing back like the sea into a broken sea wall.

It was silent in the tabernacle.

Pollon gave himself a moment to appreciate going undiscovered, and then completed memorising the *anaphoras*.

The Nest.

That certainly sounds promising.

He moved carefully to the curtain and saw the blood pooling at the edge of the mosaic floor, and then he understood the silence.

The hierophant lay dead in the centre of the floor.

Pollon wanted to hide; he considered going back into the scriptorium, or even trying the other doors again. *Go now*, he told himself.

The murderer – some underpriest? – would flee. At least at first. *I should go now*, he told his feet.

He took a deep breath and slipped out from behind the wall-hanging.

Then he made himself move to the door to the tabernacle. It was ajar, and he looked out.

He took five deep breaths, and told himself, *now*. And then again.

Don't be a coward.

I'm a scribe! Not a thief!

Two more deep breaths.

A sound from the nave. A slave, sweeping.

He went through the door, and immediately turned left, into the side aisle.

The slave never raised his head as Pollon made it out of the temple, and then, his dread increasing with every step, down the long flight of formal steps off the acropolis and into the town. And then to the ships.

On the beach, he vomited up his hasty meal, and had to sit on a rock above the tide line. He looked out to sea, and gave himself a chance to recover.

The Nest.

It was real, then. A place that *made* the resin, that was in turn made into the gods' ambrosia. And the Nest was close to heaven, or part of it; the messages made that clear.

That steadied him. He rose and went to the ships where he found Zos, stripped to the waist, with Daos and Leontas and Trayos, bartering for a load of Narmerian grain and cooked meat for three thousand people. He waited until they were done, and local merchants and farmers were setting up an impromptu market on the beach, and only then did he take Zos by the arm and drag him into the shade of the *Wave Serpent*'s stern as she was closest to the town.

'I've got access to the *anaphoras*,' he said. 'I can give you a summary in an hour or so, but here's the short form – Maritaten has fought a major action in the east, against the Hundred Cities and the gods.'

'And lost?'

'Lost badly. They're hunting her. But it's chaos – and it looks to me like they haven't found her. She escaped on the river, at least three days ago.'

'And the Jekers?' Zos looked out to sea as he asked.

'Nothing,' Pollon answered. 'It's as if no one is watching them. Or they've vanished. Or no one is interested.'

Zos rubbed his beard. 'Fuck,' he muttered.

Pollon leant forward. 'More importantly, I think I've found the source of the resin.'

Zos was still thinking, eyes on the horizon. But suddenly his eyes changed focus.

'What?' he snapped. 'Don't play with me, brother.'

Pollon shook his head. 'It'll take me a few days,' he said. 'But I think I can already guess. There's a place called the Nest—'

'Dry Ones!' Zos said.

Like Pollon, he saw it immediately. Pollon knew the warrior was quite intelligent, for a non-scribe, and he smiled encouragement.

Zos went on, 'They must have a captive nest of Dry Ones ...'

'And it has to be near heaven. Or attached to it.' Pollon shrugged. 'I need hours to go through all the reports, and I'll make a summary of the last ten days' *anaphoras*. Maybe there's something in there that I missed about the Jekers.' He paused, glanced up at the acropolis, and back at his friend. 'Ahh ... and someone just murdered the hierophant.'

'Here?' Zos looked at Pollon with an odd expression. 'Was that someone, by any chance, you?'

Zos said it in such a matter-of-fact tone that Pollon was chilled. 'Not me!' Pollon protested. 'Some junior priest. They were having a spat about the gods, and the junior was apparently too patriotic to his prince to stomach a betrayal.'

'Interesting,' Zos said slowly. 'And you say you need access to the god's eye?'

'Not the eye. I can't access everything from a single eye. I need the Nexus – a priest's access.'

Zos fingered his beard. 'Maybe they'll need us to *restore order* here,' he said. 'If they're experiencing civil strife.'

'There's no civil strife yet ...' Pollon paused. 'Oh. I see.'

Zos shook his head. 'Heaven,' he said. 'The Nest will be in heaven. That's ... what? Two or three months' travel to the south? And then we'd have to climb the mountain at Auza and get in ... That's not happening any time soon.'

'But the resin? It's the key!' Pollon tried not to sound too adamant, but his excitement showed.

Zos sighed. 'Right now, I need you to find Maritaten. And the Jekers. The delta is huge. We don't have enough force or enough food to go wandering around the side channels and rivulets. And I'm afraid to find them at sea.'

He looked back at the horizon. And let out a long sigh.

'We'd better get to scouting,' he muttered.

Chapter Four

Axe and Anenome

Axe was looking at the ruins of the temple complex north of Lukor.

'That's all very well,' he said to Anenome. 'But it looks to me like all of their best charioteers got away.'

Anenome was shaving. He was a very handsome man, slim, unscarred, and he liked to look his best before a fight. He had a bronze razor, and he was using a discarded Narmerian conical helmet as a shaving bowl.

'Their river fleet got away,' the shaving man said. 'Their whole household got away – all their best chariots. And the Guard of Swords.'

Axe grunted. 'Fucking gods. They never finish anything. Remember when you said this contract would be different?"

'Watch your mouth, brother.' Anenome pointed at a god's eye that had been hastily painted on the ruins of a wall. 'Anyway, it *is* different,' he said. 'We're getting paid in ambrosia.'

'I hear it's fucking chaos up there on Auza.' Axe spread his hands.

Axe ignored his partner's concern and crossed his arms. When he leant against the ruined wall, it groaned.

'You have a spy in heaven?' Anenome asked.

Axe gave nothing away but a shrug. 'I have a friend.'

Anenome took a towel from a slave, wiped his face, and tossed the towel back.

'Are you saying we're on our own?'

'What I hear? Enkul-Anu is in a fit because the War God died facing the World Serpent. And Sypa's in charge, but she won't lead armies. Telipinu took a hit – we saw it – and Illikumi took him home to heaven. So …'

'Fuck. So it's just us.' The smaller man took a sword from his scabbard, hanging close to hand, and began doing exercises.

'Hmmm.' Axe looked like a brutal killer; looks didn't deceive. But he was more than just cunning; he had a clear notion of strategy, and Anenome never ignored him. 'Jekers are moving into the delta. Or so I'm told.'

The rapid flow of Anenome's exercise paused.

'We don't own the Jekers?' he asked.

'That's a question for another day,' Axe said. 'One of the fucking gods has the Jekers – I'd wager my golden helmet on it.'

Anenome was drawing pictures in the sand now.

'Here's the Iteru,' he said. 'Here's the delta. Maritaten … we agree she's alive?'

'No one thinks she's dead except the gods,' Axe muttered. 'Or one of the princes is leading them. Doesn't make much difference to us.'

'Anyway, she's running west – the Jekers are in the delta. Can we … use the Jekers as an anvil and smash her forces against them?' Anenome drew a broad arrow.

Axe looked at it. 'We're running out of food,' he said slowly.

'So we let the army sack Lukor.'

The two men looked at each other.

'That's a big decision. What if the gods don't like it?'

The look went on for a while. Then Axe grinned.

'Fuck it,' Anenome said. 'The boys got out of control, and who are we to stop them?'

Axe shook his head. 'It would cost us days to sack Lukor. In fact, it's worse than that – you know what happens when you loose an army on a city.'

Anenome made a face. 'Think of the loot!'

Axe shook his head. 'There's a better way. Summon the high priest or someone, demand a pile of food and a big ransom. *Threaten* to level the place.'

Anenome was quiet for a moment; he made a cut with the sword, then a flourish. Then he stopped again.

'You're right,' he admitted. 'But sacking Lukor...'

'Imagine what we'd get for Maritaten's head, though,' Axe said. 'More resin. Immortality.'

'You think?'

Axe's smile filled his face. 'Worth a shot. They need one new war god. Why not two?'

Kursag

'I am your god,' Kursag announced.

He'd changed his body again: now he had the head of a vulture and the body of an athlete, as tall as two tall mortals. He wore a black kilt, and his vulture-wings, when he flew, seemed to darken the sky, each wing stretching out for fifty feet, their pinions a majestic, shining black.

None of the Jekers doubted him. He flew from ship to ship, demanding sacrifice and obeisance from every crew, and drinking in the raw *auratic* power as the sacrifices were made.

He drank it all in: the cheers, the cries of terror, the utter devotion...

This is all I desired.

'*Enkul-Anu is fallen!*' he roared, his voice like fifty lions

334

roaring in rage. *'I alone am God! I alone am worthy of fear and worship! Together we will destroy Narmer and take its riches!'*

There were fewer Jekers than he would have liked, but by the time they'd sacked Narmer, the numbers would swell with desperate men and women willing to do anything to keep their worthless lives.

He counted over a hundred ships spread over a vast amount of ocean, but he could fix that; perhaps five thousand warriors. Inwardly, he cursed the events that had cost him the rest of the fleet, but these would be the hardiest and best of the blood-soaked Jekers, and they would be unstoppable.

The Iteru delta was full of cities; it held the richest part of Narmer and the most developed agriculture. Danisa and Varisa were too far north to hit immediately, but Thais was ten parasangs to the east along the main branch of the river.

'We begin at Thais!' he ordered.

And his devoted Jekers lashed their slaves and began to push their war-boats upriver.

Nicté

Era had declared a day of rest and celebration, and Hefa-Asus had made the preparations to raise Nicté to master of her chosen trade.

It should have been a great day.

Instead, her anger simmered. Hefa-Asus insisted on a ceremony that seemed to her, in her present state, to stress his seniority at every turn. And he was smug – she was sure of it; smug about his Nikali mistress.

Whereas she …

She tried to batten down the thought, but it escaped. She

had bedded her pirate, and he'd deserted her before she awoke. Sailed away, as if she was a whore to be avoided.

Bad Krul, indeed.

For entire hours, she was in charge of herself; fully aware that Hefa-Asus owed her nothing, and was raising her to the highest dignity. Indeed, while he put the gold ring of mastery on her finger, she had a moment of clarity in which she was fully aware that this, *this* was the summit of her ambitions, and this man had helped her reach it.

And then the doubts would circle, and the feeling of having been *used*. It assaulted her sense of self; it left her vulnerable and angry and she knew perfectly well that *she'd done it to herself.*

The promise of a celebration had indeed brought most of the wanderers back. Old Jawat was dancing with Era, which was a sight to make anyone laugh. Era, dancing, was probably the most beautiful thing Nicté had ever seen – a purity, a grace, a subtlety of movement that ran from hips to hands.

When she fights, I see only a hint of this.

Jawat, by contrast, moved stiffly, like a mime aping a dancer. People laughed with drunken amusement, and Era grinned, and Jawat laughed with them, and all of it flowed by Nicté.

Wine and mead flowed like water, and everyone danced, sang, leapt over fires, gambled ...

'Atosa made your ring of mastery,' Hefa-Asus said from beside her.

'That's nice,' she said.

'You should thank him. Have you looked at it?' Hefa-Asus beamed at her.

'Are you drunk?'

He made a face. 'I have indeed consumed an immense quantity of mead,' he said. 'And I would not dance, just now. But drunk?'

She didn't want to talk to him. Nor, despite her inner anger,

336

did she want to snap at him. But she heard her own voice say, 'Where's the Nikali woman?'

He looked at her, and frowned. 'How would I know?'

'You mean you just walked out on her when you were done?' she asked.

He smiled, clearly remembering. 'What else would I do? I took what I wanted and left her with some advice.' His smile was damning. Oh-so-pleased-with-himself.

Nicté was utterly disgusted. 'Of course you did,' she growled, on the edge of violence, and walked away.

But the next morning, Nicté threw herself into her work. Many of their people were barely able to walk, much less work, but Era was up and moving, and Jawat demonstrated that age teaches some forms of wisdom by showing every sign of being sober. Atosa, too, was ready to work, and the Hakrans, all very modest in their excesses, were ready to go.

By midday, more than half the cargo had been shifted, and by evening, every man and woman was working except the Jeker captives, who remained chained to the wharves in the lower port, and Jawala, who remained with them.

Nicté had worked herself to near-exhaustion, and it had defended her against her own mind; she hadn't thought of Krul in hours. She had come down the falls road with Era and now she turned to the commander.

'Are we taking the Jekers with us?' she asked.

Era made a face. 'Yes,' she said. And then, 'Some of them want to kill themselves.'

Nicté shrugged. 'Let them.'

Era shook her head. 'No. I mean, maybe. But I have a hunch...'

Nicté made a face.

'I have hunches!' Era said. 'Seven hells! I don't *know* anything, Nicté. I just guess and make things up.'

337

Now Nicté shrugged.

'What's the matter with you?' Era asked.

'Matter?' Nicté asked. 'Haven't I worked like a slave — like five slaves — all day?'

Era was looking at the Jekers, but her words were for Nicté.

'You were like a spectre at the feast yesterday, and today you won't talk to anyone.'

Nicté shook her head. 'I'm fine.'

'Worried about going home?'

'No,' Nicté said with finality, and walked over to the Jekers. Behind her, Era snorted, but didn't follow.

'Want wine?' Nicté asked the Jekers.

They all looked at her, but only the former chieftain met her eye, though his eyes seemed to stare far past her.

'Yes,' he said.

She poured him some from her canteen, and he drank it off.

'You're the warrior,' he said. 'I saw you kill the *ra-wa-ke-ta* of the people.'

'The Jeker woman?' she smiled. 'Yes. It was my pleasure.'

The Jeker drank off the rest of his wooden cup. 'More?'

She poured more.

'So,' he asked, 'why are you with them? They all seem crazy to me, except you.'

'Sometimes I think the same,' she agreed. 'But they are ... very good people.'

He drank more wine. 'Good how?'

She shrugged. It wasn't a conversation she was ready to have just then.

'Good to each other. Fair and honest.'

Mostly. Suddenly she leant forward. 'We're going to overthrow the gods.'

His eyes focused on her. 'Now you are as crazy as the witch woman and the *wanax*.'

Nicté shook her head. 'I won't argue. And Trade is a bad language to speak of good and evil.'

The Jeker drank some more wine. 'Why overthrow the gods?'

'Because they're useless bloodsuckers,' Nicté said.

The Jeker looked out to sea. 'That's true,' he admitted. He'd paused a long time before he said it. 'But you'll never touch them. They're the gods.'

'We've already put two down,' Nicté said with a sharp-toothed smile.

He looked at her, his face seeming to move.

Fear? Disbelief? Rage? Hard to tell. 'You killed two gods?' he snapped.

'Not personally, but I did my part,' she said with pride. 'And some demons.'

The Jeker's chin fell to his chest. 'Fuck,' he said. 'Go away.'

She thought he was angry, but then she saw tears.

Interesting.

She poured him another cup of wine and went up the steps to the city. Their conversation had calmed her.

We're fighting the gods. Who cares if I bedded an idiot?

I do.

But sleep helped, too – and she got to sleep fast enough.

In the morning she moved a heavy load of uncast copper ingots with Hefa-Asus and Atosa, and managed to be civil throughout the movement, as patient oxen hauled the cart to the top of the escarpment.

Already, the Hakrans and most of the former slaves were loading the big wooden dugout canoes. The sight reminded her of home, and raised her mood.

I'm going home.

That was a good thought. She even let herself imagine the tattoo she'd get for killing the Jeker woman.

And when the copper was loaded, she took her ring of mastery from the deerskin pouch at her neck and really looked at it. It was fine work: the ring's shape was pure, and it held a red stone with a beautifully rendered World Turtle, her clan's sign. The stone sparkled as if it was alive.

'Oh, Atosa!' she said in genuine wonder.

The jeweller was rubbing his lower back.

'Eh?' he asked. And then, 'What? This the first time you've looked at it?'

'Yes,' she confessed in a low voice.

'Huh,' he said. 'I had ... what ...? Two days, to find a good stone, melt my gold, cast the ring, polish it all out ... and no slaves to do the polishing. And you didn't even look at it? What are you – a god-queen now?' His smile took the sting out of his words.

'The turtle is so ... noble!'

'That's better. I thought you didn't like it,' Atosa confessed.

She hugged him. 'It's magnificent!'

'It's better than magnificent!' he replied. 'And you can store a bit of the *Aura* in it.'

She looked deep into the stone.

'Ruby,' he said. 'Not garnet.'

She found that she was grinning. Suddenly she said, 'I am a master smith!'

'So you are, honey,' Atosa said. 'I'm guessing you had something on your mind yesterday.'

She twisted her grin and looked at the ground. 'Maybe.'

Atosa drank some water. 'Time to do some more work.'

He was leaving something unsaid, and she suspected it was about her treatment of Hefa-Asus.

She wasn't ready yet.

The last of the copper went into a canoe. The last southern grain went aboard, and amphorae of oil – good to trade anywhere on the river, some brought all the way from Noa – and Mykoan wools.

'The Jeker thinks we're insane,' Nicté said to Jawala, who was watching a team of inexpert former slaves manoeuvre a huge clay jar of Noa's best olive oil.

'Careful there!' Jawala shouted. 'Someone get *in* the canoe! Lift with your legs!' She didn't sound like a powerful wise woman. She sounded like every wharf rat that Nicté had ever met. But then she turned, her eyes calm and penetrating.

'We *are* insane,' Jawala said. 'I can't pretend that we're sane by any normal measure. Because the norm has become acceptance of evil, and we're going to resist.'

Nicté thought about that, and then smiled. 'Nicely put.'

Jawala grinned back. 'I like being old and wise. People listen to me. I make up wise sayings and keep them ready.'

Nicté thought she was serious for a moment, and then realised Jawala was mocking herself.

Early the next morning, before they were ready to depart, Atosa came up the road from the falls and the lower city with Jawat. The two showed every sign of having shared a last binge.

Nicté was packing her own kit into a canoe, making sure she wasn't sharing with Hefa-Asus.

'Seen Era?' Atosa asked.

Nicté shook her head. 'Still in her furs with Dite.'

'She'll want to hear this,' Atosa said. 'There's a ship in from Lazba in the islands. Says he saw Zos, leading a fleet.'

Nicté nodded. 'She'll want to hear that right away.' She even managed a smile.

An hour later, with one hundred and seventy-seven former slaves, as well as their original crew, a dozen new volunteers from the city, thirty former Jekers, and with Era in the lead canoe, they set off east into the dawn, upriver. And with every stroke of her paddle, Nicté's heart rose. The banks were lined with hemlock and spruce, and by midday there were birch trees – white birch – and deep groves of maple and beech. There were beaver dams in the side eddies, and deer.

I'm going home, Nicté thought.

And Era was grinning like a wolf. When they landed at midmorning, Era took her aside to ask her to take the lead boat, and the two woman sketched a rough itinerary with the help of a guide.

'You heard about Zos,' Nicte said.

Era grinned. 'I feel as if we're back in the game,' she said. 'Zos is headed for Narmer. We're finally headed for the Snows.' She nodded. 'Are you ... all right?' Era hesitated a moment. 'Nothing ever seems to get to you, but lately ...'

Nicté felt a flash of anger, and then calmed herself. Era was *wanax*, the war leader; she had every right to be concerned. 'I have been angry,' Nicté said. 'At myself.'

Ah,' Era said with half a smile. 'Oh, I'm very good at that.'

The two women shared a look, and both went back to work.

Zos

Zos handled the taking of the citadel of Kanun easily, lending five hundred warriors to the prince's steward after swearing an oath to hand the citadel back afterwards. There was very little civil disturbance, but Zos, Daos and Pollon did their best to keep the pot boiling, and they gave Pollon sole access to the god's eye Nexus while they 'guarded' the temples and locked down the priests.

None of it gave Zos much concern; it was very much the

kind of operation he'd run a dozen times as an elite sell-sword. It felt odd to be doing it for himself.

The prince's brother showed signs of wanting to set up his own government. Zos isolated the man and his household, and intercepted some messages that made it clear he was guilty as sin of conspiring with the gods and the hierophant against his own brother.

None of that mattered. There was news in Kanun of the defeat of Maritaten's army in the east, and that made a lot of people deeply uneasy. Pollon was monitoring it; Daos and Leontas were enlisting spies in the marketplace under the cover of hiring more soldiers, to make sure they didn't get an ugly surprise.

What worried Zos was the absence of his scouts. He'd sent Trayos south with five ships to find the Jekers, and he hated sending other people to do his own dirty work. Scouting a foreign coast for Jekers was the dirtiest work he could imagine. Every day and every night he pictured all the many disasters that could befall Trayos and his five ships – a third of his force.

I should have sent just one ship.

I should have gone myself.

I should have taken my whole force. This city is the sideshow of a sideshow.

Zos was not used to being racked with indecision, and it was like an itch that had to be scratched every minute. And almost every minute, he told himself that the die was cast: that he'd sent his best captain with the most pirating experience to do a complicated task, and he had to await the results.

He told himself that, but twice a day he started to order the rest of the little fleet to sea, and had to hold himself in check, and doubt himself all over again.

I never meant to come here, he admitted to himself.

343

He'd allowed himself to be sidetracked by the possibility of real information in a sea of ignorance.

'Daos,' he said, on the second afternoon, 'any useful prophecy? What's happening next?'

The young man – even broader and fuller in the chest than ever, and with a deepening voice and a lot of hair, all of a sudden – simply smiled.

'Nothing,' he said. 'We have left the time-line we were assigned.'

'What does that mean?'

Daos shrugged. He'd brought in another fifty Py archers – good men looking for a contract. They had just wandered up out of the desert and taken service with Zos' fleet, as if they'd made an arrangement months before. It was a small but real triumph; the tall night-hued women and men from the deep desert were the best archers in the north, and maybe in the world.

'I don't really understand it all,' Daos said. 'I mean, I guess I'm a conduit, but the source is ... gone. Or not helping me any more.' He shrugged. 'I mean, I knew we'd come to Narmer, as I knew that if you didn't train me in arms, I'd die here. But where? And why? And ...'

It had been an uncanny incident. Daos was in the big market, negotiating with the Py captain, when an assassin went for him with two knives. The man wore a long black veil like a desert woman, but when he threw it off, he wore red cloth bound tightly to his body by parchment ribbons covered in sigils and runes.

His attack was as sudden as a desert storm, and he killed one of their Py archers to get at Daos' back.

Daos backflipped like a bull-leaper, baffling the assassin's attack. The man in red never got another chance, and his sigils, however potent, did nothing to stop the poisoned arrows of the

Py. But the incident and its resolution had impressed everyone who had heard Daos predict his own death if he was not trained by Zos.

'Never mind,' Zos said.

He wanted to hit something; he understood combat, even though he feared it. But he'd had years of court intrigue, too, and this whole war with the gods was more like an endless court intrigue than an actual battle.

In the evening of the second day after Trayos sailed, Pollon sat with Zos in the hierophant's palace, which they'd taken as a headquarters, and outlined what he knew. It was a long brief, and had surprisingly little hard information.

'So,' Zos said, 'Maritaten is probably alive, since they're ordering people to look for her. She's probably north of Lukor, since her river fleet was reported passing there. The gods' army is at Lukor?'

'It was, as of yesterday, demanding an enormous ransom.' Pollon shrugged.

'Which god is in charge?'

'No god. A pair of mercenaries named Axe and Anenome.'

Zos smiled. 'I know them well. Allies and business rivals, in my old life. This must be their biggest contract ever. Riding the proverbial tiger.'

He was doodling on the big inlaid cedar table that dominated the hierophant's scriptorium.

'And the World Serpent fought the God of War in the high *aether*,' Pollon said. 'Nobody knows what happened. I mean, maybe the gods know, but we're only seeing the reports from the mortal side.'

Zos nodded, pulling on his beard.

'What's pretty obvious,' Pollon went on, 'is that no one is doing what Nisroch, Herald of the Gods, used to do. He was like …' Pollon looked up at the pantheon of the gods, painted across the ceiling in the Narmerian style 'Like a *ra-pte-re* to the gods. A chancellor – a reporter-of-things. I can't find the word.'

'Spymaster?' Zos said.

'More than just spies,' Pollon said. 'He collected all the reports from … well, everyone. I know. I was part of this.'

Zos frowned. 'So?'

Pollon shifted uneasily. 'He had mortals who put it all together into reports. Some of them were available to us, so we could keep our god-kings informed.' He met Zos' eye. 'God's eyes are only part of the collection system. Someone has to watch them, and know what they're looking for.'

Zos was impatient, and it showed. His thoughts kept sliding off to Trayos: nailed to the mast of a Jeker ship; sinking beneath the waves; killed by angry Narmerians …

'So what?' he asked.

'The system is broken,' Pollon said. 'Remember I told you a lot of reporting stations were gone? That's not the half of it. Nisroch is clearly gone.'

'We didn't kill him,' Zos said with some bitterness. 'I knew that, and the World Serpent confirmed it.'

Pollon made a face and rubbed the hair that was finally growing from his formerly shaved head.

'Well, I can't make it out, but the system's broken, and that means the gods are at least as blind as we are. Maybe more so. I can read all this well enough, but it was part of my job.' He shrugged. 'I think Nisroch's absence is very important.'

'So Maritaten is west of Lukor.' Zos wasn't paying attention to anything but his own immediate planning. Like every God-King for whom Pollon had ever worked.

'If I had to guess, she's running for her palace at Phatos. Do you know she's a former House of Pleasure slave?'

'Not exactly the stuff of warrior legends,' Zos said dismissively. But then, waving a hand as if to say *A little of this, a little of that*, in the Hundred Cities way, he said, 'Except that the rumours in the market say she fought pretty well. They wounded a godling and got away. Maybe she's a fucking genius. Doesn't matter. I need to help her if she's still out there. Our sole reason to be here is to keep the Narmerian revolt alive for as long as we can. To keep the god's eyes focused here, and not on Era and the others.'

Pollon raised his eyebrows, and Zos relented.

'I'm sorry, brother. I'm telling you things you already know. Somehow, I assumed we'd just … find her. Or the Jekers. And that either way, we'd know what to do.'

Pollon poured each of them a cup of wine from a beautiful pitcher of solid gold.

'What do we do with this place? It's a nest of vipers. Reminds me of Hekka.'

Zos drank the excellent wine with appreciation. 'This is island wine. Did we bring it?'

Pollon shrugged. 'No idea.'

Zos savoured it. 'Can you identify the man who killed the hierophant?'

Pollon nodded. 'I knew his voice the moment I heard it. He's named Ben-Turuk.'

'Well, that's easy then,' Zos said. 'We make him hierophant, and make it clear to him that we know what happened.'

Pollon drew back a little. 'Remind me never to play power games with you.'

Zos smiled. 'Oh, come, master of information. You can play as well as I.'

Pollon smiled. He looked away for a moment, as if he, too, were enjoying the wine. And when he turned back he nodded. 'I like it. What does that say about me? What am I becoming?'

Zos poured more wine. 'A person who wields power.' He raised his cup. 'We're up against the gods. It's going to be messy.'

Pollon's face was troubled. 'It is already messy,' he said, and his voice held genuine sorrow.

Zos was awakened after a bad night's sleep. He had too many dreams, and he was uncomfortably reminded that Eritha was a woman when she lay down by him after her watch.

'Lord Trayos' ship's in sight off the beach,' she said softly, and then rolled over and began to snore.

Zos felt as if the weight of the world was falling away from his shoulders, and the feeling of lightness was completed when he saw the man himself in his fine cloak waving from his ship. Zos celebrated by going back to sleep for an hour, an unaccustomed luxury.

An hour later he was listening to Trayos' report – succinct and professional. According to the old pirate, there were a dozen Jekers off the main channel of the Iteru where it flowed out of the delta, and that was music to his ears.

Two hours later, as his people finished loading their food and water to get to sea, Pollon came down from the acropolis to report that the new hierophant was installed.

'That's not the real news,' he said. 'Thais? Big city in the delta. My former master traded for gold and ivory there.'

'Spare me,' Zos said.

He'd drawn a rough picture of the delta on papyrus and used sharp flints to tack it to the cabin table.

'The priest there is screaming for help through the Nexus. He says there's a million Jekers attacking and the garrison is small and incompetent.' Pollon looked at the map.

The delta was drawn as a simple triangle, and the Iteru was illustrated in blue chalk and black carbon. The main channel ran from Phatos, past Thais, to the sea.

'Then if Maritaten is all she's claimed to be, she'll head there to save Thais.'

'Or she'll hide in her palace at Phatos.'

'Or that.' Zos found Eritha on the command deck and motioned over the side. 'Get the other captains. All of them. Council of war.'

Eritha swung over the side, landed on the beach, and ran for the *Wave Serpent*.

Daos, who was aboard, looked hurt. 'I'm your *papista*.'

Zos had to grin. 'No, you are not. You are now one of my captains. You've graduated. And you know what that makes you?'

'Sad?' Daos looked sad. 'I will still drive your chariot of fire.'

'That again? I'll settle for a ship of wood. Anyway, you are a triumph! My first ever *papista* to survive the experience. Hells, lad, I might start keeping my soldiers alive next.'

'Who will replace me?'

Zos was going to give a flippant answer, but he was watching Eritha tear along the beach, and he shrugged.

'Eritha, if she wants it.'

Daos nodded. 'A worthy woman. She will make a great warrior.'

'Is that prophecy?' Pollon meant to be funny, but Daos looked startled.

'I suppose it is!' he said. 'It just came out...'

Zos looked at the sky. 'Let's get this done.'

They were all there: Orestas, Daos, Rathor, Tuwinon, Stilko, Anturis; all of Trayos' captains and all of Leontas', too. Fifteen captains in three divisions.

Zos pointed at his rough map.

'The Jekers are laying siege to Thais. They'll burn and kill everything outside the city and then throw themselves at the walls like waves hitting a beach until they break in or fall. They won't have the skill to lay a proper siege, and they won't have the food to stay forever.'

'How many?' Orestas asked.

Trayos glanced at Zos and said, 'A hundred ships at least, and more arriving from the south every day.'

Zos intervened lest anyone get overawed. 'But remember that on our ships, every oar is a fighter. Their oars are pulled by starving slaves.'

Rathor, the former Jeker slave, had been appointed captain of a captured Jeker ship called the *Revenge*. He smiled nastily. Anturis, who'd survived two years as a slave and now commanded a captured triakonter called the *Porpoise*, showed her teeth, but without amusement.

'So they have three thousand warriors to our thousand or so,' Zos said. 'But we should have the element of surprise. And we might have a little luck. Because it's my intention to attack them from the sea, with fire, and burn their ships.'

Trayos smiled. 'Nasty,' he said. 'For Narmer. They'll be stuck there.'

Zos nodded. 'Ever been to the delta? It's a fucking swamp, interspersed with the best farmland in the world. Diseases, marshland, crocodiles, hippos, shit in the water...' His smile was as nasty as Trayos'. 'Burn their ships and watch them starve. Where can they go?'

'They'll take Thais, gorge themselves, and march somewhere else,' Rathor said. 'Sorry, Zos, but they won't just sit and starve. They'll turn the people of Thais into more Jekers, enslave every shipwright and build a new fleet.'

Zos pulled at his beard and looked at him. 'I hear you.'

Anturis spat. 'He's right, Zos.'

His first reaction was annoyance at anyone telling him how to fight a battle. But Anturis was tough as an old firebrick, and she'd been a Jeker slave like Rathor. And he wasn't enough of a fool to ignore her.

'But it will win us the initiative,' he said. 'It's like a small wound at the start of a fight.'

Anturis nodded. 'That I can accept.'

Zos shrugged. 'I'm open to other thoughts. But we don't have the ships to face them at sea, and we don't have the swords to meet them on land. We don't have the food to close the river mouth and blockade them for any length of time. So I say – night raid, burn their ships. We take every merchant in this port and turn them into fireships. The north exports sulphur and bitumen. It's all right in our laps. And it is *still* a long shot.'

Trayos made a sour face. 'I can't believe I'm saying this,' he said. 'But we could break into Thais during the confusion. A thousand hard warriors would hold the city.'

Tuwinon raised an eyebrow. 'If you said "sack the city" my people would be eager. But who's paying us to hold it?'

Zos spread his hands. 'Best I can suggest is – burn the Jekers and see what happens.'

'Well,' Leontas said, 'you're honest. And I followed you into the dragon's den. But do you see a payday here?'

'Eventually,' Zos said. 'And an immortal payday, at that. And remember, we own this fine little city now.'

Tuwinon spread his hands, as if he was sorry for what he was going to say. 'Shares?' he asked.

Zos nodded. 'Every ship shares equally. I reserve an extra ship's share which I will divide as rewards. Captains get a quarter of their ship-share, officers split another quarter, the other half is divided among the rowers and the archers and the marines.'

Tuwinon nodded. 'Fair, if there's any loot.'

'Narmer will pay us,' Zos said. 'If they don't, why, we'll just take our payment.'

Leontas grinned. 'I knew I liked you.' He paused and then made a face, as if swallowing something bitter. 'Am I the only one who mislikes burning all the slaves with the Jeker ships?'

Anturis shook her head. 'I'd have taken a burning death every day over what they did to us.'

Zos frowned. 'We don't have the time or the resources to rescue the slaves.' He met Leontas' eyes. 'But it sticks in my throat.'

Leontas shook his head. 'Mine too,' he said. And after a moment, to Zos, 'You are a harder man than I thought.'

Zos shrugged. 'I'll sleep badly for a few nights,' he admitted. 'And then I'll forget it.'

Later Pollon stared over the rim of a wine bowl, his eyes golden as a god's in the firelight, an odd trick of reflection. 'How does going for the Jekers help us focus the Gods on Narmer?'

Zos had been lying on a sheepskin close to a beach fire, making patterns in the sand. He looked up. 'Damn it, Pollon,' he said.

'Damn what?' Pollon asked.

'My gut tells me that hitting the Jekers is the best move.'

'My friend Zos told me that we were going to support this Maritaten against the Gods.'

Zos lay back and shrugged. 'I see your point,' he said. 'But if we don't hit the Jekers, we can't enter the river and we never link up with Maritaten, wherever she is.'

Pollon nodded and handed the wine bowl to Zos. 'We're drinking too much,' he added.

'So we are,' Zos admitted.

'Would it be fair to say you just want to hit the Jekers?' Pollon asked.

'It's nice to fight an enemy you can *see* and *hurt*,' Zos said.

'And if we lose?' Pollon asked.

'We won't lose,' Daos put in. 'Just wait.'

Zos jerked a thumb at his former *papista*. 'See?' he said, as if that explained everything.

The next day, when they were at sea with a dozen small fire-ships towed behind them, Pollon came up to the command deck, grinned at Eritha, who suddenly had a fine *thorakos* of bronze scales, and nodded to Zos.

'You didn't say anything about Maritaten to the captains.' he said.

Zos nodded, watching the sea to the south. One Jeker scout, and his plan was scuppered.

'I told them she'd be paying us,' Zos said. 'If she doesn't come, we might have other options.'

'You are lying to your own fleet?' Pollon asked.

'The necessities of commanding pirates,' Zos said. 'Look good, minimise the hard fighting, provide treasure.'

'Where's the treasure coming from?'

'No idea,' Zos said cheerfully. 'I'm making this up as I go.'

Kursag

He fell like a dark storm cloud. It was a cold, rainy winter day in the delta, and the citizens of Thais huddled indoors, terrified of the Jekers and oppressed by the weather.

Kursag had the sky to himself, and his black vulture wings powered him through the wet air above his Jekers. Between his taloned feet, almost two hundred ships crowded the main channel of the river. Small parties of marauders paced alongside them on the riverbanks, burning every farm and settlement they passed, looting and killing. Another river was forming on the roads parallel to the Iteru: refugees – now in their thousands, pouring east towards distant Phatos and its non-existent protection.

Oh, Narmer, do you sense my wrath?

Nothing stood before the Jeker tide. Every effort he'd made, even while wounded and betrayed, to save their ships from the titanic storm and the destruction of Dekhu was now repaid in blood as they rampaged through the richest province in Narmer. It was *exactly* as he'd imagined – better, in many ways.

He led them, his black pinions the banner and rallying point for every raiding party. Wherever they spread, they could see him out over the river, and he could see them. Undreamt-of levels of command and control occurred to him, and he began to implement them.

Fear made a wonderful tool of discipline. A hundred independently minded Jekers died in a day, and the message was received by the rest.

Kursag demanded complete obedience. Kursag was not interested in individual initiative.

As the fleet closed on the city of Thais, Kursag could look through the rain and see its whitewashed walls, its colourful houses, its wharves and shipping.

And its healthy garrison.

He should have expected what followed, but he didn't.

His forces flowed right up to the wharves and walls, and broke against them like waves on a rocky shore. The garrison was not cowed; if they were afraid, they took their fear out on his Jekers in an endless hail of arrows. And the walls of Thais were tall, and under the whitewash lay fired brick atop a base layer of giant stone secured with layered workings against all forms of *auratic* attack.

Worse, Kursag discovered that he lacked a truly potent ranged weapon like his hated father's thunderbolts. Tall walls represented a real defence, and his one experiment with flying over them and attacking the garrison there led to the discovery that being the target of fifty archers was deeply unpleasant even when it was survivable. A single near miss from an officer's star-stone arrow was a reminder that his immortality was not absolute. He tasted the poison of the star-stone and then he tasted the officer's heart blood, but it was a petty revenge.

And where did he get a star-stone arrow?

Mortals. They must be purged.

Kursag left the walls. The garrison commander put heart into his people, and the citizens of the town knew what awaited them if the Jekers broke in. Narmerians were small, and wiry; they didn't look physically imposing.

But they were tough as old boot leather, and they had nowhere to run.

As night fell, Kursag dropped fire from on high into the town, but in a culture of mud brick and tile it was less effective than he would have liked.

And the next day, flexing the inexorable muscles of his new-grown obedience, he ordained the building of a mighty siege mound – a mound that would overtop the walls and allow his Jekers to flow in on a broad front. He ordered his favourite captains to lay it out; the ships were emptied to drive the galley slaves and all the new slaves captured by the sweep downriver into the marshes around the city. Dirt was dug, baskets woven, and the lash freely employed, and the ramp began.

Hyatta-Azi was the best of his captains: a former prince of Atussa, a cold-blooded reptile of a man who'd joined the orgy of blood the moment he saw its ascendancy. A magnificent combination of obedience and ferocity.

Kursag landed before the man. Hyatta-Azi wore a silk cloak clotted with human blood and stinking of rot. His moustache and beard were filled with blood; his body was painted red. He carried a great stone axe of lapis and gold that he claimed was an ancient artifact. Perhaps it was. Behind him was a mortal woman in a cloak decorated with scalps.

Kursag didn't care. If anything, he liked the statement the cloak made.

Immediately, the former prince and his lieutenant threw themselves flat on the muddy ground.

'God of the End,' the mortal proclaimed from his servile position.

Kursag liked it all, apart from the fucking rain.

Before him, just beyond bowshot, a line of slaves' faces empty from days of fear and torment, blank with shock and incomprehension, carried wicker baskets of dirt forward into the range of the heavy bows on the city wall.

Kursag watched the confused city defenders with something approaching delight.

'They can shoot down their own people,' he said. 'The siege-mound will grow with every corpse.'

There were lines of slaves. Lines and lines of them, and the Jekers were spreading into the delta, gaining more. Thousands more. Part of the fleet had raced ahead of the refugee column and even now would be turning it back.

'I will destroy Narmer with the people of Narmer,' Kursag said.

'Yes, God of the End,' Hyatti-Azi said.

'Rise,' Kursag ordered. 'Rise, and drive these miserable animals to their deaths.'

Auza, Home of the Gods

Sypa stood in the Hall of Judgement, dressed entirely in her jewellery: a dozen necklaces of lapis and jade and carnelian; a waist-belt of gold that served only to promote her loins; anklets;

a skirt of beads; a high headdress of gold wire. She was, to all intents, nude; yet the gold and jewels enhanced, dignified, and titillated all at once.

Sypa didn't sit in Enkul-Anu's throne. She stood before it, and raised her hands for silence.

Every god was still.

'Brothers and sisters,' Sypa said, 'we are under attack. Our whole way of life is under attack. We have taken losses. It is time for us to remind the world who we are and why we rule here.'

There was cheering.

'Narmer is in revolt,' she continued. 'Not one stone will be left on another in that stinking land. Let our hands fall on them like thunderbolts. Let us bring them plague and death until they beg for mercy.'

More cheering.

'And Mykoax, and Trin – and now Lazba! We will punish them all. And Noa, that they may know we have the power to punish them.'

Now some of the gods looked worried. Noa had, for the most part, been staunchly loyal to the gods – like the Hundred Cities, like Akash.

'Noa?' Telipinu said. Only he could ask, being the son of Sypa and Enkul-Anu.

'Noa! Where their god-queen thinks herself a rival to me!' Sypa spat.

Telipinu shook his head. His wound was healing, but the star-stone had robbed his right foot and ankle of all feeling; it was as if he had a foot of metal. But now he stood on both feet.

'The goddess-queen of Noa is loyal,' he said.

'You are a boy,' Sypa said. 'You know nothing.'

And before their eyes, she dispatched Gul, the God of Death, to take the life and soul of Cyra, the goddess-queen of Noa. Gul,

God of the Dead, entered his chariot of bones, and descended to the earth below with his consort as his charioteer.

Laila thought that he wore a deathless smile.

By the time he'd reaped the horrified goddess-queen's head, Telipinu had sought out his sometime partner, the Snake God Illikumi.

'She's insane,' Telipinu said.

Illikumi looked around uneasily.

'Where is your father?' he asked.

'Mourning Ara,' Telipinu said.

'Uthu, the new Sun God, and Grulu are both saying—'

'Saying what?' Telipinu asked.

'That your father is dying. Or perhaps already dead.' Illikumi shrugged.

'Crap,' Telipinu said. 'He's in mourning.'

'Someone,' and here the snake's head looked all around in an eerie way that defied a mere mortal neck, 'needs to tell him that Sypa is as much a danger to heaven as the fucking mortals.'

Telipinu nodded. 'Do you read the reports that come through the god's eyes?'

The snake's black eyes looked at him.

'Of courssse,' Illikumi hissed.

'Jekers are assaulting Thais, in the delta.' Telipinu's great golden eyes narrowed in anger. 'Enkul-Anu gave me Narmer. Sypa wants to destroy it. That was clearly not my father's will.'

'Best get your father out of mourning, then,' Illikumi said.

Telipinu looked around, his hawk's head as flexible as the snake's neck.

'I want to save Thais from the Jekers,' he said.

Illikumi nodded. 'If you've read the reportsss, you know the Jekersss have sssort of godling leading them.'

Telipinu nodded. 'And it can fly. So it's someone big.'

Illukimi hissed. 'Get Enkul-Anu,' he said. 'I am perhapsss too cautioussss. But ... who isss thisss dark god? Ssssome forgotten entity?'

Telipinu paused.

And then enlightenment came to Illikumi. He was relatively new to plotting and he wasn't keen on risk, as he'd just said.

But ... if Telipinu was gone, Sypa's promise that Narmer could be his would become a reality, even if Enkul-Anu returned. And it needn't be destroyed, if Enkul-Anu returned.

'Or ...' He allowed his fangs to show in a wide smile. 'Or we could go and deal with thisss ... upssstart, and you could prove you are the god of Narmer. Sssave the city. Exposssse the rebelssss' weaknessss.'

Telipinu clapped his hands together. 'You and me, brother,' he said. 'We will make war on this interloper.'

Illikumi's smile spread. 'I am right behind you, god of Narmer!'

Sypa struck the door of the Hall of Mourning with her sceptre of gold and lapis.

'Great Storm God!' she intoned.

Slowly, the great basalt door hinged back.

Inside, the hall was absolutely dark. Even Sypa, who had a number of special powers, had trouble seeing anything there; the heat of her consort was invisible to her.

'Husband! Father of my sons, Lord of the Storm!' Sypa said. 'Heaven needs you!'

Somewhere in the vast hall, filled with captive shades of the punished dead chittering with powerless rage, Enkul-Anu spoke softly.

'Ara is dead, Sypa.'

'Ara is dead and we have a war on our hands,' Sypa said. 'Our son is going forth to fight in a misdirected ...'

'Silence! Sypa, leave me to my sorrow.'

'Mourn later!' Sypa snapped. 'Ara is dead. The rest of us are alive! Or are you so afraid that you cannot rise to defend your realm?'

Enkul-Anu's soft voice held no hint of fear. Instead, it conveyed a gentle, pervasive threat.

'Ara was the best of us, Sypa. Ara was noble where I am practical. Ara went boldly where I go only when I must. And I broke him. I broke him …'

'He was broken in the taking of this realm, beloved. And what other choice did we have?' Sypa's voice was wheedling. 'We couldn't have run any further. We had to make a stand.'

'Is that all there is?' Enkul-Anu asked. 'Just aeons of struggle merely to survive?'

'Survive?' Sypa spat. 'We *rule*, consort. We are gods to our cattle. We are lords of millions of beings, and we are fat on their labour. That is not survival. That is triumph.'

'Is it?' Enkul-Anu asked.

'You ask too many questions, love. Leave it. Ara fell facing the monster, and he slew her in his fall. Let us rejoice at his victory and not lament his end.'

Now her voice was deeper, huskier, more seductive, She moved towards the source of his voice.

'Did he indeed?' Enkul-Anu asked. 'Did he slay her, wife?'

He began to take shape in the centre of the hall – his true shape: titanic, many-legged, armoured.

She stopped. Enkul-Anu was always dangerous when he chose to take his true shape.

'Do you ever consider these shapes we wear?' he asked.

Sypa stroked her soft flanks. 'Only to make mine more desirable for you, King of Heaven.'

'Do you ever consider what taking mortal form says of us,

Sypa? Even in our private chambers, we wear these shapes. Why is that?'

'The easier to rule our mortals,' she said. 'You yourself said they would hate and fear us in our true shapes.'

'And now I realise that it was an admission of weakness. They aren't cattle. They are mortal creatures of intellect, and we realise that they could threaten us in our natural forms.'

Suddenly he was there in his mighty raiment as Storm God, with scarlet skin and the head of a bull.

'We put on the trappings they expect, the more easily to rule them, but we rule them as a conquering army does a hostile populace. They revolt and revolt, and our young can do no better than fight among themselves for power. It can have only one end.'

'You are deep in sorrow, husband, and dwell among shades and darkness. Come forth into the sun, and smite our foes! Feel your power and forget Ara! He lost his mind an aeon ago, and we are lucky he rose to the challenge one more time and died well. Let it go.'

'I need...' Enkul-Anu said.

Sypa, in her carnelian and lapis and nothing else, lit a fire beneath her own skin so that her mighty sensuality shone forth like a torch in the mourning darkness. The chittering shades fled her cheerful carnality.

With artless long-practised grace, she reached up and pulled out the golden pins that bound her hair, so that it fell down her back and all the way to the black marble floor.

'I need time...' Enkul-Anu said.

'What you need, Storm God,' she said, swaying forward, 'is a good fuck.'

After the fleet of river craft left Phatos behind, nothing went according to plan, and Maritaten watched the marshy ground on the right bank while she killed mosquitoes with her right hand.

To get her chariots to Thais, she had to ferry them across three branches of the Iteru. Now she wished her army was on the other bank, but that was too hard to achieve, and the far bank was mostly desert – a desert that had rolled over farmland and villages in the last three generations. Its destruction hadn't been clear to her before; tax accounts and scribal records didn't sufficiently describe the devastation wrought by the encroaching sand.

'I needed to see this,' she muttered.

That was a problem for an unlikely future in which she remained goddess-queen of Narmer. Because today her whole fleet was busy moving her chariots across one of the winding branches of the great river as it entered the fertile delta. With marshes on both banks, and a narrow road on a neglected causeway as the army's only path, the whole process took far too long. Her scouts said that the enemy had moved up behind her, laying Lukor under tribute and racing north, so that only yesterday her rearguard of Py archers, Meyay tribesmen and Guard chariots had had to fight just to hold the causeway.

'Well?' she asked Ak-Arrina. He was commanding her army, and he was still obeying her.

'We'll finish by nightfall,' he said. 'We got supplies at Phatos – horses, arrows, fodder. We can keep this up for another week. After that ...'

He was watching a chariot warrior and his charioteer carrying their chariot across a mud flat to a waiting *baris* ship, a deep-water vessel capable of sailing on Ocean.

Silently, Maritaten blessed Mari-Ye for making her spend her estate money on building ships. Right now, they were all that stood between her and disaster. The enemies behind her had no fleet, and her people were seizing or burning every boat they passed, leaving her enemies nothing to contest her river power.

But ahead...

Ak-Arrina glanced at her. 'I think we should abandon the chariots.' The statement caused him what looked like physical pain.

She was stung. 'You and... my other war councillors... said the chariots were our greatest advantage against the Jekers.'

Ak-Arrina watched the two chariot soldiers lift their car out of the mud and hand it up to the waiting ship's crew. Chariots – at least those used by Narmer – were light; one strong man could carry the whole car on his back.

'Have you ever been to Thais, Great Lady of the High House?' he asked.

Maritaten hadn't. She looked at Hehet. The former steward of the House of Pleasure was widely travelled.

The woman shook her head. 'No,' she said.

'It's a mercantile city surrounded by marshes,' Ak-Arrina's voice was dull. The campaign, the defeats, and the loss of his men was wearing him down.

Not so cocky now, Maritaten thought. *And not even thinking of my body. Interesting.*

'And our chariots will flounder in the marshes?' she asked.

Ak-Arrina nodded. 'I can't see how we'd use them,' he said, as if the words were being pulled out of him. He was a chariot warrior – a brilliant mobile commander, at least according to his own account.

Maritaten turned to Hehet. 'Get me Horat and Tudhal,' she said. And then added, 'And Mari-Ye and Timut-Imri, the sorcerer.'

Ak-Arrina didn't even have the spirit to protest the low-born charioteer and the foreign godborn sell-sword being included in a royal council.

Wine was served, and she drank hers from a golden cup while a pair of her women held woollen cloaks to block the wind. Winter in Narmer wasn't savage, but it was cold and damp. The western edge of the delta was warmed by ocean currents, but here in the east the wind swept out of the north across the mudflats and penetrated wool and linen. She wished she had furs.

Horat came on deck looking as if he'd been asleep. Tudhal had only been down in the waist of the ship, sparring with his people. He came aft and bowed low.

'Great Lady,' he said in his heavily accented Narmerian.

'First of Swords,' she said formally.

Timut-Imri came fully dressed in a fine purple robe of brilliant workmanship, and Mari-Ye came straight from his devotions, wearing the headband of his office.

'Advise us, my companions,' Maritaten said.

Ak-Arrina repeated his assertion about the chariots.

Horat drank off the offered Mykoan wine in a single long gulp and held out his cup for more. Hehet rolled her eyes.

Tudhal looked at the two charioteers, who were now moving their horses carefully over the mudflat, testing the footing before their beloved animals made the crossing. It was completely necessary, and it was very slow.

'Chariots are wonderful in their place,' he said. 'If we want to beat the Jekers, we'll need 'em.'

Horat spat over the side, and Maritaten wanted to clout him in the head. It was as if he was parading his low-born habits to offend Ak-Arrina.

'I'm with Tudhal,' Horat said. 'Listen, Great Lady — if we're going to fight in the marshes, none o' the big ships are going to be any use at all.'

'We'll have to be able to hold the main channel,' Ak-Arrina snapped.

Horat shrugged. 'All I mean is, Great Lady … leave enough ships to transport the chariots. Leave the charioteers with their cars and horses and drivers, and take all the warriors. Tell them to think of their river boats as chariots.'

Ak-Arrina brightened. He looked at Horat as if the man might have some value after all.

'I like this notion,' he allowed.

Tudhal nodded. Behind him, Hehet nodded, too. She said nothing, but she had been writing on papyrus, and Maritaten knew what she was calculating: forage, food, water – the sinews of war – and their ships' carrying capacity. Hehet didn't have it all in her head, but she had a small army of scribes and clerks who had been saved from the wreck of the battle, and she'd formed them into an efficient service.

'It can be done,' she said. 'Give me an hour, Great Lady of the High House, and I will tell you which ships are best, and how many.'

Maritaten was watching a second chariot being carried across the mudflat.

'Why don't we have engineers?' she asked. 'We build the mightiest temples in the world. Why don't we have mobile bridges and people to repair the causeways?'

Mari-Ye cleared his throat. 'Most of the engineers were priests,' he said. 'Mostly of the new gods. They're the gods who get things built.'

'If we come through this,' Maritaten said, 'we're going to need to fix that. In the short run, levy me every peasant you can and set them to building wharves and matching causeways at the next river crossing.'

'Yes, Great Lady,' Hehet said.

'Mobile bridges?' Tudhal was genuinely interested, and she liked him better for it.

She shrugged. 'I don't know ... There must be a way.'

She looked at Mari-Ye, as she usually did when she had an intellectual problem, but his face was closed.

The sorcerer nodded. 'I agree – there must,' he said. 'Perhaps I can help.'

No one said anything, which was faintly embarrassing.

Maritaten had an idea, and then she suppressed it, because the Lady of the High House didn't launch untried ideas and open herself to ridicule. She waited for one of them to say something.

The silence lengthened.

'Whatever we build, the spring flood will wash it away,' Mari-Ye said with the wisdom of a thousand years of priesthood.

Only her idea wouldn't wash away.

How bad could it be? She could see it in her mind's eye, though she knew nothing about currents, winds, tides up in the western delta ...

'We could lash boats together,' she said. 'Dozens. Maybe hundreds. And put a wooden deck across them.'

Mari-Ye shook his head. 'How would the path go over the bows and sterns?' His voice was questioning, not patronising.

'Side by side, then,' she said.

'That's a great many boats,' Hehet said.

'But it would be flexible,' Mari-Ye rubbed his bald head, a rare gesture. 'I know people I can ask. It is an idea, Great Lady.'

'Not in time to save us right now,' she said airily, content that her idea was well received.

Or are they pretending because I am the Lady of the High House?

She sighed internally. 'Thais remains the objective,' she said. 'Hehet, organise the boats for the chariot corps. Ak-Arrina ...'

She looked at him and allowed herself a very slightly intriguing smile, to engage his desire. She had few enough weapons; she'd use them all. 'Can we use this river as a defensive barrier? The enemy can't outflank us on the other bank, or so I believe.'

'Nor will they find boats easily,' Tudhal agreed. 'That's a fine idea, Great Lady.'

Ak-Arrina managed a smile. 'It *is* a good idea, Lady. I may have become too focused on running away.'

She smiled with intentional flirtation. 'All of us have been distracted, Prince. May I leave you to make this crossing as difficult as may be for the enemy?'

'My pleasure,' the prince said.

'We'll need stronger ropes,' the sorcerer said suddenly. 'If the ropes were strong enough, we could bridge...' He paused. 'Anything. A bridge of boats with a deck laid across it. You are brilliant. But you'll need ropes made with *auratic* materials.'

Maritaten glanced at him, considered a word of censure – because one just didn't praise the god-queen with a scholar's patronising air – and then shrugged it off. Timut-Imri meant well.

'See to it,' she said.

Chapter Five

Era

The first four days were difficult enough, but all that was required was hard paddling and some poling across the broad flats. There were villages on the banks, spaced roughly a day's travel apart, and Era learnt from Nicté that they existed mostly to support the tin trade and the boats. Each village had a camp-site, with latrines and a stockade, and a small market where they could trade for food. On the second day, they camped with a boat caravan coming downstream from the north-west, and the Poche city of Palanke at the edge of the wild. The heavy bark canoes were laden to the gunwales with tin ingots; every boat was worth a fortune in Noa or in the Hundred Cities. The boat crews were a remarkable group: people of many races, but mostly northerners; some Hakrans; a great many Poche and Uran; a few Nikali and Onadawega. They were strong men and women, dressed in woollens and skins, all of them armed, all smoking tobacco, and all of them drinking anything that could be found.

For Era, it was like entering another world. The trees were different, the grass was different; even in winter, the ground was a different colour from that in Narmer and the Hundred Cities. And the boat crews were loud, defiant, independent – entirely unlike the slave sailors of the Hundred Cities or the disciplined Hakrans.

On the fourth day, they came to the First Rapids: a long chute where the river had carved out the rock in a fabulous channel, smooth and curving, then a narrow canyon of solid rock, where only a few stunted spruce clung to the sides, and then over a stadion of sharp rocks.

All their boats had to be unloaded in their entirety. The more expert among them took the empty boats through the gorge, and then hoisted them over the rocks through freezing cold water. Everyone else followed a well-trodden trail, back and forth almost a parasang, carrying every load: all their remaining star-stone, all their weapons and supplies and everything they'd brought from the coast.

Some things were abandoned, to join barrels and bales left by other crews. Era picked up a bale of furs someone had abandoned, and Dite began making fur mittens.

She and Dite hadn't talked much in the last three days, and though they shared blankets, there had been no intimacy. So when Dite presented her with a pair of beaver fur gauntlets that went up to her elbows, Era kissed the other woman.

'Still angry?' Dite asked.

'Yes,' Era said. 'You manipulated me.'

Dite shrugged back. 'Every interaction is nothing but two people manipulating each other.'

Era frowned. 'No. I don't agree.'

'You are the commander,' Dite said. 'You use everything *but* sex to make them do your bidding. You wheedle, you cajole, you even fake rage. Don't lie to me, Era. I know you.'

Era didn't have the words to express herself, so instead, practising the new patience that was becoming the bane of her existence, she kissed the other woman lightly on the lips and turned away.

'These are beautiful,' she said. 'We disagree about how well you know me.'

The sixth day found them paddling furiously against a heavy current to reach the projecting wharves of Palanke, sometimes called the Forest City. Its centre was dominated by a dozen enormous Calak and Poche temples and a ball court. Aside from the ajaw's palace, the rest of the city was wood. To the west, generations of farmers had hacked a bucolic valley out of the wild woods, but everywhere else, the eye found crags and trees, and one great arm of the Northern Woods ran almost to the walls on the north side.

The walls, unique in the world, were made of huge trees laid on a foundation of stone, and stood as high as six tall men, and the gates were magnificently painted.

The waterfront was used to boat crews, and catered to them with fighting pits and taverns, and a dozen densely packed markets. In the centre of the city, a canal ran in from the river and then *through* a great timber hall, as tall as the pyramidal stone temples in the city centre, with a roof of gilded tin that caught the evening sun as if it was on fire. The Tin Hall was famous throughout the north; merchants bringing cargoes south from the mines could unload here, have their cargoes inspected, and then sell them to merchants waiting to ship them downriver, all inside and away from prying eyes and the heat of the summer sun or the driving winter rains.

Palanke was rich. Era gave her people a day of leave and some scrap silver to spend, having sold most of their last cargo of southern red wine for a truly astronomical price. Meanwhile, she and Dite and Jawat and Nicté wandered the city, staring in amazement at the roof of the hall, at the fortunes in tin left sitting on the wooden floor of the great hall, at the weapon smiths and potters and textile weavers. They went to the temples last, the stepped pyramids reaching many times the height of a man; several were closed except to priests, but one was open to all.

They climbed the pyramid together, and a priestess encouraged them to make a sacrifice.

'Ek-Chuak is a god of merchants and warriors,' she said. She wore beautiful face paint, so that the upper part of her face was painted black and the lower part white, echoing the stripes on the god's image. 'His worship is open to all.'

Era was about to voice her opinion of gods when Nicté stepped forward and made a sacrifice, swiftly and neatly and with a clear appreciation of the ritual. The priestess smiled at her.

'As we're merchants *and* warriors,' Nicté said with a sharp-toothed smile.

'We're against *all* gods!' Era hissed as they went back down the pyramid.

Nicté shook her head. 'The southern gods rarely come north. It's too cold, or that's what we joke. We have our own gods here. If they are less ... tangible, we love them the more. They don't make war on us or burn our towns.'

'Why don't I know this?' Era asked.

Nicté shrugged. 'No one in the south much cares. I lived outside Ma'rib a few years. I have reason to know.'

Dite was looking at the other temples.

'And none of these are to the true gods?'

'True gods?' Nicté asked sharply.

Dite smiled sweetly. 'You know what I mean.'

Era felt a chill.

'The great temple has niches for all the southern gods.' Nicté's smile suggested that she was ready to make more of this, but then she relented. Which was amazing, as she had been very prickly since Vetluna.

'You two might like Chin,' she said, pointing at a fine temple that had a glazed roof. 'The god of same-sex lovers.'

Dite blinked. 'But the so-called southern gods are ... real.'

Era looked at her friend, ready to step in, but Nicté shrugged.

'Are they? I suspect they're not long for this world. Whereas Acat, god of tattooing,' she smiled, 'is my next visit. And he will receive my silver and my worship. Is he less real than Enkul-Anu?'

'Yes,' Dite insisted.

Nicte's smile was no longer friendly. 'Enkul-Anu will fall,' she said. 'If not to us, then to the next rebellion, or the next. But people will always need tattoos.'

She turned and went down the steps on her own, and left Era smiling.

Dite was rueful. 'That's me told,' she said. 'Let's go and see a god who supports women in love.' She smiled beautifully. 'I might learn something.'

Era looked at her – her beautiful black skin, her magnificent eyes, her high forehead, her superb figure.

'Are you really with us, former god?' she asked.

Dite met her eyes. 'Absolutely. Which is more than can be said for the two other old gods in your train.'

Era almost stumbled on the steps. 'What?'

'The bear and the donkey,' Dite said sweetly. 'The difference between them and me is that I've sacrificed my old body and many of my powers. I am a powerful mortal, but I am just a mortal. The bear is—'

'*Temis!*' Era guessed. There she was, standing in the cold northern sun on the steps of a magnificent step pyramid, and the truth hit her like a stone hammer. 'Seven hells!'

Dite put a long-fingered hand on her arm. 'We're not friends, Temis and I, though she has done you no harm and a great deal of good. But can you trust her?'

'And the other?'

Dite's hand on Era's arm was warm and human.

'The donkey?' Dite shrugged. 'I'm not sure myself. Someone supernatural. In hiding. Someone very old and very powerful.'

Era stood stunned for long moments, until Dite, much lower on the pyramid's sides, looked up.

'Are you coming?' Dite asked.

Hefa-Asus

'Does it hurt?' Hefa-Asus asked politely. He'd used every form of subtlety at his command to get a position in Nicté's boat.

Nicté was bare to the waist, paddling hard. Hefa-Asus was behind her, in a perfect place to see the new tattoo across her right shoulder blade, showing, in wonderful detail, the duel with the Jeker champion on the beach. The black ink was particularly strong, and Nicté's red-brown skin carried it well. But he could see brighter red welts, and she kept splashing water on it – and him.

'I'm fine,' she said.

'Did you see the tin?' he asked, hoping that speaking of their craft might make her happier.

'No,' she said. 'I've been blind since birth, and could not see the tin in a city full of tin.'

'Have I offended you, Nicté?'

She turned so that he could see her eyes, slitted in anger.

At the next rest halt, he switched boats.

North of Lakamha, which his friends insisted on calling Palanke, the great river divided. The main course ran north and west, into the tin country, and the narrower branch, the River of the Mountains with different names in different languages, ran north-east, towards the Uran country. It ran *through* the mountains in a wide, deep valley that had its own people and its own culture. Here, the river was known as the Saswatatan. The Kau-te-lan lived on its banks, whom southerners called Kautlin.

Soon, he would come to the valley where he had made war as a young man. It had been an endless march for a small raid – a lesson to a young warrior about the pointlessness of war.

He wondered, given his flat forehead and ear jewels, whether the Kautlin would tolerate him. They were famous traders who protected themselves in a similar way to the Hakrans: by trading and living far from others. Kautlin women left their valley to become translators and priestesses; Kautlin men only left to trade.

These were merely surface thoughts. Because in his heart, Hefa-Asus was in acute discomfort.

What have I done to offend Nicté? he asked himself. He asked himself every day, all day. He didn't precisely have a word for what he felt for her, but it was sharpening the closer they got to her home.

She would leave them. He was sure of it. She was a master smith now; a successful warrior. She would be instantly famous among her people, and probably rise to one of the great chieftainships in a matter of years. And they would eventually be enemies, when he went home. Which he would, eventually, when there was a new ajaw. Like Nicté, he was a famous man now.

Famous enough to *be* the ajaw.

He shook his head. That was an old way of thinking. Now, he had other dreams; he was part of Era's dream of overthrowing the gods, and that was a good dream. He wouldn't leave her in order to drink balché and swive slave girls, however pleasant. Because there were magnificent challenges coming to his craft: new designs; new metals, even. Alloys of star-metal?

He shook his head. But the whole idea of fighting the gods was a satisfying dream.

I need to persuade her to stay.

Because . . .

She is a great maker, and we will need her.

And . . . because . . .

He looked into the deep woods they were passing; they seemed like home after the barren world of the south, even though, as a young warrior, he'd found them imposing and spooky.

Because I don't want to be here without her.

He confronted that thought for a moment, and then slipped away from it, because . . .

I need her . . .

That thought was almost completely alien to him.

Almost.

Chapter Six

Zos

Half a dozen ragged Jeker ships, two so small they might have been considered boats, stood off the estuary of the main channel of the Iteru, rowing or tacking to pass over the bar and into the brown water of the great river. It was sunset on a winter's day, and the north wind made getting into the river against the current a tricky piece of seamanship.

Almost as fast as the sun was setting, a dozen more ships came down on the north wind, led by four big Jeker ships, their notched sails full. The six trying to enter the river paid them little heed until the northernmost was hailed.

Then the northernmost was stormed. It happened so fast that the next two were still trying to understand what had happened as they were pinned by half a dozen ships that should have been friends. Too late, the doomed Jekers realised that the ships coming down on them were a trick – they lacked the skulls and corpses that should have ornamented them.

Only the three southernmost ships were wise enough to flee, and the only way they could flee was away south, abandoning any attempt to enter the delta and running downwind towards Kyra.

★

'Well,' Persay said with a leer, 'we've found a way to keep the Py and your desert women from killing each other.' His grin widened.

The three tribeswomen were coming back aboard. Makeda's dark skin had a red wash over it, as if she'd bathed in blood. One of the Py was slapping her on the back, and she tolerated the man's touch and returned his grin. The storm of arrows released as the ships closed had annihilated the Jeker fighting crew, and made the conquest nearly bloodless – for Zos' people.

Makeda leapt up onto the command platform amidships of the *Sea Eagle*.

'The river is yours, lord,' she said.

Zos smiled in appreciation. 'I think we'll find a hell of a lot more Jekers just upriver,' he said, and then to Eritha and Persay, 'That went well. Now there's no one to give warning.'

'Brilliantly done,' Pollon said.

Zos made a face. 'Mostly luck, brother. If that last had been a little quicker getting into the river...' He made a motion with his hands. 'But he wasn't.' He looked at the brown water flowing under the ship. 'Ten parasangs to Thais. Against the current, in winter... We need a good deal more luck to get there by tomorrow night.'

One by one, his fleet entered the river, and it took until after dark. Lacking a pilot or an expert on the Iteru, Zos made them all anchor, tossing heavy stones on long lines overboard and then testing the lines to make sure they didn't drag in the deep river mud.

But as soon as dawn turned the sky pink, the stones were hauled back aboard. Luck was with them, and Zos threw a pearl over the side in supplication, an old habit, as a wind from the west pushed his ships into the current. The river was relatively low, and after a few hours of sailing they reached a pair of Jeker ships stranded on a mudflat. Zos ordered them burned. He put all the rest of his Jeker captures, recent and old, in the vanguard as a deception, and they felt their way up a river so wide that, at first, they couldn't see both banks from the centre channel. On the south side, the mudflats rose into desert dunes with astonishing rapidity. Zos, who hadn't been this way in fifteen years, could have sworn there used to be farms and villages where now there was only sand.

The north bank wasn't much better, but the destruction was very recent. Burnt villages, a sunken merchant ship in mid-channel, the top of her masts still visible above water, and floating corpses, marked the progress of the Jeker fleet upstream.

After the sun reached her low midpoint in the sky, the wind shifted, and they had to row. It was a long, hard pull into the current, moving as slowly as an old man would walk. Towards sunset, after they had to bear away to the south bank to avoid a mudbank and a dozen floating logs, the wind came from the north and a little east, making the rowing all the harder.

Zos cursed, and ordered them to anchor against the south bank. They stayed on their ships and ate cold food, and Zos lost sleep worrying about their journey. Worries that weren't eased when, to the east, long before the sun should have risen, there was a pink glow over the horizon. He shook his head.

Pollon was awake, and looked over the side.

'What's that?' he asked.

'Something burning,' Zos said.

'Thais?'

Zos grimaced. 'Hells, I hope not.' He lay down and tried to sleep, and eventually, despite the north wind and a little rain, he fell into a dream.

He couldn't remember his dreams when he awoke, although he thought they'd been sour. His shoulder and neck hurt from sleeping on the deck, and he wondered about age, and ageing;

378

wondered what the long-term effects of the Dry One's resin would be.

He'd dreamt of the torturers breaking his body. It came back to him at midday, as the rowers beat the water with their oars in something not far from desperation. Zos even took an oar himself, and Persay, Pollon and Eritha all joined him, to give some of the rowers a respite. By evening, his neck and shoulder pains were lost in a cacophony of fatigue, and when he ordered them to anchor he went to sleep quickly.

Eritha woke him for his watch and pointed mutely over the bow to the glow in the east. It was closer now.

'Thais is afire,' he muttered.

He drank off a cup of neat wine, and began to do exercises on the deck to stay warm and loosen his muscles. The dream was still with him.

Presentiment? Or old fear?

Full daylight gave them back their west wind, and they raised sails and ran before it, the water gurgling under their bows. Zos summoned his captains.

'Unless the wind changes' he said, 'we attack tonight. I want to see all the fireship crews aboard the *Sea Eagle* an hour before darkness. And I want you to question every man and woman. Is anyone from here? Find me a pilot, or a fisherman – anyone who can lead us upriver in the darkness.'

An hour before the sun had fully set, they came aboard: fifty volunteers from every walk of life. Two men and a woman admitted to being from this part of the delta, but they knew no more of the river conditions than Zos knew himself. This worried him, but he tried to put it out of his head and instead give them a sense of their mission.

'If we can burn the Jeker fleet,' he said, 'we can change the world.'

He looked into their faces, and they looked back. They were

edgy, like anyone on the rim of the shield of war; they felt excited and afraid and a dozen other things, and suddenly he knew he had to go with them, however absurd that was for the commander. It wasn't just that he hated to send people on a dangerous mission without going himself. He trusted his luck, and he was a capable navigator.

And Lord Trayos is just as capable at commanding a battle. Maybe more so.

And I have ordered too many to their deaths. I will lead this time. In person.

'The Jekers are like rats eating our harvests' he said, his voice suddenly stronger. 'By themselves, they are a menace, but their effect is everywhere – the destruction of trade, the waste of resources...'

Slack faces showed boredom. This was the wrong crowd for high strategy.

'Destroying the fleet will make you all heroes,' he said firmly. 'And every one of you will be entitled to a double share of loot when we take their camp.'

That got a better response.

'And I will lead you myself,' he said.

He appreciated the cheers.

Instead of dying, the west wind rose. It wasn't a gale, but it was a fine wind, and as darkness fell Zos boarded the lead fireship with Persay and Eritha and became his own pilot, leaving Alektron in command of the *Sea Eagle*, which the old sailor relished. All of the fireships had a lantern set in the stern so that it was visible only from behind, and all of them raised sails and started downriver.

Eritha put a hand on his shoulder as they went down into the boat.

'You have your shield and panoply?' she asked quietly. She'd seen his sheepskin bag going into the boat.

He smiled in the starlight. 'Yes.'

'So you aren't coming back,' Eritha said.

Zos shrugged in the darkness.

Eritha was a very intelligent woman. She blinked once, her eyes flashing in torchlight, and then went down the side and into the boat. He followed, dropping in. Even here, two days' travel up the river, there was a tide, and the river was tricky.

Two hours into the journey, one of the fireships struck a floating log full on, caved in her bow, and sank in minutes, leaving her scratch crew to swim through the cold, muddy water to other ships. Zos cursed and looked east, where the pink that had tinged the horizon for the last two nights was now almost orange.

He hoped it was Thais, and they were getting closer.

The west wind meant a clear, cold sky, with the emerald stars of the Gift burning so bright that they gave the deck a pale green hue. Overhead, the Maiden was fully in the Gate, and the Gate was rising like a mighty fortress of stars over Zos' head. It was midnight.

The fireship he was piloting struck a mudbank under full sail, and the mast snapped off at deck height, falling forward with a crash. No one was hurt, but the fireship was hard aground, and the ship next in line struck, too, although she didn't lose her mast.

Eritha leapt into action, ordering their thin crew of volunteers to cut the mast free.

'We'll have to abandon ship,' Zos said bitterly. 'This is what happens when you travel at night without a local pilot.' His self-criticism was obvious.

'Can we spare a second ship?' Eritha asked. 'Give us two hours and we'll have her off.'

'And the mast?'

'Get me a crew' Eritha said, as if she – and not Zos – were captain.

He found that he was smiling, despite everything; it wasn't a moment for panic, and Eritha was a better sailor than he was and clearly knew what to do. If she believed the ship could be saved...

It took almost an hour to ferry two dozen seamen from the *Sea Eagle* to the stricken fireship; another hour to empty her flammables and cut away anything that could be spared, until she rose out of the mud with a squelch and a roll and a sudden stink of river bottom. It was yet another precious hour while the veteran sailors, led by Eritha's father Jiani, cut away the bottom of the mast to make a new post, raised the stubby mast on lines, and dropped her home. They made a great deal of noise, and the whole process seemed to take forever. Every moment Zos expected a shower of arrows from the near riverbank, or the feral shouts of a Jeker squadron bearing down on them with the weight of the river current behind them.

But then it was the tail of morning – still *almost* full dark. He had no idea how far he was from Thais or the Jeker fleet and no real idea how long it would take to get there.

Should we anchor, and hope to lie low all day and not be discovered? Press forward, and risk being mid-channel in sight of all the Jekers, and a long painful day of death ...?

They all looked to him. Even Pollon.

You always wanted to be a wanax.

Zos laughed at his boyhood desires. He would have given a year of his life to be somewhere else, doing something else, right now. Hauling rock as a slave, for example.

'Fuck it,' he said aloud. 'Raise the sails. Get underway. Let's go!'

There was a soft cheer from the borrowed sailors, and then they were slipping over the side. The fireship, lighter now and bobbing in the current, gathered way and began to move upstream.

An hour later, Zos knew he'd made the wrong decision. He cursed himself. The wolf's tail of early dawn was lighting the sky a cold and bare grey in the east, and the orange glow of the burning city seemed too far away, and in the wrong direction.

And the west wind pressed them on and left him no alternative. He couldn't turn downriver in this wind.

Fuck.

Desperate times call for …

Illikumi

The two gods came out of the east in their magnificent flying chariots, heralding the dawn. They'd flown high towards the rising sun, and then they'd followed it until they could see Thais far below them, the whole of the delta laid out like a tomb painting beneath them. At the edge of the darkness, the sunrise was chasing the night over the rim of the world. There was the city, marked by a rising column of smoke and a hundred flickering fires that lit the last dark of night. The city stood on a low promontory that stuck out into the river like a long thumb, and the mighty Iteru detoured around the rocky peninsula in a long, deep curve.

The Jeker fleet was mostly beached on the south side of the city, on the excellent beach on the west-facing side. Fifty Jeker ships had worked into the marshes further east, on the other side, beyond the curve of the river where the ground became flat again. On the west side, where the land was higher, a mound was rising, created by thousands of slaves and captives flinging river mud and their own bodies on it, even as the two young gods watched with their superhuman vision. The mound was broad and deep, and already half the height of the wall.

A charnel reek rose on the morning air.

Telipinu looked down even as the two chariots descended, and motioned to his war-brother.

'We strike their ships and their camp,' he said. 'If the interloper dares face us, this will force him out.'

They fell like comets out of the last of the night, and Telipinu's deadly arrows began to fall on the Jeker ships. Each one was like a thunderbolt, and every ship he struck exploded and burned, and the young god, son of Sypa and Enkul-Anu, did not miss. Twice his chariot raced low across the sky, scattering death along the beach.

Illikumi lacked his war-brother's magnificent arrows but he had tricks of his own. His arrows were more subtle, striking men and killing them, releasing poison that filled the air by the ground. But he was cautious, staying above Telipinu, watching...

He still missed the interloper.

They had turned after their second pass, flying straight over the city to hear the cheers of the garrison and the people in the streets below as they hauled at the reins of their auratic teams, turning as hard as they could for a third pass. The beach was chaos come to earth; hundreds of Jekers were dead or gasping their last, turning to black and green shreds as their flesh rotted under Illikumi's poison, or burning alive in the wreck of their ships.

And then, like a great hawk swooping from high on some songbird, a black monster with brazen claws and the head and wings of a vulture struck Telipinu's chariot from above. One talon pierced straight through the young god's body, and he was pulled screaming from his car. The monster drew a sword and beheaded the son of Enkul-Anu in a shower of immortal ichor that burned like white fire as it hit the ground.

Only as the chariot drawn by stags turned, uncontrolled,

beginning a spiralling descent, did Illikumi see the falling corpse of Enkul-Anu's son, and the black victor rising from a kill that had taken him almost to the ground.

Illikumi didn't hesitate. He might have rejoiced; after all, he'd only come here to lure Telipinu to his death, but the vulture-headed creature reeked of power. Illikumi lashed his immortal horses into a climb, wished he had recruited a charioteer, and fumbled for his bow.

The black monster climbed after him, and his heart almost failed him – it was so fast. He looked for cloud, and there was none; the rising sun lit a clear blue sky. The only clouds were far to the south. He ran for them anyway.

He raised his bow and steadied his aim, and loosed a bolt of deadly poison at the black vulture rising behind him, but the chariot's passage left a wake in the air and his shaft missed.

'Enkul-Anu!' he screamed, his own plots forgotten.

He had no real hope, but cries to the Storm God were, according to the legends of heaven, always heard.

He lashed his magic horses and prepared another arrow.

The vulture wings were much closer. Illikumi twisted to get a clearer shot, and his arrow went home; his immortal eyes saw it strike.

His pursuer never faltered.

'Enkul-Anu!' he roared in terror.

He went higher, and the vulture wings beat hard behind him like the rapid beats of his own mighty heart.

Zos

The first rays of the rising sun found them mid-river, just as he had most feared. They were close ... so close. Close enough that the carrion smell of rotting flesh and the war-smell of burning filled his nose, and a trail of smoke offered them a slight cover from the shore to the right, where the city of Thais stood on a low rocky mound that jutted into the river. The light showed him that the city was afire – no surprise – and showed him a hundred or more Jeker ships beached or anchored just off the city.

And … they weren't filling with men to come and swamp his squadron. It took time for him to guess what had happened: some other brave soul had put a fireship or two in among them. He could see at least six afire; the unmoving black dots might be corpses.

A morning raid from the city? A daring sortie?

It doesn't matter a damn.

'Signal to form a line,' he said to Eritha.

This had always been their plan: to spread their eight – now seven – fireships at intervals that would allow them to burn a big stretch of beached hulls. The wind was behind them; the beach reached out into the river, and there was very little steering required.

Slowly, almost majestically, the other six fireships spread more sail and drew alongside, with perhaps half a stadion between each ship. It wasn't precise – it couldn't be, with such small crews – and it didn't need to be.

And here he was, anyway.

Zos grinned.

I'm going to do something insane. Like the old days.

Behind them, perhaps half a dozen stadia away, was the rest of his little fleet – not so little, really: twenty-four ships with all the latest captures, the smallest a triakonter. Trayos would be ordering them now; he was probably the better admiral anyway. And he had wanted the command so badly …

Zos felt a pang.

386

Jealousy? Anger?

The fleet he'd raised was the largest command he'd ever have, and he wasn't going to command it.

So be it. If this is my end, it will be ... remarkable.

We will conquer. I will make you mighty, and we will slay and slay.

Zos snapped 'Shut up!' out loud.

Eritha started.

'I wasn't sayin' nothin'.'

Zos grunted, watching the shore. Now, after a long, anxious night where everything seemed to pass at a snail's pace, they were moving towards the beach at what seemed like breakneck speed.

He looked back at the fleet. His fleet.

And at Eritha.

'We can light this hooker any time, Cap'n,' she said, as if fireships were her everyday pastime. 'She's not going anywhere but that beach.'

Zos looked forward.

'Which is to say, we need to go,' she said firmly.

Astern, the rest of the volunteers were already boarding the little boat they'd towed, except one big man, who was doing something with the mainsail.

'I'll light her,' Zos said.

Eritha rolled her eyes at what she took as male bravado.

'Get to it, then,' she said.

Zos went forward. The fire kit was laid out and ready in the dry space under the peak. Picking up a firepot, he dashed it to the deck and kicked the charcoal into the flammables.

He thought for a long moment it wouldn't catch, but then the wind whipped the charcoal and the straw and wood shavings caught, and then some oiled cloth ...

387

He turned and ran back to the stern, where his shield and his armour waited under the helmsman's bench.

Eritha, who was a very practical young woman, was already in the boat they'd towed for this purpose, and she had a knife in her hand, ready to cut the painter that attached it to the ship. At this speed, and with the boat fully laden, there was a danger it would be towed under.

Zos leapt up onto the stern rail, and balanced for a moment, looking downriver at his fleet forming line abreast.

My fleet.

My plan.

'You're not going with them, are you?' a voice said from behind him.

He felt the heat of the rising fire.

'Daos?' he spat.

The young man grinned. He was silhouetted by the fire. It wasn't a monster yet, but that was coming.

Zos turned and waved to Eritha.

'Get going,' he said, and cut the painter himself. He saw the round *O* of her mouth in the darkness.

'Daos?' he asked.

'I'm your charioteer,' the man said. 'And I'm here to drive your chariot of fire. Remember?'

Zos thought of ruining the moment by asking who in the seven hells was commanding the boy's ship, but instead, he said, 'Good! Help me put on my armour, like a proper *papista*. I need to get it on before the ship goes up.'

The armour went on quickly. Daos was the perfect *papista*, aiding with the magnificent, light *thorakos* of shining bronze over his best embroidered *heton*; greaves of bronze that were themselves cunningly plated in gold, and had serpents worked on them, so that they appeared to twine up his legs and meet at his knees; his father's helmet, with a huge panache of scarlet feathers; the Shield of Taris, ancient and powerful, on his arm.

And then he went forward. It was like a dream. Time was of the essence, and yet he moved in the time of eternity, savouring everything: the clasp of his cloak; the feel of the great godlike shield on his arm; his father's helmet on his head; the drive of the ship and the rising fire.

Daos was armoured, too, and held the trident. Their ship was slightly in the lead; another of the fireships was fully caught now, and the fire bellowed like a dragon trapped below, while flames rose from the open holds.

They were perhaps two hundred paces off the beach, and thousands of Jekers were gathering to pole them off or douse the fire. Fireships only really succeeded when a foe was surprised, and their surprise was entirely lost.

Chariot of fire. I like that.

Zos couldn't help but smile. He stepped onto the small platform that steadied the bowsprit, so that he was at the very front of the ship; Daos took position at his shoulder.

'You ready for this?' Zos asked

Daos laughed with his new, deeper voice. 'You might say I was born for this.'

Draw me and we will slay them all.

Fifty paces from the packed beach, their ship burst into a roaring leviathan of flame, and only the protection of Daos' auratic power kept his red cloak from burning. And Zos drew the sword, *Terror*, and held it aloft.

The sword *moaned*.

Oh, master, this is glorious. Thou art brilliant, and their corpses will be our monument.

The fireships roared out of the last of the darkness and billowing smoke from the burning town, and the flames rose higher than their masts as the sails caught. Every Jeker on the beach was suddenly seized by an unnamed dread. Fire and darkness cut at their calloused hearts like sharpened chain, and suddenly, as if they were one animal, they broke.

Not a hand was lifted to stop the flaming behemoths that crashed into the tight-packed beach.

Just before they struck, Daos levelled his trident and blew the beached ship ahead of them to splinters, so that the fire-ship nestled into the wreckage and was caught tight between two big pentekonters. Their pitch-coated hulls caught almost immediately.

Somewhat ignominiously, the shock of striking the wreckage threw both Daos and Zos flat.

But Zos didn't care. He leapt to the sand, the sword held high, and no man stood against him. Daos stood at his shoulder as their wall of flame fell on the beach. Thirty enemy ships were caught in the maelstrom, burning like spilt oil lamps, and the rising tide of fire backlit Zos and Daos as they walked up the beach unopposed.

'Do you not feel the terror?' Zos asked.

'Yes' Daos said. 'It is horrible.' His face, which was almost always lit by a smile, was hard and set. 'It is a terrible weapon, forged for evil.'

'But you stand.'

'I am your *papista*. And I will drive your chariot of fire.'

Zos could hear the fear in the boy's voice, and the force of will.

'Wasn't *that* our chariot of fire?' he asked, pointing back.

Their fireship was going to burn to the waterline and beyond in the next few minutes, but all the ships around her were well caught – their rigging afire – and the Jekers were paying for leaving their sails unfurled. Smoke rolled over them, hiding everything but the beach.

Daos' voice was suddenly bright, eager, untouched by *Terror*. Or rather, suddenly filled with hope.

'There,' he said, and pointed up the beach.

There, waiting just above the sea-wrack line, was a chariot that looked entirely covered in gold, and was drawn by four mighty stags of burnished gold, each the size of an ox. There was no driver, no warrior. The beasts had an unnatural immobility, as if they were only statues.

'What?' Zos felt as if he'd missed something, and also touched with supernatural awe.

I will drive your chariot of fire.

In the flames of the burning ships and the red light of the rising sun, the chariot itself seemed to burn.

Closer, it was clear that the inside of the car was covered in blood – bright blue ichor, supernaturally bright like the glow of a jewel. Zos had seen it before. The blood of a god.

Zos stopped dead in the sand. Ahead, a line of Jekers were beginning to rally. They were the hardest men and women on the surface of Ocean and *Terror* could only grip them for so long. But their fleet was burning. Zos' mission was accomplished, and he hadn't really planned past this point.

But someone had.

'You knew this would be here?' Zos asked.

With the boldness of the young, Daos stepped up into the golden chariot car.

'Telipinu, Steward of the Gods, son of Enkul-Anu and Sypa, died here.' He pointed up. 'These chariots land themselves.' He shrugged. 'It's ours now.'

As he touched the immortal reins, the four great stags shook their antlers and pounded the sand with their feet.

Zos made the first motions towards sheathing *Terror*. He wore the sword slung low from his waist, and to sheathe her he had to run the blade across the lip of the scabbard until he felt the prick of the point, and then put her home. She felt him try . . .

No! No! You idiot! This is the moment of your incarnation! I will make you immortal!

He slammed her home, and felt the guard lock into the lips of the scabbard.

Idiot! Idiot!

Ruthlessly he shut her out. He was getting better at it, despite her intrusion into some of his dreams.

'Well, I'll be damned,' he said, and stepped into the chariot car.

'Eternally,' Daos said cheerfully.

And the chariot sprang into the air.

Auza, Home of the Gods

Enkul-Anu strode forth from the Hall of Mourning, tall and magnificent, his horns glowing like molten gold, his scarlet skin appearing to burn with an inner fire, the heavy tread of his massive feet sounding through heaven like the impact of his thunderbolts on a battlefield.

He passed through the Hall of Judgement and then into the Hall of the Gods, and so awesome was his presence that some of the younger gods and all of the gathered mortal servants and slaves fell on their faces in worship.

'Summon the Demonic Legion,' he snapped. 'Where is Telipinu?'

Sypa came behind him, and she, too, evoked awe – beautiful to the point of being hard to look at, her eyes flashing fire.

'I told you, love – Telipinu has gone to rescue Thais from the Jekers.' Sypa sounded bored, as if she'd had to remind the Storm God once too many times.

'Where is Gul?' he demanded, looking over the assembled gods.

'I sent him on a mission of divine importance,' Sypa said.

He turned. 'What mission?'

She drew herself up. 'I sent him to kill the goddess–queen of Noa. She offended me.'

The full weight of his golden gaze fell on her.

'You *what*?'

She set her shoulders. 'It needed to be done. She was arrogant and refused me tribute.'

Laila flinched.

The Storm God's golden eyes bored into Sypa. 'Noa? After Ma'rib, they are our strongest supporter. The heaviest tribute, always meticulously paid. And you sent Gul?'

'Gul is strong. Gul obeys.' Sypa didn't give a finger's width. 'You were lost to mourning, and it was time to make an example.'

Enkul-Anu's burning golden eyes swept the hall. The other gods were absolutely silent, while the few mortals present lay on their faces and tried not to be seen.

His gaze fell on Laila, who met it.

'Laila, bring me my demons.' His eyes swept the hall again. 'And my armour.' He looked back at Sypa. 'We will have a reckoning, you and I.'

She smiled. 'When you cast your reckoning, Storm God, remember whose *efforts* recalled you to your duty from the Hall of Mourning.'

'The tribute of Noa is a high price for a good fuck,' he snarled.

The snake god could only stay ahead of him for so long. He climbed, and that was a good choice for the snake; he wriggled and curved, but went ever higher, and the sky chariots were well built, full of potent workings, and capable of going very high indeed.

But their maker, aeons before, had cautioned against riding them too high above the curve of the world. The snake was finding out why as the auratic horses who ran so well on air began to lose traction high above the world. Thais wasn't even a speck below; the Ocean could be seen stretching away like a sheet of hammered silver. Kursag could almost see the far coast of Dardania in the fully risen sun.

The chase took time, and as they rose, his quarry shot poisoned arrows at him, and some found a mark, and none hurt him at all.

I am a Great God now. I have the worship of thousands. The sacrificial blood flows like water, and fills me with their auratic power.

Up, and up.

He had time to savour the end of the chase and to plan his return to earth. He would not kill the godling. He would take him, in pain and humiliation, and carry him to the earth. He would gather his Jekers, and he would consume the godling alive before them.

Oh, the power of it.

He could imagine the wall paintings, the statues to his triumph ... but of course, there wouldn't be any. Because he was going to destroy all of them, root and branch.

The end was not climactic. The snake god loosed his last arrow, and then Kursag slammed a talon through the young god's chest like a fisherman spearing a tuna, and plucked him from his chariot.

The snake screamed, a high, sibilant scream.

The chariot, bereft of its driver, began to spiral down to earth, as it was designed to do.

Kursag closed his vulture wings around his prey and dropped, savouring the snake-god's terror in the long plunge to earth below.

This is glorious.

Chapter Seven

Pollon

Pollon had seen enough battles by now to know how they opened, and the emotional stages he experienced: pre-battle anxiety mixed with boredom; mounting fear; growing confusion; and then his own outright terror, matched by the violent chaos.

And this battle didn't disappoint. Zos didn't return, and Pollon knew why, and thought his friend insane. Trayos stood on the command deck of the *Sea Eagle*, watching the fireships run into the beach.

When the largest ship, with Zos aboard, seemed to explode in a shower of sparks as it crashed into the line of beached ships, Trayos nodded sharply, but spoke no word. To the right and left, the fleet had formed two lines of a dozen ships each. The rowers rowed slowly, doing no more than keeping station against the current.

Time seemed to pass slowly for all of them; some of the rowers, their backs to the action, risked pulling muscles to turn and look.

Trayos strolled down the central catwalk in his fine armour of bronze and padded linen.

'Lord Zos has triumphed!' he called. 'Every fireship went into their fleet. The whole beach is afire.'

Men and women cheered. Alektron spat over the side and managed a smile, rare from him.

'In a few minutes—' Trayos began, but then Disa, in the leather basket on the mast, called 'Jekers!'

'Where away?' the merchant-pirate called.

'Coming from the marshes beyond the headland,' the young woman called, voice shrill with excitement and fear.

Pollon was watching something else – something incredible: a golden chariot rising from the beach just four stadia away. At first it was a blaze of red gold, but as it turned, his archer's eye caught the flash of the team, the shape of the car.

'Gods!' he spat, and reached for his bow. 'Trayos! Look!'

Trayos leant out under the yard as the mainmast was being taken down and laid amidships.

'What the fuck is that?' he said. 'Archers! Be ready!'

Every ship had a strong contingent of archers now.

'More Jekers!' Disa shouted.

She was riding the mainmast down, still high above them as the sailors lowered the mast in a spiderweb of working rope.

Trayos glanced at the golden chariot and shook his head.

'I can't do anything about that,' he said.

Alektron, at the steering oars with Eritha, grunted – and then broke into a rare, beaming smile.

'It's the cap'n,' he said, and pointed with his free hand.

Pollon looked up, and there was Zos, leaning over the side of the chariot at an angle which might have given any of his friends pause.

'Daos is driving!' Eritha called. 'Oh, Daos!'

He was very popular with the women in the fleet.

In heartbeats, the chariot pulled alongside the ship, the four mighty stags of gold running together. It was … unearthly, and very beautiful. The four stags, this low, appeared to run on the water.

'Fuck me,' Trayos said. But he was grinning. He leant out and shouted, 'Nice toy!'

Zos waved at the headland and the distant city.

'Jekers coming from the marshes!' he yelled. 'I counted fifty-five ships. Nothing bigger than a triakonter.'

Trayos waved back. 'We'll have the size, then.'

'Send me an archer,' Zos called. 'Send me Pollon!'

Pollon shivered with a strange pleasure. As a boy, he had never been chosen for games, and now the warlord of the mortal revolt wanted him for his sky chariot.

'Will it hold three?' Pollon shouted.

'Only one way to find out,' Zos said. 'Come on, brother.'

Pollon fetched his bow and his quiver, and then climbed carefully up on the stern rail where it started to rise into the great arching stern.

'Come closer!' he yelled.

'Jump!' Zos called.

Pollon balanced on the rail, all but petrified. At some distance, the working part of his head told him that there was a deep irony to being pleased to be chosen for the sky chariot, but being afraid to jump the dozen feet to the car.

Water rushed by below his feet,.

'We've got you,' Zos said.

The chariot nudged inches closer and Pollon closed his eyes, opened them, started to lose his balance, and then released his fear.

He leapt, both feet powering his leap.

Zos caught him in both arms like a particularly warm embrace, and then snapped something closed across the back of the chariot car.

'Got him,' he said to Daos, whose grin looked big enough to split his face.

Daos leant back, snapped his golden reins, and the chariot

leapt forward. If Pollon had thought the ship was moving quickly, now the ship fell away behind at an incredible rate, and they were also climbing. And yet, despite the attitude of the chariot, he didn't seem to be falling out of the back.

'It's magic,' Zos said 'Don't worry about it.'

Below, their fleet was forming a crescent in two lines. The Jekers were coming around the city in packets: three ships, then half a dozen, then a big clump of them, and then some stragglers just coming off the upriver marshes. From up here, Pollon could see it all.

So could Zos. He directed Daos to fly along the peninsula of the city, and then back to the *Sea Eagle* to report his findings to Trayos. By then, the three leading Jekers were only a few stadia away

Trayos nodded. 'And you?'

Zos smiled. It looked both malevolent and boyish. 'I'm going to see what these javelins do,' he said.

With a nod, they were off again, and Pollon steadied himself. It wasn't cramped in this chariot car built for gods, and he had time to string his bow, and look at the arrows in the crossed quivers on the sides. They were all too big for easy shooting, but he thought he could get them off his bow at full stretch. He tried the bow in the bow case but it was impossible for him to string it, much less draw it. It was designed for a nine-foot-tall god.

Muttering, he took an arrow, a foot longer and much heavier than any arrow in his quiver, and shook his head.

'What do you think these do?' he asked.

Zos pointed to the thunderbolt glyph on the golden head. 'Explode?' he asked in a sarcastic tone.

At Zos' direction they'd passed over the leading elements of the Jeker fleet, and now they approached the main body in a circle, coming in behind. Half a dozen arrows came from the trailing vessels, but archery wasn't a Jeker speciality.

As they drew level with the trailing ships they were moving at perhaps only twice their speed, and they were maybe a hundred feet above the masts. Pollon leant out with his heavy arrow, did his best to calculate the trajectory, and loosed.

The arrow flopped around in the air and then fell, striking the water aft of the last ship in the group, where it detonated with a thunderclap.

'Fuck,' Pollon said. All he'd done was make a hole in the water. 'I don't want to waste these, but they're very hard to shoot.'

'I'll go closer.' Daos looked delighted.

Pollon took another arrow and leant out over the back of the car.

Daos was as good as his word, and came down over one of the ships at mast height.

Pollon loosed. He understood that he had to compensate for his own speed, but he really had no idea how the arrow would perform. On the other hand, right now he could almost touch the ship. He loosed.

Before he could draw a breath, the ship opened like a flower in spring, debris rising in the air and buffeting the chariot.

Zos was standing above him, ready to grab his waist if he fell. Daos was turning them hard. Under them, the Jekers' main body of ships was suddenly splitting up.

They went low over another ship, and Zos leant out with one of the chariot's javelins, which was like a heavy spear for him. But Zos had thrown heavy spears all his life, and his javelin went home amidships in a triakonter, the slaves straining to row, their eyes locked on the golden chariot that hovered over them...

And then they were gone. Bits of them scattered against the

underside of the car, and a piece of some flying debris cut Pollon's face. He turned his head and saw that the first Jeker ships had already been rammed and taken, swamped by Trayos' crescent. Their fleet was re-forming to receive the main body.

'Again!' Zos roared. 'We can win this for our people.'

Again Daos drove the golden team down, this time so low they appeared to run along the river, and Pollon shot from the right side while Zos hurled a javelin from the left.

The Jekers couldn't even reply. They just died.

Pollon's initial joy at the power of the arrows – at his own success in figuring out the shooting problem – gave way to horror. By his fourth arrow, he didn't want to look at the result. He felt nothing for the Jekers, but every ship was rowed by people whose lives had been made a nightmare, and he was killing them.

They were turning from their fourth run, and the Jekers were slowing, unable to deal with this new attack, when Daos suddenly banked away.

'What the hells of deepest Kur?' Zos barked.

Daos pointed at a black dot hurtling from the heavens with his free hand.

'A god,' he said.

Zos frowned. 'I should have expected that,' he acknowledged.

Daos looked at Zos. 'Fight or flee?'

Zos made a face. 'No way am I leaving my people to die. I've done it before. It sucks.'

'Fight, then.' Daos looked pleased. And he swung the chariot through a long banking turn, gaining altitude rapidly.

'Which fucking god is that?' Zos said.

Pollon was watching as the hurtling black dot grew. It seemed to explode towards them, but that was just the effect of the closing speed of two very fast objects.

There was a flash of an onyx claw; Zos was driven to his knees under his magnificent shield, and the black thing was gone, past them.

Zos stood. 'Fuck,' he said.

The Shield of the goddess Taris, once Queen of Heaven, was unmarked. So was Zos.

Daos was already pulling them into a turn so tight that all three men were virtually pinned against the chariot side, and yet Pollon had some control of his bones; he could feel the strain of auratic power all around him.

'Here it comes again!' Daos shouted.

This time, Pollon was ready, and shot an arrow as they closed. He must have hit, because the detonation caught all of them, and then they were through the cloud of fire, the chariot bucking as it hit the superheated air of the wave front.

They were turning again, and he was trying to get a thunderbolt arrow from one of the crossed quivers. Zos had a javelin in his hand and a set expression on his face.

'Which god is that?' Zos asked again, over the rush of air. His hair and his cloak were blown almost straight out behind him.

Daos shook his head. 'No idea.'

Pollon said, 'It has something in its claws ...'

Then they were going head-to-head again, now only five hundred feet over the water, which was engulfed in chaos. Trayos' tactics had played out; his two lines had collapsed to one, and every ship in the river was locked with another in mortal combat.

All that in a flash.

'Did we get him?' Pollon asked hopefully.

Zos was already up. 'I don't think so,' he said. 'But it was a good shot anyway.'

The ebony god with vulture wings was turning above them, either baiting them or indecisive.

'We didn't touch him,' Daos said. 'He's very strong. If not for that shield, he'd have destroyed the chariot by now.'

They levelled out, and Zos cocked back his arm. But this encounter was different. As they joined, the vulture wings cupped the air and the dark god turned with them, hammering the chariot with a sword that moved like blue lightning.

Pollon didn't know the god, but the sword looked familiar.

He shot, and missed.

The blue lightning struck, and Zos parried with the shield.

And the sable god swooped in again …

Zos threw the spear with the whole weight of his body behind it. It struck the vulture-headed figure full on, and the explosion drove them apart. The vulture-wings lost their beat and the god tumbled away into the air.

So did the chariot. It took Daos an eternity to control it, and when he did, they seemed to be running on the water again. Zos looked horrified, and Pollon saw why: the immortal shield had a gash in it.

'Fuck,' Zos said.

'*Godkiller*,' Pollon said. 'The mightiest weapon in heaven's arsenal.'

'He's coming for us again,' Daos said.

Zos looked up and back, where the vulture-god had regained control and was flapping after them. He still carried the golden body of a snake-headed god in one claw. Closer, Pollon could see with horror that the snake-headed god was … one of the young ones.

Illukimi? Illikumi!

'We're not touching that thing,' Zos said. 'We're not even hurting it.'

Pollon readied another arrow.

'Have any star-stone?' Zos asked.

Pollon could have wept with frustration.

'Two,' he said. 'I never thought—'

'Make 'em count,' Zos said. 'I can't imagine *Terror* will have any effect, though I may try her.'

Pollon hoped Zos wouldn't have to; the hideous sword always left him feeling as if he'd been coated in a filthy grease and left to rot.

He took a star-stone arrow – made by Hefa-Asus, and gleaming coldly in the winter sunlight. His hands were shaking. Then they entered a cloud, white and fleecy and so brilliantly lit by the sun that everything around them seemed to be on fire.

Daos was turning. 'I'm going to make him climb up under us,' he said. 'He'll have to go straight and he'll be …' He shrugged, not having the language to describe air-to-air combat. 'Anyway, the cloud might confuse him.'

'He'll be slower relative to us.'

Pollon had more faith in his own archery skills with one of Hefa-Asus' arrows. But he feared the vulture god hitting them *in the cloud*.

They rose further, until Pollon could no longer see his target beneath him, and then they burst through the top of the cloud into a pure blue sky and Zos said, 'Oh, fuck.'

Pollon turned. 'What?'

Daos groaned. 'I wondered,' he said to the air.

Off to the south, not much higher than their chariot, came a phalanx of flyers – perhaps fifty, led by a burning scarlet figure.

'That's the Storm God,' Daos said.

'Thanks,' Zos said with some sarcasm. 'I wouldn't have recognised him.'

Kursag

He blew through the cloud into the open air, his head turning to find his prey. He felt wonderful – on top of the world.

There was the golden chariot, fleeing his wrath.

And there …

There …

The shock of it was awful, and he took them all in with one glance: the legion of demons, and their leader – his father, Enkul-Anu, alive, and in full battle harness with his mighty thunderbolts to hand.

Enkul-Anu. Alive.

Alive!

Then who did I kill over the star-kissed sea? Kursag asked himself. *Who else would rise to fight the World Serpent?*

Oh, no.

Ara would.

Enkul-Anu

He saw Telipinu's chariot off to the east, fleeing, apparently, and then he saw what was in pursuit: black against the white clouds, vulture-headed and vulture-winged.

The chariot turned due east, running from the fight. Enkul-Anu was disappointed, but the vulture thing looked tough, and had Illikumi clutched in its claws, his snake's head dangling limply. That settled whose side the fucking thing was on.

It turned north, lazily, as if unable to decide what to do.

'Bashmu! On me! Udug! Take the rest of the legion and kill the Jekers!' he ordered. He pointed at the river, clear in the sunlight below, with the long thumb of the Thais peninsula like a stone carving on a crystal sheet. 'And I mean *all the Jekers*!'

Bashmu's four comrades joined him, and Udug took the rest of the demonic legion down in a steep dive for the river far below the clouds, where the mortal ships could be seen on the river like bugs racing across calm water.

It didn't take an eternity of interplanar warfare for Enkul-Anu to know that the vulture was connected to the Jekers. Symbols mattered – he knew that.

'Get him,' he said to Bashmu.

Together, the six of them gave chase.

The Bear and the Donkey

They were deep in the valley of the Saswatatan, and the flow of the river was sufficiently strong that every man and woman had to paddle. The enormous trees on either bank crept by in an unending flow of ancient forest.

The donkey sat up and brayed.

'What?' growled the bear.

'The mortals. The *other* mortals. They're … fighting.'

'That's all they ever do …' the bear replied.

'No, they're fighting the *gods*. Fuck, what happened to planning?'

'Nothing we can do,' the bear growled. 'We're stuck here.'

The donkey's liquid eyes met the bear's yellow ones.

'Even now, I can raise a storm over the ocean. A storm in the delta where they're fighting.'

'What good will that do?' the bear asked.

The donkey shook itself. The men and women paddling were looking a little fearfully at the two big animals shifting, growling and braying.

'Cover?' the donkey asked the sky. 'Distraction?'

The bear said, 'The mortals said they were going to try something in Narmer.'

The donkey brayed again. 'Well, they're trying. And they're dying.'

'You'll give us away!' the bear growled.

The donkey *glowed* for a moment, and just for that moment, there was a crackling blue outline of a huge man with the tail of a fish. And then he was just a donkey again, snuggling down into the big bark canoe, and the paddlers looked at each other, and kept paddling.

Six boats ahead, Dite missed her stroke with a scream.

Nicté, on her other side, stiffened.

Era grabbed her lover's strong shoulder.

'What happened?'

Dite looked harrowed. 'Oh, no,' she said.

Zos

'Back to the ships!' Zos shouted.

'The demons …' Pollon was pointing at them.

'Back to the ships!' Zos insisted. 'I'm not leaving them to die.'

Daos turned and gave him a long, questioning look.

'I brought them all here,' Zos said. 'I led them into this, and it's a trap. I'm not running off to fight another day. If necessary, I'll just fucking die with them.'

Pollon blinked, but said nothing.

'All right, then,' Daos said. 'Here we go. Hang on!' He sounded *cheerful*.

The bottom dropped out of the world. Their dive was so steep that it was more like a fall, and Pollon squeaked. Whatever mechanism compensated for the speed and turns of the sky chariot, Daos' steep dive was too much for it, and all of them were pressed back in the chariot car. Only the chariot's own protections, the invisible barrier at the rear, saved them from tumbling out.

Zos could see straight down. He could see Phatos as a dark clump on the desert surrounded by green off to his right, and the ribbon of the river, and part of the delta, laid out like a picture. They had come well east of Thais when the demon legion appeared, and now …

They fell faster than a dropped stone. Zos was overwhelmed – angry, frustrated …

'How many star-stone arrows do you have?'

Pollon counted again. 'Two.' He was parchment-white.

Down, and down.

Off to the west, over Thais, the demon legion was falling as well, if not as fast.

'They're going to beat us to the fleet,' Daos said.

'I know,' Zos snapped.

So much was rushing through his mind that he wasn't thinking much of anything.

One thought occurred to him out of the maelstrom of failed ideas.

We were supposed to focus the gods' attention on Narmer. I guess we've done that. Is this it?

Of course, Enkul-Anu has come. But why? To help *the Jekers? That's insane.*

Or is it? Who is the black vulture god?

'Ships on the river, Zos,' Daos said.

'Yes,' Zos said, trying not to snap.

Stop panicking. No more fear and hopelessness. You've already been tortured to death once. What more can they do? It's all been borrowed time since Hekka.

Pollon nudged him. 'Not our ships. And not Jekers.'

Zos realised he'd closed his eyes. He opened them again. They were still diving almost straight down, at an enormous speed, and the four mighty stags were running flat out, the brilliant sun shining on their golden hides. But over their backs he could see the river, a parasang or two west of the marshes. They were lower now, and Daos' dive was headed west, back towards Thais. He really was a divine charioteer.

It was a considerable fleet: sixty or more ships.

Pollon's face was still white, but there was strength in it now.

'It's Maritaten. It must be. We heard she'd preserved her river fleet.'

Zos felt as if blood was returning to his brain.

'Kur's fucking icy hell,' he said, with some pleasure. 'Daos, lay me alongside the largest.'

'They'll shoot at us, Zos,' Daos said with cheerful practicality. 'They'll think we're gods.'

'Damn it, we don't have time to mess around,' Zos said. 'Lay me alongside that big ship. The one with the rising sun on the sail.'

'Narmer has the best archers in the world,' Daos reminded him.

'We're out of good choices. I'm going to jump aboard that ship. Now put me where I can make a leap.'

'That's insane,' Pollon said.

'Give me a better idea.'

Zos was stripping off his armour. He wouldn't need it and it would only impede his leap.

Pollon looked at him. 'All right,' he said. 'We leave the battle to chance and run for heaven, right now.'

Zos paused with his hands on the pins of his breastplate.

'What?'

'Enkul-Anu is *here* with his legion of demons,' Pollon said.

'We have a flying chariot. There will never be a better moment to try for the resin store.'

'Almost there, Zos,' Daos said.

The helmet followed the breastplate, and Zos went to the rear of the chariot.

'Hold that thought,' he said.

They were moving more slowly; Daos was reining in the team, and the deceleration should have pinned them to the front of the chariot car, but instead it was just a series of jolts. The chariot was slowing in a long parabola over the south bank, and then they were over water.

Slowing …

Slowing …

Arrows started to reach out for them, but they were always behind them, and low. There was a frightening volume to the archery, though. Then a shaft hit the underbelly of the car; then two. A shaft struck one of the stags and glanced away.

'You're sure this is how you want this to go?' Daos asked. 'I never saw this in my dreams.'

'I don't know whether that's good or bad,' Zos said. 'Pollon, it's an excellent idea. But we need Maritaten. We need about ten miracles, and Maritaten here is one. Don't die. Come back for me.'

'I'm your *papista*,' Daos said. 'Of course I'll come back for you.'

A dozen arrows struck the car, and the team were hit almost constantly, though they were moving at the speed of a normal gallop, or maybe a little faster.

Pollon forced a fake smile. 'Good archers,' he managed.

Zos watched *under* the chariot as they lined up with the ship – the *Rising Sun of Arrina* – and descended. An arrow just missed creasing his scalp and ricocheted off the adamantine axle, splintering.

He was ready. He felt right.

'Lower!' he roared.

The chariot seemed to be the same height as the ship, and it was only going a little faster. The arrow strikes were almost constant, but still didn't seem to do any damage.

'Steady!' he roared, and leapt.

He tumbled twice in the air, measuring his landing. He'd never jumped from so high, and he hoped that he had the right angular momentum to roll it out, and then...

He was rolling. He'd hit the magnificent awning that covered the stern and it had broken a great deal of his fall, as he'd hoped. Then he hit something with his back and popped into the air, struggled to get his feet under him, rolled forward over his hands, his back screaming with pain. At least it wasn't broken. He *knew* how that felt...

He landed on one knee, facing forward. His back muscles hurt so badly he couldn't stand; something was like rampant fire in his hip and his head was spinning.

But he was down. Two hundred faces were turned to him all along the deck: rowers, sailors, perfumed courtiers, archers. But they were still in shock, and he was moving, ignoring the terrible pain with a lifetime of practice.

Actually, the pain was already lessening.

He turned.

In the stern, under the wreckage of a magnificent royal canopy, a dozen soldiers were attempting to clear fallen cloth from a throne of gold. On that throne, apparently untroubled by the intruder who had fallen from the sky, was a beautiful young woman: small, elegant, with the piled hair of Narmerian royalty.

'Great Lady of the High House, Maritaten, goddess-queen of all Narmer!' Zos called in a firm voice. His Narmerian was not bad. 'I am Zos of Trin. We need your help.'

She looked at him for a moment, and a smile twitched the corner of her mouth.

'A kilt for my naked guest,' she said.

Zos realised that the leap and landing had stripped away his kilt, his loincloth, and all, so that he stood before her in only a sword belt.

'Great Lady,' he said, 'right now, there is a battle before Thais. My fleet is fighting the Jekers. In the last minutes, Enkul-Anu has entered the fray with a legion of demons. There is another god – a vulture god. He may be a third force. He may be the god of the Jekers. He may, in fact, just be another one of the fucking gods.'

An older priest handed him a magnificent white linen kilt, pleated in the Narmerian fashion and decorated beautifully with dandelion silk embroidery in red and blue.

'Please order your archers to cease fire,' Zos continued. 'My sky chariot is coming back for me, and I am going to my fleet to face the gods. I wanted you to know that we came to help you, and ...' He thought her eyes were the most magnificent pale brown he'd ever seen. Was that a hint of jade in their liquid depths? 'And we will die trying, if that's what fate requires. Great Queen,' he said with a deep bow, 'there is a revolt against heaven. Take heart that this is not the end.'

Maritaten rose from her throne. She wasn't tall, but she was graceful, lithe, and her face carried quick intelligence.

'What would you have of me, stranger?' She walked straight up to him and put a warm hand on the centre of his chest. 'I am the Lady of the High House, and I, too, am ready to die for my people. See my armour? See my archers? My hand is not light. I have weapons that even the gods might fear.'

He smiled down at her. 'So do we, Great Lady. We stole one of their own chariots.'

'We go to the battle, then.'

'And the demons?' he asked. 'And Enkul-Anu?'

Maritaten paused.

Zos looked around. There were some very competent killers around the throne – plus one smaller man with a face full of scars, who actually had the point of his long *khopesh* pressed lightly to the side of Zos' throat. His face was unreadable.

'May I offer the Great Queen of Narmer some advice?' he asked.

She nodded. Her hand was still flat against his chest, and he wondered if it was a sign of protection to keep her bodyguards from gutting him.

'Speak,' she said.

'Get off the river. Here, the demons can hunt your ships. Do what you can from the cover of the marshes and woods instead, and live to fight again.' He looked at the small man with the sharp *khopesh*. 'I need to go. I offer no threat, I am at your service.'

'Cease fire,' she said without taking her eyes off him. 'Let him go where he will. Zos of Trin, I preserved my river fleet to own the river power. I will not lightly abandon it.'

'Very well,' he said. 'But it is my intention to move the fighting into the marshes. If I can.'

She nodded. 'Go then. Let what must be, be.'

She took her hand off his chest and snapped her fingers, and the armed men shuffled back.

'How are you doing against the Jekers?' she asked.

'We've burned two thirds of their fleet,' he said, 'and the rest would have been destroyed, had the gods not come. As we speak, the demons are killing the Jekers. It is *not* a simple battle.'

She nodded. 'I hope to see you again at the end of it,' she said. 'I feel that there's more to this than you are telling me.'

He laughed and rubbed his back. 'So much more,' he agreed.

413

The golden chariot was coming alongside the ship again, and no arrows flew.

'I take my leave, Great Lady of the High House,' he said.

The short jump to the chariot car took all of his energy, and he sagged against the side as Daos whipped the golden team into a long accelerating curve away.

'Well,' Pollon said, 'I see we're all still alive.'

Zos nodded. 'So far. Back to the fleet.' He smiled at Pollon. 'If we survive the next half an hour, we go for the resin store. If I die, you two do it.'

Pollon nodded, and Daos flashed them both a smile.

'I don't think you die,' he said. 'But all I've seen of any of this is the chariot.'

Maritaten

'That was exciting,' Maritaten said to her councillors. 'Who was he?'

Tudhal grinned. 'That's Zos the sell-sword, Lady of the High House. I thought he was dead. There were rumours he'd hurt Resheph, the upstart plague god.'

'You know him?' she asked with interest.

Tudhal nodded. 'Yes, Great Lady. We've crossed paths and spears.'

She watched the golden chariot fly west.

'We live in interesting times,' she said. 'Pass our star-stone to the best archers.'

Mari-Ye raised a cautious hand. 'Great Lady! The stranger may have been rude and barbarous, but his suggestion that we get off the river...'

Maritaten met the old man's eyes and held them. 'Will be ignored. It is all or nothing, today.'

Mari-Ye drew a deep breath as if to speak, but then said nothing.

Maritaten set her shoulders. 'To Thais,' she said.

Enkul-Anu

The vulture-headed god fled for the lower air, using clouds to hide.

Enkul-Anu wasn't in a mood to play hide-and-seek, and he and his band of demons plunged into the fleecy cloud, shot through it, and emerged on the other side. Enkul-Anu felt a blink of a moment when all was not right with the world ...

'Where's Pazu?' Bashru bellowed.

The rest of the demons emerged from the cloud, but not Pazu.

Enkul-Anu's anger began to foam to rage.

He dived.

Below the high white clouds, the sky was clear all the way to the winding ribbon of the great river Iteru far below, and Enkul-Anu had no trouble finding the demon Pazu, falling away. Enkul-Anu circled, swearing, and then his golden eyes narrowed.

Whoever that is, he has Godkiller. *That was the blink.*

'Follow me,' he said. 'This is serious.'

'Boss?' Bashru asked.

'He killed Pazu and he's falling under the body, trying to escape.'

'Could still be in the cloud,' Namtar said. 'Lord Boss.'

'Then you check the cloud – and be careful. Whoever the fuck this is, they had the ability to kill Pazu.'

Enkul-Anu motioned with an arm, and Namtar rose. Demons were not the swiftest flyers, but they were tough. Very tough.

Too tough to be killed by a single blow. Unless with a weapon designed to kill their kind.

Enkul-Anu's superhuman eyes were still tracking the falling body of his mostly loyal and now dead demon. To the west, rain clouds over the ocean were being pushed inshore over Narmer. Visibility was going to suffer.

Let's get this over with. One rebel god is not a rebellion of the gods.

Unless it is. I need to be cautious. And I want Illikumi back. And where the fuck is Telipinu? The boy can't just be running.

'On me,' he said, and dropped.

Trayos

It all went so well, for a while.

But this wasn't Trayos' first naval battle – or his twelfth – so he anticipated the moment when tactics and plans went to shit and everything came down to fighting.

For him, today, that moment came when, having rammed and sunk their second victim, their third fouled his ram. Suddenly two of the little Jeker triakonters were grappling him, stuck like limpets. Each had thirty oars and a dozen hardened killers.

He had fifty oarsmen who were not broken slaves, and another dozen marines, and now it was down to brawn.

He got his big figure-of-eight shield up and locked with Jiani and Alektron, backed by Persay, Eritha and the rest of the marines holding the gangway in the middle of the command deck. The Jekers came at him. His archers decimated them, but they came on.

It took the Jekers three rushes to understand that the oarsmen would kill them. They'd run down the gangway at him, and be tripped and killed.

By the fourth rush, there were six ships grappled to the *Sea*

Eagle and his best bronze sword was a broken scrap at his feet. He threw the crystal and gold hilt into the face of one Jeker after using the broken shard as an improvised brass knuckle against another. The Jeker was straddling Eritha's father, who was bubbling out his life, and old Alektron had a gash on his thigh that didn't look good.

Trayos laughed. 'This is the life, eh, Alektron?'

The old sailor looked at him as if he was insane.

'You want to die alone in a hut, forgotten by everyone, with some puking disease?' Trayos asked.

He drank a little watered wine and handed the old sailor the canteen. Then he found the best sword among the dead men scattered at his feet, found a spear he liked with a wicked barbed head, stretched out his back, and drank more wine.

'Here they come again!' Eritha sounded very tired. Her voice was flat, as if another rush of Jekers wasn't really worth working herself up for.

The Jekers came over the bow and sides and stern, all together to the sound of a brazen trumpet. There were now *eight* Jeker ships grappled to them.

Trayos wondered who everyone else was fighting, and risked another swig of precious wine.

Hate-rictused faces filled the bow and forward quarter, and the Jekers came forward warily over the abandoned benches. Trayos had Zos' crew drawn up in something like a tight battle circle around the command deck.

Something exploded out of the bodies in the forepeak and a Jeker died, his head flying from his body to splash in the sea.

Persay, covered in blood, leapt over the back of the Jeker line to land in the midst of them, wielding only a bronze dagger, or a very short sword.

The stern was difficult to storm because of the shape of the ship, but two dozen Jekers tried. They came over the curved wood to meet the three nomad women, who screamed like keening widows and cut into them with their whirling, long-bladed spears.

Trayos knew the vital moment in a fight when he saw one. 'On them!' he yelled, and led the way.

Persay was somewhere in among the confused brutes, and Trayos thought the man had gone down under the benches after his initial leap, and was cutting their hamstrings. The Jekers couldn't look down into the bilges and up to fight his people at the same time, and the result was a massacre.

Trayos drove one opponent over the side and watched him start to sink in his bronze armour. He turned, his reflexes honed by years of combat, and used his big shield to fend off the next two men, but a blow slipped past the figure-of-eight shield and cut him just above his greave.

He was alone, and they were coming for him.

So this was the end. He grinned, slammed his big shield into the man nearest, and cut his hamstring under his shield at the moment of contact, determined to sell his life dearly.

And then the other fighter, a woman, looked over her shoulder and backed a step. Trayos tried to leap forward, but his wounded thigh didn't allow it, so he went to one knee.

She didn't finish him. She was backing away, and then her expression changed. It took Trayos a moment to see that she had an arrow shaft under her raised spear-arm. She was already dead, even if her body didn't know it yet.

And past her, just forward of amidships, a big red pentekonter was disgorging men onto his deck. There were Py archers, led by Leontas. His own survivors gave a thin cheer as the tall warrior began to clear their deck.

Trayos couldn't do much more than breathe, and watch the blood flowing from his thigh to pool on the deck under him. There was a lot of blood there; it couldn't all be his.

'Someone help me up,' he called weakly, and then the world exploded.

He was flat on his back, his face burned like fire, and he couldn't see.

'Lord Trayos! Lord!'

That was Eritha's voice.

'What …? What? I'm blind!'

Another voice – higher, a little mad: Persay. 'Blind? Fuck, that's not good.'

'What …?' Trayos muttered.

Eritha's voice: 'Boats are exploding. There's demons in the air hurling gouts of fire!'

Trayos could hear the screams. He'd never noticed that battle sound had so many layers before: the dying; the merely wounded; the terrified; the hate-filled or berserk; the sound of flames licking; the sound of …

The smells …

'Are we afire?'

Eritha said, 'Not any more. Leontas' people helped us put out the fire.'

Trayos sighed. 'Are we winning?'

He grabbed at her in his intensity, and a spurt of blood came from his abdomen. He could feel the heat of it, and the sticky place where other blood was drying next to his skin, and there was a large wood splinter straight through the bronze. He felt it with a jolt of hard reality and more than a little shock.

Eritha touched his face.

'The Jekers are destroyed,' she said.

Trayos smiled, and a trickle of blood came out of his mouth.

'On my deck, in victory,' he said with the relish of a con-noisseur. 'Fuck the gods! I think I'm …'

'He's dead,' Persay said. 'Now who's the *Naumachos*?'

Eritha was looking down at her father's corpse. Trayos had been a pirate, and fishermen and pirates aren't friends. Her father had been her whole world until a month before.

'I don't know.' She felt hollow. Off to starboard, another Jeker hull caught fire from a demon stooping low over it, its bat-like wings beating the air. The smoke was thickening and her weather sense noted that there were rain clouds racing in from the west, and the wind was freshening. 'Lord Leontas, I suppose.'

'He's already boarding another ship,' Persay said. His mad eyes glittered.

Alektron was pale from blood loss, and he looked even worse than usual. 'Let me do it,' the old salt said. 'I know the sea and I know what to do.'

Persay laughed his mad laugh. 'I can't choose you, mate. Zos doesn't have elections.'

Eritha looked along the deck at the twenty or so remaining crew.

'You have an idea?'

Alektron nodded. 'I do.' He didn't sound like a petty tyrant now. He sounded…

Like she felt. Beyond the mortal plane. Exhausted, but somehow … more alive than ever.

Persay grunted. 'Right, then,' he said.

Alektron made an effort to stand taller, his bandy legs straighter.

'Right,' he snapped. 'I need oars out and way on her. Eritha, you're steering. Persay, gather five people you like. You're the marines. The rest of us are rowing.'

'Give me the three nomads and we'll kill anything that comes aboard,' Persay said.

Alektron looked forward. 'Oars!' he roared. 'Sort your shit out, there. Evens an' odds. You, Serissa! You hurt too bad to beat the stroke?'

The big woman shook her head. 'I got it,' she said.

'Disa! Into the bow and watch for shoals!' Alektron's voice was crisp, confident.

He ran up the gangway towards Eritha, who already had a steering oar in hand.

'You! And you! Get the dead over the side.'

He was shouting at desperate, wounded people, and they responded, which was its own miracle. Then he picked up Zos' old shield – the one the captain had had plated in gold for signalling.

From the helm on the slightly raised stern deck, Eritha could see a little further, but the smoke was everywhere and the rain would start soon.

'What are we doing?' she asked.

'Running on the wind,' Alektron barked. 'I don't know why, but the demons are only killing Jekers. Let's leave before someone sorts that shit out.'

'There's the *Shark*,' she said. 'And there's the *Trident*. Leontas can't be that far …'

'No way on us yet,' Alektron said. 'Signal for me. Signal *Follow me!*'

She picked up the shield. They only had three signals: one for stop; two for go; three for follow.

She caught the sun, and flashed the shield three times. Waited for a long moment while another Jeker ship died in a maelstrom of fire, and signalled again.

Now she could see Leontas, deep in the billowing smoke closer to the beach, and the fires there. He was poling off a stricken Jeker ship.

'The *Trident* is responding,' she said as an answering flash came.

The steering oar was live under her hand and she could hear the oar-rhythm being beaten on the deck. Twenty oars wouldn't move a pentekonter very fast, but it was something …

'I want to pass as close to the city as we can manage,' Alektron said. 'Right inshore with the smoke, and then around it and into the current.'

'Aye aye,' she said.

'Look,' he said. 'I'm not a fuckin' cap'n. I'm an old salt. But here's what I think — it's all gone to shit, and we can get out and fight another day, or stay an' get cooked. An' if the demons come for us when we're close to shore, well, maybe a few of us can swim and live.'

'Better 'an anything I have,' Eritha said.

The next ten minutes were still brutal — slow, agonising, frustrating, terrifying. And in a way, dull. The battered *Sea Eagle* crept in towards the beach where the fireships had struck. The whole beach was either aflame or a smoking ruin, and the smoke drifted on the fitful wind. They passed almost directly astern of Leontas' red ship, and it responded with a flash of a shield, and turned as if in pain to follow them.

One by one, the scattered survivors of their fleet spotted them, and the recurring flashes of the golden shield. One by one, the ships followed.

And then they entered the smoke. High above, the sun was a pale disc in a smoky hell, but the rest was a choking nightmare. Eritha had to wet her headscarf and tie it over her face just to breathe until they had crossed the length of the beach and passed through it. Rich palaces loomed above them on the high ground that formed the city; the walls stood on rock instead of mud, and the water under their keel was deeper … but they had no more smoke for cover.

Back in the belly of the river bend, where the battle had been fought, fat, predatory demons flew, rending and tearing with an inhuman delight even compared to Jekers. Whatever fire weapon or spell they'd used at first was exhausted, or perhaps they'd simply enjoyed playing with their mortal prey, but now they were landing on the surviving Jeker ships and killing their mortal foes claw to hand.

Out of the clear sky to the east, a ball of gold hurtled at them.

Eritha squeaked, 'Is that Zos?'

Persay rushed to the rail. So did the three nomad women.

'It is!' Persay said. 'And I see Daos and Pollon.'

The breeze from the west was freshening.

Alektron ignored the onrushing golden chariot.

'Avast rowing!' he ordered. 'Get the mainmast up, you lubbers! Off your benches and get to work!' He turned to Eritha. 'You stay with the steering oars.'

'What about Zos?' she asked.

Alektron shrugged. 'He'll manage!' he said, and leapt into action, bellowing orders.

The golden chariot came alongside and Zos stepped onto the *Sea Eagle* as if he and Daos had been practising. He looked down the deck once; there were still bodies everywhere. Eritha's father lay under the helm bench, and Trayos lay in the middle of the command deck, as if the whole ship was his funerary barge.

'Shit,' Zos said.

Eritha felt too much had happened for words. She stared at him dumbly, and finally said, 'We're running upriver.'

Zos looked forward, at the big bend in the river as it passed the city, and aft, where the *Trident* and the *Shark* were just emerging from the smoke off the beaches.

'That's a good plan,' he said.

'It's Alektron's plan. He's ... captain.' Eritha lacked the words to explain.

Zos was looking at the bodies. 'By all seven of the hells of Kur. I should have been here.'

Eritha didn't even shrug. 'My father's dead.'

'Damn it, Eritha...' He paused, caught her shoulder between his hands. 'I didn't mean... Hells... Listen to me, Eritha – don't die. And don't let Alektron die. Beach the ships and run into the marshes if you must. The demons can't hunt every one of you...'

'Zos!' Daos said. 'The demons have seen us.'

Zos blew out a breath. 'Stay alive. We're not done. Maritaten is just downriver. She has more ships and people than we were led to expect.'

'We destroyed the Jekers.' Eritha realised she was crying, and she didn't know why. 'We beat them. And the demons are pounding their survivors.'

Zos nodded, as if any of it made sense.

'I'll find you all. If I don't come back, look for Maritaten of Narmer. She's...' He smiled. 'She's capable. And I think she's more likely to save us than we are to save her.'

He was standing there because leaving felt like desertion. He went over to Trayos, seeing the man was dead of many wounds. For no particular reason, Zos put his hand on the dead merchant prince. Beyond him, a pair of wounded sailors were throwing a dead Jeker into the sea with the slowness of utter exhaustion.

Alektron came up. 'I'm—'

Zos nodded. 'I know. You're the captain. I wasn't here. Damn it, I meant to be here.'

'Can you do anything about the demons wi' yon fancy gold ride?' Alektron asked. 'Gi' us half an hour an' we'll be gone.'

'Maritaten is just around the bend,' Zos said.

Alektron shook his head. 'More meat for the demons, if'n ye ask me.'

Zos nodded. 'I'll see what I can do. Save what you can.'

'Got that right,' Alektron said.

With that, Zos stepped back into the golden chariot, and it shot away.

'Well?' Daos asked.

'They don't need to be saved,' Zos said. 'They're saving themselves. But they need time.'

'So we fight the demons?' Daos asked.

Three were already turning towards them with heavy beats of their gigantic wings.

'No,' he said. 'We're going for heaven.'

Pollon looked at him.

Daos raised an eyebrow.

'All right. Yes. Let's see if we can get one or two. Is this thing faster than a demon?'

'Yes,' Daos said with youthful confidence.

'Take us out over the river,' Zos said. 'Pollon, can you spare one star-stone arrow for a demon?'

Pollon shrugged.

'You have to use one. They won't know we only have two.' Zos was looking out over the smoke as they rose. 'And I'll see what a thunderbolt does to another.'

'And then?' Daos asked. He was turning towards the demons; half a dozen were rising from their feasts to intercept the golden car.

Zos pointed west. 'Run through the weather front. We'll have to kill or outrun any who follow us.'

'Where's Enkul-Anu?' Pollon asked.

Zos shrugged. 'No clue, brother. Let's just keep staying one step ahead of the gods, eh?'

'Is that what we're doing?' Pollon asked.

Zos laughed. 'We're still in the fight,' he said. 'And we're up two miracles to none.'

The black vulture emerged from under its kill and turned north, flying low to the dunes. Enkul-Anu grunted with satisfaction and followed, flying higher and slightly faster. He spread his mighty wings, slowing, pacing the fleeing godling, preventing it from rising again.

His demons began to spread out.

The storm out over Ocean was like the rage of some god, and the God of the Storm glanced at it like a man who can't stop scratching an itch.

This is an open rebellion. But whose? How many gods are involved?

Why the fuck did Sypa order the death of the queen of Noa?

And who made that storm?

The storm front was gathering strength over the open water, and lightning forked from the increasingly dark clouds along the front, which stretched as far as his immortal eyes could see.

His quarry turned west, towards the storm front. Of course he did.

Enkul-Anu glanced at his demons. They were well spread out now, and the flankers were already pacing the fleeing vulture godling, a little above and on either side.

Time to end this.

Enkul-Anu dropped, adding speed, his magnificent wings beating faster and faster as he came in behind his prey.

And then the vulture's head rotated, and suddenly the black god pivoted on a wing tip and struck north, right at Gallu. Gallu spread his bat-wings and fought back, rocking the monster, and black feathers flew...

Blink.

Within two beats of Enkul-Anu's wings, the demon Gallu started to fall away, and then began to tumble.

Whoever we are facing, they stole Godkiller.

Who is he?

What is this? Conspiracy? Rebellion?

Enkul-Anu roared his challenge, and the vulture turned in the air, more tightly than his frame and wings should have allowed. *Godkiller* glowed in one black claw, and Illikumi's bleeding body still dangled from the other.

Enkul-Anu used his wings to brake as the vulture's head fixed a black-eyed stare on him.

Bashmu tossed a fireball and the vulture dodged under it, letting it burn, towards the earth below.

'Who are you?' Enkul-Anu roared. 'Stay and fight me!'

'You and your three demons?' The voice sounded slurred. 'That's hardly fair. Though you're never *fair*, are you?'

The vulture flew at Bashmu, who just avoided the shining tip of the deadly sword.

With visible contempt, the vulture opened a claw and dropped the screaming snake-god.

Enkul-Anu didn't hesitate. He powered into his dive, reaching for the boy, who'd suffered a dozen terrible wounds. But he was a god, and he could still scream, and they rang through every octave and into regions of sound that no mortal ear could hear.

Enkul-Anu put his undying will into his dive and reached for the falling snake-god. The ground was rushing at them, and it was close …

So close …

His mighty fingers closed on the snake-god's leg, his wings shot out, and Illikumi was snapped up like a whip by the force of his deceleration. But the boy was still alive.

Enkul-Anu looked up in time to see the vulture turning west again. It was definitely faster than his demons. Bashmu, no fool and a veteran of a hundred fights, contented himself with throwing fireballs from a distance, but the vulture dodged, weaved, and then plunged through the black clouds to the west and was gone.

Enkul-Anu powered up, towards the surviving demons, and handed Bashmu the wreck of Illikumi. 'Take this boy home and fill him with resin,' he said.

Bashmu nodded. 'What was that thing, boss?' the demon asked.

'I hate to think,' Enkul-Anu said. 'Go.'

And he turned west, into the storm.

Pollon

Daos set them right at the demons who, as veterans of many campaigns, formed up to take them from several directions at once.

'I'm going to go right through them,' Daos said. 'And then I'm going to accelerate away.'

Zos and Pollon looked at each other. Pollon's insides were turning to water and he thought of all his many missed shots as he readied his arrow.

Daos lashed the team, and they stretched out, golden hooves somehow biting the air as the chariot began to gain speed.

The nearest pair of demons came at them from either side, slightly staggered.

'Close with the right-hand bastard,' Pollon said.

Daos turned them slightly and they were racing directly at the fanged monster. Suddenly it was no longer a fat black dot, but a bat-winged entity, every trace of the veins in his wings visible. The monster had a fireball playing on its talons, but it was hesitating to throw.

Their closing speed was phenomenal, but the target was steady in terms of relative angles of approach, and Pollon loosed without conscious thought. He saw the arrow strike home and the demon seem to melt ... and suddenly he was looking at a winged crustacean, something more suited to ocean depths – many-legged, covered in chiton-armour, with a dozen ragged antennae and a pair of enormous mandibles. The shaft had gone deep just below the huge armoured head, and Pollon thought he saw blue fire licking at the wound, and then they were past. There was a sudden pitch as an explosion rang out beneath them, and he was flat in the bottom of the car.

'Got one,' Zos said. The big warrior was lying over him.

'Rrrugh,' Pollon said.

Zos rolled off him, and Pollon felt as if he'd bruised every limb, but he got to his feet.

'We've definitely got their attention,' Daos said.

Pollon looked back to see demons rising from all over the deep belly of the river. Behind them, smoke rose like a storm front from the ships burning on the beach and the fires started in the town. And ahead ...

'Icy hells!' Pollon muttered.

The storm clouds were turning from grey to black, and lightning forked along the front of the storm.

'Hang on!' Daos said. 'This will be bad.'

Pollon grabbed the rails on the side of the car and braced himself.

They suddenly rose, and then fell, faster than the auratic compensation could handle, and the black wall now towered over them, rising too high to see the top. They were close; he could feel the air change – colder, damper, and carrying a definite tang of the sea.

'Hells!' Zos roared. 'Where did this come from?'

Behind them, the demons were gathering into a flying wing. They were well behind – perhaps five stadia. But they were clearly in pursuit.

And then, out of the front of the storm, burst another black shape: vulture-winged, immense, and moving so fast that he had passed them almost as quickly as he appeared.

The vulture-god hit the wing of demons like a hawk hitting a flock of starlings, as the golden chariot passed through the wall of black cloud. The chariot gave a mighty heave, as if a giant hand was slamming it to the earth below, and the clouds closed around them like curtains in a temple's inner sanctum.

Pollon was bombarded from all sides – lightning, thunder, turbulence, palpable blows to the sides of the chariot – all in a stygian darkness lit only by the thunderbolts. He hung on grimly; it was like riding a nightmare and with every instant, another sense was assaulted.

And then they were merely wet and cold.

'How exactly are we getting into heaven?' Zos asked.

Daos spoke up over the buffeting wind and the rain. 'There's an entrance high on the south side of Auza.'

Zos leant forward. 'And you know that because …?'

Daos shrugged, his eyes still on the thick grey cloud all around them.

'The same way I knew I'd drive your chariot of fire.'

Zos glanced at Pollon, who was huddled by one of the side panels of the chariot car. He gave a minute shake of his head.

Zos blew out his cheeks in frustration. 'And then we have to find the resin store. If – and it's still an *if* – it's somewhere inside Auza, and not off in the southern desert or elsewhere.'

'Of course it's on Auza,' Pollon said, with more confidence than he felt. 'The resin store can't be anywhere the Dry Ones can get at it. It can't be in the desert. We'd know if it was in any of the cities and I followed the message traffic on the Nexus for days …'

Zos shook his head. 'In a lifetime of pointless risks, this seems to me the greatest risk.'

Pollon huddled down further. All of them were dressed for war: Zos had a cloak but Pollon, as an archer, wore only a brief *heton* and he was cold, wet and miserable, none of which made him better at reckoning their risk.

It was surprisingly cold in the storm. He shivered.

Zos looked back at him, saw, and then stripped the red cloak from his shoulders and settled it around Pollon.

'Sorry, brother,' he said.

'I'm fine.' Pollon knew as he said it that his tone suggested that he was anything but fine.

'His lips are blue,' Zos said. 'Is there any way this magical device can warm us?'

Daos frowned. 'Not that I know of. I'm sorry – the gods are immune to heat or cold.'

And so are you, thought Pollon with a tinge of bitterness.

But Daos redeemed himself a moment later. 'As soon as I think we're clear of the demons, I'll put us back outside the storm front,' he said.

He was as good as his word, and after what seemed like an interminable time in the cold and wet, they rode the tumultuous winds back into bright sunlight. The storm front had passed well inland, and was raining down on empty desert and the ruined city of Hekka beneath their feet. They ran south. Before they passed Ugor, the wind was dying and the storm front began to fall away behind them.

Zos was watching it. 'Very convenient, that storm,' he said. 'Just where we needed it. *Everything* is very convenient, except the number of my dead friends.'

Pollon hadn't recovered yet and wasn't ready for conversation. His wet wool was still warm, and Daos had done something to mitigate the rush of air. He was recovering.

Eventually he began to look out and down. The view was spectacular, even awe-inspiring: the world of his professional life, the coast of the Hundred Cities, laid out like a toy beneath his feet. There was great Weshwesh, and soon enough, mighty Tur, and then the magnificent multi-layered city of Ma'rib, and always the ribbon of the coastal road running along the edge of the sea. It was a bright winter's day in the south; the sun was warm, and there were farmers in the fields, preparing a second crop of wheat or barley. They were low enough that they could see people look up ... and see some fall on their knees in worship.

From this height, they could see the long peninsula of Akash, and the sparkle of the southern sea alongside the endless brown of the great southern desert. And, rising from the south of Akash, the awe-inspiring majesty of Mount Auza, which rose higher than any other mountain in the world, its mighty shoulders snow-capped and its high crown sparkling against the sky.

Pollon felt something like the shock of a wound as he realised the scale of the mountain – and the task before them – and he closed his eyes for a moment.

Zos had a stone in his hand and was touching up the edge of his bronze shortsword, a plain *xiphos* in the style favoured by Dardanians.

'We're never ...' Pollon began.

Zos smiled. It was a hard smile, and for a moment he looked like a deadly mercenary and not Pollon's friend.

'The knucklebones are cast,' he said. 'This is what we're doing. For good or ill we – a scribe, a washed-up sell-sword, and a boy – are storming heaven. And for all that, we are three deadly men with a chariot full of thunderbolts. If we can get there, we'll scare the piss out of the gods.'

Pollon, who was much warmer than he had been an hour before, nonetheless shivered.

Daos looked back. 'Demons,' he said.

Zos shook his head. 'Where?'

'Below us and well back. I can see them – they cast long shadows in the *Aura*.'

Pollon had been searching the horizon, but he turned to look at the charioteer. His voice was deeper, and his shoulders broader again.

'Daos is growing before our very eyes,' he said to Zos.

Zos nodded. 'If he grows any faster, he'll be older than I am by the end of the day.'

Daos blushed. 'I'm not in control of it.'

Zos put a hand on his shoulder. 'I know. But your beard is growing while I watch. I can't call you *boy* any more, and who has a bearded charioteer?'

Daos smiled, and Zos winked at Pollon.

They began to climb out of the warm lower air and into the cold. Zos' cloak was dry now, and Pollon pulled it tighter around himself and watched Zos. The big man was clearly cold himself, but wasn't willing to say anything about it.

Pollon had a fleeting memory of his former life as a scribe, and he laughed aloud.

Zos turned. 'What's funny?'

Pollon shrugged. 'I used to be a scribe whose greatest adventure was going to archery practice. And having sex with my landlady.' He thought again of Mura. Dead? Alive?

Zos grinned. 'Sex is almost always an adventure.'

Pollon wondered if he could use the nexus to find Mura. But he was too concerned about Zos to hold on to the thought. Zos was slumped against the chariot's side, and Pollon had seldom seen him look so bad. His back was hurt, perhaps badly, and there was blood flowing over his right instep.

And he was still making jokes.

Daos blushed. 'One that I'm eager to try,' he admitted.

They all laughed. But Zos was pale.

None of them were laughing an hour later, as night began to fall over the world below. It was very cold; Zos and Pollon were unashamedly sharing Zos' cloak, and still the golden chariot climbed towards the distant stars. Auza filled the sky on the right side of the chariot, and the eye could make out details that showed the vast scale of the mountain: the pilgrims' stair wandering back and forth up the mountain, free of pilgrims at this hour; the hostels set into the mountainside so they could rest as they climbed. It was a four-day hike to the top for most, and neither horses nor donkeys were allowed on the stairs. Every pilgrim, godborn or peasant, had to make the climb themselves.

And above it all was the glitter of the facades of some of the halls of heaven, their visibility at this distance indicating their sheer size.

'The halls of heaven,' Pollon sighed.

'At least we didn't have to walk,' Zos said. 'I always wondered if it would come down to a long fight up the mountainside. Now that I see it...' He grimaced.

They flew up and over the western shoulder of the mountain, and at last could see the Gate of Air cut into the side of the mountain like a temple portico rendered for Titans.

Zos stood, abandoning the cloak to Pollon.

'Incredible,' he said.

'A trifle vulgar,' Pollon said, aiming for humour.

'No, I mean, we're here. We're going to try this.' Zos' grin was triumphant. 'I assume the gate is guarded?' he asked Daos.

Daos shrugged. 'I have no idea.'

Zos knelt. 'Then here's what we do: Daos looks like a young god, and he probably is, right?' He laughed. 'So Daos takes us in, we land, and you have a star-stone arrow ready on your bow.'

'And then?' Pollon asked.

Zos shrugged. 'We fight whatever we find, and make it up from there.'

Pollon nodded. 'I do like a detailed plan.'

Zos glanced at the yawning Gate of Air and its immense pillars, then back at Pollon.

'I've stormed a few fortresses in my time,' he said. 'There are two ways you succeed. One involves a lot of careful planning. The other is all done on the cutting edge of chance. Honestly? They both require luck, and since we can't pray to the gods, let's just hope for luck.'

'A bucketful,' Pollon agreed.

His hands were shaking and he couldn't feel his fingers. He put his right hand in his armpit until a little feeling was restored and then, very carefully, nocked his one star-stone arrow. He imagined fumbling it, and watching their last best weapon fall away into the upper air…

Daos nodded. 'Everyone ready?'

Zos nodded.

'Here we go.'

Chapter Eight

Zos

They passed through the Gate of Air without opposition. Zos, despite his banter, had feared some sort of supernatural guardian, or an invisible wall, but the designers of heaven hadn't thought they'd need a lock on their door four thousand feet above the desert.

From the floor of the chariot he could only see up, and above him was a staggeringly detailed mosaic – superb, immense, and the usual display of Enkul-Anu, Sypa and the other gods, each in their full aspect: cavorting, defeating the old gods, dragon-slaying or lying on couches.

He tried to imagine how this had been built, and then he heard the golden team's hooves ringing on stone as they slowed and came to a gentle stop no different from dozens of other chariots he'd known.

Zos looked over the side.

There were two demons guarding a single majestic bronze door – one red, one a bilious green. They were a hundred paces away, and seemed utterly bored. Next to their chariot on the white marble floor was another that appeared to be carved from old bone, with an unmoving team of six skeletal horses.

Zos shivered, recognising the chariot of Gul, the Lord of the Dead.

And then he put that behind him, too.

Zos stepped out of the back of the car, taking three of the chariot's thunderbolt javelins with him, and Pollon followed, arrow on string. It was much warmer here. The air was perfumed as if there were incense burners somewhere close – a musky reek that Zos didn't particularly like.

Daos stepped out of the car, holding his trident. He looked bigger, and so did the weapon.

Zos didn't pause. He walked towards the bronze door, flanked by his friends, seeing the demons stand unmoving. It had the feeling of a dream; a certain distance, an unreality of texture.

Finally, when they were twenty paces away, the left-hand demon spoke.

'Stop. What is your errand in heaven?'

'Mayhem,' Zos said.

The two demons shared a glance, and then each produced a sword which burned with red fire. Pollon raised his bow. He didn't draw, yet; he let the demons feel the *Aura* of the star-stone first. It had occurred to him that one star-stone arrow couldn't slay two demons, but it could threaten both of them.

'Star-stone!' the red demon spat. 'Bastards!'

He snapped his sword forward, and it became a lash that fell on Zos, who raised the Shield of Taris to catch it. The blow drove him to his knees but did no damage.

Pollon sighed over the irrationality of his foes and shot the green one. The arrow went home in the centre of the creature's chest, and the thing turned from a bat-winged horror to an insectoid horror even as electric blue fire played all along it, and it screamed in despair.

Pollon took another arrow from his quiver: a perfectly ordinary stone-tipped shaft he'd made himself.

The red demon looked at its mate, whirled and charged.

Daos stepped past Zos, raised his shield – a tower shield

437

that seemed to have grown with him – and thrust one-handed with the trident. All three blades went in to the crossbar, and the demon folded over the weapon as if he'd received a much greater blow. It fell in two pieces, each of which began to transform.

Zos was almost used to the changes now. And he was delighted to see the effectiveness of the trident, because he'd had doubts about his own weapon.

'Come on,' he said, but Pollon lingered.

When Zos looked back, he saw the once-priggish former scribe cutting his arrow out of the rapidly decaying corpse of the green demon.

'It's still intact,' he called happily.

'Watch out for the blood,' Zos called. 'It's acid.'

Pollon glared at him – the scholar who hated being patronised.

'I know,' he muttered.

Zos tried the huge bronze doors, and they opened under his hand with a simple push.

And so the three of them strode into heaven.

Auza, Home of the Gods

'Where is Sypa?' Gul asked.

Laila was weaving in the Hall of the Gods. She and Sypa each had looms there. Sypa hadn't managed to fully set hers in an aeon, whereas Laila's piece, despite her various other pastimes, was nearly complete: a closely woven rectangle of dark blue cloth without any apparent decoration.

'My lady goddess cannot be disturbed,' Laila said. 'The snake god Illikumi was brought to us, wounded, just minutes ago.'

The God of Death gave off a palpable aura of cold fear.

438

'Fetch her for me,' he demanded.

Laila rose and made a bow, handmaiden to greater god.

'Great God of Death, my lady ordered me not to disturb her. She is healing Illikumi, and he was sore wounded.'

Gul frowned, his skeletal face hideous. 'Sypa sent me on an errand. It was unpleasant. It is done. Now I desire to speak to her. And I have news of greater import than any foolish snake god.'

'If you tell me . . . ?' Laila suggested from her position of respect.

'I did not come her to bandy words with a whorish servant,' Gul spat in his hollow voice. 'Fetch me your mistress.'

Laila looked at the other gods gathered there. Gul's arrival had done nothing to dispel the atmosphere of tense anticipation – a tension that had been enhanced by the arrival of two tired and frightened demons and a desperately wounded godling. Everyone in heaven, from the servants and slaves to the gods themselves, knew that there were great happenings in Narmer, and that Enkul-Anu had gone in person.

Laila had learnt to be a handmaiden in a hard school. She grovelled, but took no further action. As she expected, Gul turned away to the other gods.

'Is there no one here in a position of authority?' he demanded. 'Who rules heaven in the absence of the Master?'

None of them spoke up, not even Grulu, who might have liked to. Timurti sat with spittle running down her absent face. Anzu, in his winged lion aspect, roamed up and down like an angry tomcat writ large, but said nothing.

Above them, a gong rang, soft but insistent.

'Someone has come,' Laila said. 'Great God of Death, perhaps our master has returned. Someone had entered the Gate of Air.'

Gul ignored her. 'Sypa is hiding her pretty head,' he said in contempt, 'while a war is being fought in Narmer, where I should be reaping corpses, and none of you is regent?'

Laila stayed silent.

'Call Sypa forth!' Gul whirled to face her, and the smell of grave dust billowed from his black cloak.

Laila rose to her feet. 'I will do what I can.'

'Do as I order, and quickly, or see whether your good looks can defy my scythe.' Gul spoke in a hollow voice that portended doom.

Laila slid behind a massive wall hanging and went out through the hidden portal that led directly to Enkul-Anu's chamber. If any of the other gods knew she had access, many questions would be asked. But she risked it. She was in a hurry and doubted that any would follow her.

She went out of the other end of the great Storm God's chambers and into the massive corridors behind the halls of the gods. Sypa had apartments directly across from the Storm God; hers were opulent where his were plain to the point of being empty.

She went to the door. 'Great Goddess of Lust,' she said. 'The God of Death requests...'

'Begone.' Sypa spoke lazily from within. 'I told you not to disturb me.'

'The Great God Gul is insistent, Sypa!' she called in her best 'helpless slave' voice.

'I am healing a wounded god. Send more ambrosia, and quickly.' Sypa's voice lingered with a seductive air that made Laila shake her head.

Whatever the Great Goddess was doing while her husband was at war, it wasn't a traditional healing method. Laila sprang to obey, though, mostly because fetching ambrosia would keep her from the Hall of the Gods and the wrath of Gul.

Everyone feared Gul.

Ambrosia, the finished product based on resin, was very closely guarded. Every mortal wanted it: a few sips could end disease or close a wound; taken regularly, it conferred virtual immortality.

So it wasn't left lying about. Only specially chosen servants were allowed access.

Like Laila.

She went to a server's chamber located self-effacingly between the chambers of Ara and Sypa, but the spell-protected gold ewer holding the ambrosia was almost empty. Laila finished it off herself with a sour smile, and turned to go deeper into the palace. The ambrosia store was a level below – and if that was empty ...

She went down the magnificent steps, rendered in pink marble and worn dangerously smooth by the passage of feet over an aeon. She was barefoot, as always, and moved confidently down the one long flight that led to the quarters of the lesser gods, and the key storerooms. She passed the chambers of the godling Nisroch and paused. She'd made it her business to monitor the Nexus; none of the other gods seemed interested except Sypa, and Sypa was not good at technical things.

Or so she pretended.

She went past, wondering what had happened to Nisroch. He had probably been caught and destroyed in the mesh of someone's plotting—

She stopped in the doorway of the ambrosia store because she had heard something. Her hearing, at least, was godlike.

She had heard someone coming up the steps from the lower levels. She was instantly alert. Servants, demons and slaves came and went this way all the time; the stairs connected to the Gate of Air just below her, and below that they were really just servants' stairs. The gods had other ways of moving about.

But it wasn't the sound that alerted her. It was the tone. Laila was quite expert at tone.

These were mortals, and they sounded ... bold.

Mortals.

There were a handful of very trusted mortal slaves allowed on this level, although she hadn't seen any since the Great God killed his mortal attendants. And they certainly wouldn't sound so confident.

Laila checked the long, slim knife she wore along one thigh, and peeked out of the door, which was itself wrought of bronze and gold and cunningly fitted to its marble frame.

There were three of them, she saw, as they crested the stairs. Her heart was suddenly hammering as if she was in the climax of sex; her eyes narrowed.

Mortals. In heaven.

It's happening!

Oh, Druku! Are you here?

She thought about it for several rapid heartbeats, but in her immortal soul, Laila was the most passionate of creatures, and the mortals were not the only bold ones in the palaces of heaven.

She stepped out into the corridor and confronted them.

The short one raised a bow, and the tip of the arrow reeked of the poison star-stone. The prettiest one – tall, slim, but wide-shouldered – flourished a trident... and Laila flinched. It was *the trident. Earthbreaker.* She knew it immediately, because she'd stolen it herself. And replaced it with an auratic reproduction.

The third was large, for a mortal: big, broad and scarred. And he held a magnificent shield that shouted of its auratic power, and sheathed at his side was a sword...

Terror. She knew it immediately – the magnificence of it, the size, the smell.

'Who are you?' she asked. And then, before they could answer, she shook her head. 'Do you know Druku? I am Laila. Take me to Druku.'

'Do you know Druku?' the goddess said. 'I am Laila. Take me to Druku.'

Pollon's arms were quivering as he held his bow at full draw. Daos was peering over the top of his shield at the magnificent apparition.

'Laila,' he said aloud. 'Aurora!'

Laila's eyes widened. 'What?'

Daos grinned. 'You're Aurora!'

The beautiful goddess's confusion was evident, and she stepped back as if preparing to flee.

Zos had never thought so fast or so clearly in his life. Somewhere in his head, he ran it all together, and he remembered the fight on the island, months before.

'Who are you, lady?' Zos asked again, and the bear growled.

'This is Druku, God of Drunkenness and Orgies,' Era said. 'You witch. We're against all gods.'

Dite-Druku gave a small shrug. 'I came to help,' they said. 'And in mortal form, I'm as human and vulnerable as you. Cut me with your star-stone, my darling, and I'll bleed red, not ichor.'

Era tested it, cutting very lightly to the woman's shoulder, and a seam of red mortal blood appeared.

'Ouch,' Dite said.

'I know Druku,' Zos said. 'He's not here, but we can take you to him ... them.'

The goddess paused. She was like a statue of beauty, one shoulder of her modest *peplos* unpinned to show her strong neck and fine shoulder; her neck flushed over her light brown skin.

She was eight feet tall.

She looked back at Zos, her almond eyes shining.

443

'He's not here? But…' She looked as if she was going to say more, but decided against it. 'Where is he?'

Zos struggled for a moment with the pronoun 'he' and then moved on.

'Druku is in the far north,' he said. 'With my friends.'

Laila took a deep breath. 'He was supposed to be here.' Her voice was like silk combed with fine oil; it slipped into you effortlessly.

Zos could make no sense of that. 'Great lady, if you are a friend of Druku's, help us.'

'Can you take me to him?' Laila was pleading, if a goddess could plead.

Daos spoke for the first time. 'Aurora, you belong with us anyway.'

Laila shuddered and took a step away.

'Daos, stop that,' Zos cut in. 'Let me handle this.

'But—'

There was a sudden shrill, commanding tone. Laila looked back at the sound.

'My mistress,' she said.

Zos stepped forward, trying not to look at her beauty but rather to read her expression, as if she was a mortal. Her size was imposing, her scent…

Zos closed his eyes and remembered his torment when he'd been broken on the wheel, and it cleared his head.

'Great Lady Laila, we can take you to Druku, although, to be honest, it could take some time.' He met her eyes, which was difficult as they shone with… something untameable.

Laila took a deep breath.

'Sypa is calling,' she said. And then, as if the two things were connected, she said, 'Very well. My usefulness here is almost at an end anyway. Take me.'

Zos took a deep breath of his own. 'First, we need you to take us to the resin store.'

'The resin store?' she asked, turning the words over as if considering them.

Pollon spoke up. 'Where heaven stores the resin from the Dry Ones? You call it the Nest.'

Laila shrugged. 'I don't know what you mean. This room is an ambrosia store – these alabaster and faience jars each hold a measure of ambrosia. And down below us is the Bright Farm, where the resin is … extracted.'

Pollon's 'Extracted how?' clashed with 'Take us there' from Zos.

'It is far below,' she said. 'Below the gate.'

'Gate?' asked Pollon. 'To outside?'

Laila looked at Pollon as if he was a small child.

'No, mortal,' she said. 'And please put that poisonous thing somewhere else.'

Pollon looked embarrassed.

The shrill sound came again.

Zos was considering taking the goddess and running. And he was starting to wonder how many gods would defect, and what they'd do with them … Weren't they *against all gods*?

He shook his head to clear it. Then he took his cloak and used it to bundle up as many of the amphorae of ambrosia as he could carry.

Pollon slipped half a dozen into the front of his *heton* and tightened his belt.

Daos was staring at Laila as if transfixed.

'You live,' he said, several times.

Laila tapped a beautifully arched bare foot impatiently 'The same might be said of you, if you are who I think, boy,' she muttered. 'And I see you have the trident.' She pointed at it. 'Which I stole for someone else.'

'Tyka,' Daos said. 'She arranged for me to have it.'

Laila shook her head. 'So many plots. What now?' she said. 'Sypa will come, if I am not quick.'

'Take us to ...' Zos looked at Pollon.

'Are there captive Dry Ones at this Bright Farm?' Pollon asked.

Laila nodded. 'I believe so. It's not ... not my area.'

Zos looked at his friend. 'What are you thinking?'

Pollon hesitated, as he always did.

Zos slapped his back. 'Speak!' And then he shook his head. 'Here, drink this.'

He knocked the top off a priceless faience flask with his bronze sword and handed it to Pollon.

Pollon looked at the jagged glass with some trepidation, but then he poured it into a wooden cup he carried on his belt, and drank it off.

Laila looked at him. 'He might die,' she said, without sounding particularly concerned.

Zos shook his head. 'Not our first time.' He used Pollon's cup to drink another.

Daos quietly and urgently emptied five. With each one, he grew, and Laila eyed them with real fear now. Zos was surprised to see the tension around her beautiful eyes.

'How?' she asked. 'How do you yet live?'

Pollon turned to Zos, his voice full of an un-Pollon-like fire. 'They must have hundreds of Dry Ones prisoner.'

Zos, used to thinking of the Dry Ones as dangerous foes in the desert, shrugged. But then he remembered one Dry One, leaping through the air to engage the demons over Dekhu.

'We release them,' Pollon said.

Laila shuddered. 'Druku would never allow that!'

Zos blinked. And then said, 'We release them,' with an immortal clarity. If his brain had been running fast and well before, now he felt ...

446

Godlike.

Laila began to strip the ambrosia store methodically. She could carry a great deal, and she produced a magnificent *peplos* and used it to make a bag.

That shrill sound came again.

'We must go,' Laila said.

'Take us to the Bright Farm,' Zos said.

She shrugged. 'Very well. You're sure you know Druku?'

Daos nodded. 'Druku is currently in another aspect, as a woman,' he said.

'Ah,' Laila said, pleased. 'Yes, that's what they said they would do.'

Obviously mollified, she led them down the corridor, which was itself twice her height, as wide as a mortal palace's great hall, and fully decorated in embossed bronze and mosaic – floor, ceiling and walls. The craftsmanship was superb. The subject was the same: the new gods' conquest of heaven and their subsequent revels. Over and over.

Zos wondered if the gods ever grew bored with those motifs. He was bored by the end of the corridor, where two polished bronze pillars outlined a trellis worked in mosaic roses so perfect that he thought they were real for a moment.

'Zos,' Pollon said.

Zos looked back.

Pollon was staring at his star-stone arrowhead.

'It's making me feel ill,' he said.

Zos felt it too – like there was an itchy heat coming off the thing in sluggish, oily waves.

'It must be the resin,' he said. 'The ambrosia.'

'Come.' Laila stepped *through* the flowered trellis. 'Take my hand.'

Zos took a deep breath and took her hand ...

447

Enkul-Anu

The storm tasted like an old, old enemy, and Enkul-Anu's fears deepened until he was tempted to flee the field and run for heaven.

What the fuck is happening here? he asked himself as he powered through the wind and rain of the great storm.

Every levin bolt tasted of the last war; he sent his massively augmented senses down and outward. Down into the sea, where he had always suspected one or more of their enemies had lingered; out, into the storm.

This was no natural storm, and it battered his senses and left him blinder than was quite right. And nowhere could he find his foes, new or ancient.

He turned and drove east, back through the wall of storm. He was more exposed within it than he cared to allow; the storm, instead of augmenting his powers, was eroding them. He emerged north of Thais, and one glance showed him his error. The vulture god had eluded him in the mayhem and was now contending with his demon legion.

Enkul-Anu summoned a thunderbolt and drove towards the battle raging in the air over the delta. His demons were wise; they had ringed the vulture and they were pelting it with auratic power, each as their own talents allowed. They'd taken losses – he could see that – but he could also raise more demons.

But the vulture didn't abide his coming. As soon as he closed, the vulture made one of his impossible turns in the air, changed shape, and dropped almost to the ground like a black teardrop. The storm was coming in; the demons threw gouts of power, and Enkul-Anu lost their foe somewhere near the surface of the great river.

He swore, and his curses were powerful enough to wither the winter wheat in the fields of the delta.

You were never fair.

It must be someone who knew him all too well.

He has Godkiller.

Someone who had stolen from heaven itself.

And there was the storm raging over the delta. Raised by an ancient enemy.

The human rebellion is a bait! he concluded between one heartbeat and the next.

'Demons!' he roared. 'On me! To heaven!'

They formed up on his right and left like two vast wings, and he turned for Mount Auza, far to the south.

I'm not only surrounded by idiots — I am one.

But is it Sypa? Gul? Druku?

Or are they all against me?

Kursag

He went through the wall of storm and it fought him like a live thing, reaching for his powers, pushing a fog into his mind to match the disorientation of his other senses.

He ignored most of it.

He lives! Enkul-Anu lives!

He twisted in shame that part of him reacted to that with joy, and tried to crush that feeling.

I am the destroyer. I will destroy the weakest part of me first.

Then, as he weaved through the terrible storm, he thought of his Jekers.

They were crushed.

They weren't all crushed. The thousands on the beach — they were stranded, but alive.

I must save them. Without them, I have no base of power.

And besides, breaking Narmer is still the fastest way to break everything.

Zos

They emerged from an undecorated trellis: no roses, no mosaic, no pillars of bronze. Zos didn't need a guide to know that they were now in the working portions of heaven; everything here was a plain slate grey. Down at floor level, a single bead of unpolished bronze, green with verdigris, ran along just above the joint with the filthy floor.

Laila reached out and touched a plate on the wall.

'I'm not even sure it functions any more,' she said.

'What?'

'The curse, embedded in that wire,' she said, pointing at the corroded bronze. 'It melts your flesh, or so I was told.'

'You said you've never been here before,' Pollon said steadily.

Laila blinked. 'Perhaps I just heard...'

Pollon raised an eyebrow to Zos, and Zos understood: the goddess was a liar. But he couldn't be more ready for an ambush; his heart was pumping double time, and the ambrosia had sharpened his vision and his hearing.

Zos wondered if ambrosia was addictive. He certainly wanted more. The taste was... marvelous. Incredible. So was the effect.

'You first, Lady,' he said to Laila.

She hesitated.

Zos nodded. 'You first. Let's see if the curse is invoked.'

It took Laila a moment, but then her hand shot out and she slapped the bronze plate on the wall again.

Daos nodded. 'We could all feel it. You can't trick us.' He went forward towards her. 'Why are you with them at all, Aurora?'

Her face contorted, and she said, 'I'm a survivor.'

Zos's sword was shouting in his head.

Draw me.

Shut up.

Kill her. Seize heaven. Rule.

He drew *Terror* the width of a finger and slammed her back into the scabbard.

Laila's eyes widened and Pollon's hands shook. Daos looked at Zos.

'Must you?'

'Yes,' Zos said.

I'm having a spat with my sword.

They were moving down the forbidding stone corridor; it was dark, poorly lit, and smelt faintly of old urine.

'This is heaven?' Pollon asked.

Laila glanced back. 'You know that thing is utterly evil,' she said. 'I can't trust you.'

Zos shrugged. 'Not really important to me just now.'

Laila stopped. 'Interesting,' she said. 'All these doors lead to the Bright Farm.'

'Many servants? Workers? Guards?'

Laila wrinkled her nose. 'I don't think so. The current administration wants as few people to know what happens here as possible.'

'You seem to know a bit about it,' Pollon said.

Laila shrugged. 'Druku told me to learn what I could. So I did.'

'Whose side are you on?' Pollon said. 'Druku's?'

'My own,' Laila said. 'I'm a survivor.'

'Aurora was the Goddess of the Dawn, the beautiful child of Love and the Sun.' Daos spoke in his prophetic voice. 'She refused to fight the newcomers, and said all violence was an affront to the cosmos.'

Laila produced a bronze knife. 'Well, I'm not afraid to use violence, godling, and my only interest in you is if you can take me to Druku.'

Zos was looking at the huge double doors, more like the entrance to a warehouse than he'd expected from the immortal gods.

'Open them,' he said.

Laila looked at him. 'I'm not sure…'

Zos put a hand on *Terror.* 'This evil thing wants me to kill you.' The goddess took a step back. 'So instead, just open the doors for us and get out of the way. Pollon, Daos – there's no way through this without blood. When those doors open… be ready for anything.'

Pollon's voice was shaky, but his sense of humour was apparently unimpaired. 'I've been ready for anything since breakfast,' he said.

Daos said, 'Laila… Aurora, I promise we'll take you to Druku.'

Laila shook her head. 'When I open these doors, everyone in heaven will know.'

Zos nodded reasonably. 'Are there other doors that won't set off an alarm?'

She shrugged. 'I don't know.'

Pollon frowned. 'I think she's lying.'

Daos shrugged, and slammed his trident into the dark basalt double doors.

They exploded inward.

As the dust settled, the opening revealed a massive cavern; indeed, it appeared that the whole mountain might be hollow. The cavern stretched beyond sight, and was lit by rows of magelights hung high above. The floor was a scattered, organic mosaic of hexagonal stone cells.

But there was an atmosphere of decay and even despair here; many of the magelights were out, leaving long areas of the massive cavern in shadow. Many of the hexagons were broken or damaged; there were viscous puddles on the floor, and the whole place smelt...

Like honey. Honey and cinnamon and something musky.

There were *thousands* of cells. The scale was staggering.

'You really shouldn't have done that,' Laila said.

Scattered across the floor were dozens of workers, although for the most part they appeared to be mortals; a few were obviously demonic. Off to Zos' left was a guard station, or perhaps an office – three low doors, a big dirty window looking over the cells and lit from within. Otherwise, the entire cavern was dedicated to the hexagonal cells.

'Hells,' Pollon spat, pointing at the ceiling.

Zos noted with a shudder of revulsion that there were *things* crawling on the ceiling.

The scale of it defeated him. He'd expected a store of resin – hundreds or even thousands of amphorae of raw resin, like the ones he'd seen in the hold of the *Untroubled Swan*. Instead, he was looking at stadia of cells.

Each cell must hold a Dry One. He knew that much. There were catwalks of wood above the cells, and dozens of men and women walked along them with long poles and buckets. They were, he saw, skimming resin from the tops of the cells.

He took that in with a glance. The seed of an idea came into his head, and he blinked.

'I think they're *wyverns*,' Pollon said in his matter-of-fact scribe voice. He pointed almost straight up. 'A magical flying creature. A snake with wings.'

Daos was looking up, too.

Laila hadn't entered the cavern yet.

'Pollon, don't let her go,' Zos said. 'Daos, open that door.'

He pointed at the guard station, but the door was already opening and a demon and a dozen men came out, all armed.

'Who the fuck are you?' roared the demon. 'I'm going to fucking skin you alive! I'm going to cut your head open and fuck your skull. I'm—'

Zos threw one of the thunderbolt spears at the demon. He had three behind his shield.

The demon ducked it with inhuman reflexes. The armoured man behind him took it full in the chest, and vanished in a cloud of blood and bone fragment. Several of his companions died with him.

The demon leapt for Zos, snapping a white-hot flail at him.

The shield turned it. The demon lost a beat in shock, and Daos struck him with the trident, which slammed the demon all the way across the entrance to the cavern and into the guard station's wall.

Draw me! Slay the demon! Slay the goddess! Rule here forever!

Zos glanced at Daos, who winked. Then Zos ran forward…

I'm too fucking old for this.

He leapt. The demon was fast, but not as fast as a bull-leaper; its attempt to bat Zos from the air with its flail was slow and late. And it was changing form.

Even as Zos landed high on its malformed back, between its fast-extending wings, it tried to slam him back into the cavern wall. Zos didn't fully land on its insectoid carapace, however; he touched down and leapt again, this time for the roof of the guard station.

The giant centipede thing that the demon was becoming turned to follow him, and Daos thrust the trident in between the plates of its newly forming carapace.

The result was spectacular, but messy, and Zos was suddenly covered in … former demon.

The three remaining human guards were stunned, and Zos leapt again, feeling the landing in his knees and thighs. But the

454

ambrosia had done its work; his shin was suddenly healed after three bad weeks, and his back and hip were... fine.

He had made it, and now he was between the soldiers and Pollon.

He drew his mortal sword. It was just a good bronze short sword, but he was facing men, and he was leery of drawing *Terror* in heaven.

The shield drew the soldiers' eyes, as did the helmet.

'Who the fuck are you?' asked one guard, moving forward with deadly competence.

'Killed the manager,' muttered the other. He was moving cautiously towards Daos.

Zos was in a hurry, and he moved in, smashing his magnificent shield into the guard's shield with brutal intent. The man was staggered. As he tried to keep his footing, Zos cut his left hamstring under his shield, and as he fell, killed him with a thrust to the temple just under his conical helmet.

Daos simply struck the other man on the tower shield with *Earthbreaker*, and the man was blown out over the retaining wall to fall into the cavern and break his body on the cells.

'Yikes,' Pollon said.

Laila sighed. 'Let me go. You are all doomed now.'

Indeed, a booming knell was sounding through the cavern, and the bat-like creatures were beginning to drop from the roof. Only as they extended their wings did Zos understand their size.

He ran for the door to the guard station, Daos at his heels.

There was a lone mortal inside, cowering behind a stone desk like an altar. There were cold burning in the ceiling, which was perhaps three tall men high, and the walls were covered in scratch marks and hash marks, as if they were used for calculations.

A shelf full of baskets of clay tablets lined one wall, and there was a bronze pedestal in the centre of the room, decorated to look like an enormous grasshopper. The enamel plaques on the pedestal were illuminated by something inside.

'Who are you?' Zos demanded.

'This can't be happening,' the man muttered, shaking his head.

Zos stepped past the pedestal and put the point of his sword to the other man's cheek.

'Who are you? Be quick.'

'I'm the chief herder of heaven,' the man said. 'Where are the gods?'

'Where indeed?' Zos asked with a certain sarcasm. 'What do you herd? The Dry Ones?'

The man looked as if he might burst into tears. 'You killed the demon!' he said. 'That's not possible!'

'Surprise,' Daos said.

He was looking at the device on the pedestal. It was far more complex, more aesthetic, than anything else in the room, and Zos dismissed the idea that this was a guardroom. It was a records centre.

'Pollon!' he shouted, but Pollon and a very unwilling Laila were already through the door. Pollon slammed it shut just as a predator's scream to chill the blood rang through the vast cavern.

'Wyverns,' Pollon said, somewhat unnecessarily.

Daos looked back at the chief herder.

'What does this do?'

'Don't touch that!' the man shrieked, as Daos put a hand on the bronze grasshopper, next to its prominent handle. 'Are you insane?'

Pollon was looking at the basket of tablets, then at the scrolls of papyrus revealed on a shelf that had been behind the door.

'Where are the resin stores?' Zos asked.

'I don't know.'

Zos nodded and slashed the man's face with a casual cut.

'Where are the resin stores?' he asked again.

Laila sighed and said, 'They are the next two doors down the corridor outside.'

The chief herder looked as if he might cry.

Zos left him, to look at the device on the pedestal.

'Looks to me,' he said at a glance, 'as if the coloured lights correspond to groups of … nests?'

Outside the big window, a long, dark green wing tip flashed, and something heavy settled on the roof wall above them, making the room shake. Plaster fell from the ceiling. The gods and their magnificence didn't extend to the records shack in the caves where resin was made.

'We're trapped,' Laila said. 'The wyverns will rip us to pieces. Even me. They respond to intruders …'

Zos touched the grasshopper's handle and watched the herder flinch.

'What does this do?' he asked.

'Don't touch it!' the man screamed. 'Gods! It's a release for the cells! We only use it when we kill off a season's worth and want to clean them out!'

Daos put the butt end of the trident under the man's nose.

'Dry Ones?' he asked.

The whole cavern shook.

Zos looked up from the window. 'Do you mean the Dry Ones you have captive for your resin supply?'

'How do you even know about that?' the man whined.

Zos looked at Pollon. 'You are a fucking genius, you know that?'

Even through all the fear, Pollon was pleased, and showed it. 'I have my moments.'

Laila looked at Zos as if he'd grown a second head.

'Why? Why is he a genius?'

Zos ignored her. 'When I draw *Terror* and open the door,

457

either the wyverns will be affected, or they won't. Either way, we're running for the hallway. I don't think the bastards will fit through the doors.'

Pollon shuddered. Daos turned his head away. Laila looked as if she might scream.

The chief herder's knees gave way and he sat suddenly.

'No,' he said.

Zos smiled. Whatever happened next, he was about to strike a death blow to heaven.

He put his hand on the bronze grasshopper.

'Nooo!' shouted the chief herder. 'You have no idea what will happen. The gods will flay us all ...'

'Oh, Kur's hells,' Laila said. 'Now I understand. You are serious about this. You are insane.' But she smiled, and her smile lit the room. 'You are the rebel mortals.'

Zos pulled the handle.

The cavern rumbled, and a high keening noise filled the air, as if thousands of bronze sword blades were being rubbed against each other. It was a terrible noise.

All of the wyverns, and there were a surprising number of them, exploded from their places on the walls and ceiling into the cold air of the cavern. They shrieked and called – a cacophony which obliterated the senses and made it difficult for Zos to think.

He went to the door and opened it. Daos was close behind him; Pollon had an arrow on his bow, and Laila looked as if she'd grown. Her smile held.

Outside, chaos ruled. Thousands of Dry Ones were dragging themselves from the now-open cells. They were covered in resin, and they were slow to emerge, sluggish, alien, hideously coated in their own magical substance. And, far off across the cavern floor, something very large was emerging from a huge cell.

Wyverns began to pounce on them, seizing them, tearing them apart and eating them.

The Dry Ones tried to resist, especially those who were relatively free of resin. Suddenly, a cloud of blue fire enveloped a wyvern and the smell of roast pork filled the air.

A long beak shot out over the roof of the guard station, and Zos whirled.

Another wyvern came up over the railing and flew straight at them, while a third dropped from high above with a long screech.

Zos drew *Terror*.

Laila screamed. Pollon writhed. Daos' face went as hard as stone.

Era

They had a dozen good fires lit, and food was being cooked. It had been the hardest day of the whole expedition, and Era wanted to lie down on her furs and sleep, but instead she went from fire to fire, listening to complaints and making sure there was enough hot food. It was cold – really cold. Colder than any winter day in the Hundred Cities, or anywhere else she'd ever been except Vetluna, and it was far colder here. There was snow under the trees, and the trees were everywhere: the hemlock and pines stood hundreds of feet tall, and a thick carpet of needles ran right to the edge of the river. Paper birch grew in clumps that looked like ghostly fingers reaching for the river or the sky in the dark.

At the fourth fire she found Jawat ordering Lefuz, one of their veterans, to set a night watch well out from the fires. She complimented both of them on their alertness and moved on. Jawat was reliable, unless there was a brothel handy, so in the deep woods of Dendrowna he was a prince. And Era treated him as such.

This is not so bad, she thought. *We're going to make it to the high country before the ice sets in on the river. We're on schedule.*

She was at the seventh fire and accepting a cup of hot wine when Mawat ran up behind her.

'*Wanax!*' he called.

Most of them called her *wanax* now: King. An odd title for a former dancer and singer of epics. It made her glow inside, that they thought of her this way.

'What's up?' she asked.

'The Dry One, *Wanax*. It is … emerging.'

Era shrugged. 'Not for the first time. Maybe we won't have to carry it—'

'Jawat says come now.'

Jawat was a reliable officer and Era sighed. She did drink off the hot wine before she ran back up the streamside trail, dodging roots and jumping holes to avoid a tumble into icy water at the edge of darkness.

The Dry One's cocoon had been placed close to the third fire, where it could be warmed. A trio of big women were supposed to turn it every few minutes.

Instead, two of them were cowering under a huge tree, while the third was oddly positioned beside the cocoon. Only when Era was very close could she see that the cocoon was split open; she could see the shape of the Dry One's head and its wing cases, and one of its talons …

… which was through the woman's arm. She wasn't screaming; her expression looked absent, and she looked at Era just as the Dry One's head fully emerged from the cocoon. Its faceted eyes met hers, and she realised that the woman and the insect were moving together.

'The hour foretold has come!' the woman's voice said, but

it sounded like a thousand women speaking quietly. 'Now we take back what is ours.'

The bear burst out of the woods behind them and roared, 'I know who you are! Damn it! We're allies!'

The Dry One pulled its long limbs out of the cocoon with a squelch that sent chills through every mortal present.

'Now,' the woman said in her many voices.

The Dry One looked directly at Era and nodded.

'Now we win,' it said. 'Now our queen is free. You wet ones did well. We are allies!'

The bear stood up on its hindquarters, ready to fight, as the donkey knocked a man down to get into the fire circle.

Dite pushed her way in.

'No!' she shouted. 'What is happening?'

'The war begins! We will take back what is ours. But ... never forget ... allies.'

The Dry One withdrew its talon from the woman's arm, leaving no wound, no mark, though the woman slumped.

The Dry One spread its wings, leapt into the air and was gone.

Era looked at her lover across the fire.

'What the fuck was that about?' she asked.

Dite closed her eyes and slumped in turn. 'It can't ... They can't ...'

The bear growled. The donkey brayed. And Dite turned her beautiful eyes, now full of tears, towards Era.

'What have they done?' she asked.

Auza, Home of the Gods

Sypa emerged from her apartments, shouting for Laila, but when she reached the Hall of the Gods she found chaos.

'We're under attack!' Grulu whined. 'The alarm has been

sounded. It hasn't sounded in five hundred years. Someone should have done something…'

Sypa glared around, her own troubles forgotten.

Gul stared at her from the deep sockets of his eyeless face.

'Where have you been?' he hissed.

Sypa held his black gaze. She had no time for him; he wasn't interested in her and she had no power over him, but then, he had no power she desired, either. And she'd always disliked his access to power and the way he used it.

She could hear the gongs sounding in the marble rafters.

'What is going on?' she asked archly. 'And where is my Laila?'

They're not gods, she thought, looking at the ruin of Timurti and the flock of sycophants gathered around Grulu. *They're like sheep. Senescent sheep.*

Anzu, in his usual lion form, growled. 'I'll rip them to pieces. I'll rend their flesh.'

'*Whose* flesh?' Sypa snapped.

They all looked at her.

'Send the demons,' she said. 'Where are the demons?'

No one spoke.

Finally Uthu, the newly minted 'God of the Sun' said, with far too much hesitation, 'Um…That is… uh… the Great Storm God… He took most of the… um… Demon Legion… with him.'

Sypa took a deep breath to calm herself.

'Fine,' she said. 'I'll go and look myself, shall I? The great god's consort wandering the corridors looking for intruders.' She sneered. 'Because I'm the only one with the wits and balls to do it.'

Uthu hesitated, and then said, 'I … uh …'

'Send me, Goddess of the Twisted Sheets,' Anzu said. 'Let me fill the corridors with blood and meat.'

Sypa favoured the mad lion-god with her best smile.

'Someone knows what's wanted,' she purred. 'Take the young Sun God with you. Bring me a report, or some heads.'

She looked around, surprised that Laila had still not appeared. She had other handmaidens, but none were capable of much. She fixed her gaze on one – a former mortal called Hannah.

'Go with them, Hannah. You may return once you know what's happening.' The immortal woman looked horrified, and Sypa glared. 'Go!' she shrieked.

The last thing she needed was for Enkul-Anu to return and find…

…and find the snake god in her private chambers. She swept the great hall with her beautiful eyes.

'Don't go anywhere,' she said to the assembled host of heaven, and moved to her apartments as swiftly as dignity permitted.

Anzu and Uthu led the way, with Hannah accompanying them; they left the hall through the Gods' Gate and went to the broad Corridor of the Gods, where all the principal deities had their private homes.

The alarm gongs were louder here.

Anzu leapt down the main corridor and Uthu followed more cautiously, with Hannah creeping along well behind them, peering at every door as if a winged demon might leap at her. Sypa let her pass and then went into her own chambers to the young god, who was still desperately wounded. She didn't want him wounded. She wanted him healed.

But that was for another day, now.

'Take him to his own chambers,' she ordered her other hand-maids. 'Find him ambrosia. When I catch Laila, I will whip her until she's red as a berry, the tart.'

She had a moment – just a moment – where she wondered if Enkul-Anu and Laila were together. It was a thought that raised her anger, but it wasn't possible. Enkul-Anu was fighting a war.

So where in ten thousand hells is Laila?

As it proved, none of the wyverns could withstand *Terror*. Zos didn't bother to cut at the nearest, but looked back, caught Laila's hand, and dragged the goddess through the double doors into the corridor beyond. Out on the cavern floor, twenty combats raged, and blue fire warred with red fire as wyverns and Dry Ones fought. At first it had seemed like a slaughter of the sentient insects; the wyverns had simply eaten a dozen of them.

But there were *thousands* of Dry Ones. Many were helpless; hundreds were more like larvae than like fully fledged Bright People, their colours dull, their bodies coated in resin, their movements feeble.

But many were complete, and they drew themselves out of their cells and stood drying their wings. Those that survived took to the air, until the cavern was filled with swirling combats in three dimensions. Dry Ones were clawed from the air; wyverns fell to the cells and were swarmed by those who could not yet fly.

Zos stared for too long – or rather, stared for long enough to ascertain that his initial observation had been wrong: the Dry Ones were going to massacre the wyverns. Despite some claim as to having rescued them, Zos didn't want to stay around and find out what happened next. Especially as the distant blue glow of the titanic Dry One was now pulsing with a brilliant blue-white fire.

He finally saw the two promised doors. He motioned, and Daos struck the first with his trident.

Beyond it, thousands of earthenware amphorae of resin were stacked from the floor to the vaulted ceiling.

'We should…' Pollon began.

Laila looked at Zos with horror as he took a thunderbolt from behind his shield, flung it into the nearest stack, slammed

Laila against the wall and pressed himself against her, using all his wrestling skill to move her tall bulk.

His instinct was correct; the explosion was immediate and the resin caught fire like naphtha.

'Damn,' he muttered. 'I should have burned the far room first.'

For sure, the heat of the resin fire was so intense that there was no way he could get past it and reach the second chamber.

'Time to go,' he said to Pollon, and sheathed *Terror*.

Laila's eyes were closed tight.

Zos still had her hand.

'Go!' he roared. 'Get us back up to the Gate of Air!'

She shook her head. Her eyes opened. 'You have ... destroyed ... I don't understand. Druku *can't* have wanted this.'

Zos pulled her towards the trellis-gate through which they'd come, but it was glowing a fiery red. Laila looked as if this was one blow too many.

'Are we trapped?' Pollon asked, a little wildly.

Daos was now as tall as Laila, and he put a hand under her arm to steady her. 'Beautiful Aurora,' he said. 'Heaven must fall. Druku and I have our differences, I admit, but we ... are in this together. Now please get us out of here.'

Laila could be seen to steady herself. She looked back at the burning resin store with distaste, and then at Daos.

Perhaps she yielded to him, or perhaps it was just the survivor in her coming to the fore, but after a long hesitation punctuated by the screams of dying wyverns, she nodded.

'This way, then. But we will have about seventy flights of stairs to climb. Come!'

There was a broad staircase of cut stone in an alcove to the side. The treads were slippery with wear, and the stairs wound up and up and out of sight, with a central well in the middle. Zos peered up, and couldn't see the top, although there were lights. He went back and picked up his cloak full of amphorae of ambrosia.

'Go!' Daos called.

Zos wasn't one to hesitate. He sprang up the steps. The tall goddess was behind him. Daos still had her by the shoulder.

'Let me go!' she shouted. 'Let me go!'

'I thought you wanted to go to Druku,' Zos snapped as he climbed.

Laila moaned. 'He can't have wanted *this*,' she complained. Zos wanted to argue, but he didn't have the breath. After five flights of steps they were no longer running; the treads were inhumanly high, and each set of stairs went on too long, up and up and up in an endless rising square around the central shaft.

There were sounds beneath them now, and more above them.

And then a Dry One flew up the central shaft. Its body was alight with sorcery, its wings moved too fast to see, and it landed, glanced at them, and leapt again, wings pushing it higher.

Laila gave a little scream.

Above them there was a roar, a flash of fire as bright as the sun, and charred bits of Dry One fluttered down the central shaft of the stairs.

'Not good,' Pollon said, and Daos shook his head.

Laila took a deep breath. 'Follow me,' she said, and raced up two more flights of stairs. Zos pushed himself to follow.

They emerged on the first landing they'd seen in many flights of stairs, and a Dry One landed with them, as if invited. Its quick and alien head movements tracked each one, as if memorising them, but it offered no violence.

Another landed, and another, and then all three went up together in a whirr of wings, and there was a roar and another flash of sunlight.

This time, there were blue flashes as well.

Laila was at a door now.

'They have unleashed Anzu,' she said, and touched a ring she wore to the key-plate. 'He will kill me as willingly as you.'

Another alarm sounded.

The sound of wings became a rush of air, and more Dry Ones came up the shaft. One died in front of them, and its resin-coated body fell to the landing, cut in half.

They could hear what sounded like a huge lion, roaring very close.

'Come,' Laila said.

Zos pushed an exhausted Pollon through the door and then waited while Daos backed through, before going in himself.

He stopped dead as soon as he turned.

He stood on a black marble balcony perhaps twice as wide as a chariot, with a richly worked gold handrail gripped by the sculpted talons of black marble demon statues. The marble was magnificent, veined in green and blue, and the balcony went part of the way around a great chamber the size of an arena, shaped like a massive beehive, or the tomb of mighty Atrios in Mykoax.

Down on the floor of the chamber was a pattern in many colours of marble, and another bronze pedestal, standing at a man's height from the floor. The whole vast chamber was lit from the very top of its beehive roof by a single massive magelight.

Laila hadn't stopped for the view. She was hurrying along the black marble balcony, and Zos tugged at Pollon's shoulder and followed her.

Daos was transfixed.

'Come on!' Zos shouted.

Daos turned back to close the door, and suddenly there was a shining figure with a spear as bright as sunlight. The spear lashed out, and Daos covered the thrust with the trident. White fire traced the air where the two weapons crossed, and Daos stumbled back.

Zos dropped his cloak full of ambrosia and passed Daos the way he had been taught to protect his charioteer: his shield arm wrapped the other man's left side so that the Shield of Temis covered the other, just as the bright spear struck again.

The sun-spear struck the dead goddess's shield and bounced away. Tendrils of white fire filled the air.

'I am Uthu! The Sun God!' shouted the spear-bearer.

The glowing godling had a shield of shining gold and white-blond hair. He stood a two feet taller than Zos, and his skin crackled with sun-fire.

'Zos!' Daos said, but Zos was past him now.

'Run!' Zos said.

There were blue and red flashes like strobes through the open doorway to the stairwell.

'Run, boy!' he shouted again.

I am not losing another papista.

Uthu attacked again – a heavy blow. This time, Zos angled his shield as he would against a mortal foe, trusting the shield to turn the attacks. The flare of light told him he'd succeeded. He didn't have a weapon in his right hand; he'd been holding the cloak full of amphorae …

He reached for his short sword and realised it was useless against the godling; bronze wouldn't bite, and *Terror* would hurt his comrades as much as his foe.

The godling struck again. It was the same blow over and over.

Fools. They don't train – they have their powers, and that is enough for them. I wonder if he's ever wrestled?

Zos backed away, and the godling came on.

'Foolish mortal! Whatever trick you have to protect you, nothing—'

Uthu struck in mid-sentence, so he knew at least one trick.

468

Zos didn't so much plan his response as simply let his body execute it.

The godling's blow came in, hard, lightning fast, but on the same line and against the same target.

He had his shield up, but it was almost parallel to the line of the attack, and the spear scored into his side, a bolt of pain, but he used the rim to pick up the spear as it came back out of his side. He rolled it aside and powered by the pain, stepped in, stepping *forward* into the godling's chest even as his shield pushed the deadly shining spear farther aside, opening the godling's centre and even slightly turning his body. The rim of his deathless shield ripped into the young god's spear-arm like an axe blade. The godling stumbled back, wounded, and dropped his spear. It rang on the marble like a bell.

Zos followed through on his shield attack, now pushing the shield into his foe's shield, so that they went in close, body to body, shields locked. Zos had momentum, and skill, but Uthu was huge and heavily built. Despite his size, he was pressed back a step, his massive right leg going back to brace and coming up against the balcony's wall and rail.

Zos' face was inches from the godling's own.

'Foolish mortal!' Uthu spat, and Zos felt that strength pressing at him. 'You are weak and I am strong! I have *power*. You have …'

His empty right hand went down, and he got his fingers under the godling's left knee where it was exposed under his shield and he pulled …

With one long, controlled movement of his whole body, he broke the godling's balance and tipped him back on one leg until Uthu was leaning out over the railing …

And dropped him. Fifty feet to the black marble floor below.

'Training,' he spat at the unmoving body far below.

The fall won't kill the bastard, but he'll have a long time healing.

He turned, aware that the light had changed, and saw three

dead Dry Ones in the doorway, their shattered carapaces smoking. And over them loomed the deranged face of a giant lion with flaming eyes.

Zos lifted his shield, but Anzu's blow knocked him back against the rail so hard he felt as if his back had snapped. The pain in his side was intense, constant.

Again.

He had no feeling in his legs, and so he slipped to the black marble floor.

I got another one, he thought with intense pleasure. *And I saved Daos, so this ... is all right.*

But the mad lion-thing had other problems, and it whirled to face new attackers — all Dry Ones, as they filled the stairs and the central well. Zos watched with a distant detachment as Anzu fought them. Unlike the little sun god, the lion was ferocious and fast and brave — insanely brave. His eyes poured fire on his foes, and he held the doorway, burning a dozen of the Dry Ones and taking little enough damage in return.

But Zos' military brain, which never really stopped analysing any more than Pollon's did, told him that the Dry Ones didn't care if they killed Anzu. They were trying to get up the stairwell; the lion god was an irritation. And they seemed to place little value on individuals, much like insects. A few could die to distract Anzu while the rest went ...

Where the fuck are they going?

The shock is wearing off. I need to get out of here. Worth a try.

Zos found that he could, in fact, crawl, if he ignored a great many warning signals from his body. He half-rolled, and his back hurt; he got his right leg under him, and his side hurt, and now there was blood; bright blood. But a lifetime of getting hurt told him that his back wasn't broken, and that meant he was still alive. He used his arms, walking on the rim of the magic shield, and his right fist, eyes ground shut against the pain, and went what seemed an immense distance, only to find when he opened his eyes that he'd almost come the length of the bright spear which lay in his path.

He reached for it hesitantly, but it didn't burn, and he closed his hand on it, hoping for a thrill of healing or some magical miracle.

Nothing happened so he crawled on, dragging his left leg, which appeared to have taken most of the damage. His hips were already better and his right leg was moving more smoothly.

Of course, any moment that lion-thing is going to burn me to ash.

Instead, a pair of strong hands grasped his right arm at the wrist and the rim of his shield, and dragged him.

He screamed. The wave of pain in his hips and lower back was so sudden it overcame all of his restraints.

'I have you,' Daos said.

Pollon

Pollon saw Daos grab Zos and begin to drag him along the balcony floor. Zos was screaming, but he wouldn't relinquish his prize – the burning spear.

That was Zos.

Pollon's attention was focused on Laila, although in his peripheral vision. She thought he'd stopped paying attention and made a lunge for the gate. It was another wicket, a lattice of gold-covered bronze set with mosaic flowers, like the first one they'd seen. But she had to touch a pad on the wall first, and before she managed it Pollon's star-stone arrowhead was pressed firmly into her beautiful back.

'Uggh!' she spat. 'Take it away!'

'Listen, Goddess,' Pollon said. 'If you try again, I'll kill you.'

'You'll never leave here alive without me,' she said.

'Please understand,' Pollon said, 'we're desperate people and there really isn't anything I won't do right now.'

Laila quailed.

'Back away from the gate,' Pollon said.

'Please move that poisonous thing,' Laila said. 'I'm on your side. I'm just terrified.'

'I'm afraid I don't believe you,' Pollon said.

He had a flash of a very different Pollon: a man who respected the gods, and treated them with veneration and awe.

Was that a year ago? Less?

'Back against the rail, Goddess,' he said.

'I'm not really a goddess,' she sighed. 'I'm more of a demi-god.'

'Perfect.' Pollon was looking past her now, but the arrowhead was steady.

There was a roar, and a flash of red light, and suddenly the terrifying lion-thing was coming along the balcony, straight for Daos.

There was no time to shout or plan. The lion-god would be on Daos in three bounds, and he still had his trident across his back as he dragged Zos.

Pollon thought fast, like a scribe, and then acted, like a warrior.

He dropped Laila with a knee behind her knee and a sweep of his bow-arm, and she fell a safe distance from the gate. He had an arrow on the string; the bow came up, and he shot. He never aimed; he didn't even really think.

And luckily, Anzu was quite large.

The star-stone arrow struck the god where his left foreleg met his amber-furred trunk and sank deep, and the god gave a roar which echoed off the beehive-shaped chamber.

The god didn't turn into anything insectoid. It took Pollon a moment to realise he was shocked by that.

Instead, its left foreleg began to turn black.

The lion god's red-lit eyes flashed down with insane speed and precision, and it severed its own leg just above the arrow's entry wound. And then it lifted its head again.

Daos had stumbled backwards, seeing his end nigh, and had relinquished his hold on Zos, who had rolled himself on to his back.

As Anzu's head came up, so did Zos' immortal shield, and the flash of its eyes was reflected in a shower of white-hot sparks.

Daos leveled the trident. Pollon got another arrow on his bow and held it, half drawn, in Laila's face. Zos struggled to raise the bright spear.

'Stay down,' he said.

She grunted.

Pollon figured he had a few heartbeats until she realised it wasn't star-stone. That had been his last one.

The lion god crouched for a leap, but then appeared to reckon the odds, and instead, turned with a bound...

... And bolted.

'Come on!' Pollon roared, sounding a lot bigger than he really was. 'It's a gate. Get over here!'

Laila's eyes couldn't focus on the arrowhead. But she had figured it out; he saw it in her eyes. But before she could act Daos was there, and Zos, dragging himself along.

'We only get through the gate if we're touching her,' Pollon said.

'Nonsense,' Daos said. 'I can use the gates.'

He turned and bounced off the gate-wall. 'Or maybe I can't.'

Anzu was scattering Dry Ones at the other end of the balcony. Even three-legged, it was incredibly tough.

Laila rose, glaring at Pollon.

'I won't forget that,' she spat.

Pollon shrugged. 'We can't trust you.'

'Too right,' Zos said through gritted teeth.

Daos seized one of the goddess's hands and touched the bronze plate set into the mosaic. Then he pushed her into the gate, almost embracing her.

Pollon had slung his bow by the string and grabbed the bright spear.

'The ambrosia!' Zos called.

Pollon got a hand on the cloak-bag – some of the amphorae had clearly broken – and hauled it along the smooth floor as Zos grabbed his hand and pulled them through ...

Enkul-Anu

They were still far enough from heaven that Auza was merely a shape looming against the stars when he flinched at the auratic power pouring out of the mountain. In his vision the mountain seemed to flare as if it was on fire. And actual fire, and columns of smoke, poured out of the air vents in the sides of the inhabited levels. Enkul-Anu saw them as heat, but deep in his gut, he knew something was *very* wrong.

Bastards. But who?

Is it Sypa? Gul? Who in all the cold and endless hells is behind this?

Gul's never shown any interest in the affairs of heaven. He lives in his own realm and rarely comes here.

While Sypa ... would never have sacrificed Telipinu for some plot.

Temis is in the Outer Darkness. Ara is dead.

I never saw his body. Is Ara dead? And who was that vulture thing? That was a god – in some new aspect, and with new worshippers ...

All of those thoughts and a hundred more swirled through his mind in the time it took him to frame a command.

'Something's rotten in heaven!' he shouted to the demons. 'We go through the Gate of Air. Assume we'll have to fight.'

All around him, the demons began to raise their weapons. Those with fire ignited it; those with poison or lightning summoned it. A few had shields, and they brandished them. But they were tired, and even Enkul-Anu was admitting to himself that he felt he had been beaten.

There's nothing in this world that can stand before me and my demons, Enkul-Anu thought, reassuring himself, and they raced for the Gate of Air.

Laila

They emerged into a corridor that they'd seen on entry: the hallway that led to the Gate of Air. To their left, the stairwell opened into the depths of the mountain, lit from below by strobes of red and blue light.

'There,' Laila spat.

The tall godling didn't let go of her. He was as tall as she, now – a tall, broad-shouldered god-man with a heavy beard and piercing sea-green eyes. Even amid this chaos, she had to admit that he was as handsome as the handsomest gods, and he had that air of assurance that only Enkul-Anu and Ara had shared.

He wasn't a mortal. She could see that now, and it changed her views on many things.

'I thought you were coming with us?' His voice was deep, and pleasant, and apparently untinged with panic.

'Druku would *never* have allowed this!' She said it with less emphasis than she'd meant to.

'Hmm,' the young god said, with a slight smile.

Then he turned, rummaged in the cloak that Pollon had dragged through the trellis, and cracked open an amphora of ambrosia. He drank some, gave some to the archer, and forced the rest on the one they called Zos.

The effects were immediate. The archer seemed to grow before her eyes; their wounded leader gave a moan and then stood up. 'Let's go,' he said, and began limping down the hall towards the open portal to the Gate of Air. Blood was coming from his side.

The young god nodded, but instead of moving he took one of the remaining javelins from the wounded man's shield and threw it at the trellis.

There was an explosion like a bolt of lightning and a powerful smell of burning metal. Laila covered her face in her hands and ran.

'No one will come that way now,' the young god said.

Laila wanted to weep. 'You are *destroying heaven*! What's the point? Are you fools? Who will want to rule a ruin?'

The wounded man was almost to the doors, which towered above him, slightly ajar. He stopped in the great marble entrance, small between the massive engraved bronze doors.

Laila wasn't looking at him. She was looking back, hearing calls and movement from the hall above them.

Sypa. I hear Sypa coming.

But...

Whose side am I on, here?

Besides my own.

Almost without her own volition, she said, 'Sypa is coming, probably with other gods. From the stairs, there.'

She pointed at the broad, fantastically decorated stairs that led up into the halls of the gods, so very different from the workmanlike, if enormous, basalt steps that led down to the workshops and the Bright Farm far below.

The young god still had her hand. He tugged, gently, and she found that she was moving with him.

But who is he? she asked herself. *He must be Nammu ... But Nammu was old ...*

'Company coming!' the wounded man shouted.

He wasn't as wounded as he had been; he was barely favouring his left leg, now. But the blood continued to trickle down his side.

Laila looked back as she reached the bronze doors.

'Gul!' she said weakly.

There, emerging from the stairs, was the God of the Dead. He had a bone shield on his left arm and a spear of night in his right hand, and his eyeless skull looked out from under his high, Narmerian-style crown of dull gold.

'Gul,' she said again.

Sypa

Sypa put a hand on the God of Death's shield arm, despite the cold he emanated.

'Hold your strike,' she commanded. 'That's Laila!'

Her handmaiden looked back at her, a despairing glance, and reached out with her free hand as if begging for succour, just as she was pulled through the massive bronze doors to the Gate of Air, and they were pushed shut with a clang that rang through the halls of heaven.

Gul said nothing, but strode down the corridor with his wife Urkigul at his heels and a dozen of the lesser deities in his long shadow.

He struck his black spear against the bronze doors, and they turned green with verdigris. The green deepened and bubbled up as a thousand years of decay struck in heartbeats; pieces flaked off, and then, without even a whimper, the great doors fell to green dust and chips of corroded bronze.

477

The cool air of the outer world washed over them.

To Sypa's left was the stairwell down – in her mind, the Slaves' Stair. There was a rapid pulse of blue light reflected on the beautiful white marble of the coffered roof above them, and then a long blue flash. Anzu, the lion god, maimed and burnt with a hundred wounds, suddenly appeared at the top and faced them.

'Flee or fight, you idiots!' he roared. 'The Bright People are loose in heaven.'

Sypa's heart hammered in her chest and Gul turned to face the mad lion god.

'The...?' he began in his sonorous tones.

A trio of winged creatures with faceted eyes and long, insectoid faces rose from the central well of the Slaves' Stair. Blue fire strobed; one of the bolts struck Gul and blackened his high golden crown, showing the bare skull beneath.

He raised the black spear and returned black fire for blue, and all three turned to dust that hung in the air and then rained down slowly. There were suddenly more – more than she could count: a dozen, fifteen, more, and blue fire flew in every direction. Anzu's red fire burned hotter; the black spear reaped the Bright People like a farmer cutting wheat with a sharp flint sickle ... but the numbers were against them. Gul took one step back towards the apartments of the gods – and then another, his black spear moving back and forth, back and forth. Urkigul stepped up next to her consort, her dead-white face calm, and added her violet fire to his.

The Bright People died.

Anzu stood with him. Sypa had never liked the mad thing; they'd inherited him when they'd taken heaven and she'd never trusted it, but it was fighting like a lion, even short a leg, and with Gul and Urkigul, they stopped the blue fire.

The Bright People stopped coming.

'Back,' Gul ordered.

'I am the queen of heaven,' Sypa said. 'I will not retreat.'

'There's a thousand of them, Sypa!' Anzu spat.

'Back!' Gul ordered.

And they went back.

Zos

Behind him, Daos slammed the bronze doors of the Gate of Air closed.

'You may regret that,' Zos said.

Their chariot was a hundred paces away, the golden stags waiting patiently next to the bony spectres who drew Gul's chariot. But out in the night, fires burned. And winged demons flew at them.

'Demons,' Zos said. 'And that's Enkul-Anu.'

Daos still had the goddess by the hand.

'We can get to the chariot,' he said.

Zos didn't argue. His hip was better; his left leg would almost take his weight, and he hobbled as best he could, relieving Pollon of the cloak full of amphorae and the bright spear. His precious shield was across his back and he was almost happy; he'd certainly had some triumphs, and he was willing to die trying to get away. And he was reasonably sure that he was dying; his side was leaking blood, and his left leg was wet and sticky with it, and cold.

No point in not trying, anyway.

They ran. Or rather, Daos ran, dragging Laila; Zos hobbled, and Pollon moved as if stunned.

'Run!' Zos bellowed in the former scribe's ear.

Pollon blinked ... and obeyed.

Daos made it to the chariot just as Enkul-Anu, in all his glory, alighted at the edge of the gate's broad terrace, fifty paces away.

'Who the fuck are you?' he bellowed.

'Oh, for one more arrow,' Pollon moaned.

Laila screamed.

Zos dragged himself a few more steps. Demons were landing now – three … five … a dozen …

'Fuck,' Zos said.

We were that close.

'Save me, Great Storm God!' Laila screamed.

Enkul-Anu had raised a thunderbolt. Unlike the javelins, the great Storm God's thunderbolts shone like leashed lightning in his hands – long and forked and wicked. The weapon hummed and crackled.

But the Great Storm God hesitated, his bull's head cocked to one side.

'Laila?' he asked.

Zos got a hand on the chariot rail and dragged himself in.

'Save me!' Laila begged, stretching out a hand.

Enkul-Anu hesitated. 'Who are you, mortals?' he demanded, and his voice rang off the columns and the roof.

Daos laughed. His voice boomed with the power of godhood. 'Wouldn't you like to know, Great Storm God?'

Zos was having trouble focusing his eyes. The Storm God hesitated a moment in confusion, or anger. Behind them, something struck the great bronze doors. Even the demons turned to watch as the vast gates decayed to verdigris and flakes of metal and fell in a shower of dust.

'Gul, and Sypa!' Laila shouted. 'They come!'

It finally struck Zos that the goddess was playing Enkul-Anu like a lyre. She wasn't trying to be rescued. She was playing for time. And lying.

And Sypa and Gul were suddenly lit with blue fire.

'What the fuck is going on?' Enkul-Anu snarled.

Gouts of red and blue fire flashed through the now open doorway, six men tall and two chariots' wide, and the whole interior of heaven seemed to be on fire.

Enkul-Anu ran forward, his great feet slapping the ground as loud as his thunderbolts, and he shook the Gate of Air in his wrath.

'Go!' Zos said.

The golden chariot leapt into the air.

Zos couldn't resist the opportunity. He had the bucket of thunderbolt javelins under his hand, and as the chariot made a tight turn under the mosaic ceiling high above them, Zos threw one at Enkul-Anu's head, but his vision was tunneling and it was a near-impossible throw, as the chariot turned in three dimensions and accelerated away. His bolt struck one of the mammoth columns.

Demons opened their wings, but they were too slow to intercept the golden chariot.

The thunderbolt exploded, and the column cracked. A fissure opened in the high mosaic ceiling, and tesserae fell like rain on the demons below. A demon tossed a fireball that detonated against the straining chariot team. The car was blown sideways through the high air, a sickening jolt. Pollon pinned Laila to the side of the chariot car to keep her from falling.

Enkul-Anu was turning, his arm cocked to throw his own thunderbolt, when the first Dry One flew through the broken doors and into the night air. The moment seemed to crystallise: Enkul-Anu at the head of his demons, ready to throw, his head turning; the lone Dry One flitting through the broken doors and already rising towards the ceiling of the Gate of Air; from below, a flash of red and blue, and then more blue.

Blue and blue and blue, like fireflies of blue on a lazy summer evening in the fields of Lazba.

Zos held on, unable to reach another javelin, and they shot between the last two pillars and out into the bitter cold night.

Daos put the chariot into a dive. Laila screamed. Pollon held the chariot rail, and Zos looked back at the Gate of Air, the massive temple roof and columns already vanishing behind them.

And then a flare of blue, and more blue, and more, until the sky above him was full of points of blue light that came and went.

No demons pursued them as they levelled out. Red light pulsed, and blue, and more blue.

'Where to?' Daos said.

Zos took a deep breath. He was savouring the moment. Even through the pain, he felt the triumph.

'We stormed heaven,' he said.

Pollon, clearly very cold, still managed an unaccustomed grin. 'We did, too,' he said.

Laila looked at Daos, and then at him.

'I saved you,' she said.

'I know,' Zos said.

'Now take me to Druku,' she said.

Zos nodded to Daos.

'Maritaten, first,' he said, and slumped into the bottom of the chariot. There was blood pooling under his feet, wetting his heton.

Pollon looked down at him. His eyes were full of concern.

'You are wounded,' he said.

'Dying, I'd guess,' Zos said. He was having a moment of clarity, as if the universe was some sort of crystal lattice and he knew every piece of it. *Is this what death is like?*

Laila leaned over him. 'Move back, you fools. Level this thing out so that I can work.'

Zos wanted to push her away. He didn't trust her. But he couldn't raise his hands.

'What?' asked Daos. His voice was very far away. He said something more, and …

Epilogue

Hefa-Asus

They hadn't quite had to build their own village, but it was near enough. Another week's travel on the Saswatatan had led them to the very edge of the Kautlin country. The Kautlin had been welcoming, especially when they discovered their newcomers had wine, oil and Mykoan wool to trade, and neither he nor Nicté had excited any comment.

The Kautlin had offered them a site for a 'trading village' just before the great waterfall that led to the last navigable part of the Saswatatan. Beyond it were the high mountains of the icy north. The Kautlin assumed they were very clever to offer it; who would the newcomers trade with, north of the mountains? Their matrons must have laughed over their beautiful wood and feather fans.

Old Jawat had laid out a palisade and earthwork; Nicté and Hefa-Asus, more familiar with local materials, had altered a few of his choices, and Era had insisted on local style longhouses for warmth. They'd offered bronze tools as rewards, and had a flood of local volunteers to help them build, so the longhouses had gone up like magic. Era had looked very pleased with herself for choosing a local building style. Hefa-Asus thought that she was right to do so.

The workers were mostly led by a woman who had become

Jawat's wife in a matter of days, moving into his blankets and the role of official Kautlin translator. Her name was Jiila; she was a middle-aged widow and her lineage was apparently something special. Hefa-Asus liked her; she was used to being in charge and worked easily with Jawat. She had found the workers, organised them, and had seen them paid. By the time they went back to their winter villages, a dozen other men and women of their party had partners.

And that was good all by itself. Jawala had helped, learning the local language quickly, and she also seemed to form an instant bond with the local matrons.

She was laying out bark from a pile of ready material she'd purchased, and Aanat and Miti were working high up on the seventh longhouse. Hefa-Asus was dressed in a mixture of local furs and southern garb for a trip to look at 'stone that burns' with Atosa and another Kautlin man, when Jawala stopped him.

'Nicté is working on your forge,' she said sweetly. 'Alone. Perhaps you can look for the "stone that burns" another day.'

So he apologised to Atosa.

'Can you do this without me?' he asked.

Atosa looked long-suffering. 'I ran a shop with fifty smiths,' he said. 'I can handle a walk in the snow to look at coal.'

Yal, the local guide, grunted a laugh. He glanced at Taha, Era's scout, who was learning a whole new environment

'If we kill a deer, more for us,' he said. 'Big men eat too much anyway.'

Atosa, who was anything but big, gave an appreciative nod.

Hefa-Asus went into the large, cold structure they'd raised for the forge. It wasn't covered in bark; it was more heavily built, and would eventually have a roof of something relatively hard to burn, although Hefa-Asus wasn't sure what that would be yet.

There was a pile of undressed stone waiting to line the hearth, and he went over to it and looked it over.

'This would look better if I dressed the stone – made a cut-stone circle,' he said.

'Sure,' Nicté answered. And then, after he'd started, 'Yeah, good idea.'

They worked in silence for a few minutes.

'Jawat's so hellish smug,' Nicté complained suddenly. She was digging under the soon-to-be hearth to bury a bronze pipe that would feed air to the forge.

They were building big, and to last.

Hefa-Asus thought that this was important; she'd shared a confidence, even if it was banal. He considered various answers while he adjusted his furs. It was very cold here – colder than anything Hefa-Asus had encountered in the Poche lands, which were not so very far away. He had a brown bear-fur robe for which he'd traded a good plain sword; for some reason he'd never worn the black fox-fur robe.

Nicté was wearing a light deerskin shirt and a Mykoan shawl; she just didn't seem to get cold. He was watching her too intently. He felt like a fool – not a feeling he had often.

What to say? How to respond?

Talking to Nicté used to be easy as breathing.

'Who's smug?' Hefa-Asus asked.

He struck a blow with his bronze hammer, trimming a big piece of field stone. He wasn't a great stonemason, but he was competent enough, and he'd made a couple of very effective chisels from their dwindling supply of star-stone.

If I keep working, she'll talk. Working is what we share.

'Jawat. He has a woman, so now he owns the world.' She sounded bitter.

Hefa-Asus looked at her and considered saying nothing. He offended her very easily these days; if Jawala hadn't arranged this, he'd never have been alone with her.

He cut another stone so that the hearth would be laid on a

neatly matched circular foundation, and tossed back his bearskin to free his arms.

No point in being silent when what you want to do is talk.

He swung another blow and cracked his stone – ruined. He swore at the gods of his homeland, and the Mischief Maker, and then glanced at her. After selecting a new stone, he said, 'There's probably comfort in having a partner.'

She looked at him. 'Really?' Her sarcasm was obvious. 'Where's your Nikali witch, then? Why isn't she keeping your fat arse warm?'

The insult was more like a compliment – certainly, more like their former ease. He took a little heart from it, and her eyes weren't slitted in anger ... but there was an edge to her tone.

Oh, really? he thought. *Am I that blind? Is that what this is about?*

Wait. She bedded the useless pirate and I ...

'I gambled with her,' he said cautiously. 'I didn't take her to bed.'

He saw her turn her head; saw the surprise in her carefully trained body.

Aha.

'Gambled?' she asked. 'For what?'

Inspiration came to him, as it sometimes did when he was making. In fact, when he thought about it ... The bearskin, the fact he'd never even opened the furs he'd won ...

'Wait here,' he said, and trotted back to his bedroll on the sleeping platform in Longhouse Three. He avoided puddles, and thought vaguely about solutions to the muddy nightmare that spring would make of their little encampment. But that was in the future.

I'm trying not to think of what I'm about to do.

She was already laying up the stone for the hearth when he returned.

'For you.'

He handed her the black fox robe. It was long and magnificent. The fox fur shone like a dark sun; light rippled along it like the finest southern oiled wool, and she made a sound between puzzlement and awe.

He dared. He came up behind her and put the robe around her shoulders.

'I gambled with her and won it for you. To give to you. That is, I'm not sure…' He shook his head. 'To be honest, I think I just…'

She looked up at him.

'He fucked me and left, Hefa-Asus. I've never felt so…' She shrugged. 'I can't even tell you. Ugly? Stupid? Used? Ignorant? Things I don't want to be.'

Not a tear in her eye. Just a flat denunciation of herself.

'So I thought you'd gone and…' She paused.

'Done the same to a Nikali woman,' he finished for her.

She nodded.

He nodded. 'I have, too.' He looked away. 'In the past. I wouldn't, now, but I have.'

She narrowed her eyes. 'Why the cloak? Is it my Mastery present?'

He was very tempted to say 'yes.' It was an easy way out – all solved, and they could go back to work.

Fuck it.

'Because I love you, Nicté. I love your strength and courage and craft skills. You are… magnificent.'

She looked at him for a long moment… and then Mawat came in with a bag of locally produced charcoal on his shoulders and broke the spell between them.

'Fuck, it's cold,' he said.

Mawat and Tarhu were well along the road to being real apprentices; they now felt free to talk. Ordinarily, Hefa-Asus would have been all about encouraging their banter. Right now, he wished the southerner and his charcoal were in a particularly icy hell.

Nicté gave him a look he couldn't interpret and shook her head.

'The hearth won't build itself, master,' she said.

'Nor will it, master,' he grunted. But then he grinned.

The ice between them had melted. The rest would come, or it wouldn't. No one became a master of craft without deep reserves of patience.

He could wait.

Era

Dite stood before her, swathed in furs and wearing one of Hefa-Asus' excellent swords.

'I have to go,' she said.

Era shrugged, biting down hard on her feelings.

'May I ask where, former god?' She tried very hard not to sound angry or arch, or even sarcastic.

'I'm going to find Antaboga, the World Serpent. She's just the other side of this mountain range – I can feel her. And, no doubt, she can feel me. More important…' Dite looked away. 'I rescued her eggs, and I'm going to return them. I had a different plan, but…' She shook her head. 'I can't believe how fast you mortals live. How fast you act. How many actions you must pack in to so short a time. The pace of your lives is relentless. I thought I had years for my plans to come to bloom. In fact, my plans are already ruined, if the rumours of the *Aura* are to be believed.'

'What rumours?' Era asked.

'I'll tell you more after I visit Antaboga. Right now, suffice it to say that something huge has happened in heaven, and that even that is a guess. I lack all access to information. I'd kill for an entrance to the Nexus. But I came north of my own free will, and now, my only way of learning more is to visit the enemy of my whole race.' She smiled.

'Perhaps I should go with you?' Era asked carefully.

Dite smiled. It was a brilliant smile and Era thought it was genuine.

'Honey, I'd love to have you. But let's be honest. You are in charge here and you make a hundred decisions a day. I'm not much more than your leman. No one will miss me. I'm not an *officer.*'

'I will,' Era said. 'I will miss you.'

Dite looked sad – defeated. And unsure of herself, not anything that Era expected from her.

'If I don't come back,' she said, 'then I'm sorry. We had fun.'

'So this is goodbye?' Era asked.

Dite winced. 'You know, admitting to emotional involvement and then talking about it is pretty much not my way of being. A drunken orgy with fifty well-oiled participants is more my speed.' She looked up. 'Yes, it's goodbye, unless events prove very different from what I imagine. I will come back to tell you what I learn – I still want your rebellion to succeed.' She shook her head. 'But … nothing has gone as I wished.'

Era clamped down hard on everything she felt.

'I wish you good fortune,' she said carefully.

And then, suddenly, they were in each other's arms in a hug, and it lasted a long time, and it was Era who finally broke it.

'Fuck,' Dite said, sounding almost angry, and then went out into the snow. 'Now I feel …'

Era watched her as she bound the snowshoes to her feet, and joined a pair of Kautlin hunters waiting for her in their furs. Even twenty feet away, the tears glistened on Dite's cheeks, and Era shook her head.

Dite turned, as the hunters started out across the snow. But she didn't say anything, and then she was walking away.

I liked her. But I didn't trust her, and this moment was coming. But she's crying and I don't think she's lying.

Behind her, Pavi cleared her throat.

'Yes?'

Era turned to find her Hakran friend and virtual second in command waiting with a scrap of birch bark on which she'd marked an agenda.

'Right,' she said. 'Let's get to it.'

Antaboga

She lay in her comfortably heated underwater cave, relishing most of what she saw in the world. Her eggs were coming to her, carried by Druku. A decade ago, that would have seemed impossible – indeed, even a month ago.

Now, Druku seemed as likely an ally as any. And there was no way they would bring her eggs closer and intend anything but alliance.

She looked out over the world and was pleased. To the north, and not very far away, were seven pits in the ice, each holding a massive lode of star-stone that had fallen from the sky. The star-stone was not poison to *her* kind, but she could find it, and she knew who wanted it, and that made her smile.

And to the south ... someone had raided heaven. Someone had released the Bright People and their queen.

Antaboga watched the slow approach of her mortal foe of a thousand years ago, carrying her eggs as a sign of peace, and she began practising shapes and spells she hadn't cared about in aeons.

It's good to have allies.

It's good to have people to betray.

And it's wonderful to be back in the game.

Auza, Home of the Gods

Enkul-Anu was looking at the ruin of the Nest, with Sypa stood by his side.

'We fought them as hard as we could,' Sypa said.

Enkul-Anu said nothing.

'I don't know how they got into heaven,' she insisted. 'The demons let us down.'

Enkul-Anu said nothing.

'And they took my Laila!' Sypa muttered.

Enkul-Anu said nothing. He just stood in his immortal form, looking down at the smoking ruins of their source of immortality.

Sypa's voice changed, from the wheedling seductive note to another, plainer and coarser.

'Are we ... in trouble?'

Enkul-Anu looked at her. It wasn't a glare, or an accusation. Just a level stare, and she wriggled beneath it.

He took a great breath.

'We're in trouble,' he agreed. 'We're running low on fighting gods, and we just lost most of our resin. We can't make more, and the fucking queen of the vermin is free again. Free to raise her hosts in the deep desert. Free to give her resin to any she chooses.'

He spoke without bitterness, and his words were as level as his gaze.

Sypa put an arm around his waist. 'Perhaps we should run,' she said quietly.

492

She looked at him. His eyes narrowed.

'We can't run,' he said.

'There are other worlds. We can take our best and start again.'

'No,' he said gently. 'I destroyed the gate behind us when we came here. We can't leave unless the Gate Makers come.'

'They've been dead for a hundred aeons,' she said.

He nodded, looking over the wreckage. 'The gate is shut. We live or die here.'

Sypa nodded. 'We will defeat them. Gul is very strong; Urkigul also. Anzu will heal, and Illikumi, and Telipinu.'

'Telipinu is dead,' Enkul-Anu said, his voice flat. 'The Vulture God killed him.'

Sypa choked. 'What?' she shrieked. 'What? Telipinu is dead?' She seemed to swell with rage. 'What *Vulture God*?'

Enkul-Anu looked at her and wondered if he could trust her at all. 'The Vulture God of the Jekers,' he said, the words like aloe in his mouth. 'He attacked Narmer.'

'Always Narmer,' she spat. 'Always Narmer. I say, flatten Narmer until not one stone sits upon another.'

Enkul-Anu just looked at her.

Lawesa

There were three slaves waiting in the stone-walled basement of what had once been a prosperous shop high in the city of Ma'rib.

Lawesa was cloaked in a straw rain cape and wore a big straw hat that covered his face, which was masked anyway against the winter downpour outside.

'Tell me a riddle.' he asked from the basement door.

'How do you light the secret fire?' the female slave said.

493

That was the correct code. Challenge, response, counter-response.

'Flint and star-stone,' he said.

She nodded gravely.

'Tell me quickly' he said.

'Our godborn overseer is a monster. His name is Shari-Kushuh. He's brutal, and he uses us like animals.' She spoke boldly, but wildly – someone who had reached the point where she had nothing left to lose. 'Since the war in heaven, he is insane.'

Lawesa nodded. 'I have heard his name. He is bad, even for a godborn.'

'I request that he be made an example.' She spoke well, and her eyes glittered with something: hope, and also fanaticism.

He looked at the three of them.

'And you are agreed?' he asked.

The two men nodded. 'We'd rather be dead than ...' one man stammered. 'Than take another day.'

Lawesa nodded again. 'You know you will not survive rising up against him.'

'We will kill ourselves after we put him down,' the woman said. 'I promise.'

Lawesa felt his stomach tumble at that, but this was the secret fire.

'You will be the first,' he said. 'But you will not be the last.'

He gave them instructions and a star-stone nail, and left without showing his face.

That night, he packed his few belongings and left the city, heading for Weshwesh, dressed as a peddlar.

**The Age of Bronze cycle will be
completed in Book Three,
Breaking Hell**

Credits

Miles Cameron and Gollancz would like to thank everyone at Orion who worked on the publication of *Storming Heaven*.

Editorial
Gillian Redfearn
Claire Ormsby-Potter

Copy-editor
Steve O'Gorman

Proofreader
Saxon Bullock

Editorial Management
Jane Hughes
Charlie Panayiotou
Tamara Morriss
Claire Boyle

Contracts
Dan Herron
Ellie Bowker

Audio
Paul Stark
Jake Alderson
Georgina Cutler

Design
Nick Shah
Tómas Almeida
Joanna Ridley
Helen Ewing
Rachael Lancaster

Finance
Nick Gibson
Jasdip Nandra
Elizabeth Beaumont
Ibukun Ademefun
Sue Baker
Tom Costello

Inventory
Jo Jacobs
Dan Stevens

Marketing
Lucy Cameron

Production
Ameenah Khan

Publicity
Javerya Iqbal

Operations
Sharon Willis

Sales
Jen Wilson
Victoria Laws
Esther Waters
Frances Doyle
Ben Goddard
Jack Hallam
Anna Egelstaff

Rights
Flora McMichael
Ayesha Kinley
Nathan Kehel